I0667545

GRAB

BAG

10

A Gay Erotica Anthology

FOR LITERARY HEAT

BarbarainSpy
Toronto, Australia

Grab Bag 10

by

habu

Table of Contents

Introduction   7

Director's Choice   11

Searching for the Exotic   20

Men of Mykonos   30

Need to Be Needed   61

24 Exeter Place   88

Swinger Christmas   103

Becoming Key West   121

I, Mannequin   148

Rehabilitation System   158

Slave to Two Hung Masters   171

Tea with the Prince   185

Beware the Coach   202

Fist of Gold   216

Misdelivered Mail Male Sex Training   242

The Lighthouse Keeper   273

About the Author   284

Other Books from BarbarianSpy   285

Introduction

Tenth in the series of eclectic gay male short story collections by habu, the fifteen stories of *Grab Bag 10* offer a variety of gay male stories in terms of theme, sexual interest and fetish, setting, and time period. Laid out in the order in which they were written, these are stories composed during the late fall and winter of 2015–16.

As usual, several of them reflect the current world swirling around habu at the time they were conceived, so they include stories related to his travels during this period, such as "Men of Mykonos," "Becoming Key West," and "Director's Choice" They also include seasonal holidays, such as "Swinger Christmas," and sports events he attended, such as the male figure skating story, "Beware the Coach." This was a period in which habu was writing to little-served sexual fetishes, which helped surface stories of particular exotic fetishes his mind was toying with, such as "Searching for the Exotic," "Becoming Key West," "I, Mannequin," "Tea with the Prince," "Fist of Gold," and "Misdelivered Mail Male Sex Training."

Two stories evoke famous men of the past, the political novelist Gore Vidal in "Need to Be Needed," and the movie star Rock Hudson in "The Lighthouse Keeper." One, "Slave to Two Hung Masters," dredges up habu's own memories of his Bangkok "beginnings." The stories cover the world in setting—from California to New York to Virginia and Florida, in the United States, and, internationally, to London, the Mediterranean, Thailand, East Asia, and Africa.

Habu likes to write of the pre-AIDS days of freer, more intimate sex, and thus several of the stories are set in the past. These include "24 Exeter Place," set in a late nineteenth-century London male brothel; "Tea with the Prince" set in early World War II Japan and China of the 1930s; "Fist of Gold," and "The Lighthouse Keeper" set in the 1950s; and "Becoming Key West" and "Slave to Two Hung Masters" set in the 1970s.

As with previous Grab Bag collections, habu has striven to make his stories fresh and complex and the homosexual couplings graphic, inventive, and hot. As usual, there should be something here for every taste and something new to explore for everyone seeking stimulation.

The first two stories in the collection are set in Virginia in the present. Right off the bat we get a transvestite story in "Director's Choice" of an actor hired to play Romeo against a cross-dressed Juliet in a very private, all-male-cast play at the Shenandoah Valley Shakespeare Theater in Staunton. Across the state, on the coast in Norfolk, an Old Dominion College swim team member is taken to the Norfolk waterfront to engage in fetish sex with sailors in "Searching for the Exotic."

From there, the stories take us to the Mediterranean, where, in "Men of Mykonos," inspired by habu's recent visit to the island, a submissive novelist, recovering from the grief of losing his dominant partner, is comforted by an assortment of studly Greek men on the island of Mykonos. The fourth story in the collection, "Need to Be Needed," was inspired by the life of America's answer to Oscar Wilde, Gore Vidal. In this story, a young singer, trying to make it in New York, comes under the spell of a charismatic, dominating, and self-centered bigger-than-life novelist and fights for an equal share in the relationship.

The fifth story, "24 Exeter Place," takes us to London and back into the late nineteenth century for a look into the life of the male prostitutes in a "gentlemen's club" male brothel.

"Swinger Christmas," habu's entry in a 2015 winter season writing contest, is a bisexual male perspective of the staff party machinations in a hedonist "body beautiful" gym franchise.

Habu almost always has a story to fit in a collection that's set in one of his favorite playgrounds, Florida's Key West. In "Becoming Key West," a businessman escaping Baltimore in the 1970s slowly learns to unwind in the keys and to become "Key West."

"I Mannequin" is a bow to the weird in which the protagonist is bound on an Internet service date and worked over by a man with a tailor's dummy fetish. "Rehabilitation System" is another hard look at man-on-man sex and the result of the sexual reality of incarceration and how prison terms often "reform" men in a direction contrary to the plan is exhibited.

Habu often includes a semi-memoir of his early days in Bangkok and the Mediterranean in his collections. "Slave to Two Hung Masters" is such a "some major elements altered but maintaining the essence" remembrance. The title pretty much says it all as far as story theme. This is an intense one, which includes the fetish of fisting.

"Tea with the Prince," is a period piece covering a long-term control relationship of a young American placed with a Japanese prince and German military officers in Japan and China during the 1930s early, Asian, phase of World War II.

Competition in the world of figure skating can be nasty, as evidenced by the kneecapping of an American women's champion. It also, in the men's field, seems to be dominated by gay men and at least one famous American coach has been talked of as making sex slaves of his male skaters. Habu captures these themes in "Beware the Coach."

The more extreme gay male fetishes are underrepresented in stories in the marketplace, and, from time to time, habu includes extreme fetish—frotting, docking, sounding, fisting, for example—to provide reads for those seeking such shock and stimulation. "Fist of Gold," is a relatively mild use of the fisting theme in which an archeologist flying into Mali to meet up with a mentor who indoctrinated him in the technique of fisting finds more than one man willing to meet his need.

"Misdelivered Mail Male Sex Training" illustrates how costumed role playing can rev up stagnant sexual relations.

Having taken hints, habu tries to conclude his collections with a Romance story. "The Lighthouse Keeper," the story of a closeted gay movie star retreating to the isolation of a lighthouse in Delaware Bay following revelations in the press of a high-profile gay relationship, is just such a Romance story of redemption and new opportunities.

Therefore, as is the standard fare of habu's Grab Bag collection, something for every reader of gay male literature to rev up their engines with. Enjoy.

Director's Choice

I gazed into the dressing room mirror as I sat contemplating applying my stage makeup. Looking past my own image, I viewed the androgynously beautiful face of Kim, chin perched on my shoulder. All of my senses went on alert as Kim's fingernails scraped down the side of my bare torso, firm buds of breasts pressed into my shoulder blades.

"Relax. Go with it. You're too tense," Kim murmured, lips then going to the side of my neck. I shuddered as I tilted my head away to give maximum purchase to those lips and Kim's hands moved around my chest to cover my pecs, thumbs and forefingers latching onto my nubs and making them pucker up. I was going hard and began to pant. I'd dreamed of this but never had been here before. For the $5,000, though—not to mention having dreamed of it—I would "go with it" as Kim suggested. I knew Kim was only trying to help.

I could tell from the script what sort of performance this would be—or would simulate, I trusted.

"A kiss," Kim murmured. "We should do this before we are on stage, don't you think? On stage it should come across as natural, not forced."

I did think, I supposed. It was just two matinees for $5,000, and I'd already memorized the lines—and I had dreamed of this, even if I'd never had the nerve to do it.

"Ooo, such muscles; you're a real hunk," Kim cooed.

Kim licked up my cheek, urging me to turn my face, which I did, my lips meeting Kim's and opening to a pressing tongue. I shuddered again as I followed the progress of a hand down my belly, the unlacing of the codpiece of my tight costume leggings, the fishing out of my hard cock, and the start of the rhythmic hand stroking, letting nature take over, as I moved my hips, sliding my cock inside the loose sheath being provided.

My thoughts of simulation for the performance were beginning to melt away. But was I really ready for it?

"Give me your cum," Kim murmured, long dark hair draping down and tickling my bare chest as my lips briefly were freed. "It will make the work on the stage so much easier. You know it will."

I couldn't disagree. I'd had no intention of doing this, despite my suspicions about the abbreviated script of *Romeo and Juliet* I'd been given, but there was the $5,000 for just two matinees of work, during what I'd been afraid would be a down time in my production schedule, and also, I couldn't deny, there had been the longing to explore the possibilities of this side of me. When I signed the contract, could I really say I wasn't attracted to it by the other possibilities?

Overwhelmed by the new sensations, the sensuality of the circumstances, the sweetness of Kim's kisses, the sliding of Kim's sheathing hand on my throbbing cock, I let my pelvis relax and Kim's hand take control. It didn't take long to give Kim what was asked for.

"Sorry," I mumbled.

"I'm not," Kim responded, with a smile.

* * * *

"That's just as well," VanDerGrifff said, with a little laugh and a smile. He removed his hand from my forearm where we sat at the bar. I had to strain to hear him over the noise in the room, packed with gyrating bodies—all male. I had to strain equally to understand him as I'd had a drink or two too many in my nervousness to the alien—but dreamed of—position I was in. "It actually is just as hoped for what I have in mind. Consider what I proposed. I'll put it more formally in writing and mail it to you with a contract for you to sign if you're interested."

We parted then—or I should say, I left the gay bar, Tony VanDerGrifff, the play director from Washington, D.C., saying he was staying as he wanted to make a hookup. Before he had swung off in whatever direction he was going in, he'd called over a willowy transvestite in a gold lamé slip of a rag that barely covered anything, stuffed a fifty in her cleavage, and told her to give me a good time. Immediately pulling into me and running her hands over my biceps, she seemed willing and tried to drape herself over me even closer, but, embarrassed, I begged off and left the bar quickly.

I wondered if VanDerGrifff was mistaking whatever I'd said in my drunkenness about my dreams with some sort of reality.

I hadn't known he'd take me to a gay bar after my Off-off-Broadway performance as Stanley in a sexy production of *Streetcar Named Desire*. I'd been keyed up from the moment I'd discovered it was a gay bar and had taken another look at Tony, finding him intriguing and showing a comfort in this venue that I'd never taken the chance to develop. I'd just had the last of a mountain of fights with Petra and had left her with her slicing into me the parting declaration that I probably liked men better than women. I hadn't thought of that before—or had made an effort not to—but I'd given a whole lot of thought to it since. I just hadn't done anything about it.

I was in my bad-boy beefcake role phase on the stage and, in this production of *Streetcar*, had moved around the stage nearly throughout stripped down to the waist and being sullen and sultry. I'd had no idea that the Washington stage director who approached me at the end of the performance, invited me for a drink, and said he might have a short but lucrative gig for me, had done so for more than my stage performance. When we got to the gay bar in the Chelsea section of Manhattan, though, I began to think that his interest was purely sexual.

I learned that it was both, but he dropped the personal interest in me with the comment, "Pity that we want the same thing," after we'd had a discussion over too many drinks that had me revealing too much about my current state and frustrations and saying what I only barely could remember when I woke the next morning that I said. His interest in my stage work had been sustained though.

He was contracted to stage two privately commissioned, closed, all-male-cast matinee performances of a stylized *Romeo and Juliet* production at the American Shakespeare Center in Staunton, Virginia, in a month's time. I was being offered the role of Romeo. The remuneration was beyond satisfactory, I had dead time between productions that both the gig and the $5,000 would fill nicely, and it wouldn't take long to learn my lines. I had done *Romeo and Juliet* before. Mostly I had to remember which lines of Romeo to excise in this limited outing. The script concentrated on a graphically sexy relationship between Romeo and Juliet, with the normally unrequited love angle being very much requited. I signed the contract.

* * * *

Bare to the waist in a hip-hugging tight leather legging outfit, with a laced up codpiece, and writhing on top of Kim Hunter, decked out in a diaphanous wrap, atop the prominent altar and/or tombstone dominating the Shakespeare Center's stage in the first rehearsal of the abbreviated Romeo and Juliet production, I began to fully admit to the thrust of this production. Tony VanDerGrifff sat in the center of the hall, giving directions.

"Now fuck," his voice boomed out from the darkened hall.

"Fuck? Really fuck?" I lifted my head toward the spotlights and asked, incredulous.

"Yes, really fuck Kim," VanDerGrifff bellowed. "And make it really sexy. Show us hard dick in hole. Why do you think this high-roller client is willing to pay big bucks for this?"

Dutifully and willingly Kim reached a hand down between my thighs, which were encasing his legs, and started pulling at the lacings of my codpiece.

In shock, fool that I was for not fully accepting the lay of the land before now, I stopped Kim's hand with mine and sat up on the side of the altar, looking out into the audience.

"I can't," I said, breathing heavily. "I've never before . . . and with others watching." I had almost said I'd never fucked a man before. It was too late for VanDerGrifff to know this. I needed this money.

"Well, shit," Tony's voice rang out. "Let's cut for the day anyway. Maybe you and Kim can . . . later . . ."

Kim sat up beside me, lacing his arm around the small of my back and resting his hand on my thigh. "Let's go home. I'm sure we can work this out," he murmured.

Going home with Kim, who was playing Juliet. He was a bit-actor transvestite from the area, living in a small cottage in a town called Port Republic, where one river fed into the Shenandoah, in the shadows of the western slope of the Blue Ridge mountains. I'd just arrived in Staunton earlier that morning. It had been arranged that I would bunk with Kim Hunter during the production. I was only now aware of what bunking with Kim meant. There was only one bedroom in his cottage—but at this point I didn't know that. I'd come directly to the theater in downtown Staunton.

Assumptions had been made—probably my fault. Who knows what I told VanDerGrifff in that bar when I was drunk. At the time, I'd thought I was taking the first plunge with him. Naïve as I was, I hadn't been giving any thought to configurations of bottoms and tops. I obviously had gotten across to him, though, that I was interested in topping even if I hadn't specified how new the whole idea was to me.

I stewed about this as we drove northeast from Staunton late in the afternoon. I couldn't figure out what was holding me up. I'd dreamt of trying this out, and Kim was quite attractive, in an androgynous way. It would be an easier transition, taking a transsexual first as a progressive move to men.

I was still stewing, with Kim, at the wheel, turning a face of beauty to me from time to time, giving me an encouraging smile and murmuring, "Don't worry, we'll make it work. We'll work into it. I find it a turn on for me, actually, breaking in a hunk like you."

I had to admit that I found it all rather a turn on too. I just had to find a way to turn myself on—to get past my own natural inhibitions.

I was still mulling that when a convertible veered around us on the two-lane road leading into Port Republic, giving me only a glimpse of two young woman in the front seat, hooping and hallaring in drunkenness as they sped past us. But they didn't get much past us when the convertible went off the side of the road ahead and into a tree. Kim was already reaching for his cell phone to dial 911, as he eased his Mustang onto the shoulder of the road behind the flipped-over and smoking convertible.

Both girls were bruised, bleeding, and barely conscious as Kim pulled the driver and I her passenger out of the wreck that was popping and giving off flames. I held and rocked the passenger while I listened for the progress of the far-away sirens. She couldn't be out of her teens. She was too young for this—maybe to die.

At Kim's cottage, shaken, I lowered myself into a front porch chair as Kim continued on into the house, saying she'd get us a couple of beers and would be back in a few minutes. I was confused on whether to think of Kim as a "him" or a "her," but it helped at this point to lean toward the "her."

She took longer than a few minutes, and I'd stopped quaking and having my mind possessed with the sight of the overturned convertible before she came back out onto the porch and handed me a beer. She'd taken the time to change into a slinky red satin shift that couldn't have come much below what she was swinging between her thighs. Moving behind me, she handed me a beer over my shoulder and I took a big gulp of it. But after that one gulp, I had to put the beer down on a side table because she was tugging at my T-shirt, wanting to pull it over my head.

"I can't get over how magnificent your torso is, big boy—and a dick to die for," she was murmuring as she tugged on the T.

When she had my shirt off, she perched her chin on my shoulder as she'd done at the dressing table in the theater, and ran her hands down my chest. I was going hard in anticipating where she was going with this—where she'd been before. I was also panting lightly, which she seemed to appreciate.

"Tony picked a divine Romeo," she murmured in my ear. "You are one beautiful hunk of flesh. We'll work through this."

Then, as before, she turned my chin toward her face and we kissed as she ran a hand down to my crotch, unzipped me, and released my engorging cock. She didn't stroke me for long, though, before she'd come around to in front of me, straddled my legs with hers. She wasn't wearing anything under the shift. I shuddered in the shock of it—and a flash of pleasure went through my body.

Taking my head in both of her hands, she pressed my face into her belly and gave me a deep moan. A hand moved my hand under the hem of the dress, and I was encasing her cock and stroking it. A new, not unpleasant sensation, encouraged by her moans and her hands cupping my head and pulling my face into her. Then the hands were gone, and she was slowly pulling the shift up and off her body. My lips went to her belly button, opening over a gold ring there.

"Take me to heaven," she murmured, as her hands went back to cupping my head and pushing it down. My mouth opened naturally over the bulb of her cock and then down the sides of the shaft. I'd long fantasized over this act. Now that it was here, I just relaxed and took it naturally, guided by her sighs and groans.

This didn't last for long—I was quite willing to continue with it—before Kim was sinking down between my knees, taking my cock in her mouth, and quickly sucked me to an ejaculation.

This was a whole new, pleasurable sensation to me, too.

I could have done more, progressed further then, but with a laugh, wiping her mouth with the back of her hand, Kim popped up, laughed, and said, "That made me hungry. How about you? Let's go in and have some supper."

Yes I was hungry. A whole new sense of hunger. I wanted to take Kim then, throw him down on the grass, and fuck the stuffing out of him. Him, her, whatever. The shift off, I no longer could think of Kim as a "her." He was a trim, willowy young man, albeit there had been some work done on his breasts. I had sucked the cock of another man and been, in

17

turn, sucked off by a man myself. The transition in my perceptions was happening—and it wasn't the trauma that I had expected it would be. I wanted more.

But Kim was already moving into the house. Whether or not he wanted me to be enflamed and frustrated to the point of going all the way without giving it deep thought or falling under the wheels of inhibitions, that was the way this was working.

The dinner conversation centered on the two young women we'd sent off in ambulances earlier in the day, assured by the EMTs that both would make it—that they were lucky to have gotten out of the car before it went up in flames.

"I take it as a sign that we must grasp life as we can," Kim said. "That we never know how much more life there is for us. If we want something, we shouldn't take too long in grasping it."

Although intellectually I could have argued that if the girls hadn't been half looped and taking a great risk, life wouldn't have given them a whammy. But I got the point and I was trembling from want, sitting across the table from Kim, seeing the androgynous beauty of him and his half man, half woman shape in the red shift he had slid down his body again when we entered the house.

"I get the point," I said in a low, hoarse voice. "Which way is your bedroom."

Kim smiled and rose from the table.

Still in his shift, me naked and on my back on the bed, Kim rode my cock, facing away from me, initially maintaining control of the fuck and doing the rising and falling. As I became engulfed in the flames of desire, though, I sat up in the bed, ran my hands under the hem of the shift and up to cover the little mounds of breasts plastic surgery had given him, and started thrusting my hips up, reaching new depths and greater thickness inside his channel and making him cry out for me and bounce with increased rhythm on the staff.

After we'd cooled off from the fuck, I turned him on his belly, pulled the shift over his head, mounted his ass, and deep thrusted to another ejaculation, the two of us reaching it almost simultaneously now. He had gone up a bit on his knees, lifting his buttocks to me to receive me as deep as I could go—

letting me know he wanted what I was giving him, making me want to give him all that I had. From the back he was all man now. I had completed the journey; I was fucking another man. No pretenses of being with a woman.

After firing off again, I collapsed full length on top of him. Now it was me brushing aside the long strands of his hair, finding the hollow of his neck with my lips, and then coaxing his face around for a deep kiss.

"Again?" he murmured as we came out of the kiss.

"Yes, again and again," I answered, exhilarated by the new-found pleasure and release of it all.

"What now, though?" I asked.

"I guess Tony will know you can fuck me on the altar during the performance now." he answered in a dreamy voice.

Searching for the Exotic

Padding out of the communal shower in the apartment at Old Dominion University—ODU—that the father of Steve Tenley, a senior and the captain of the swimming team all us guys were on, rented for us, I heard the sounds of sex coming from the TV in the living room. Wrapping a towel around my waist, I padded in there to see what sort of DVD the guys had on.

There were six of us in the apartment, sharing three bedrooms. We all were on the ODU swim team—as a freshman, I was the youngest one of the group—and we all were actively gay too. That's why we were sharing an apartment. Most of the guys on the ODU swim team were gay. That's how we'd been recruited. Coach Wilson checked the high schools across the Mid-Atlantic region out real well. When he was pretty sure of the guys he was targeting, he'd come check us out our senior year as long as we had hit eighteen. He already knew our swimming credentials. He would wine and dine us, promise us all sorts of privileges and extra stash to come to ODU, and then, if we went back to his hotel room with him and let him fuck us, we'd get a scholarship offer.

The DVD running on the TV arrested my attention when I entered the living room. Really exotic. Three guys were going at it. They all were studs and hung. Two of the guys were spiking the third guy—together, at the same time. I took in my breath and felt the immediate arousal going through me. I'd seen a lot of gay porn DVDs before and I'd been fucked by

Coach, Steve, Chip, and a couple of the other guys. But I hadn't seen two guys with both of their dicks inside a third guy at the same time before. The third guy was grimacing, but he seemed to be enjoying it.

The DVD wasn't running just for its own benefit. Both Chip, a junior, and Jason, a sophomore, had their eyes glued to the set. Jason was bent over an ottoman on his belly right in front of the TV, and Chip was crouched over his back, hands on Jason's hips, and was fucking Jason in long, deep strokes. Jason was wearing a cut-off T, but otherwise both were naked. Their toes were buried into the carpet behind the ottoman to give them traction. Chip was thrusting, but Jason was thrusting back too. Both of them had classic swimmers' bodies—long and lean. Aerodynamic. I was more muscled than the two, and not so tall. Like Steve, I relied on muscle power to pull me through the water.

Jason was coaxing Chip's face around for kisses while they fucked, but both were paying attention to the movie too. I watched them for a couple of minutes, my butt twitching from the remembrance of Chip's cock, which wasn't thick, but it was unusually long and was curved up, so that the bulb dragged along the wall of a guy's channel as he stroked. Chip was gulping and shuddering with each stroke, which was pretty much the same reaction I had when Chip fucked me. In contrast, Coach's cock was like a beer can and he was a stuffer and pistoner, manhandling a guy and getting off as quick as he could. Steve was a finesser, the best mix of length and thickness, and spending time—caressing all the walls, taking his time, bringing a guy close to jack off and then backing off. Each approach to shooting off raising a guy to a new level of arousal.

As interesting as what Chip and Jason were doing was, what was happening on the DVD was newer and more fascinating to me—I'd been bent over that ottoman and fucked by Chip before myself. Seeing two guys fucking a third one at the same time was taking my breath away. I let my towel fall, took my erect cock in my hand, leaned back against the wall next to the door, and began to stroke myself, my eyes boring into the action on the DVD. My other hand went to tweaking my taut nipples.

"Come over here, Troy." It was Steve's voice—coming from somewhere over at the side, in the shadows.

I looked over into the corner of the room. Steve, naked, a towel at his feet was slouched in a straight chair. He had been leaving the shower when I entered it; he'd told me to stay in the shower so he could fuck me, but I said I had to get right back to the books but that I'd sleep in his bed that night, if he wanted, so he moved to the chair. He was watching Chip and Jason fuck and had his own hard on in his hand and was stroking himself.

I looked at Steve but then turned my eyes back to the TV set. I couldn't get enough of what I could see on the screen. When I'd come in, two of the guys were standing, with the third, a smaller guy—like I was smaller than most in the apartment—suspended between them, his legs off the ground, his knees hooked on the hips of one of the muscle-bound studs, and his fists locked behind the guy's neck. The other guy was crouched behind him, his hands covering the little guy's pecs. The camera shots made clear that both big guys had their dicks in the small guy's ass and both were pumping him.

When I looked back from seeing Steve over in the corner, the three had changed positions. They were on a bed now. One of the big guys was on his back, and the little guy was riding his cock, facing him. The third guy came up on his knees on the bed, straddling the other big guy's thighs. He palmed the belly of the small guy and used his other hand to work his cock inside the small guy's ass. That done, he cupped the small guy's chin with a hand, arching his torso back. The big guy under the small guy grasped the small guy's cock, and the three were set in motion.

The small guy on the DVD moaned deeply. So did I.

"I said come here," Steve growled from the corner of the room. I turned my eyes on him again. He was rolling a condom on his cock, and holding it erect. "Sit on it."

"Facing me," he commanded when I'd gotten over to him.

"No, I want to watch the DVD," I answered. But that didn't mean I wasn't going to sit on his cock. I slowly came down on it in his lap, my back to his chest. He let out a long sigh as I skewered myself, wrapped his arms around my chest, dug his teeth into the line between my shoulder blades, and started pulling me on and off the cock.

I continued watching the DVD as he fucked me. Even when he pushed me down on my hands and knees on the floor in front of the chair and crouched over my hips, pumping me deep and fast, I had my head raised, watching the double fuck on the DVD.

He shuddered, came in the bulb of the condom, and lowered his face to the hollow of my neck. "You like watching that doubling shit, don't you?" he whispered.

"Yes, I like that double fucking," I answered.

"Clean my cock. Suck me."

"After I see the two big guys shoot off," I answered.

"Fuck it," Steve growled, with a deep exhale of air. He pushed me down on my belly, as he pulled out of me, rose, and padded off toward the john.

He passed Coach Wilson by the door, who took the situation in, stripped off his sweatpants and jock as he walked over to the chair, put a foot on either side of my thighs, reached down and pulled me back up to my hands and knees, mounted my hips, and thrust inside me.

I groaned at the thickness of him and how hard and fast he started to stroke. He grabbed the hair on the back of my head and arched my torso up to his chest as he stroked me. I didn't mind. I had my eyes on the DVD, where the two big studs were now hovering over the little guy and pumping their cocks to arced ejaculations on his chest and face. Coach reached under and fisted my cock. Three strokes and I was spouting out on the carpet.

* * * *

I had been laying my head back on the passenger headrest, trying to keep it from spinning. We'd left The Wave in downtown Norfolk, where I'd had a few too many beers and where I'd gotten to the point of being felt up by a couple of guys before Steve had intervened, telling me to save it for later. There had been no later, though, and I was aching for the need to be laid.

We'd kissed and he felt me up some more when we got out to his truck in the parking lot. He unzipped for me and I leaned over in the seat and gave him a blow job, but when I thought he was going to pull me over into his lap and onto his cock, he didn't. He pushed me over toward the passenger window, put the truck in gear and nosed out onto the street.

"This isn't the way back to ODU," I said, having opened my eyes and taken a look out the passenger window.

"No, we're going over toward the naval docks," he said. "There's a club over there—the Continental—that I want you to see."

I lifted my wrist to where I could see my watch and concentrated on bringing the numbers into focus. "It's already nearly 2:00 a.m.," I said. "Everything should be closing."

"Not the Continental. It's just revving up. We're gonna get you done by some sailors."

"That sounds nice," I said vaguely, and closed my eyes and let my head fall back on the headrest.

The next thing I knew we were parking in a dark lot in a seedy-looking neighborhood of strip mall stores and he was herding me down the street. After a few blocks, there was an area that was lit up by neon signs. A few storefront bars and derelict-looking three- and four-story building with blinking signs that claimed they were hotels. Rising above them in the distance were the gray-steel superstructures of naval vessels, which told me we weren't far away from the naval yard.

As we drew closer, I could see that there were men milling around on the sidewalks—some were dressed like I was, in shorts, boots, and tight T-shirts. In my case, I was wearing a cut-off T in black mesh. In contrast, there were guys walking—or staggering—around in naval enlisted dress whites—tight white trousers, with wide bottoms, and white jumpers with black string ties. I had no doubt we'd found a red light district for gay sailors.

Steve, holding my arm—and almost holding me up as close to pass-out drunk as I was—waded into the crowd, ignoring propositions left and right. We came up to the head of an alley between two storefront bars. A naval guy was leaning up again the corner at the opening of the alley, a leg bent with his booted foot flat on the wall behind him. He was smoking a cigarette. He smiled and inclined his head toward us as Steve turned us into the alley. There was a quizzical look on his face. Steve didn't react to him, though, so his eyes went back into a "bored" setting and settled back on the wall.

Steve guided me down the alley, which was dimly lit from the street from which we had entered. Three quarters down the alley, we came upon two tall, muscular sailors, one white and one black, who were stripped to the waist, with their tunics hung over their shoulders. They were smoking and standing close together.

As we passed, the white guy reached out and run his fingers down my bare arm. "Hey, babe," he whispered.

"Inside," Steve muttered and kept dragging me down the alley.

The two sailor studs fell into step behind us and followed us to the back of the alley, which dumped into another alley. We made a left and then down some stairs into a basement. The word "Continental" was lit in a small neon sign over the area way we entered under the building. I could hear the raucous noise of men talking over loud music on a juke box. The black sailor moved around us, punched in some numbers on a keypad, and the large metal door opened into a large, square smoke-filled room. The place was overrun with muscular guys in various combinations of white enlisted naval dress. A bar ran down one side of the room, Across the room from that was a small stage, where a small, Hispanic guy in a red G-string was gyrating to the loud music on a pole. Round tables and scattered straight chairs were spread around the room. Guys in white mingled among these, all drinking beer, most feeling each other up.

Prominent in the club room were the blown-up art posters hanging around on the walls. I recognized the art work of Tom of Finland, the elongated, muscular bodies of sensual hunks in suggestive—some beyond the suggestive—poses. All of the subjects were sailors. What was going on in the club matched the randiness of the art in the posters, which seemed to stream down off the wall to materialize in actual sailors rutting around inside the testosterone-charged room.

Some guys were still in full dress. Others wore only their tight trousers, showing their arousal in bulging baskets, a few were only wearing the naval tunic, their dicks poking straight up from the bottom of the tunic hems. One small black guy was naked and on his back on top of a corner table. Two sailors were on either side of him, holding his legs up and spread. Another sailor was hunched over him between his legs, fucking him. A couple were standing in line behind that guy, stroking their cocks with their fists. The black guy's head was flopped over the other side of the table, and yet another sailor was feeding his face with a fat cock.

"Beer?" I heard Steve ask the two guys who let us into the club—they were both busy moving their hands on my body. The white guy said "Sure," and Steve went off to the bar. The white guy hustled me over to a table, sat down in a chair, and pulled me onto his lap. He sat me down sideways on his lap, my right leg suspended over his right leg. He unzipped me, and pushed my shorts down as he pulled me down into his lap. His right hand went immediately under my thigh and back up and grasped my package through the thin material of my briefs.

"I'm Jack and this here's Hook," he muttered, nodding at the black guy who was sitting down on the other side of us. "Gonna show you a real good time," he then said.

That was enough talking. His mouth went to my nipples then, pushing the lower hem of my mesh cut-off T up above my pecs. My back was pressed into the muscular chest of the black guy named Hook, who brought a hand around to palm my belly and cupped my chin with the other, turning my face to his for a kiss.

When I came out of the kiss, I could see that Steve had returned not only with the beers but also with a sailor of his own, who was sitting beside Steve by the table, the two of them kissing and with Steve fondling the sailor's package.

Out of the haze, I heard Jack say, "Wanna get fucked?"

"Sure," I answered. It was what I'd come out with Steve for tonight. It hadn't happened at The Wave, and I was hot for it.

The little black guy wasn't on the top of the table back in the corner anymore. I was. Guys were on either side of me, lifting and spreading my legs. With their free hands, one was pressing my belly down, holding me down on the surface of the table, and the other one was fisting and stroking my cock.

My head was flopped over the end of the table, and I had some guy's cock in my mouth. He was still in his tight trousers, and I reached up and held his hips on either side. First Jack, and then Hook and then I have no idea how many others, were between my legs. I jerked and groaned at the entry of each of the cocks, but I settled down for however each of the guys wanted to pump me.

Next thing I knew, I was being hustled back down the alley toward the street, Jack on one side of me and Hook on the other. I was dressed again. I had a beer in my hand. Steve sauntered behind us, arm-in-arm with the sailor he'd picked up.

A small hotel lobby, with a key being passed by an uncurious bearded guy in a cage. Then the stairs, with the two bulky sailors carrying me between them, my boots thumping on the steps.

A small, dimly lit bedroom, the light tinted red from the flashing neon sign outside the open window. Two twin beds. Steve and his sailor already naked and fucking on one of the beds. Hands stripping off my shorts, briefs, and T again.

Hook was sitting on the end of the other bed, lifting his big hands to me, pulling me down onto his lap—onto his cock. Skewering me deep and slowly bouncing me up and down on his shaft, his arms around my torso and mine around his. Jack was behind me, close. His hand came around; he had a bottle of poppers in it, which he placed under my nose. I inhaled and saw stars. Floating off in the clouds.

Hook laid his torso back on the bed, and with his hands on my waist, Jack pushed me forward. I felt the bulb of Jack's cock at my entrance, on top of Hook's buried shaft, and I murmured something. Whether it was an objection or a welcome, I knew not. Nor did it matter. I was writhing and groaning at the pain of Jack pressing his cock inside me, slowly sliding in on top of Hook's. I moaned deeply, and he cupped my chin and pulled my face around to his to possess my lips as he began to pump. Moaning and groaning, I was moving from dancing on the clouds to plunging to the depths, stretched to near splitting. Slowly, slowly accommodating to having two cocks inside me, moving against each other, filling, stretching, counterthrusting inside me.

Later, how much later I didn't know. Empty bottles of beer on the nightstand next to the bottle of poppers. I was on my back, my legs spread. Steve between them, pumping me, while Jack fucked the other sailor on the other bed. Then Jack inside me. Then Hook.

Doubled again, Jack on his back and me riding his cock, Hook coming in behind, pushing me forward on Jack's chest, and then pushing his cock inside me, on top of Jack's. Easier to take now, but still taking my breath away as they both pumped.

I woke up with a headache and tracings of light coming in through the window, diluting the red tint of the neon sign so that I no longer felt like I was swimming in a bloody sea. Steve was stretched out beside me, embracing me, his face buried in the side of my neck. He felt me stirring, though and raised up on an elbow and looked down at me.

"You OK?" he asked, in a low voice.

"Yes, I think so," I answered.

"Hurting anywhere."

I was, of course. "Not too bad," I answered. "Where . . . ?"

"You're in a hotel room. The guys from last night had to get back to their ship early this morning. You get what you wanted to try? You OK with it?"

"What I wanted to try? You arranged this?"

"Yes, you were safe. I know these guys. You wanted to try DP. I know you did. You OK now?"

"Yeah, I guess so," I answered. I did an inventory of my body. The worst was the headache from the beers and I'd done most of that damage myself.

"I'm gonna fuck you again now. Then we'll shower and leave. I paid for the hotel room. You OK with that?"

"Yeah, I'm OK with that," I answered. And I was. "Those two guys. Jack and Hook."

"You want them together again, don't you?"

"Yes."

"OK, I'll arrange it. Coach said to keep you happy."

* * * *

28

I was sitting on Steve's lap, facing the TV set in the apartment living room, and rising and falling on his cock, while he held me with hands on my waist. My eyes were glued to the DVD that was running.

"What in the hell . . . ?"

"It's called sounding," Steve answered. "Fucking a guy's piss slit with steel rods they call wands. Gotta be careful, but I understand the feeling is incredible. Really brings up the cum."

"Fascinating," I whispered, not being able to take my eyes away from the two guys on the screen. They were sitting yoga style, facing each other, their legs encircling each other's waists. One of the guys was holding the cocks together with one hand, as the other leaned back, supported by his fists buried in the carpet beside his rump. His face was pointed at the ceiling, he was making soft mewing sounds, and he had the look of ecstasy on his face.

The guy holding their erect cocks together with one hand, was using the other to alternately slowly spin metal rods that he'd buried in the piss slit of each of their cocks. The cock of the guy who was looking dreamy had foamy precum coming out around the sides of the rod buried in his cock.

The ecstasy on the guy's face had me mesmerized. I'd give anything to be as aroused and satisfied as that.

"You want that. You want to be sounded, don't you?" Steve asked.

My lips felt dry and I licked them. "Yeah, yeah, I want that," I answered in a whisper, not being able to take my eyes away from it. Frightened, yet drawn by it, aroused by it, at the same time.

Steve sighed. "Well, I know a guy, and Coach said to keep you happy."

Men of Mykonos

Kenton stood on the terrace of the rental vacation villa and watched Georgiou enter the taxi on the street down the steep incline at the base of the complex. The bullet-headed bald, yet otherwise hirsute, Greek with the physique of a wrestler didn't turn to wave back. He just folded himself in the taxi and was gone from Kenton's life.

Kenton hadn't really expected more—but he had hoped. As gruff and all-business matter-of-fact as Georgiou had been, he'd filled the void in Kenton's life since Kenton's long-time lover, James Fendall, had chosen to die and leave Kenton in the lurch. The death had been unexpected. James had been the decision-maker, the doer, the businessman who knew how to get everything done and who wasn't afraid of the telephone as the younger writer, Kenton, had been.

Kenton had held his own financially—his novels sold well—but he hadn't had a clue what to do with the money—how to translate it into goods and services to support himself. James had provided all of that, including the domination and guidance in bed.

When James had had the terminal heart attack, Kenton was suddenly left on his own. There would be a considerable inheritance, but he wouldn't be able to touch it for a year or more as it went through probate. That wasn't a real problem. Kenton had money of his own. The real problem was how he was going to take care of himself. James' estate was large enough that his lawyer took interest in it and in Kenton.

Knowing the relationship and preferences of the couple, and knowing that Kenton was a novelist, the lawyer had not only suggested that Kenton retreat to the quietude and simpler life of some Greek island for the fall, so that he could get his life reoriented, but he also volunteered to connect Kenton with an LGBT travel agency that would handle all of the arrangements, including a guide to handle everything right up to the door of the rental villa—and to handle the client, as requested.

"Knowing how you are about decisions, I asked that your guide be a power top," the lawyer had said, without blinking an eye.

Kenton had been leery of making such a big change, but one night after returning from James' internment in New Orleans to the penthouse Philadelphia apartment that he and James had shared was enough to tell Kenton he couldn't just continue here on his own. He found he had no idea how the heating or air conditioning system worked or even how to answer the main telephone console before it reverted to voicemail. It only then dawned on him how much James had taken care of, leaving Kenton to live in his own fantasy world as he spun out his mid-market gay male romance novels.

The lawyer accompanied Kenton to New York to meet with the travel agency. Kenton had remained skeptical and a bit spaced out on everything until that evening when they met for drinks with the prospective personal guide in Kenton's New York hotel.

"This is what we do. I will take care of everything," the guide had said, laying out documents on the cocktail table in the hotel bar. Georgiou was a muscular man in his late forties—probably five years or so older than Kenton was, who was built well enough himself, but along much trimmer lines than the guide, obviously a native Greek, was. Georgiou was definitely the take-charge, self-assured man. The way he'd put his hand on Kenton's arm, or back, as they moved to the alcove in the bar showed aggression and assertion. Kenton couldn't help but feel a comfort with this man that he hadn't felt since James died. But beyond the basic comfort there was a slight nervousness at the assertiveness of the man. James had been much smoother and had put more effort into manipulating Kenton while not making Kenton feel how dependent he was. Of course, when James died, Kenton instantaneously learned how dependent he'd been—or slowly had become—all those years the two had been together.

"I have a cock of twenty centimeters and three and a half centimeters in girth," Georgiou had told Kenton matter-of-factly, "and I can penetrate hard again in ten or fifteen minutes, depending on how attractive I find the man."

Kenton had nearly choked on the olive in his martini. He'd never known a man as direct as this. It all seemed just to be business information to Georgiou. And centimeters always made a man sound like a superman.

"You will stay in this villa on Mykonos, a Greek island not far south of Athens, for three months," Georgiou said, showing Kenton the brochure for a line of two-story stucco houses with terraces on a rocky mountainside. There was a swimming pool on a terrace below, and then, shown in other photos, a steep, rocky slope down to the cruise ship docks and a shoreline that snaked around the base of the mountains and the C-shaped Mykonos harbor. The town and villas perched above on the mountainside were mostly of brilliant—white stucco, with ochre- and natural rock-walled ones blended in. It was a scene of cleanliness, sunshine, and relaxation, punctuated with bougainvillea, hibiscus, and oleander. "It's the best of Greece. I come from there myself. You are a beautiful man; you will find men there very soon who will service you. If you don't, we will provide a stallion for you."

There was no choice. This was the statement of where he would stay. And the agency would provide for his sexual needs, if necessary. Kenton felt comfortable with this, whereas most probably expected more input. The lawyer had done well in describing his client and his needs.

"We will fly to Athens, I will give you three-days of tour there and will bed you every night, and then a Greek cruise boat to Mykonos. Just one night cruising. Nothing fancy in a boat, but sufficient. The hotel in Athens, of course, will have a good view of the Acropolis. Five days and you will be there. I will take just carryon, so you have double baggage allowance for your three-month stay in Mykonos. Three months later I come for you, we fly to Rome for tour there, and then back to New York. I take care of everything. And I sleep in your bed and service you two times a day by contract, unless you request less."

"I don't know," Kenton said, looking at the lawyer a little dubiously.

"I take good care of you," Georgiou interjected himself into whatever the lawyer might say. "Need your passport to do documentation. I do it all. I service you expertly—in all ways."

Kenton hesitated, looking at the lawyer, who was giving him encouraging, "just go with the flow," looks.

"Give to me your room key," Georgiou said, assertively, holding out a beefy hand, the reverse side of the palm covered with curly black hair shot through with gray. "We go to your room for your passport now, yes? I take good care of you. I service you now. I fuck you good."

Kenton glanced over at the lawyer, who smiled and parroted the Greek. "Go with Georgiou. He will take good care of you. I will talk with you in the morning. Say the breakfast bar at 9:15?"

Georgiou propelled Kenton to the elevators and then down the corridor to the hotel room with a beefy hand at the small of Kenton's back. Georgiou had the room key card, maintaining complete control. Kenton felt himself falling into a comfort zone. Someone else was making all of the decisions.

Inside the hotel room, Georgiou said, "I take care of you now. I handle everything for you on trip. Take off your clothes now. I fuck you good now." And when Kenton was slow getting to that, Georgiou reached over and started pawing his clothes open. Kenton stepped away from him, and stripped himself, as, standing close to him, close enough for both of them to know that the Greek was in full control, Georgiou quickly stripped down as well.

Kenton sucked in his breath. The Greek was magnificently built. He had a great, muscular, hirsute wrestler's body for a man his age—and he was hung and in half erection. He grabbed Kenton's biceps on both sides and held the younger man at a stretch, looking his naked body up and down. Kenton could only look at the Greek's cock, which was elevating into an erection.

"You have beautiful body," the Greek said. "A dancer? A model? I could reload for penetration hard in ten minutes or less for a body like this."

"A novelist," Kenton answered nonsensically, his voice came out in a squeak of arousal. "But, yes, I was a male model when I was younger."

"Handsome face. Good body. Nice cock. I fuck you good. Under thirty?"

"Thirty-six, actually," Kenton said. But he was flattered.

"No matter. I forty-eight, but no worry. I eat my olive oil. I fuck like a younger man. You sign for trip, I fuck you two, three times a night, more than contract says. I stay hard good. Turn around and hold your cheeks open, please. I want to see the hole." And then, when Kenton complied. "Ah, I fill that good."

Kenton could readily see that the man had no trouble getting hard—and thick.

"I fuck you good. I take good care of you. It's easier when the man has beautiful body, like you. Go down on your knees and suck me now. Then I fuck you good. I take good care of you. You will be well-fucked all the way to Mykonos. No worry about that."

Kenton was on his knees at the end of the bed, with Georgiou covering him close from above. Georgiou was grunting, one arm wrapped around Kenton's chest, two lube-slathered fingers of his other hand working Kenton's anal entrance hard. Kenton, forehead to mattress, was groaning from the probing of the fingers. Once Georgiou had gotten him into the room and started giving directions, it hadn't occurred to Kenton to object or question. James had always controlled what was going to happen. Kenton had been the total submissive with James. He just slipped into the same subservient role with Georgiou, even though Georgiou was rougher. Somehow the cruder, more demanding manner made him more submissive.

"You take big cock, yes? Lawyer tell travel company you like big cock. My cock big. Very, very big."

"Yes, I like big cock," Kenton admitted with a whimper, as a third finger entered his ass. What hadn't the lawyer told them? And how did the lawyer know James had a big cock? Just how close had James and his lawyer been? And there was no questioning that this Greek muscleman had a big cock—an extra thick one. What did three and a half centimeters work out to in inches anyway? Something thick, for sure.

What perhaps the lawyer didn't know was that it wasn't always just James' big cock Kenton took. Kenton was unbelievably elastic that way, and what James sometimes gave him—and what he missed the most—was an extra man in the bed—and inside Kenton. But it wasn't something Kenton felt he could talk about with anyone now. It had been James' and his secret. He wasn't likely to experience anything like that again, he didn't suppose.

"They call on Georgiou for you because Georgiou has extra big cock; twenty centimeters long and three and a half centimeters thick," the Greek said, his voice full of pride. "I take good care of you. No other travel company take care of you like Georgiou take care of you." He was taking good care of Kenton now, fingering him forcefully.

"Oh, god, oh, god, I think I'm going to come."

"You not come yet," Georgiou directed, and the voice of authority was recognized and accepted by Kenton's ball sac, although it was aching for release. Kenton hadn't been fucked since before James died. It had him on edge.

He moaned. "I need to—"

"I fuck you now," Georgiou said, ignoring any need Kenton might want to express, pulling his fingers out, and turning Kenton to a seated position on the bed. He had a Trojan Magnum condom packet in his hand. "You must put rubber on as agreeing you want fucked. Company policy."

With trembling hands, Kenton crowned Georgiou, who then turned him back to his knees on the bed and slowly penetrated him while Kenton huffed and moaned. When fully saddled, Georgiou grabbed Kenton's biceps and, wham, wham, started stroking him hard and deep, as Kenton groaned and moaned under him. Half way to Georgiou's ejaculation, the Greek reached around Kenton's belly with a hand, grasped Kenton's cock, and jacked him off.

Afterward, as Kenton lay on the bed and watched Georgiou get dressed, He asked. "Do you need anything else other than my passport? Shall I get that for you?"

"Don't need anything now," Georgiou said. "You can hand documents in at travel office when you sign papers for the trip." And then he was gone. In the end it had all been rather perfunctory and businesslike—as was the eventual five-day trip from New York to Mykonos. But Kenton couldn't say that Georgiou didn't take good care of him in sexual terms—at least in numbers of ejaculations—and in terms of those twenty and three-and-a half centimeters.

But there had been no affection in any of the servicing. Thus Kenton had no reason to be surprised—and wasn't—that Georgiou just got in the taxi at the Mykonos villa rental at the end of the trip without even a look back.

As the taxi pulled away, Kenton's eyes lateralled to the complex swimming pool two levels lower on the mountainside, where a young Greek god in a blue Speedo was skimming the pool. He had to be in his mid twenties—tall, lithe, but well-muscled, black curly hair, pouty lips. He was gorgeous and knew he was. His forearms, thighs, and pecs were lightly dusted with black curly hair. As he skimmed the pool, he was looking back up to the terraces of the line of small villas, each with an eight-foot, bougainvillea-covered pergola outside the terrace doors. Kenton fancied the young man was looking directly at him, as if checking out the latest arrival at the complex.

Georgiou's "you will find your own man soon enough" prediction went through Kenton's mind. Kenton had always gone with older men, but maybe it was time to change that.

"A beautiful young man. Alas, his and my preferences are the same." The voice was a deep baritone. Kenton turned his face to the terrace of the neighboring villa. An older man, perhaps in his late fifties, was sitting on a rough-wood, thatched-bottom village chair, a beer bottle in one hand and a cigar in the other, and was moving his gaze from the pool below to his new neighbor at the side. "His name is Panos. He works maintenance here at the vacation villas in the morning and has a charter boat down in the harbor in the afternoon and evening. He goes for 200 euros for the night."

36

"He takes people out in the sea at night?" Kenton asked. He took a closer look at the man who had addressed him. He'd had a physically demanding life. He was probably shorter than Kenton and a bit grizzled, but compact, muscular but lean. His face was craggy, but full of character, his hair was wavy, dominated by gray, but once had been black, and curly black hair peeked out of the neckline of his T-shirt.

The man arched his head back and produced a hearty laugh. "No. That's for sleeping with him—being fucked by him, two or three times in the night, if you can take it. He's a male prostitute. He has a very nice cock. Not as nice as mine, of course, but quite presentable, and he knows how to use it, I'm told. Probably a very interesting experience, although he and I like the same thing. I think he might not be for you, though. I heard that man who just left talking to you. He lays you, doesn't he? You must like older men than you."

Kenton didn't know what to say to such a forward statement, so he simply said, "He was the guide who brought me here for the company who rented this villa for me for the season. We came from Athens—well, from New York, actually." Kenton thought of the overnight sail from Athens in the creaking Greek cruise boat that was all small portholes, no balconies. They were in a suite, so Kenton could only feel sorry for those in the regular cabins. But it had only been for one night—and Kenton indeed had lain under Georgiou three times in the night, his legs wide spread and bent, Georgiou lying between them and deep inside him and moving for what seemed to be forever, so there was little to think or complain about concerning the amenities of the Greek ferry.

"I'm sorry if I have seemed too forward," the man said. "but I think it's best to know who does what, who is looking for what, here. It saves time. I'm sure you know that these villas are for gay men—and that much fucking goes on here. So, that much really is not much of an assumption. My name is Santos. I am here for the fall season."

No, Kenton hadn't known that the villas were exclusively for gay men. He should have known, of course, considering that that was what the company that arranged it specialized in. "My name is Kenton, although you can call me Ken. And I am here for the fall season too."

"You are a beautiful man, but you look sad. Was that your lover leaving you just now?"

"No, that was the guide who brought me here," Kenton repeated. "I had a long-time lover who died and I am here to recover from that."

"But the man who just left. He was your lover too, I think."

"Only for the days traveling here from New York."

"But he covered you, no? You submitted to him. I think I am right about that."

"Yes, you are right about that," Kenton said, a tone of slight resignation in his voice. The man was going to chip away at him until his soul was naked. He somehow was sure of that.

"And what is the sexual attraction of this man, this guide of yours?"

"He has a cock twenty centimeters long and three and a half thick." Kenton meant it to be a flippant answer, to embarrass the man from talking of such intimacies, but the man laughed and bored in with his questions.

"A good answer. A very good answer. And you must have it often, I think, big like that. And missed it when your lover died."

"I missed it, of course," Kenton answered. "But this man who just left, he was just part of the travel service."

"And he walks with the assurance of a hung man. I believe the measurements you give. Your lost lover—he was hung too, I think?"

"Yes, both of them hung like bulls." Kenton felt the layers of his privacy being stripped away. The older man—he must be Greek, as Santos was a Greek name and he had all of the physical characteristics of a Greek man—was stripping him bare. But he came across as a dominant, self-assured man. And Kenton so easily slipped into a subservient role.

"Once a man is hung, that never changes. And a good lover improves with age and experience. I, for instance, am hung like this bull you speak of, and I have considerable experience. We Greeks—it is because we eat pure olive oil, I'm told—we are still great lovers at an old age—sometimes better when old, more experienced and in tune with what the men lying under us want and need. You are a beautiful man. I would like—"

"My life is changing so much now," Kenton broke in. "I'm not sure what I want anymore. I need some time . . ."

"But, of course. I don't want to seem too forward. Most men come to these villas looking for companionship. For immediate sex. But I am here for the season and you are too. So there is time. When you want me to fuck you, you will come to me."

That's not how my psyche works, Kenton thought. Men take me; I don't pursue them. They tell me to lie down and open my legs for them and I do. Would he do that for this forward, self-assured man if he demanded it here and now? Probably, he thought.

Santos stubbed his cigar out in an ashtray on a side table, put the empty beer bottle down, and stood. "There is, of course, a young stud like Panos down there. He's looked up here several times, so he has noticed you now. Remember, 200 euros for a coupling with Panos. And then there is experience—for free." He gave a low whistle, which prompted Kenton to look around to him. His fly was open and his cock was exposed. He was hung and in half erection. "As you can see, more than twenty centimeters. I can give you more than your guide gave you."

Kenton shuddered and looked away.

"Whenever you want it, it is here for you," Santos said, as he pushed the cock back inside his shorts and zipped up. He turned and went back into his villa.

Kenton turned toward the rail of the terrace, his eyes taking in the stretch of the harbor. The clutch of buildings down at the town center; the scattering of white, ochre, and stone buildings on the sides of the encircling mountains; the translucent blue-green of the water; and the ships—the balconied cruise ship just at the dock below the line of gay-resort villas and the Greek ferry slowly moving out of the harbor, taking Georgiou back to Athens. His eyes then came back up the hillside to the pool below. Panos was standing there, looking up at him.

I wonder how many centimeters, he thought. Then he shuddered, pulled away from the rail and walked back into the

39

villa. It was a self-contained unit. They had stopped on the way up the hill and Georgiou had bought him enough provisions for a week. The kitchen was at the other end of the unit from the sea. It was separated from the dining and living room section by a counter. A metal circular staircase went up to the second floor, which had a small bedroom, with a single bed, above the kitchen; a bathroom; and, on the sea side of the building, a master bedroom opening out to a balcony above the pergola over the terrace below.

Standing in the living room and looking down at his unopened luggage, Kenton thought, Now what? He already felt alone and lost—and not having any idea what to do next.

He took one of the suitcases upstairs to the master bedroom and placed it on the floor. He was drawn to the balcony and once there, he realized that he had come out to look at Panos again down at the pool. But no one was at the pool when he looked toward it.

Disappointed, he came back into the bedroom and then down the stairs to retrieve the other suitcase. When he got to the bottom of the stairs, though, he heard a knock on the door. He opened it to a smiling Panos.

"Hello. My name is Panos. I help with what needs to be done here. You are new, I think. Are there any services you are needing?"

Involuntarily, by instinct, Kenton drew out his wallet and extracted a 200-euro note and lifted it for Panos to see. Panos laughed, smiled broadly, put a hand on Kenton's sternum to move him back from the door so that the young Greek could enter, and pulled a condom disk from the waistband of his Speedo.

Despite the 200 euros, Kenton had to do most of the work at the beginning. Panos lay on his back on the master bed, his wrists locked behind his neck, and grinning up at Kenton, as, facing Panos' head and riding his pelvis, Kenton fucked himself on Panos' very nice cock. After Kenton had ejaculated on the young Greek's chest, though, Panos began earning his fee. He pushed Kenton over to the side and then onto his back. Standing by the bed, he pulled the condom off, grabbed Kenton's head by the hair, and brought Kenton's mouth to his cock, almost brutally face fucking Kenton and creaming his face.

"You got beer?" he asked almost immediately after coming.

"Downstairs, in the refrigerator," Kenton answered, meekly, running the back of his hand over his face to wipe away Panos' cum.

"Stay here. I give you a special for the first time. No more charge."

Kenton watched the lithe, dancer's body move gracefully down the stairs. The young man's cock was nice, but it wasn't anything close to the size of James' or Georgiou's, or, for that matter, what Santos from next door had shown him. Still his body was young and hard. Kenton had always gone with older men. There was something exciting and different— and a bit dangerous—about this young man. Kenton had never been with a male prostitute before—young or old. What wasn't different was Panos' self-assurance. All he need do was tell Kenton what he wanted, and Kenton likely would do it.

Thus, when Panos came back with a length of nylon rope he'd found somewhere downstairs and started tying Kenton's wrists together and then pulling his arms over his head and tying his wrists to the headboard, Kenton only looked on with wide-open eyes. He'd never been bound and fucked before.

He was now, though. Royally fucked.

Panos stuffed pillows under the small of his back to raise and turn up his hips, rolled the condom back on that he'd used earlier, grabbed and wishboned Kenton's ankles, and pushed his knees under Kenton's buttocks. He cupped Kenton's face in his hands, staring hard into Kenton's eyes. Kenton panted, feeling the bulb of the cock resting just inside his rim. Panos patted him on the cheeks, moving his face back and forth and then, coming in for a French kiss, plunged his cock deep into Kenton's channel, as Kenton tried desperately, and unsuccessfully to break the kiss so he could scream. Panos fucked him hard and long.

After he was done, Panos slipped on his Speedo and, while untying Kenton's wrists, declared, "You are a good fuck. I charter a boat down in the harbor. I take you out sometime and fuck you good and proper on the sea where no one can hear us. Try it; you'll like it. For you, only 100 euros."

At the head of the stairs, he looked back and said, "Welcome to Mykonos."

Yes, welcome to Mykonos, Kenton thought when Panos was gone. He immediately felt the loneliness sweep in again. This was the wildest fuck he'd ever had. But Panos had suggested he could do wilder. Was this what Kenton was looking for?

* * * *

Kenton came slamming out onto the terrace late the next morning wrapped in a robe and fuming. Santos already was out on his terrace, this time with a bottle of wine and two glasses sitting on the side table beside him. He was only wearing shorts and sandals.

"*Kalimera*," Santos said in a pleasant voice, not showing whether or not he saw the mood Kenton was in.

"Excuse me?" Kenton said, turning toward the neighboring terrace. He hadn't seen Santos sitting there when he'd come out. He ratcheted his ire down. He was taken aback by seeing the older man bare chested. He was deeply tanned and in quite good muscular shape. The salt and pepper hair on his pecs was profuse and tapered down his belly.

"*Kalimera* is good morning in Greek," Santos said. "It will be helpful for you in the village if you learn a few Greek phrases. They won't expect much. This is a tourist town, so almost everyone speaks English, but they will appreciate the gesture. I'll be happy to teach you some phrases—perhaps while we are making love, while I am inside you."

Ignoring the last part, Kenton said, "*Kali* . . ." but couldn't go any further.

"*Kalimera*," Santos patiently repeated.

"*Kalimera*," Kenton repeated.

"Very good. But you seem upset this morning. I would have thought you felt quite satisfied after yesterday afternoon."

"Pardon?"

"The walls. They aren't too thick in these villas. And you make considerable noise when having sex. Panos is good at bringing out passion in a man, isn't he? I can bring out passion in a man too—maybe better than Panos can."

"Ah," Kenton said. So that's why Panos had said they could go out on the sea to make love—that they could go where there was no one to hear them.

"So, was Panos good for you? You seemed nervous yesterday—like you needed a man inside you. I was quite willing to help you with that. I'm still willing. Perhaps you can come into my villa now, and—"

"Yes, Panos was very good," Kenton answered, too exasperated to try to deflect the bluntness and openness of Santos' conversation.

Keying on this, Santos continued, "Something seems wrong this morning with you, though. I heard you curse a few times in the night. I hope you don't have the traveler's curse."

"No, no sickness," Kenton said.

"Good, because it's no good fucking a man who has the shits."

Once again Kenton let this baldness pass. On some level he found it arousing, though. And now that he'd seen both Santos' cock and his bare chest, Kenton was finding this bold, crude bantering welcome. Somehow it was more honest than he was used to get during the mating dance in the States.

"It's the lights in my villa over here. They won't come on. I kept looking for some way to turn them on. I guess I'll have to try to track Panos down this morning. He said he was the maintenance man here in the mornings."

"And perhaps spend another 200 euros on him?" Santos said, with some amusement in his voice.

"Perhaps," Kenton said, beginning to fall in with Santos' conversation style.

"Do you like young cock? Is he not too vigorous for you?"

"I usually go with older men. He's different. A little hard to keep up with, yes. But I suppose I'm here for the adventure."

"Older men like me have more experience. I would bring you with me. We would peak at the same moment. I can peak a man again and again until his balls ache and he begs for release. Have you ever had your balls ache and enjoyed it? Ah, no, probably not. But I could do that for you. I would take good care of you. I could give you three climaxes in quick succession too, if you wish. Make your balls ache for want of it and then bam, bam, bam. Cum everywhere. We would need a mop."

Kenton felt himself warming to the innuendo. But it wasn't really innuendo. It was more explicit than that. The "I would take good care of you" was just what Georgiou had said, and in many ways he had, indeed, taken good care of Kenton. From the way Santos talked, though, Kenton thought that perhaps Santos would give him more attention in sex than Georgiou did and this was warming him up.

"I could show you the magic of the lights in your villa," Santos said. "There is a secret to it. I could teach the secret to you."

"You could? You will?"

"For a small price."

"And what's that?" Kenton said, now a bit amused and also a bit relieved. Perhaps there was something simple that needed to happen with the lights. Maybe he didn't have to be as upset as he'd gotten in the evening and the night. Having something like that not work was a reminder of how dependent he'd been on James—and then, in several ways, on Georgiou while they were traveling.

"Tell me, do you sleep naked?"

"Yes, why?"

"Are you naked under that robe?"

Kenton didn't answer right away, which was answer enough for Santos.

"Stand and open your robe and let me see your body and then I will show you the secret of the lights in your villa."

"Oh, hell, why not?" Kenton said. He turned toward Santos and opened his robe.

"As I thought, a beautiful body. I could make music on that body. And you are aroused."

Closing his robe again, Kenton said. "You are quite forward in your talk. That would probably arouse a statue. I don't think it means anything today, though."

"You don't think? Or you know it doesn't mean anything today?"

"It doesn't mean anything today."

"But perhaps some day?"

"Perhaps. But you were going to show me about the lights."

"I can tell you, unless you wish me to come over there inside your house, where I can show you how to fix the lights and you can invite me upstairs, and, speaking of lights, I could fuck your lights out."

"The lights. The secret of the lights. If you can tell me from here, that would be best." Kenton was smiling, though. He had already decided that he would try this man out someday—not today, though. His thoughts went to the size of the man's cock. More than twenty centimeters apparently. How much more? How many centimeters was James? What's eight and a half inches in centimeters?

Panos had worn him out, but it was more from the athletic positions, being bound, and the vigorous thrusts than for where he could reach, what he could stretch.

"Just inside the entrance to your villa, on the wall by the kitchen, there is a box. I don't think they shot home the breaker for you that connects the lights to the electricity. They turn that off when the villa isn't occupied."

Kenton went in and threw the switch, and, sure enough, the lights came on. He thought it only polite then to return to the terrace and thank Santos for the help.

"That's too bad," Santos responded.

"How so?"

"If you truly had a light problem, you could have come to my bed tonight. I don't have a light problem."

"Then that opportunity has been lost," Kenton said, with a laugh.

"Since I helped you, perhaps you can help me."

"With what?"

"This bottle of wine. I'm told that it's healthy for me to drink the wine, but not the whole bottle. That raises a conundrum. I need someone to help me drink this bottle of wine, and I just happen to have two glasses here."

"You just happen to have two glasses," Kenton repeated, still amused.

"Come over here and drink this wine with me. When we are done, I can put you on my lap and fuck you. Do you remember how big my dick is? I can tickle your tonsils with it inside you."

"I'll share the wine, but for today, I will sit over here on the other side of this fence and vine."

"For today? So, perhaps on another day, I can put you on my lap and fuck you? You have a beautiful body. It needs to be used."

"Perhaps on another day. Not today, though. Today, I have to go see the village."

"And let Panos take you out in his boat and fuck you on the sea?"

"Perhaps."

"For 100 euros? He offers a discount for those he likes."

"Money is to serve one's needs."

"I will pay you 300 euros to let me bed you." By now, Santos had filled a glass with wine and delivered it across the fence. Both men were at the rail and looking down into the Mykonos harbor.

"If I thought you were serious . . ."

"Of course I am serious."

"You don't look like a man who can waste money like that."

Santos laughed. "Looks can be deceiving. I am a rich man. See that yacht down there in the marina? The largest one? Over toward this end. That is mine. These vacation villas—they are mine too. The villa you are renting is mine."

Kenton didn't really believe him. Santos was just playing him, he thought.

"Besides, I have seen your body now. I pay that much for the prostitutes down in the town and they don't have the beautiful body you have or even the one I have. Look at me, Ken."

Kenton turned his head again and gasped. Santos had stood and dropped his shorts. He was as naked as Kenton was under his robe. And this time his cock was in full, magnificent erection.

"Have you ever been fucked raw, Ken? I am checked regularly. I like to bareback fuck. I can bring you pleasures skin on skin that Panos never could. Don't ever let Panos fuck you raw. He goes with whoever pays 200 euros. I am pickier than that—and checked each time I fuck a new man. I will pay you 400 euros to bareback fuck you. Just show me a doctor's certificate."

"Which couldn't happen today," Kenton answered with a shaky voice. He knew now that, yes, Santos would fuck him—someday—unless the man was just toying with him.

"No, not today. Today, we enjoy this bottle of wine. Then you say you wish to go down into the town. I will give you the address of my doctor. I will call ahead and make the arrangements for the check. No need to pay. You just need to let him taste you bareback too. We share, and when I send him a man for check that's how I can be sure the man checks good—Doctor Mavrades must fuck him raw too. Mavrades willing to do that, I know test is valid. OK? You go to the doctor while you are in town?"

"Perhaps," Kenton answered. He was so keyed up now, though, that he regretted that there would be a wait. He decided just not to take Santos seriously about giving the doctor privileges in exchange for a bill.

Santos saluted him with the last dregs of the wine in his glass. "You have me excited now. I must give myself relief."

Kenton could see over the separating fence that Santos had his cock in hand and was stroking himself. If anything the cock was longer than it had seemed before.

"You wish to watch? Or this time I could use a rubber and service you. How about it? You come over the fence and onto my lap? From the noises you made with Panos, I know you are a passionate man who enjoys it."

"Let's leave it as a 'perhaps later' for now," Kenton said in a shaky voice, as he struggled up from his chair and started backing into the house.

"Tell me before you retreat, Kenton. You are going to let me fuck you someday, aren't you?"

"Yes, Santos, I'm going to let you fuck me someday." He turned, entered his villa, and raced up the circular stairs to his bedroom, lay on his back, and jacked himself off.

He had no idea why "yes, someday" couldn't have been a "yes now."

* * * *

There was no more intent going for Kenton that afternoon when he descended the hill and walked into the harborside town of Mykonos—having the same name as the island—than to acclimate himself to what was there. He had the address of Dr. Mavrades tucked away in his wallet, but that whole scenario that Santos had spun for him—intending to bareback him and gaining assurance that the doctor had thoroughly check him for disease first by barebacking him himself after a clean bill of health—seemed quite outlandish. Santos was a funny little man, plying Kenton with sexual innuendo to the point of arousing interest in Kenton and then making demands on him that included being fucked by another man first.

It just wasn't going to happen—at least in that way. He would let Santos fuck him—but with a condom—and he hoped to hell that he wasn't disappointed that Santos' cock couldn't fuck him as well as the man's tongue could. Could a man ejaculate just from lying on his back and listening to a man like Santos make love to him with his voice, Kenton wondered. It would be a good experiment.

Kenton wasn't even thinking of the dangerous young man, Panos, when he walked down to the harbor and sat on a bench overlooking the marina, either. He had a sense that Panos was too wild and vigorous for him for an extended, deepening relationship. Conversely, he was a complete departure from what Kenton was accustomed to in a coupling. But Kenton couldn't stop thinking about sex with him.

He was embarrassed by what Santos had said about the noise he had made while Panos was fucking him. He couldn't doubt it—Panos had been rough and had provided no mercy when Kenton had begged for it—and the helplessness of being bound had pulled something out of Kenton that no other lover—certainly not James—had done. Being noisy in sex was something new for him—as was being fucked by a younger man.

The thought of what Panos had said about sailing him out to the sea and fucking him where there would be no inhibitions for Kenton to scream his head off if Panos pulled that reaction out of him caused Kenton to scan the marina for the possibility that Panos' boat was there.

It was there and so was Panos, still only in a Speedo and looking oh so sexy. The younger man was scrubbing down his boat. Involuntarily, Kenton rose from his bench and walked out on the dock and to Panos' boat.

"No business yet today?" he asked as he reached the boat.

Panos looked around at him and grinned. "Not until just now. You want a private sail? 50 euros for the boat and 100 euros for me."

Kenton understood exactly what services Panos was quoting prices for. He felt his hand go to his wallet. He certainly had more than enough money, but he had no intention of availing himself of the services.

Panos came over to the side of the boat and reached a hand out. He still was grinning. "Let me help you aboard," he said.

Kenton hesitated.

The smile faded a bit and Panos' voice took on an edge of steel. "Come on board. I will take good care of you."

Kenton meekly took Panos' hand and stepped over the gunwale.

"Check out below and I will prepare to cast off," Panos said, as he gestured to the cabin door leading down into the boat and moved toward the bow. "Strip down and have your legs open for me when I'm at sea and come down into the cabin."

Kenton took in his breath when he had descended into the cabin. He found there a black leather sling that Panos no doubt would tell others was a hammock, but that Kenton, seeing the restraints attached to the four chains, knew would have another purpose. There was no explaining away the riding crop and extra-thick dildo that were laying on a nearby tabletop.

He shuddered. He just couldn't do it. This wasn't anything he was looking for. He was out of the cabin, back over the side of the gunwale, and half way back toward land on the dock before Panos had time to notice that he'd bailed out.

He walked the streets of Mykonos, fighting with himself and why he turned away from the adventure, being both drawn to and frightened by Panos. Why couldn't he decide what he wanted? There was no real secret there, though, he knew. He hadn't made a decision of his own—or done anything to take care of himself—for years. Could he just change as quickly as he would need to do for Panos? He sensed that Panos would drain him dry financially, just using him—and roughly so, without real respect or affection for him. How and when would a relationship like that end?

Panos' version of taking care of him seemed so much like Georgiou's was. Just using the aging American as long as he had money for it. When Santos said he would take care of him, Kenton got an entirely different impression. Santos had made no material demands. Indeed he claimed to be richer than Midas, which Kenton doubted, but in making such a claim he was signaling that he wanted nothing from Kenton except sex. And the only demand he'd made was shared proof that the two of them were clean, because Santos wanted to have the ultimate pleasure of raw sex with him. This Dr. Mavrades was supposed to show Santos' documentation to Kenton at the same time as he established that Kenton was disease free.

Santos would be an adventure too, but an entirely different kind of one than Panos would be.

Kenton found that he had been blindly walking the streets and when he stopped and looked up, he saw the sign for Dr. Mavrades' office just up the narrow street. He took that as a direction, as the sign of what he should do.

A female nurse was at the reception desk of the second-floor office, where three men were sitting in the waiting room, and as soon as Kenton announced his name to the receptionist, the nurse intervened.

"Yes, Mr. Kingston, we were told to expect you. Please come directly back with me. I will take the necessary samples and you may come back at 7:00 p.m. to consult with the doctor on the results—if that is convenient with you."

It was real. Kenton had expected it all to be a joke. He wasn't at all sure he would make that appointment, but he was here now so he at least would start the process.

He spent the early evening sitting at the harborside Babylon bar in the Paraportiani Waterfront area, a gay district that had figured high in the suggestion that he spend time on Mykonos, watching the sunset starting over the water, and half flirting with and half deflecting the attentions of fit and beautiful young Greek men interested in hooking up with a rich American, which Kenton registered as with anyone who saw him. At several points he had intended just one more glass of wine and then the climb back up to his villa, but when he finally found himself getting up from the café table, it was close on 7:00 p.m., and his feet took him back to Mavrades' office. The flirting of the young men at the gay bar had put him in the mood to carry through with the last part of the examination.

The office was dimly lit and the receptionist was closing up as he arrived.

"I'm sorry. You're closing?" Kenton asked. "Did I have the time wrong? I thought I was told 7:00."

"No, it's your appointed time, Mr. Kingston. The doctor is coming for you directly. You two will be alone in the office." She gave Kenton a meaningful look, and he blushed, realizing that she knew why this appointment was set for the time the office closed.

And as she departed, Paul Mavrades was walking down the hall toward Kenton. He was wearing a weary, distracted look until he caught sight of Kenton and then he gave the American a smile. Kenton couldn't help smiling back, the thought running through his mind that this might not be so bad. Mavrades was a tall, unusually handsome man with gray hair, mustache, and short beard. His eyes were a piercing blue, and Kenton got the impression that they lit up in unexpected pleasure when they were cast on Kenton for the first time. A little chill when down Kenton's spine.

"Mr. Kingston? Welcome. Just come back to my surgery, and we will take care of this matter as quickly and professionally as possible. It is an unusual requirement, but Santos Cleridhis is an unusual man—and he is used to getting what he wants."

51

For the first time Kenton contemplated that perhaps Santos was as well-heeled as he had claimed to be.

Ushering Kenton into a spacious office with a desk and a couple of club chairs off to the side and an examining table prominently located in the center of the room, Mavrades bade Kenton sit in one of the club chairs and then went over to the desk.

"The circumstance is unusual. Perhaps a bit of wine and conversation before we begin. Wine?"

"Yes, please." It came out like Kenton had cotton in his mouth, so he cleared his throat and repeated the "Yes, please."

After delivering the wine, Mavrades took three sheets of paper from the desk, returned to the chairs, sat down, and handed the papers to Kenton. Kenton had to set his wine down on a side table and hold the papers in two hands because he was trembling. Mavrades was wearing a long, white surgical coat, which gave the impression that that was all he was wearing. When he sat down, the gown tented out at the groin—alarmingly so. His eyes took on a dreamy look as he looked at Kenton.

"You know you are a bit of a surprise," he said.

"How so?" Kenton asked. Once more having to clear his throat to get the answer out.

"You are a very handsome man. And you seem highly refined in character. Santos doesn't usually pick his partners so carefully. That's probably why he has them checked like this. You don't seem the kind of man to get involved with this."

"I'm surprised as well. I guess I'm footloose and searching. I recently lost a long-time lover to death."

"Ah. An older man?"

"Yes. Considerably older. But the death was an unexpected one. He was in very good condition until the heart attack. He hadn't been diagnosed with heart disease."

"And you were satisfied with him. An older man."

"Yes. I prefer older men." Kenton blushed at that, realizing that the doctor was a good ten years older than he was.

"Because they aren't so demanding?"

Kenton blushed again. "That wasn't an issue. I need frequent attention and James was able to give that—and, being older, he was experienced."

"Ah. And this perhaps is why you have agreed to lay under Santos—you are frustrated by the lack of attention—and you appreciate a man who is experienced? I ask, because Santos is quite direct and can be crude. We are the best of friends, understand, but I believe you must be quite frustrated for servicing to fall under his sway. As I said, I haven't had a man as handsome and refined sent to me for this."

"Yes I suppose that must be so," Kenton said, looking away, unable to maintain eye contact with a piercing gaze that seemed to reach the quick of him. "Tell, me, Doctor," Kenton said, suddenly turning, the question having just popped into his head. "Santos is quite a talker about his prowess. Do you have any idea—?"

"Yes, I am quite sure that Santos can deliver on everything he promises in sexual services," the doctor said, giving Kenton a level stare.

"Uh, thank you," Kenton answered, a chill going down his spine.

"Ah, yes, well. The good news is that you are disease free and so are Santos and I. You have the certificates there in your hand."

"The good news? There is bad news?"

"Possibly. With Santos there is another element that I check out with the men he wishes to cover. Not all men are capable of handling him. Tell me, has he exposed himself to you?"

"Yes," Kenton answered, blushing again.

"In erection?"

"At least partially so."

"Do you have any discernment of the dimensions of his equipment? Can you manage twenty-four centimeters? Santos does not mine at a shallow depth. More than one man has had to come back here for treatment *after* being penetrated by Santos."

"I believe so," Kenton said, and then, warmed by the wine and aroused now by the doctor, he boldly continued, "My lover was unusually hung. I had come to expect to be filled and stretched. If you must know, I think this is what has drawn me to Santos. It was just playful banter from him until he exposed himself to me. I have grown to expect the size. To need it—to be challenged by more of it."

It hit Kenton at that moment that this was the base reason Panos failed to fully satisfy—it wasn't that he was young, perfunctory, and kinky. He wasn't big enough to challenge Kenton's channel.

Kenton's eyes were drawn to the doctor's groin. The tenting there now was much more pronounced.

"Well, I will check for that," the doctor said. "It is one thing to say what you want and yet another to be able to accommodate someone like Santos without debilitating pain. We will proceed with the necessary examination. I will be clinical and as quick about it as possible. It will involve you taking a rubber member of Santos' dimensions, with most of the examination time being taken by you adjusting to the size of it. Then I must, by Santos' direction, penetrate you myself— without protection. That need not be long, to meet the requirements, or deep. I am not unusually thick, and though I could tax you with the depth I can reach, I can control myself. So, if you'll stand and take off your clothes and go up on that examination table, we will take care of this as quickly as possible. For clinical purposes you will be restrained. I hope that isn't a problem."

"No, I guess not," Kenton said as he stood and started to strip down. He felt a bit woozy as he stood. Obviously he'd drunk too much wine over the afternoon and evening. It was evident now that he'd been working up the courage to carry through with the doctor's examination. Even though his head was hazy at the moment, he was quite clear of the understanding that he was willing to go through this because he craved having his channel filled and stretched again by a cock such as Santos'.

And what about the doctor's cock?

"Will you have any trouble managing what you have to do?" he suddenly asked the doctor, as his briefs were being pushed down his legs.

"Do you think I'll have trouble," Mavrades asked in a hoarse voice as he unbuttoned his medical coat and Kenton gasped at the sight of the miles long—but not thick—cock in full erection and with a gold bead pierced into its head.

"If you are contemplating twenty-four centimeters, you should not be troubled by twenty-one."

Kenton swallowed hard. He didn't have an answer for that. But twenty-one would be more than Georgiou so proudly flaunted.

"The good news there is that, with Santos, as with me, it is mostly in length. If you can handle Santos' length, you should be able to handle two men of his length and his girth at once. Tell, me, Mr. Kingston, have you ever had two men inside you at once."

"Rarely," Kenton answered, not wanting to pursue that further.

"Ah, so. How old are you?" Mavrades asked, seeing Kenton naked. "Your body is magnificent."

"I'm thirty-six."

"You have the body of a much younger man. It's almost a crime for a face that handsome to crown a body that beautiful. I have never before envied my old friend Santos as I do now. Do you do sports?"

"Tennis, some squash, running, and I do lift weights. James wanted me to keep in shape."

"I can only repeat deepest envy of Santos, and I can only ask again if you are willing to risk your body with Santos. I can assure you that if he told you he can—and will—ravage you, he can and will. Be sure to keep my card and to call if you need medical attention afterward. I will be very discreet and will come to you."

* * * *

Kenton was groaning and gasping, strapped to the examination table, his feet in stirrups, his legs spread, his wrists attached to restraints on the side of table. The doctor was standing between his spread and raised legs, crouched over him, his lean chest covered in a down of gray hair mere inches from Kenton's heaving chest. The doctor's eyes were locked on Kenton's for signs of distress, but Kenton could only give him the flare of pleasure, his mouth hanging slack, answering the doctor's questions in breathy staccato replies of how well he was accommodating the Santos-sized dildo the doctor was working inside him.

The dildo was extracted. "You knew what you could take," the doctor whispered. "You opened right up for it. Santos will be deeply pleased."

"As will I," Kenton admitted in a hoarse voice. "It's more than I've taken before. It's what I want."

"You did well. And the examination is nearly over. Just a bit of penetration to validate to Santos that I declare you clean."

"Oh, god, oh, god, the gold bead. It found my prostrate," Kenton cried out. "Oh, no, please don't stop."

"If you wish, I can work that and make you come," Mavrades whispered. "I don't wish to impose, though. I can do it quickly, clinically, without deep penetration."

"Oh, god, yes. Make me come. Shit, fuck, fuck, fuck. Yesss!" Kenton had already been keyed up. It took just a few strokes of the gold bead over his prostate to pull an ejaculation out of him. And when he had done so, to Mavrades' surprise, Kenton raised his face to the doctor's and took his lips into a deepening kiss. Breaking away from that, Kenton cried out, "Give it all to me, Doctor! Go deep! I want to take you too."

"Are you sure? It's not clinical."

"Fuck me! Fuck me hard and deep!"

With a grunt from him and a groan from Kenton, Mavrades dove deep, then pulled back, and then dove deep again.

"Release me!" Kenton cried out, and Mavrades immediately released him from the wrist restraints. Kenton clutched the doctor's shoulder blades, holding Mavrades' chest hard against his and set his pelvis in a counterpistoning to the doctor's strokes that had the doctor wildly fucking him to his ejaculation and a second one by Kenton.

Afterward, as they cooled down, Mavrades said, "will you be my guest for dinner? There's an excellent meze restaurant just down the street, with a good view of the harbor."

"And then will you bring me back here and fuck me again?"

"But of course, if that's what you want. But we can go to my flat. It's just above the office here."

"Is that what you want, though?"

"But of course. Santos won't mind. We share. In fact, I think we . . . you might . . . no, I won't say it."

* * * *

Back arched, taking his weight on his shoulder blades, feet flat on the mattress under his haunches to raise his pelvis just so, Kenton cried out at the depth Mavrades' cock was reaching, as the doctor knelt between the American's legs, hands grabbing Kenton's knees, and grunting at the effort to bury his cock so that curly blond and gray pubic hair wove together.

Kenton had never experienced such a snake-like cock, dragging that gold bead across his undulating channel muscles until Kenton's legs gave out and he went flat on the bed. Wrapping his legs around the small of the doctor's back, he held them loosely there, going with the rhythm of Mavrades' long slides out and in, raw skin sliding across shimmering channel walls, while Mavrades glued his forehead to Kenton's, closely gauging the effect of his all-wall's attention with his beaded cock, his eyes capturing Kenton's. Pulling back to where he dug at Kenton's prostate with the bead. Once twice, while Kenton writhed under him, mouth slack and blowing bubbles until Mavrades captured it in a deep kiss, until Kenton tore his mouth away and howled his ejaculation to the ceiling of Mavrades' bedroom.

It was only much later that night when Kenton was staggering up the hill to his villa that he started to wonder if the disease check was as much a protective requirement of Santos' as it was a means for the two old friends to share their men. Somehow, Kenton didn't care if it was the latter.

* * * *

Kenton slept the sleep of the dead that night. When he woke, he put his robe on and went down to the kitchen to start the coffee. There was no water from the faucet in the kitchen.

And none in the bathroom either. Once more he was reminded of how dependent he'd always been on someone else.

He went out on the terrace to look down at the pool to see if Panos was there to report the lack of water too.

"*Kalimera*," came the chipper voice from across the fence between his villa and Santos'. "I would expect you to have coffee in your hand."

"So would I," Kenton asked.

"I happened to have a fresh pot here and an extra mug. Would you like a cup?"

"I'm dying for a cup of coffee. There isn't anything I wouldn't do for coffee at this moment," Kenton answered.

"Not anything?" Santos asked, a mischievous look on his face. "No matter, though. Did you enjoy Paul yesterday? Have you ever been fucked by a hung man with a bead in his cock before?"

"Yes and no. I have the documentation in my house on the tests."

"No need. Paul called me this morning. He enjoyed you immensely. You stayed with him for some time. He claims three ejaculations."

As you perhaps planned? Kenton thought, but he didn't say that. He moved on. "I came out to see if Panos was here. I have no water today."

"You do need a man to take care of you, don't you?"

"Yes, I surely do," Kenton said, with a sigh.

"If I come over and get your water fixed, will you let me be a man for you today."

"Yes," Kenton said, in surrender. They had reached that point. "If you come over here and fix my water you can do whatever you wish with me."

After Santos went under the kitchen sink and turned the water valve back on that he had come in earlier in the morning and turned off, he stood up, and swiveled to Kenton, who had been standing close behind him. His hands went to the sash around Kenton's waist, which, when dealt with, caused the robe to flare open. Santos' hands moved inside, and Kenton sighed and moan as Santos expertly worked his torso, cock, and balls with his hands, while their lips met and Santos backed Kenton into the dining room.

Kenton's butt met the edge of the dining room table and he just laid back on that; spread his legs, hooking his ankles on Santos' shoulders; and groaned as Santos spent considerable time getting his long cock inside Kenton's passage.

"Oh, God, oh shit. You're enormous, a snake," Kenton whined.

"It's what you want," Santos said, simply.

"Yes, it's what I want," Kenton admitted. "Oh, shit. Oh fuck. Drill me deep. Yes. Yes! YES!"

There was some time of no talking as both men worked to get the maximum pleasure from the huge cock barebacking Kenton on the dining room table. Kenton grunted with the progress of each inch, each time assuming— wrongly—that it was the last inch Santos had to give. As Santos sank deeper into him, he instinctively gaped his mouth wide, expected the bulb of the cock to pop out there at any second. They managed to come almost together—or, rather, Santos, in his expertise managed to bring them off almost simultaneously.

"Best lay I've had for as long as I can remember," Santos murmured after they'd come and he was laying his chest on top of Kenton's. "You do like them big. You opened right to me. There is room for . . . well . . ."

"Take me upstairs. Fuck me into tomorrow," Kenton murmured.

"Better yet, I'll take you over to my villa," Santos answered. "And perhaps later you can pack and move in with me over that. You need a man to take care of you obviously, and you bring out the youth in me in the fucking."

"Now? Come over to your villa with you now?" Kenton asked. "You will fuck me again now, won't you?"

"Yes, I will fuck you again now. We will take good care of you."

We?

Kenton didn't think about that until they had gotten to Santos' bedroom. Paul Mavrades, naked, was waiting for them on Santos' bed. He was sitting at the foot of the bed. He opened his arms to Kenton, and Kenton moved to him on the bed. The doctor was in full erection, and Kenton, without direction descended on his lap, facing him, and slowly descended on the doctor's cock. In just a few moments, Santos was behind him, his hands gripping and spreading Kenton's buttocks and rolling the buttocks up to him.

"Can you? Will you? Both of us? I know you can manage," Santos was whispering in Kenton's ear.

"Oh, God, yes," Kenton murmured, now understanding just how fully Santos and Paul liked to share their men.

Need to Be Needed

"That's one sweet ass. You are one sexy piece of ass."

"I can sing too, and will look good in front of your band," I said, trying to keep the focus on why I was there, in the sleazy hotel room, tinted red by the "O" and the "L" of the flashing neon sign just outside the window.

I wondered if he could hear the pain in my voice, although chances were that he'd be proud that he'd put it there. Phil Gauteau, the huge French Canadian of the trendy band of the same name currently playing the Chelsea Bathhouse, had his back propped up on pillows against the headboard. He was smoking a cigarette and had an open bottle of bourbon and a water glass on the nightstand beside him. He hadn't offered me either. There was a small pile of Magnum condom packets on top of the nightstand as well. One of the packets was split and empty, the used condom now on the floor beside the bed, fat as a sea slug with his cum.

I vaguely wondered if there was a smear of blood on the condom, as well. He was a monster of a man, with a cock to match. It wasn't appreciably long but was one of those known as a beer can dick. I'd never had a man that thick inside me before, and he had given me little time to prepare for it and had fucked me mercilessly, seeming to have enjoyed my cries of distress immensely.

I wanted something from him and he knew it. So, I was in no position to ask for more consideration.

I was stretched along his side, my right leg bent, the sole of my foot pressed into the surface of the thin mattress. I was doing what I could to keep from squeezing my anal channel shut, which was throbbing and was swollen, I was sure. I'd felt the opening for tears and found none, but the channel had been reamed wide open and hadn't closed yet.

I had no illusions that it would close anytime soon. He'd taken me hard and fast, missionary style, as soon as we'd entered the room, him saying that he'd hardly been able to keep his hands off me until we got into the room—a good sign for what I was after.

"I don't know what it is about you that's so sexy," he'd said. "You were born to be fucked."

I couldn't explain it either, but it had been my experience through life—for men to want to fuck me. None as cock big as he was, though.

I'd had no idea he'd be that thick—although his height and burliness should have given me a clue—and I'm sure anyone in the hotel at the time could hear my screams and grunts and groans as he spiked me, the sound backed by the rhythmic thump of the headboard against the wall and the squeaking of the springs as he pounded my ass.

I half thought he'd listened to the beat of the headboard and the squeal of the springs to set a rhythm. That's what he did in the Phil Gauteau Band, in addition to putting the musicians together—my interest at the moment. He was the band's drummer and manager. I was a singer—a singer badly in the need of a job and a breakthrough.

Moving from running my fingers through his chest hair, I let my hand drift down his belly and into his thatch. The cock fascinated as well as frightened me. It wasn't just because it was so thick—surely nearly as thick as a beer can—but also because it was almost jet black. The skin of both his cock and his gigantic balls were black. There was no sign of blackness in him otherwise, but the color here bespoke of an interracial mix. I encircled the shaft with my hand, barely being able to touch my fingers together. It began to swell instantly.

He laughed. "Ready for it again? So soon?"

Not hardly, I thought. But I wanted this gig badly. My way to standing in front of the band in the Chelsea Bathhouse and singing like Frank Sinatra went straight through this monster dick. Gauteau had made it quite explicit what I had to do to get the chance. And that it was an audition of long duration.

I bent over his belly and, while still encasing the base of the cock with a hand, opened my mouth wide over the bulb and began to suck. He groaned for me, which was a good sign, and after a few minutes, during which the shaft engorged so much that I had to unhinge my jaw to keep it in my mouth, I felt a nudge on my shoulder. I looked up to see that he'd split open another condom packet.

"Crown me. Then we'll go to town again."

Every ounce of my attention was on the baseball bat moving inside my passage, as he gripped my wrists, my torso cantilevered over his legs, my legs running up the side of his torso, his pelvis jerking back and forth as he pulled my body on and off the thick shaft. Grunting and groaning, I kept my eyes plastered to the red neon flash of the "O" and the "L" outside the hotel window and counted the strokes as he surely came closer to ejaculation and my liberation for now. The flashing sign was red; the tint of the atmosphere in the room was red, my swollen passage walls were red—my whole world was red, as I concentrated on surviving the fuck without split channel walls.

And then, slowly but relentlessly, I opened to him and the pleasure of the fuck—the satisfaction of accommodating a monster cock—flowed in, and I was crying out for it. "Fuck me. Fuck me hard!" and he was increasing the pull, striving for deeper penetration, crying out, "Take it, baby, take it!" as he filled the bulb of his rubber.

Later, our breathing having calmed down and his cigarette crushed out on the scarred top of the nightstand, the bottle of bourbon nearly spent, I felt him snuggling in behind me, his arms embracing me, his hand going to cupping and fondling my cock and balls.

"Such a sweet lay. I could fuck you for days."

It seemed to me that he had.

The fireplug of a cock was pressed into the small of my back. I couldn't tell if it was hard or not—I certainly hoped not. My passage was throbbing and, I could tell, was gaping open.

"So, is it set, then?" I asked tentatively, in a whisper. "Will you give me a chance to sing with the band at the baths?"

"One thing is sure," he muttered in a low-throated voice, "You've got one sweet, tight ass. You must sweat arousal juice."

I began to tremble as I felt his hand fumbling between the small of my back and his groin. There was no mistaking it, he was rolling on another condom.

I moaned deeply as he turned me on my stomach and came down on my back. I opened my mouth in a silent scream and my eyes bugged out as he began to enter me again. pulling my knees up, I raised my buttocks and spread my legs, trying to be as open to him as I could be.

"Oh, shit, of fuck. Fuck, fuck, fuck," I moaned, my eyes latching onto the blinking neon "O" and "L" outside the window as he began to pump again—in rhythm to the blinking neon lights.

I couldn't help myself. I begged for more of what he was giving and set my hips in motion, meeting his thrusts with counterthrusts.

"Oh, baby, baby. Yes, baby. Give it to daddy."

"Yes, YES! SHIT YES! FUCK ME!"

* * * *

We were celebrating in our small loft room at the edge of Chelsea—well, in Zane's small room. I was still living off of what little of a startup fund I'd brought to New York with me from Delaware. Somehow Zane, an aspiring actor, and I had hit it off well after meeting at one of those "aspiring artists" roving parties in Manhattan, getting half drunk, and coming back here for Zane to spike the night away on my ass. He too had remarked on how fuckable I was; I was beginning to think it was my only asset. I'd been sleeping here since then, on his nickel, and eating my principle meal of the day here, too, at his sufferance.

He'd said it was worth sharing the meal with me if I cooked it—that he would burn half of whatever he tried to cook anyway.

Zane had come back to the room with the news that he'd gotten the young hunk supporting role in an off-Broadway play, and I, of course, was full of the news that I was going to begin that weekend singing with the Phil Gauteau Band in the Chelsea Bathhouse. It really was a gay male bathhouse, but these had become trendy lately as places of entertainment as well. Some had gone so far as to be attractive to heterosexuals, but the Chelsea Bathhouse was still all gay male, with much open sex going on even in the main room during the shows. Certainly no women would chance it and a good-looking straight man would be raped in no time flat. The Phil Gauteau Band had gained a "to see" reputation as well, and it worked in the band's favor that, unless you were willing to take in a gay venue, you'd have to pay big bucks for a private gig. The underground press loved advertising largely forbidden venues and limited-access bands.

For the first time, that night, both Zane and I felt that we were "on our way" at last.

I had wanted to celebrate by sharing a bottle of cheap wine, but I was at a disadvantage with this, as Zane would have had to buy the wine. Zane, instead, wanted to celebrate our familiar, costless way—costless because Zane didn't believe in condoms and this was the early seventies, before the scourge of AIDS set in. Neither one of us could have afforded the cost of the condoms we would have needed anyway. Sex was nearly our only form of affordable entertainment in those days.

Zane couldn't keep his hands off me when we were together.

Both naked, we were sitting on Zane's air mattress on the floor, me encased in his arms, facing away from him, between his legs. That was the bedding we had: two camping blow-up mattresses on the floor, with sleeping bags on top of them, although mine was rarely used, as Zane liked to sleep with his dick in me. Between the two, they took up nearly all of the floor space in the room, where a kitchenette took up one wall and the only other room was a small bathroom, with a tight shower.

That was the major regret that Zane expressed about the small apartment—that it was physically impossible for us to shower together.

Zane was a real hunk—a Nordic blond, with a perfectly formed athlete's body that placed him squarely in the romantic "second man" love-interest roles—not always too bright, but always a hunk—in plays. In contrast, I was smaller, dark complexioned, Jewish, and with a sleek, young-man's body that was well proportioned enough, just not muscle bound. And there must have been something to that "scent of sex" thing men talked about when they were with me, because it was so often mentioned and I never was without propositions. Phil Gauteau had admitted that his arousal with me had been both a scent thing and the image of stuffing that beer can cock of his into the hole of a man as small as I was. It was a wonder to me as well that he had managed it earlier that evening—three times. Sometime during the third time, I'd adjusted to it well enough to have hoped for a fourth.

Zane had his arms around me, with one hand stroking my cock. His lips were buried in the back of my neck. What he had rising up the small of my back was getting harder and harder. His cock wasn't thick, but he was what we termed a "foot long" in length. Not nearly a foot long, of course, but close enough—it certainly seemed as long when it was inside me.

"Such a coincidence for both of us to get good work on the same day," I murmured.

"Yes, isn't it? I'm ready to celebrate. How about you?" Zane asked, his voice dreamy. He coaxed my head to turn with cheek pressure from his sexy five-o-clock shadow beard that he perpetually groomed. I opened my mouth to his, feeling the heat and insistence of him.

I wasn't sure I was ready for this. My passage still throbbed from Gauteau's beer can cock assault earlier in the evening. I didn't know if I could have sex again for a day or two.

But then I was having sex, whether I thought I could or not. With his mouth still in possession of mine, he slowly pitched my torso forward, raising my buttocks to him. The cock slid right in. If he had any sensation that I'd been reamed

66

huge and still hadn't closed, he gave no reaction. His intent was to make me come before he took his pleasure. It was what he always wanted.

I moaned and writhed within his grasp as he invaded with his cock only far enough for his glans to reach my prostate and start to work that, while his hand stroked my cock. Where I expected pain, I was getting only pleasure and the slow, sure buildup to an ejaculation.

"Oh, God, Zane. Yes. There. Just like that. Oh shit, FUCK!"

I shot my wad out across the mattress and collapsed in his arms, as his long, thin cock now began its journey deep up inside me. My passage walls constricted over the familiar shaft and began to shimmer. No pain—nothing left over from the rougher, near-splitting attention of Phil's cock. I set my pelvis in motion, riding back on the cock as it moved ever deeper—reaching for my stomach. He began to pump me deep, and I moaned and moved my lips back to his for a deep, all-tongues kiss.

I went down on my elbows onto the mattress, my cheek pressing into the mattress in front of me, the surface of the mattress slick from the cum I'd shot off there. Zane went up on his feet, crouched over me, gripping my waist with his hands, pumping me hard and deep, his golden pubic hair mingling with my silky, black curls, in to the hilt, reaching for my tonsils.

And then, with a "Oh shit, Mike. I'm gonna come," he did so in three long, wet spoutings deep inside me.

We both, panting, fell off to the side, him embracing me with his arms, still sheathed deep inside me.

"Congrats, Mike," he whispered.

"Same to you, Zane," I whispered back. "I hope you didn't have to sleep with the director to get the part."

I felt him stiffen. I don't know what had made me say that. Guilt, I guess, considering what I'd had to do to get my gig. I didn't have any reason to think he'd had to get the part this way. I was the one getting my job that way. He'd mentioned before times when it seemed he was expected to let a man fuck him to get a part, but there was no evidence he'd done so. He was a top. It would take serious consideration for him to submit to a man.

It hadn't taken that much for me to decide to do so to get ahead. But then I was a submissive. And I'd never had trouble giving it to a man with a good body and a stiff cock. Ever since my senior year in high school, starting with the former Marine living next door on the first day I could give consent, I'd willingly opened my thighs for any muscular, half-good-looking man demanding entry.

"No, of course not," he said defensively. "Besides the director is a woman."

"A good-looking woman?" I asked, digging myself even deeper.

"Yes, she is."

"So, are you going to fuck her?"

"If I can. But I didn't do it to get the part."

"But does she react to you like she wants you to fuck her?"

"OK, OK, I've fucked her, OK? But it was after she told me I got the part." He pushed me away from him and sat up on the floor next to the mattress.

It had been somewhat of a raw edge between Zane and me. He was bi. He fucked women too. He was fine—or least showed as such—about having me stay here and mooch off him. But he didn't rely on me for anything and was as easy sticking it in a woman's box as in my ass. I was the one who had needed him.

"And, how about you?" he asked, each word separately enunciated, like rifle shots. "This Gauteau drummer who gave you the job. He's got a monster dick, doesn't he?"

"Excuse me? I didn't sleep with anyone to get the singing gig."

"Really? You want to go with that? How many times did he fuck you? Did you think you'd come to me open enough for a Mack truck to drive up in there and I wouldn't notice?"

"Three times," I admitted meekly. "It was excruciating. Dick as thick as a baseball bat."

"But you've had a lot of dicks, haven't you?"

68

"Not that many," I said defensively. "I'm not a slut." Then, after a pause, "None that thick."

"But you'll take him again, won't you? to keep the job."

"Yes."

"And you'll enjoy it, won't you? Now that you're reamed to his size. You are such a slut."

"Yes," I shot back. "Now that I could take a Mac truck, there's no reason not to take him again. He fucks really, really well."

It was true. It had been painful, until half way through the third time when I just relaxed and went with it fully, already reamed to the drummer's needs. I already was thinking of having Phil Gauteau inside me again. Then, after a pause, "Quite the pair, aren't we?" I murmured.

But I'm not sure Zane heard me. He had risen from the floor and stumbled off to the bathroom.

By now it was late in the night. I turned on my side, away from the bathroom door and, with a low sob, closed my eyes to try to fool sleep to overcome me. I didn't want to think about what I'd had to do—what I'd had to give.

I felt Zane's body come down on the mattress behind me, stretching along mine. A hand clasped my right leg, low on the thigh, and I allowed him to raise the leg. I jutted out my buttocks and sucked in air as his cock invaded my ass and slid deep inside me.

"Sorry, sweetheart," He murmured in my ear, before sticking his tongue in my ear and swabbing it.

"You just want to have your way with me," I said, making it sound like a whimper. "You just want to get your dick in me again."

"Yes, I just want to get my rocks off again," and then, more seriously, "we're quite a pair, but we're going to make it, you and I."

I sighed as his tongue started fucking my ear in the same rhythm as his cock was slow pumping my ass deep, sliding freely in the cum he'd deposited there earlier. I clamped my passage as tight as I could, my channel muscles undulating over his pumping cock, eliciting a moan from him that I harmonized with an octave higher.

"Fuck me, Zane. Fuck me hard."

"With pleasure."

I groaned as the cock picked up plowing speed.

* * * *

It was uncanny. Every time I looked out into the audience, he was looking at me. This despite having two young men hanging off him. And I knew that look. He wanted me. With all the young men at the Chelsea Bathhouse who were available to him, he wanted me.

Cole Temple was a legend at the bathhouse. He was even a bigger legend than just in the New York bathhouse scene. He was one of the foremost political novelists of our age. A lion of a man, the body of a Zeus into his forties and movie-star good looks, he famously was perhaps the most openly narcissistic and egotistical public figure in America in the current era. He was bigger than life, flamboyantly homosexual in an Oscar Wilde way before that became any sort of fashion and able to bring it off while still being acceptable in the halls of power and entertainment. His was the only opinion that mattered when he was holding court at a gathering. He sucked all of the air out of the room and still everyone there willingly laid down and opened their legs to him—emotionally, certainly, but also physically when he demanded it.

And he demanded servicing daily—often nearly hourly.

His father had been a major baseball player, his mother a raving beauty, whose father, a U.S. senator, had been the head of a political dynasty. Cole was related to a first lady on this side of the pond, and multiple royal houses on the other side. He was the last person leading families wanted to invite to gatherings, but he was the first one they wanted to hear give a acid-tongue riff on other members of the family. Therefore, he never was left off the guest list.

His homosexual affairs with novelists and actors and more than one royal when he was barely legal were legendary. And he had become a major novelist and political commentator and book reviewer in his own right.

He had shown up at the Chelsea Bathhouse from the day it had opened, and was reputed to have fucked at least one young man at the bathhouse and taken another one home each night. He was both insatiable and ever hard. A joke was making the rounds that a molding of his cock was going to be marketed as a dildo.

And now he was sitting at a table in the first row as, I, wearing only a gold lamé G-string, wrapped myself around a pole on the stage in front of the Phil Gauteau Band and sang my little heart out.

Two young men bracketed Temple at his table. One was naked and had his face plastered to the side of Temple's head. The other, as good as naked, sat on the other side of Temple, who was only in silky boxer briefs, and had Temple's cock pulled through the fly of the briefs and was stroking it. As was obvious from Temple's reputation, the man was hung. From what I could see, a thick vein running the length of it, I could readily believe that it would be modeled for a dildo.

Despite the attention he was getting from the two young men, Temple had his eyes on me. When he was sure I was looking, he even smiled directly at me and cupped his package—a sure declaration of intent in the bathhouse. I shuddered and felt myself going hard.

It had been a euphoric four weeks since I'd been fronting the Phil Gauteau Band at the Chelsea Bathhouse. I had made a splash, yielding great reviews in all of the underground newspapers. I felt that now men were coming to the shows at the bathhouse to see and listen to me.

He wasn't the first one declaring he'd come to fuck me. And there had been patrons who had done just that, leaving me fat tips. I had never received action like this before. I decided I craved almost constant cock.

Having Temple sitting there, with his eyes on me, was some sort of peak I had achieved. Temple was the biggest catch of them all—not just at the Chelsea Bathhouse, but in New York and beyond.

I needed the boost. I'd gotten two whammies earlier in the day. I'd walked in on Zane fucking a woman in our room that afternoon. In the last four weeks, life had looked up for both of us. We both had real beds in the room now. But it also was becoming obvious that we were on the cusp of a change in living arrangements. We each could afford better now. But we

71

hadn't had the conversation about whether we would relocate together or go our separate ways at this point.

We had had the conversation about bringing others back to the room, however. I might have managed if I'd caught him in the room with another man, but I still wasn't comfortable with his bisexuality.

The woman was considerably older than he was, but still was trim and with shapely legs that went on for miles. Zane's pelvis was inserted between those legs and he was holding one of them raised from her body, which was arched back, her head hanging over the side of the bed and her long, straight, blonde hair swishing on the floor to the rhythm of the fuck. From the door into the room, I had a clear shot of his "foot long" taking long strokes inside her. I turned and left. This wasn't what we'd agreed too. I realized that this probably was the director of his play and he was just solidifying his run in the part, but I thought we had an agreement that neither of us would bring someone else back to the room.

At the same time, I realized that this was his room, not mine. He didn't need anything from me—certainly not permission to bring anyone to the room to fuck. He had brought me to the room to fuck. It had been my need that had brought us together. It was obvious, though, that the time for new digs had arrived—and that they would need to be separate digs. The thought depressed me; I had been avoiding it.

And then, when I had arrived at the bathhouse and sought Phil Gauteau out, I found him in his dressing room, fucking a young man on a divan. Later, when we rehearsed, and the young man showed up standing behind the keyboard, I realized that I no longer was the last person Gauteau had auditioned for a job in the band.

Inevitably, I was being moved down a notch and would be receiving less attention than before from that beer can dick I now had learned to crave—if at all. I just hoped that the next young man Gauteau auditioned wasn't another singer. My reviews gave me some hope, though, that he wouldn't be releasing me any time soon.

When I returned from a break and started into a new set of songs, I noticed that Temple no longer was at the table in the front row. If legend held, he was off fucking one of the young men I'd seen him with and had the other one in reserve to take home.

I was wrong, though. When I left the stage door that evening, a Cadillac coupe was taking up most of the room in the alley. As I passed it, the driver's side window rolled down. I saw the face of Cole Temple through the open window.

"Get in," was all he said.

Feeling numb and hopped up at the same time, I went around to the passenger side of the car and climbed in. I had reached a milestone. The famous novelist, Cole Temple, was taking me home to his bed.

Temple lived in an oversized penthouse apartment on Fifth Avenue, overlooking Central Park. We rode up in the private elevator to the top without a word. Inside the foyer, he turned to me and said, "The bedroom is in that direction. Take a shower and clean yourself out," and I walked, feeling like I was walking on air, down a long hallway to what had to be the master bedroom.

I wasn't all the way down the hall, though, before I heard his doorbell ring and him opening the door to a large, boisterous gaggle of people. They streamed into his living room with much noise.

I took a shower, padded out to the bedroom, which was dominated by a bed that had to be nearly twice the size of a king-sized bed, and slipped between the covers. I could hear a raucous party going on down the hall—a party I wasn't being invited to.

At length, I dozed off, only to be awakened in the dark sometime later, with Temple pulling up the sheets, climbing into the bed on top of me. He pushed my legs apart with his knees and stuffed a pillow under the small of my back. He covered me close from above, and, half awake, I began to gasp and groan as his cock forced itself inside me. It was as all-consuming as the legends foretold.

He was both Phil Gauteau and Zane in one—both thick and long. I writhed under him, moaning and begging him to go slow, as his cock relentlessly dug deeper and deeper, ignoring my wishes completely. It was all about him. Cole Temple taking his pleasure on the body of a young man. On one level, being a submissive, I reveled in not being given any consideration. Struggle was useless. He was too big and strong for me, and what resistance I did try to give he took as a coy game and enjoyed breaking down, grabbing my wrists and forcing my arms above my head as he drove the cock ever more vigorously.

For a forty-year-old man, he had remarkable stamina and vigor. He fucked me for nearly an hour straight. I ejaculated twice while he was pumping me deep.

When he came, in a flood, I realized that condoms were not in his repertoire.

I was still lying there, panting, with him going flaccid, but still big meat, inside of me, him laying full length on top of me, asleep and snoring.

I woke in the light of morning, on my belly, Temple lying full length on top of me, with his dick pumping me deep again.

I'd never had it so thick and long together. With a moan, I raised up on my knees a bit to give him even deeper purchase and began to move my pelvis in rhythm with his thrusts.

Once again he fucked me for more than a half hour, not finishing before I had ejaculated into the sheets and collapsed onto the bed.

He rolled off me and sat on the side of the bed. "I'm taking a shower. There should be everything you need in the kitchen to make breakfast. I prefer regular coffee in the morning to decaf. I trust you can cook."

My mother had died in childbirth when I was ten and I had two younger brothers, so, yes, I could cook.

Naked and hobbling, bowlegged, I padded out to the living area while he was in the shower. The living room was a mess from the party the night before. I couldn't resist bringing some order to it—replacing cushions on couches, uprighting lamps, and collecting butt-filled ashtrays—on my way to the kitchen.

All I could think of while I was moving about was how he had pinned me to the bed with that monster cock of his—and how I ached for him to do it again.

When he came out, his beautiful body only half covered with a robe that was gaping open, with him scratching his balls as he moved, he gave the living room an appreciative look. While breakfast was simmering, I'd had time to tidy up even more.

It was obvious that he appreciated the cheese and mushroom omelet I'd worked up as well.

"I demand absolute quiet between 10:00 a.m. and 1:00 p.m.," he said as I watched him eat the omelet. If he wondered what or when I'd eat breakfast, it didn't occur to him to ask. He lived up to the legend of his self-centeredness. "That's when I'll be in my study writing. Phones turned off; no answering the door. Tiptoe around beyond my hearing."

"Yes, sir," I said, confused on why he was telling me this. What did I care what his daily routine was? His legend held that, although he took a young man home every night, it was a different young man every night. I'd had my Temple fuck—and a fuck to remember it was.

"I'm lunching at the Plaza today. Expecting a plumber, though. The household money is in the kitchen drawer by the stove. Don't tip him lavishly. Don't tip him at all if he leaves grease on the floor."

"Yes sir." So I was expected to stay until the plumber had come and gone.

"You can use the bedroom behind the kitchen," he said, "although I want you waiting in my bed every night unless I tell you otherwise."

So, he expected me to be here beyond the plumber. He wanted me in his bed again. I suppressed a moan as I went hard again.

I probably should have asked him what the hell was going on here. But he'd pushed my buttons. I was a total submissive. As long as he told me what I was to do and didn't ask my opinion, that's what I'd happily do. It aroused me. It made me go hard. There was no hiding from him that it did.

"Do you give a good blow job?" he asked, brushing his robe more open as he sat on the stool at the kitchen counter. He was in magnificent erection.

"Um, I . . ."

"Well, don't just stand there. Suck me off," he said, pulling me to him with a grip on my arm and forcing me down on my knees before him.

75

Afterward, after he'd told me to hold off twice because he didn't want to come then, he guided me into the living room, turned me over the arm of a sofa on my belly, and fucked me hard for some twenty minutes, cupping my chin and arching my torso back cruelly as he mined my passage deep and slathered my passage again with his cum.

He finished at nearly the strike of 10:00 a.m. "Remember, not a peep out of you until after 1:00 p.m.," he said. "My luncheon appointment is for 1:45. There's a number for a grocery service on the refrigerator door. Call for whatever ingredients you'll need for supper."

He left me there, draped over the sofa arm and moaning from the thickness, length, stamina, vigor, and prodigious cum of him.

I didn't return to the Chelsea Bathhouse that night—or the next—or ever again.

Although he didn't live up to his "every night" legend after that, he didn't completely change his spots. He still went to the Chelsea Bathhouse some nights—unabashedly telling me he did—and fucked a young man, a new one each night, there—again having no embarrassment in telling me he had—and he still occasionally brought a young man home to fuck—rousting me out of his bed to do it, but bringing me back after he was finished and had sent the young man home and with me waking every morning in his bed with his dick pinning me to the mattress.

He also frequently held court in the living room to a gaggle of raucous guests before coming to me at night, and he never invited me to the party.

I would have thought that I was just his housekeeper if he didn't keep me so well fucked. I wondered what he'd done for a housekeeper and cook before me, but I never had the nerve to ask.

* * * *

"What have we become, Cole?" I asked, beyond frustration. Not at all comfortable, at least at this moment, of where Temple had taken our relationship after ten years.

"You didn't say no to it," he retorted.

"When have I ever said no? When have you ever shown the least regard for what I think or want? Do you realize I've been with you for ten years now and you've never let me out of the bedroom to meet any of your friends?"

"You couldn't hold your own with any of my friends," Cole spat out. "They would make mincemeat of you. They had razors for tongues; I've protected you from them. You are fulfilling the role you can handle. I would toss you out otherwise."

He was standing beside the bed, nude. The young black man who had been in bed with us and who I'd just sucked off as Cole fucked me missionary style at the side of the bed, rolled off the other side of the bed and headed for the bathroom.

We had come a long way in our sexual activity since the early years.

"Toss me out? Just like that? Like I meant nothing to you? Like I haven't given up everything to cater to your every need?"

"You're getting what you want, what you need."

"I don't think so," I answered, angrily. I started to rise from the bed, but he pushed me back down with a fist to my sternum.

"This is what you're good for. This is what you stay here for," he retorted, wagging his cock at me. "Here, suck this. You want to." Grabbing a fistful of hair he jerked my head forward to his groin.

Sobbing, I opened my mouth to his cock and took as much as it in as I could, gagging, as he released my hair only to grab my head between his hands and face fuck me.

"Here, up on the bed," he commanded, as he pulled out of my mouth and scrambled up on the bed onto his back. Pulling at me, he demanded, "You want my cock. Ride it. Fuck yourself."

Still sobbing, I dutifully threw a leg over his hip, positioned the head of his cock on my entrance, descended on the shaft, and started rising and falling on the thick, long cock that I couldn't get enough of.

The black man padded back out of the bathroom.

"You want Nate's cock too, don't you? Be honest. Tell me. You live for the cocks."

"Yes, yes, I want Nate's cock too," I answered, with a sob. And I did. I'd just passed thirty and nothing had become of my life other than serving Cole Temple's needs. And I'd done it all for his cock. I wasn't getting any younger. He seemed suspended in time. He'd started bringing more young men home—and then had moved to bringing them into bed with me, moving from them fucking me in sequence to sharing my ass passage. How soon would it be before he pushed me out his bed, and his apartment, and his life? And I'd given the entire ten years to him, my chance at a singing career—any career—had been choked off in the first night he'd brought me home.

How much longer would he keep me in his home?

"You want us both together, Nate and me, don't you?"

"Yes," I answered, fearful of what would happen the first time I said no. And this wasn't the first time in the last year I'd said yes to two cocks at once.

"Nate, catch," Cole commanded, as the well-muscled and hung black man came up behind me and straddled Cole's legs. What Nate caught was a condom packet. In the years since Temple had first fucked me, we'd come face to face with the threat of AIDS. Unwilling to declare monogamy when I was willing to, he bowed to the needs for protection, although neither of us were pleased with the loss of the feel of barebacking. Nate had fucked me earlier in the night, as Cole watched and beat his own meat. Increasingly, Cole had wanted variety and had wanted me to participate—and to provide him entertainment.

I cried out as the black cock started working its way inside me above Temple's already-buried staff. Nate wrapped his brown arms around my chest and his lips went to the hollow of my neck.

"Such a sweet, tight hole," he murmured, which took me back years to what Phil Gauteau had said about my channel's reception of his black cock.

"Oh, God, oh shit," I muttered, shuddering at the invasion of the second cock, but managing it. "Fuck me, fuck me." How much longer would any man want to fill me like this? How could I deny that I wanted this as long as possible. I couldn't. "Fuck me hard, both of you," I muttered, with a moan. "Yes, fuck me, YOU STUDS!"

Temple laughed. "Yes, you want it. It's what you're here for," as, moaning, I began to rise and fall on the two buried cocks.

"Yes, shit, work me, work my ass!" Someday I would have to do without. But not today.

* * * *

"So, here you are at last, Mike."

I felt arms going around me in the shadow of the wings of an auditorium stage. Cole Temple was on stage, sitting in a wing-back chair, and conversing with a microphone with another political pundit on the implications of the recent national elections. The auditorium was nearly full. People always came out to hear Temple. He was known to be not only scathing and controversial in his pronouncements but on the mark as well.

"Zane," I exclaimed, turning my face back to the man who was standing close behind me. "My God, I haven't seen you in years."

"Not since you disappeared from the face of the earth," Zane said. "Although I and others knew where you were—that you were being held prisoner in Cole Temple's apartment."

"Hardly a prisoner," I answered.

"What would you call it? One day you were the toast of the town as a singer for the Phil Gauteau Band, and the next day you were gone, only to be found in Temple's bed. Nate Jackson tells me that he and Cole fucked you together. I might add that one day you were rooming with me and the next day you were gone."

"I'm sorry. Events took over."

"What happened to your life, Mike? Is Temple's cock worth giving up everything for?"

"It was my choice," I said, defensively.

"Was it? Was it really, Mike? I know Temple. I know it's all about him and he has the power over people to make it all about him."

"It's a good cock," I answered, trying for flippant. "Even after ten years. It's a great cock. it's the greatest. His cock is legendary. They've made a dildo from it."

"And I think more men have ridden the real one than the rubber one," Zane shot back. He calmed down immediately, though and spoke in a softer voice, "I've missed you, Mike."

"Have you really? Your career really took off. I thought you were in Hollywood now."

"I am, but I'm in town for a premier. I'm footloose tonight, though, and I have a hotel room nearby. How about a toss in the sheets for old time's sake?"

"I can't. Cole will need me after he's finished with this program."

"Do you really think so? I bet it doesn't matter to him a jot that you're here. He's preening for the public. Just look at him out there, in his element. I heard him propositioning a stage hand before he went onstage. Are the two of them going to fuck you together tonight?"

I just grunted in answer. I wondered which stage hand he meant. There were hunky ones and there were some not so presentable. Some were thuggish. I couldn't help but shudder at the prospect.

"I bet you could come away with me and he won't even know you're gone," Zane continued. "Does anyone else fuck you now, Mike? I know you need regular attention."

"Yes, of course."

"Anyone else beside who Temple brings to bed? I know that he's become increasingly jaded over the years. Anyone you've chosen for yourself?"

I couldn't answer that in the affirmative. "I'll need to be here when he's finished with the program," I said. But there was a catch to my voice. Zane was running his hands over my body in the shadow of the stage wings. He was clutching my cock through the thin material of my trousers.

"You're hard. You're hard for me, Mike."

I actually was hard for the image he'd brought up of a stage hand coming home with us, but I didn't say that. I let Zane continue his silky seduction. It seemed important to him, and it had been years since a man had tried to seduce me. I could be hard for him, so it wasn't really wrong.

"I bet we can go back to my hotel room and Temple won't even know you were missing."

"Of course he will." I was panting lightly, though. I couldn't hide the pull of my former lover now that he was rubbing my cock through my trouser material, and my mind went to that "foot long" cock of his, which I could feel hardening at the small of my back.

"You can't win the bet without testing it," Zane whispered in my ear. "Remember how fast I can make you come. You will come to my hotel with me, now."

Well, when he put it as a command . . .

* * * *

"Oh, God, oh God, oh God," I chanted, panting, as I lay on my back at the foot of the hotel room bed, with Zane standing on the floor between my legs, my right leg running up his chest, and the bulb of his cock rubbing across my prostate.

"Oh, shit, I'm going to come," I cried out and then I did. I cried out then as he went deep with the cock.

"Bet I can make you come again before I do," he muttered. And he did.

"That was as good as of old," he murmured, hunched over me, his kisses covering my face, pecs, and nipples. "But, no, not quite as good," he added. "It will never be as good as when we could bareback."

"No, not that good," I admitted. "But very good."

"As good as Temple can do?"

I didn't want to lie, so I didn't answer. Nobody had the talented cock that Cole did.

"Come to California with me, Mike. Leave him. He's cruel to you. You've become a nonperson. You deserve better. We can be monogamous. I can bareback you again."

"He needs me."

"I'm sure he does. But I'm sure he doesn't know it. You've given him too much, too easily."

"I have to go," I said, rolling over and away from him, and reaching for my clothes. "He'll wonder where I am."

"I have bet he won't," Zane said.

Zane won that bet. When I got back to the apartment, Cole wasn't there—and hadn't been there. I showered and, naked, slipped under the covers of the bed. Well after midnight I heard the mob arrive and move into the living room. Cole's voice rang out over the hubbub, so I knew he was home. I drifted off to sleep, and when I woke, all was quiet. But Cole wasn't in the bed.

I came out of the bed and padded into the living room. The place was tossed into the usual chaos after one of Coles' frequent parties, but he wasn't there, or in the kitchen, dining room, or study. Absentmindedly, I put the living room back in order. On my way back to bed, I heard them in one of the guest rooms. Cole was covering a young blond missionary style. I recognized the blond as an apprentice stage hand at the lecture—not one of the thuggish, seasoned stage hands I had fantasized about.

Both were grunting like rutting animals. The young blond was rubbing Cole's buttocks with the heels of his feet in tune with the rhythm of Cole's thrusts—something I'd never done before. Cole was grunting like he enjoyed it. I stood there and watched for a bit, but I knew that Cole could fuck for longer than I could stand watching. The two began bouncing up and down wildly on the bed, the young blond crying out at the hard taking. I turned and went back to the bed in the master bedroom.

Near dawn, Coles came to bed, nudged my thighs apart with his knees, and fucked me in the same position he'd used on the young blond and just as vigorously, bouncing our bodies up and down on the mattress. I even rubbed his buttocks with the heels of my feet as he thrust hard inside me, again and again and again. If he related the heel rubbing to what I'd seen the young blond doing, he didn't remark on it.

If I'd said all was right with the world because Cole, in the end, had come back to me, I would have been lying. Zane had been right. Cole showed no hint of having known that I'd left the auditorium during his program. He couldn't have come looking for me afterward—he'd gone looking for the stage hand apprentice. He was completely innocent to any thought of where I'd been or how I'd gotten home.

I doubt he'd even have cared if I told him that I'd let Zane fuck me.

And, worse than that, the young blond's name was Jared. He was twenty-one and gorgeous, and when I woke the next morning and went out to the kitchen to make coffee, he was still in the guest room, once more being fucked by Cole— making enough noise that I knew he was being fucked good by Cole.

* * * *

"We meet again. That's quite a pile of packages. Doing your Christmas shopping?"

I turned to see that Zane was there, at my side, in the Third Avenue Bloomingdale's department store. It had been five days since I'd slept with him in his hotel room. I had assumed he'd finished his business and gone back to the West Coast. He hadn't. I'd also spent the five days mulling over his request that I go to California with him.

It gave me a little thrill to know he hadn't left New York yet. I'd already decided that if he asked me to his hotel room again, I'd go.

"I'm doing Cole's Christmas shopping," I answered.

"I could have guessed," Zane said. "So, did he miss you the other night?"

"No," I said. I almost added something, but didn't. Zane noticed that.

"There is more to that, isn't there?"

"Yes, but I don't want to talk about it."

"Yes you do. He didn't come home alone, did he?"

"No, he didn't."

"The young, blond stage hand—picked out for Cole and not for you?"

"Yes."

"And the next night, yet another young man—younger than you? Fucking him longer than he fucked you?"

"Yes."

"That one's name is Sean Runion. He's the new singer in the band now playing the Chelsea Bathhouse," Zane said.

"Temple has been fucking him for over a month now. He's twenty-three."

"You knew."

"Everyone knows, Mike. I didn't want to be the one to tell you. But it adds to my reason to ask you to come home to California with me. Temple is all about Temple. He won't make an honorable break with you. He'll just follow his dick on to new conquests and let you slowly fade away—in the end just using you as his housekeeper. It's a miracle that you've been with him for ten years. Runion stayed the night, did he?"

"He's still there after four days," I said, almost choking on the words. "He's rarely been out of bed ever since." At least the blond stage hand had only been a one-night stand.

"And Temple?"

"In bed with him. For the first time I've known him, Cole isn't keeping his strict writing hours. He fucks me too, but not as often as he's fucking Sean—even when he should be writing."

"Come to California with me, Mike. I'll treat you right."

"He needs me."

"Apparently not enough."

"If he'd just admit that he needs me."

"Cole Temple admit that to anyone? It's not going to happen. What are you going to do now?"

"About Cole?"

"No, about us. Are you going to come back to my hotel room with me?"

"You don't know how badly I wanted to do this back in that room we shared," Zane told me as he pushed my belly against the tiles of the shower in his hotel room bathroom and fucked me from behind under the cascading water. "You remember that the shower wasn't big enough. I did fuck you over the sink once, though."

"Yes you did. I remember," I murmured, as I widened my stance, wanting him to reach ever higher inside me.

"And over the toilet."

"Yes"

"And on the floor. We were young and wild. We could at least be wild again."

"Could we?" I dearly wondered if that was possible again. And, yet, here we were in his shower, with him covering me from behind.

* * * *

The doorbell woke me. I turned over and moaned. I couldn't close my legs. Zane had fucked me through the night as if had he'd taken that long dick of his out of me, I might have escaped and bummed my way back to the East Coast. Despite the soreness deep inside me—the feel of his accumulate cum—what, four, five times in the night?—since Zane's answer to safety was regular checking and a pledge of monogamy rather than condoms, I found myself reaching for him, missing the possession of my channel by his cock.

Somewhat of a revelation had hit me between the second and third fuckings, though. I was tired then and told him so. I begged for a respite. It didn't matter to him. He'd slapped my legs apart, pinned me to the mattress with his cock, and pumped me hard. This was about him and what he wanted. He thought no more about me and my needs than Cole did. I was as much just a trophy ass channel for him as I had been for Cole. With Zane, it was all about Zane too. Could I help it if I aroused men like this—even at my age? Was it all about sex?

I reached out for him, as interested in a cuddle as a fuck. He wasn't there, though. That's when it caught up with me that there had been a doorbell ringing.

I heard him call up the staircase from the foyer of his Hollywood Hills mansion. "A visitor for you, Mike. I'll put him in the living room and go make coffee." His voice sounded flat, like he was of two minds on whether to let me know someone was here to see me. I had no idea who it might be.

I quickly pulled on jeans, a T-shirt, and sandals and clumped downstairs.

"I had a hell of a time finding you." Cole's voice sounded hurt, on the edge of anger. "Sorry, I shouldn't have put it that way," he continued, visibly calming down, forcing himself to release tension. "I just was worried as hell."

"I couldn't talk to you about it, Cole," I answered. "We never seemed to be able to talk to each other about it."

"I need you, Mike. I need you to come back. My life is all fucked up. You gave it order." His voice was choked up and I could see the glisten of tears in his eyes. Feigning such an emotion was beyond his capability, I believed. I must take him seriously. This was well beyond the natural arrogance of Cole Temple.

"That's something you've never said before, Cole," I said.

There was a catch in his voice when he answered. "I know. You know me. You've been everything to me for the past decade. I couldn't function without you. I can't function without you."

"Do you mean that Sean can't cook or clean house?"

"Sean is gone. I realized that you misunderstood about him."

"What's to misunderstand? Sean is young; his body is supple. He is in awe of you, which we both know is something you must have. Do you mean you're giving up fucking men in the baths and bringing them home?"

He gave me a blank look. He didn't have the foggiest notion he was doing anything out of the ordinary—for him.

"No, you can't stop doing that, can you?"

"You're different," he said. "You're above all of that. Those are just casual lays. I've kept you with me for a decade. We've been together for a long time. Doesn't that tell you anything?"

"It tells me that I can't expect you to change, certainly, but I can expect something else from you."

"What? Whatever it is, I'll say it, do it. I need you. I need what you give me, what you are to me. I can't function without you. What is it that I need to say or do?"

"You just did," I said, with a sigh. "I can't expect you not to be the great, legendary Cole Temple, I guess, but we'll have to work on a little more recognition of that need you are talking about."

Temple rose from his seat and extended his hand. "Let's go home, Mike. Life isn't perfect, but we can work at it."

When Zane came into the room with coffee cups on a tray, he found the room deserted, the front door yawning open, and Cole Temple and me gone.

24 Exeter Place

"Thank you," the monsignor said as I handed him down from the carriage in front of 24 Exeter Place in a quiet pocket garden not far from Victoria Station. I had told him my name was Luke, but he'd managed to go all afternoon without directly addressing me—like I wasn't wholly there. This was the first time he'd thanked me, though, and I thought there was reason enough to be thanked earlier in the day.

"Can we possibly be here?" he asked, looking up at the façade of a brownstone, whose edges blended in with the brownstones of the crescent on either side of it.

"Discretion," Your Eminence, I murmured. "The hallmark of the gentlemen's clubs of London."

"Ah, yes, I do appreciate that," he said, his English good, but with a heavy Spanish accent, as we mounted the steps and I raised and lowered the door knocker. Stewart Brandon, the imposing majordomo met us at the door. "Ah, Your Eminence . . . Luke," he said as he swept aside for us to enter. "I trust everything was satisfactory," he said to the Spanish monsignor, an emissary of the Vatican to the Court of Saint James, who had been introduced to the club by the marquis, Lord Fitzwater of York, one of the club's major patrons.

"Quite satisfactory," the monsignor said. "The young man can see me back to the hotel later?"

"Certainly, as you wish," Brandon said, as he ushered the priest into the drinks parlor, where several members had already gathered. Turning to me, he said, "Mark will need some help with the service; Matthew and John are otherwise occupied."

"Yes, Mr. Brandon," I answered, moving toward the kitchen at the back of the building for a tray of drinks. The four service men of the club were known as Matthew, Mark, Luke, and John no matter what their real names were. It made identifications easier for the members, who barely noticed who was serving them in the public areas of the club, although when we put our trays down, they generally brought us into the orb of their conversations at least long enough to acknowledge our presence, to make small chit chat, and to voice their interests and expectations.

The atmosphere in the drinks parlor was one of boisterous conversation, whiskeys and scotches, and cigars and cigarettes. There were several centers of discussion, focused on the careers and interests of the gentlemen, most in their middle age, all notable beyond the confines of the club walls. I passed by the "courts" group with a tray of drinks. The Right Honorable Peter Bowles, judge of the Appeals Court, was discussing the intricacies of the naval impressment case before him, including the scandalous indignities the press claimed were being imposed on the young sailors, with Admiral Stanley Thornton and the leading barrister of the day, Bradley Thaw.

"Nothing that the noblest of our young men don't encounter in public school," Thaw was saying.

Bowles laid a hand on my forearm and pulled me into the group for a moment. "I looked for you earlier today, Luke," he said. "I believe this was our afternoon." I doubt he'd been to court that day. He was dressed for riding, including having a riding crop in his hand that he kept flicking against his leg.

"Yes, Your Lordship," I answered. "It is, indeed, sir. I'm sorry that we have missed—"

"I don't intend it to be missed. I intend it to be fit in."

"Yes, of course, Your Lordship. I'm sorry. A guest of Lord Fitzwater's was in town and I was sent to him at Grosvenor's for the afternoon."

"Ah, the priest who has just entered then. I didn't recognize him."

"He's Spanish," I said. "Manual Alvarez. Apparently sent here on some diplomatic mission by the pope. Lord Fitzwater was very definite about wanting him to be made comfortable in London and to have someone escort him around."

As we conversed, I saw John come down the stairs behind the Earl, William Yates, and, at Stewart Brandon's beckoning cross to the Spanish priest. I felt the relief that John was seeing to the priest, as I was being torn between my obligations to Alvarez and Lord Peter.

The remainder of the drinks on my tray went to the politics discussion group near the door to the foyer, which included a viscount, Lord Charles Beaumont; the fiery orator in the House of Lords, Sir Travis Compton; and a gentleman so much farther up in the royal house that we never spoke his name or title in this club—just referring to him as "Your Highness."

I passed Mark in the foyer as he was arriving with a fresh drinks tray and I was returning to the kitchen to replenish mine. As I passed the staircase, I caught a glimpse of the Spanish priest's white cassock, denoting his tropical origin, near the top of the stairs. I didn't make it to the kitchen, though, as the door to the music room opened and the baronet, Sir James Stockdale, the club member nearest my age, a reputed ne'er-do-well and dandy the world knew as Dickie, accosted me.

"We are in the need of a singer of a new song Felix has written," he said to me in a slightly slurred voice. "You are the best singer in this establishment, Luke. Get thee in here."

He was a member—and also the one I liked the best—so I entered the music room and he closed the door behind me. This obviously was where the artists were gathering. Among them I marked the current leading man of the theatre, Sir Dennis Winston; and the celebrated novelist, Sir Henry Duwright. Felix, the black musician, who was the toast of Covent Garden underground cafés by night, was at the piano. I didn't escape for the next fifteen minutes while I was forced to warble Felix's new song, with him playing at the piano. Dickie saw to it that I couldn't leave by standing close behind me, holding me close, and giving me sloppy kisses on the neck

90

while I endeavored to make out the crude markings on notes on the score Felix handed me.

Back in the foyer, Peter Bowles caught my eye and nodded and, instead of going to the kitchen, I mounted the stairs to the second floor.

Curious, before I went to my assigned room, I opened a cupboard door between two of the other rooms that led into a narrow secret passage between the rooms and went to the spy holes into the rooms on either side. It was church day on the second floor of 24 Exeter Place. On one side, the bishop of Leeds was on all fours on a bed and Matthew was mounted on his ass and giving him quite a ride. On the other, as I suspected, John was lying belly on the bed, wrists bound to the headboard above him, and the Spanish monsignor, Manual Alvarez, cassock open, flared, and trailing behind his thin body, was plastered to his ass and making like a camel crossing the desert.

The Spaniard had taken me, similarly bound and in the same position, at the Grosvenor that afternoon. There was a hint of the Inquisition in him even when he was fucking a young man.

I came back into the corridor just as the Right Honorable Peter Bowles was reaching the top of the stairs. I regretted the riding crop he was flicking against his leg, but he was a senior member of the club and Stewart Brandon kept pointing out that I should be proud that he scheduled me so often. He paid extra in dues and some of the extra trickled down to the young man who serviced him. That may or may not have made up for the whip, but Stewart Brandon didn't care either way, so the issue was moot.

Today was bothersome, though, as he was a man quick to anger and he'd been made to wait for my services. He was a cruel cocksman when he was angry.

He too made use of the wrist restraints we all had attached to our beds, in addition to the ankle restraints had had me spread-eagled on the bed. He left them loose, however, as he enjoyed my writhing and throwing my body around as he made me rise to my knees under him and he rode me as he'd ridden his horse earlier, my rump between his knees, and his riding crop flogging me on the back, buttocks, and thighs.

Afterward, knowing what the servicing would be, Brandon sent a servant from the kitchen staff—my best friend, the African giant Kwame, to my room to apply unguents to my welts before they could take hold and fester. Kwame was the best of salves himself, taking me in his arms, stretched along my body—he was a good foot taller than me and much meatier—lifting my leg to expose and stretch open my passage, and slowly entering me with a long, long cock as his hand, slathered in the unguent, gently massaged my slight wounds— the judge hadn't got out of control or left much evidence of the exercise of his fetishes—as his staff worked my passage to a mutual ejaculation.

The Right Honorable Peter Bowles never was concerned for whether I came in his use of my body—today, despite having been made to wait, having been far less demanding than the days when his cases weren't going as he liked and he used his fists. It was only his own pleasure that he paid the extra dues for. On his bad days, the next day or two were bad for me too, causing me to lose sessions. We were paid by the session—and for each client ejaculation in a session—having to keep and report a tally of each release by way of discreet chalk marks on the inner walls of the night stand top drawers.

As I was descending the staircase, ready to take up my first-floor service duties again, the baronet, James Stockdale, was standing at the bottom of the stairs, looking up expectantly, and barring my way.

Stockdale was young, hung, athletic, and inventive. Usually I welcomed his approach as being a fresh break from the older members, whose repertoires were largely limited to the missionary and doggy positions and whose ejaculations, generally, were weak and rapid and their erection incomplete. Even the weak ejaculations were recorded and paid for, though.

There was nothing incomplete about Stockdale's erections or weak and rapid about his ejaculations. And he was a master of the male Kama Sutra.

But coming so soon after being worked over by the judge . . .

He walked up two steps of the stairs, his gaze still expectantly boring into my face, and, with a sigh, I turned and preceded him to my room.

No restraints with Stockdale. He fucked me all over the room, manipulating my body into various inventive positions. During the hour-long process, in which he showed he could make me come twice but save himself for one, long, prolonged gush, I, first, watched the dust motes build up under my bed as he doggy fucked me on the floor, and then all four walls, as he took me in a standing fuck, me draped on his chest, my knees gripping his waist, as he walked around the room slamming me up and down on his cock. Then it was the ceiling I viewed as he put my weight on my shoulders, jackknifed my legs and hammered down inside me from above. He saved his coming for tenderly embracing me on the bed, taking me in a side split, and capturing my eyes with his as we kissed deeply and he pumped my ass full of cum.

Stewart Brandon found me some minutes after Stockdale had dressed and left, on my back on my bed, my legs bent and spread to provide relief to my throbbing ass channel, Stockdale's cum dribbling out of my hole, and still moaning over the athletic man's attentions.

"The Spanish priest is ready to go back to the Grosvenor," he said, making no remark on my state of exhaustion as I lay on my bed. "Give him an hour there, but be back by dinner. You are accompanying the marquis to the theatre. I don't expect you back on duty before morning."

I groaned and rolled over to the side of the bed and searched for the floor with my bare feet. How could he consider a night with the marquis, Lord Charles Beaumont, not being on duty? Why were there only four of us to service these men. The members were a randy bunch. The club should hire two more prostitutes.

Monsignor Manuel, well serviced before, including two torturous fuckings of me in his Grosvenor hotel room earlier than afternoon, didn't need the whole hour. He was done and ready to bathe, take confession from Spanish residents of London, and attend a mass after no more than twenty minutes of plowing my ass, as I lay on my back at the foot of the bed, bending and pulling my legs up toward my chest and spreading them wide myself, while he crouched between my thighs, his cassock open and flaring behind him, and slammed me hard with a thin, upcurved cock rising out of an unruly black, curly thatch. He only managed a trickle of cum, but there was no way they could claim that the 24 Exeter Place gentleman's club hadn't fully met his expectations and needs.

I arrived back at the club in time for an early dinner, which I enjoyed with John and Kwame in the servants' hall off the kitchen. It was my habit to go out for a long walk after dinner, not only to settle my meal but also to have a few moments to myself and to exercise the limbs that kept my body in trim rather than the muscles I more frequently used to grasp a gentleman's cock with to make shimmering love to it.

However today that was not to be realized. Stewart Brandon came to me at the door as I was about to leave the club. His demeanor was one of excitement rather than regret to interrupt the time of the day I enjoyed the most—other than those nights that Kwame crept into my room and worked me over with an impossibly thick and long cock and stamina that no members of the club other than the baronet Sir James Stockdale could equal.

"His Highness is on the third floor, the Swan Suite. He's asked explicitly for you."

"Matthew?"

"It doesn't matter. His Highness has asked for you to attend him. Matthew is pouting, but that isn't your concern; I will knock him together."

With a sigh, I turned and mounted the stairs—first to my own room, as a call to serve such a royal required some special preparations—and then to the third floor. Till now Matthew had been the sole server for the man. But he'd asked for me, so there was nothing else to consider.

Afterward I was plied with questions on the encounter. Who topped? What positions? Is he hung . . . thick . . . long? Does he have a Prince Albert? (This last question bring twitters all around.)

Like Matthew, I kept the details to myself, as Stewart Brandon expected and would find out if I didn't, only responding to one of the questions. "Aren't all of the royals thick?" I asked, which was met with appreciative laughter.

First, we weren't alone. The guy in the corner was much too small and cute to be a bodyguard, I thought. And I was informed he was a dresser. His Highness couldn't undress himself by himself? OK, the extra man's cute, I thought, I can go with that—imagine myself with him rather than this walrus. It wasn't unknown for one club member to want to watch while another club member—or two, although doubles were John's specialty more than mine—fucked me.

The imperial walrus indeed was thick—as thick as I'd had—and, surprisingly and appropriately, he did have a thick Prince Albert ring in the head of the cock. Otherwise, he was quite royal. He laid on his back, his arms crossed behind his neck, and viewed me with a somewhat distant and amused look in his eyes as I straddled his hips and did all of the work for the first ten minutes, which wasn't easy considering the thickness of him; it took nearly the full ten minutes to bottom him out—all this until he engaged and decided that I had something he wanted to take from me, and then he swiftly turned our bodies, slapped my legs apart, thrust inside me, and completely dominated and pulled every ounce of value out of me for his own pleasure. In other words, the British Empire in a nutshell.

All of this within the span of thirteen or fourteen minutes. It was a blitzkrieg, and it was all about him—which was no surprise to me—once he took full control, it was wham, bang, five strokes and an ejaculation. And a world-record ejaculation to boot, itself a production of a good twenty seconds, multiple eruptions, and a tidal wave of cum.

As I lay on my side, his cock still inside me, and panting, he patted me on the rump and said, "Good show. I will want you again in a few days."

In the end, he said he wasn't in the mood for seconds, just a cock sucking. The gold of his Prince Albert clicked against my teeth as he forced his royalty down my throat and creamed my tonsils with his regal nectar.

Again, Steward Brandon found me laying all akimbo on the bed and panting hard in the suite after His Highness' dresser moved from the corner of the room and draped and smoothed the man out. The dresser was young and cute. I could only imagine what His Highness did with him. He gave me a shy, sympathetic smile, and I felt my cock harden. As with most of the rest, His Highness did nothing about any needs I might have and he'd fired off and gone soft just when I was beginning to get revved up. I still had a need after this onslaught. The dresser seemed to understand that. We shared smiles and I winked at him, moving my hand to my cock, which was half erect and unsatisfied. Brandon was all smiles too when he entered the room as the dresser left.

"He is very pleased," Brandon said. "He will ask for you again."

"That's what he said to me," I answered, not trying to make my voice sound flat, but I'm sure it did. All hail the gods, I thought, but rather than say anything else, I just tiredly waved my hand in an imperial salute.

As I had intended, the dresser slithered back into the room after Brandon left.

"Excuse me, sir. Is there anything I can do for you?"

"There certainly is," I murmured, taking my cock in my hand and shaking it at him.

In no time, he was kneeling between my legs and taking my staff in his mouth. When I was fully erect, I pulled him up to me, turned him, fumbled a bit in getting his ass bare, and then split his cheeks with my cock. He sighed and moaned as I pumped him slow and deep. There were club members who wished to be bottoms, but never enough for my tastes. I had built up a lot of cum over the day, and I gave it all to the dresser as he gasped and fell over himself in telling me how good I was.

"Better than . . . ?"

"Yes, much better."

I dropped my idea of having a Prince Albert added to my equipment.

I made another, unsuccessful stab at getting out of the club for a walk on my own. The encounter with His Highness had taken practically no time at all. Once more Stewart Brandon was waiting for me at the front door in the foyer.

"The marquis is in the library and is asking for you," he said.

"But it's too early for us to leave for the theatre," I said.

"He says he is tense now."

"Ah. And I suppose he'll be tense after the theatre too," I couldn't resist saying.

"I have no opinion on that," Brandon said, and leveling his eyes on me, "and neither to you."

I got the message.

"I hear that you are a bit tense, Your Lordship," I said as I entered the library. Other than the marquis sitting in a wing back chair with a scotch and a lit cigar on the table next to him, the library was deserted. I left Brandon standing at the door, and assumed he was on guard. It was against the club rules to engage in sex on the public floor. The marquis didn't care much about other people's rules, though.

"Yes, Luke, I am. Kindly service me."

With a sigh, I went down on my knees between his spread legs, unbuttoned his fly, fished out his erect cock, took it in my mouth, and, looking up into his eyes as I knew he liked, gave him a slow, deep-throating blow job that had me sputtering to capture and swallow his prodigious load. The marquis could build up cum like no other member of the club in my experience—and I had experienced nearly all of the members. All members of this club were interested in the services that I and Matthew, Mark, and John provided—that's why they joined and paid the exorbitant fees here.

On the carriage ride to the theatre, the marquis returned the service, although it didn't have anything to do with what I would want. He enjoyed giving head as much as he did taking it. In the darkness of the back of the carriage, he leaned over, took my lips in his, murmured about how handsome I was in evening wear, unbuttoned my fly, and lowered his face to my lap. He was wearing gloves and inserted a hand under my balls, running a gloved finger into my channel, and found my prostate. Rubbing there enhanced the rise of cum up from my ball sac. I pulled out the handkerchief I had brought with me for this contingency, and held it nearby as his head bobbed up and down on my cock. At least he was permitting me to come. I couldn't always count on that, even in circumstances like this. I warned him when I was coming and he pulled his mouth away, keeping his hand fisting the base of my cock and stroking and watched the expression on my face, as I folded the handkerchief over the bulb of my cock and spasmed my release three times.

As the carriage pulled up to the front of the theatre, I was reminded of the major reason I had taken the position I had—the position of lying under powerful men. The courtyard was lined with beggars. The economic situation was terrible. Without my handsome looks and sleek body and the ability to take cock after cock, I could well be one of these beggars myself. It was something to think about when I was tempted to complain about days like today. I was well paid, especially given that I had little opportunity to spend money, I was well fed and had a roof over my head. The men who fucked me were clean and wealthy. A few of them were generous. A couple had offered to set me up in my own apartment just to await their visits. I was saving that option for a few years when I felt I might be losing my charms. But I was not inclined to open my legs for only one man.

Even if I had taken another type of job altogether, I would still crave the cock. A variety of men and a variety of cocks. Even penetration by a cock as soon as one had pulled out of me. I was addicted to being fucked. "Whore" was a term of release for me, not a dirty word. All in all, it was the perfect job for me—as long as I could keep my looks and my channel was able to take a cock.

I had been given no idea what we were seeing at the theatre, nor did I care. It was time not spent on my back with a cock up my ass on a taxing day. It gave me the respite I had wanted to get by taking a walk and nothing was required of me. I sat in the last row in the box. The marchioness was there, sitting by the marquis, the two of them putting on a display for the world. She didn't ask who I was and obviously didn't care.

At the interval, they went to wherever the glitterati go and I went to the men's cloak room.

"Luke. You've come to the theatre." It was said in surprise. I turned to see the baronet, Sir James Stockdale, standing there, licking his chops like he'd like to eat me— which, in fact, he'd already done that day. Standing behind him was the novelist, Sir Henry Duwright. He hadn't eaten me out today, but did so on alternate days. Was this an even or odd day? I wondered. I'd lost count. Today was the type of day that I lost count of cocks as well.

"Great seeing you here," Stockdale continued. "Henry and I were just discussing what we wanted to do after the theatre. If you're free and would like to earn a little extra, we would love sharing you."

I knew what he meant by sharing me. A double—both of their cocks in me at the same time, the two of them making love with each other while having sex in me. It was a pity they both were tops; they would have made a lovely couple. They'd pay me a pound or two for that, at least. They loved taking me that way. I didn't mind it myself. But it had been a taxing day and I wasn't really free. "I'm here with the marquis," I said. "I'll be with him the whole night."

"Pity," Stockdale said, sounding like he meant it. "Another time, then. I'd book you at Exeter Place, but I know you wouldn't get much out of that for yourself."

"No, I wouldn't," I answered. I bit my tongue from pointing out right then that I always could be tipped directly at the Exeter, although I'd never known the baronet to do that.

"Perhaps on your day off."

"I don't have days off," I answered. And then I went for it. "Of course, there can be a bit extra under the sheets at the Exeter. You and Sir Henry could always—"

"Yes, that's always a possibility," he said. But his eyes were already roaming. I had little doubt that, as handsome as he was and with his reputation for prowess and startling equipment, that he and Sir Henry would be able to find some fellow to accommodate them this evening for free and for the bragging rights of having had the cocks of two such notable men in him at the same time.

When I returned to the box, the Bishop of Leeds was there, insinuating himself into joining the marquis' party of two for the rest of the evening. I could tell that Lord Fitzwater wasn't entirely pleased, but I could also tell that the Bishop of Leeds had some sort of control over him. I'd heard something about a land dispute that the bishop had come down on the side of the marquis in, but I couldn't remember any details.

After the theatre, we went to dinner—or rather the marquis and the bishop went to dinner and I was just along for the ride—and to be ridden. I wasn't asked if I had eaten—and thank goodness I had. I only was asked if I'd heard of the new men's dinner club, the Tombs, which, indeed, was in a subterranean chamber entered from an alley and was not the type of place that could advertise publicly.

I also didn't know that the entertainment included a young man engaged to periodically swing on a trapeze over the diners. Tonight I was volunteered to be that man. It was all part of a game. The orchestra played and I swung. When the orchestra stopped playing abruptly, I had to take off an article of clothing and toss it down into the crowd—not any part of the tuxedo I'd walked in with but a costume of billowy white silken shirt under a velvet vest; long, silken hose attached to a garter belt; and two layers of skimpy underdrawers. The man who caught the last article of clothing—my inner set of underdrawers—was given twenty minutes with me beyond a doorway covered with a beaded curtain beside the orchestra stand.

I was paid, but not nearly on the scale of the 24 Exeter Club.

My man was a burly thug who dressed like a gentleman but wasn't one. It took him less than fifteen minutes to slam me, belly against the wall, against the stones in the corridor behind the stage, release a thick slug of a cock and low-hanging hairy balls, skewer me from behind, and unload his ball sac.

When I returned to the table where the marquis and bishop were sitting, they didn't bother to ask me anything about the experience—and they were ready to leave for the drive back to the club. The bishop said he was quite happy to go to the club too, and what could the marquis say? The bishop was a member.

Neither of them asked me what I thought about it.

"You were so arousing swinging on the trapeze that I wanted to be the one to catch your underdrawers," the marquis said. "I'm not sure I can wait until we arrive back at Exeter Place."

"Why make the effort to?" the bishop helpfully said.

"Why, indeed?" Lord Fitzwater answered.

The bishop helped strip me of my trousers and underdrawers and to set me on the marquis' cock as he sat on the plush carriage seat. Helping to hold me there as I took the responsibility to rise and fall on the staff, the bishop lowered his head into my lap and took my cock in his mouth.

The bishop doggedly followed us into the club and up the stairs to the third floor, where the visitor suites were kept in readiness for the club members who decided to stay the night. The marquis had booked a room. I could tell that the marquis wasn't pleased that the bishop stayed with us, but it wasn't up to me to voice an opinion or do anything to hold the bishop back.

He watched for some time as Lord Fitzwater started out by fucking me missionary style at the foot of the bed, but he soon tired and laid himself out on the bed on his back and bid me mount the cock and do the riding. It was at this point that the bishop decided he wanted to be included. He approached the bed from behind me as I was facing the marquis' head and rocking back and forth on the cock. He had stripped. He muttered something about permission, but didn't wait for an answer. In short order the bishop had nestled in behind me; pushed my torso forward, causing my hips to roll up; and was forcing his cock in above Lord Fitzwater's.

So, after having negotiated with the baronet and the novelist over this very activity this night, here I was being double penetrated by a marquis and a bishop. I closed my eyes, relaxed as best I could, and went with the flow of the members' preferences.

The bishop didn't stay with us past his ejaculation, and both the marquis and I were tired enough that we just went to sleep in each other's arms.

The next morning we both woke to the sound of a knock on the door. Ever the servant, I rose and went to the door to fetch the tray of coffee and croissants that had been sent up for the marquis. I brought them back to the bed, sat, and placed the tray where the marquis could reach it. I hadn't had the least bit of a problem in discerning from his naked body stretched out on his back that he was erect and in need of attention.

As I twisted around and took the cock in my mouth, the marquis reached out for the coffee with one hand and for my head with the other, running his fingers through my unruly blond curls.

"Even in the morning, you are a beautiful young man," he murmured. "I hope that you had an enjoyable day yesterday."

"It was much as any day here at the club," I said, momentarily pulling my mouth off his cock to respond to his question.

"I wish for your day today to start with me," he said. "Please take this tray away, come into the bed, and open your legs to me."

Yes, just another day like any other here at 24 Exeter Place, I thought, with a sigh of resignation, as I lifted the tray and moved it to the top of the bureau.

The marquis was on his back, covers off, holding his cock erect and steady, patiently waiting for me to sit on it. All so civilized and gentlemanly here at the 24 Exeter Gentlemen's Club.

Swinger Christmas

Cody moved over to the corner of the floor-to-ceiling plate-glass window of the penthouse party room at the top of the high-rise. At one angle we was looking down at the busy E. Colfax Avenue in Denver. The other wall of window overlooked the Denver Zoo. He took a swig of his drink more so that it looked like he was drinking than that he wanted to drink. In truth, he would have liked to get drunk, but this was definitely not the time or place for it.

He did what he could not to look back into the room where a cut black dude had his wife, Pam, backed up against a wall. She certainly didn't look like she minded. They made a body-beautiful couple. In fact everyone in the party room on this Saturday night three weeks before Christmas looked like body beautiful. That's why they were here.

Cody himself outshone most of the men present in looks and perfect proportion if not for muscular development.

Cody had tried to pass on the annual Christmas-season conference of the Hayden Key Club Gym and Hotel empire at its Denver headquarters—and he would have skipped it if Tyler Hayden hadn't specifically asked Pam if she was bringing her husband. Pam, as manager of the Chicago facility, was the direct employee of Hayden Enterprises. But the company was Cody's biggest modeling account as well, so, in many ways, he was as much in thrall to the enterprise and Ty Hayden as Pam was.

Hayden had already taken Pam for a spin a couple of times and she had said more than once that it wouldn't be long before he took Cody for a ride too. The Hayden clubs were for no-holds-barred swingers, and Hayden himself was a prime example.

So, here Cody was, at the company Christmas party at the top of the Denver Hayden club tower, with rented retail on the ground floor, three floors of parking garage above that, rented office space on the next two floors, the Hayden Hotel on the next four floors, the gym services the two floors above that, the national headquarters offices the four flights above that, and the party floor at the top.

The Hayden gyms were for very special people. They not only had to be rich, but they also had to be body beautiful. Most were bisexuals who worshipped the full potential of pleasure they could get out of their own bodies. The gym and spa services were for maintaining their hard, cut bodies, not to create them. And clients didn't even bother paying the price unless they were swingers. That's why each of the company's facilities had not only party rooms but hotel space, as well— not to mention very discreet parking.

But the company Christmas party wasn't for the clients. It was for the company managers—all of whom had to maintain body beautiful as well. They displayed this at gatherings such as this by coming topless—women as well as men. This eased the casual sexiness of the parties, where assignations were made—and, as the night wore on, were carried out either right there or in one of the hotel rooms below. Before the night was through everyone would be naked—if they hadn't left early. Even then few left alone or with the one they came with.

Cody had planned to leave the party early—and he planned to leave alone. He knew his wife would stay to the bitter end.

Although some came as couples, either both spouses working for the company or the employee's spouse meeting the rigorous requirements, most came unattached, and all came prepared to swing—and not just heterosexually.

Some had to swing literally. There was a trapeze suspended from the ceiling of the two-story party room and Ty

Hayden had the privilege of designating who would swing. Often this identified who Hayden would fuck that night. Several would swing on the trapeze, and Hayden would fuck several—women and men alike. Cody's wife, Pam, had already had a turn on the trapeze and Cody had heard rumors that this was the night Hayden would send him, Cody, up on the swing as well.

That's what had Cody on edge. It didn't bother him all that much that Pam would be swinging with or without him at this party. Theirs was a marriage of convenience anyway. Pam liked being escorted in Chicago by a high-profile male model and Cody was happy using the camouflage that he was a lady's man, when, although he didn't indulge much, he preferred the attention of men. Being married gave him the ability to shop discreetly without being taken for granted. The demographic of those turned on by the ads he modeled for was mostly female, so Cody was in the closet with the door closed.

What had him on edge at the Denver gathering was knowing that Geneva, the manager of the San Francisco facility would be at this party and was bringing her husband, Gordon Clay, who owned a modeling and performers' agency in California and was putting the rush on Cody to jump ship from his Chicago agency and come out to the West Coast. Although he was tempted, Cody didn't want to be tempted. He was happy in Chicago and a move, with Pam in Chicago, would be messy. The kicker was that Clay was well known for agenting gay men, including porn stars.

Cody was struggling with the thought of leaving Pam anyway, but he just wasn't up to the change and the aggravation. It didn't help that Gordon was a real hunk, was openly bisexual, and was suggesting more benefits of coming to California than just more money.

The temptation was maddening. Cody had camouflage now—although his camouflage could be wearing thin if the rumors were right that Ty Hayden, who was actively bi, was thinking of sending him up on the trapeze. Working for Gordon would bring him out in the open—and once his preferences were publicly known, his life would face a whole new set of complications. Ty Hayden wouldn't be the least of the complications.

And here Gordon was, walking over to where Cody had isolated himself in a corner at the window as everyone else was getting serious about hooking up. He realized now that he should have picked out some stacked bimbo to hook up with to avoid Gordon—God knows a few had signaled their interest. Too late for that now, though. He couldn't even count on Geneva to come looking for her husband. Geneva had just come down from the trapeze and Ty Hayden himself had cut her out of the herd and had an arm around her over by a conference table. Although he was older—in his fifties—Hayden didn't make any demands on his employees that he didn't follow himself. A former Mr. America, he had maintained his muscularity and tone.

Geneva was an ambitious woman. If Hayden wanted to lay her, they would be at it for the next hour or so and Gordon would be at loose ends. Cody looked over occasionally and saw that a young muscle man from the New Orleans gym had joined Hayden and Geneva in a touchy-feely-kissy buildup to something—something quite soon considering where Hayden had several fingers of a hand buried in Geneva.

"I'm glad to see you here, Cody," Gordon said, as he approached. "I think you've been avoiding me."

"I avoid nearly everyone, Mr. Clay," Cody answered. "I'm afraid I'm pretty much of a recluse."

"Rather a strange thing for someone to be who models in Speedos for national magazines and billboards," Gordon said, with a laugh. "I would think it was more a job for an exhibitionist."

"One would think that, yes," Cody answered, looking down at the hand Gordon had placed on his arm until Gordon dropped his hand. "But not everyone is who you'd think they'd be."

"Funny you should say that, Cody. One would think you were straight unless they'd done their research."

Cody gave the man a hard look. There wasn't much else he could do. He felt the wind going out of his sails. Gordon knew. It had seemed he did considering the offers he'd been making, but nothing had been baldly stated until now. Clay was a dangerous man to have such information in his control.

"Have you considered the offer to come West and work under me?"

"You mean for you?" Cody asked.

"I meant what I said—under me. I am going to have you one of these days. Make no mistake about that. I think it would be in your best interests to consider the offer quite seriously. It may become quite problematical for you to continue to work in Chicago and stay married to Pam. It would make quite a social splash story on both of you."

"Pam—"

"Is Pam and is addicted to black cock. I know all about your arrangement with Pam."

"She isn't—"

"Don't even bother to say it, Cody. Look over where she is now."

Cody looked across the room. The black stud, manager of the Houston gym, who Pam had been flirting with, was fucking her now. He had her backed up against the wall, with her knees hooked on his hips and her skirt gathered up at her waist. He was pounding her hard and she had an ecstatic expression on her face. No one was paying much attention to them; much of the rest of the party had already transitioned to orgy mode.

"So, what did you want to say about Pam?" Gordon asked, his voice full of acid. "Aren't you going to go to her rescue?"

"Pam does what she wishes," Cody answered in a tight voice. "She doesn't need to be rescued."

"But you wish that the black bull who is fucking her now was fucking you instead, don't you?"

"How about Geneva, your wife?" Cody countered. "Isn't that her going off with Ty Hayden and that Dennis guy?"

"It certainly is. Geneva and I have the same arrangement that you and Pam do. And now that she'll be occupied for a while, how about you and I going to my room? The book on you is that you melt for muscle men and horse hung, and I can satisfy you in both realms. After I fuck your lights out, we can discuss when you'll be moving to the West Coast and contracts. And maybe later Geneva will come back

107

to the room and we can share her like Ty and Dennis are going to share her now. Which would you prefer? Me cunt and you ass? But no, I think perhaps you cunt and me your ass."

Cody was saved from answering by a couple of West Coast gym managers who saddled up to Gordon and him, but with interest only in talking business with Gordon. Keyed up— not least because Gordon was right, Cody opened his legs for muscular, horse-hung men, with Pam not being the only one in the family who enjoyed black bulls And Rashad Jackson being a black stud Cody would enjoy—Cody withdrew and left the party room. This was all too hot and heavy for him. And he couldn't deny that Gordon fit the profile of handsome, muscular, and horse hung. He also, though, was a sure avenue to Cody being outed, which Cody was still avoiding. His modeling career very likely would go down the tubes if he lost his sex appeal with women.

He was tense and on edge in leaving the party, though, and, since he spent half his life in the gym sculpting his body, that's where he went—to the gym floor. The lights were on in the gym, but the facility was deserted. Stripping down to his briefs, he started working his way through the machines.

He was on the bench press with an inclined back support, with a heavy set of barbells being lifted from his chest to the full extension of his arms when Gordon walked into the gym—completely naked.

Cody sucked in air. He already knew that Gordon's torso musculature and arms were perfectly—if massively— sculptured. Now, though, he also knew that Gordon was magnificently hung—and in full erection. Gordon picked up a couple of leather leads as he strutted up to Cody. Cody was mesmerized by the man's body, feeling himself trembling, and the constant need he had rising inside him. His cock was rising too, and Gordon could see that it was.

Cody had barely been able to resist the arrogant mastery of the man in the party room. Here, where they were alone, he didn't stand a chance.

"I told you that I was going to fuck your lights out," Gordon said. "If you fight me, so help me, your preferences will be spread across the Chicago tabloids by the weekend. Put the barbell down in its stand, but don't let loose of it."

It was a command, in an authoritative voice, which linked into another of Cody's weaknesses to other men. He wanted to be told what to do, to be dominated. Gordon knew how to dominate. Cody didn't have a chance against him. He watched, meekly, while Gordon bound his hands and wrists to the ends of the barbell resting on its frame.

Gordon straddled Cody's chest when he was done. "Suck me hard," he commanded as he moved his pelvis in to Cody's face. As far as Cody was concerned, Gordon already was hard and mammoth, but he opened his mouth to Gordon's cock and found that it could get harder, thicker, longer.

Pulling out of his mouth, Gordon backed off far enough to grab the waistband of Cody's briefs and pull them off his legs. He laughed. "There, see, you want me."

He reached over to a bookshelf next to the bench press and pulled out a condom packet. This was that sort of gym, condoms there for client instant gratification if they so desired and made a hookup. Part of the thrill of coming to one of these gyms was to be able to watch couples and threesomes fucking while you exercised.

Cody panted and moaned as Gordon pulled the Trojan Magnum on his cock. He squatted on the bench below where Cody sat, his legs bent at each side of the bench press and leveraged on the soles of his feet pulled back to the head of the bench.

Gordon's cock was projecting out a mile and a half, it seemed, toward Cody's hard cock, nudging under it, the bulb pressing into Cody's balls. "Raise your ankles to my shoulders," Gordon commanded, but Cody hesitated. "Saturday morning, in the *Chicago Tattler*," Gordon barked, and, with a sigh, Cody raised his legs and rested his ankles on Gordon's shoulders.

"Roll your butt up." With a whimper, Cody did so. "Impale yourself on the cock." Panting and whimpering, Cody slid his buttocks forward, stopping and panting hard as the bulb of Gordon's cock was pulled inside him. Suddenly, cruelly, Gordon thrust his cock forward, giving Cody lots of inches. Cody cried out, shuddered, and babbled a bit about how impossibly long and thick Gordon was.

"Shut up. Fuck yourself on the cock," Gordon demanded. With a whimper Cody moved his hips back and forward on the cock, until, with a groan, he shot off up Gordon's belly. With a laugh and a "Knew you wanted it," Gordon grabbed Cody's waist and took over the sheathing and unsheathing of the cock until he too had come with a jerk. He stood immediately, pulled off the spent condom, and presenting his dick to Cody's mouth, commanded, "Clean it." Cody took the cock in his mouth.

"Now I'm taking you up to my room and give you a proper fucking and we'll talk about the West Coast job." He untied Cody's wrists and moved back to the doorway to retrieve his trousers as Cody, whimpering, felt around for his own briefs and trousers.

Geneva had already returned to their room before Gordon and Cody arrived. She was sitting on the end of the bed, having started to unclip her stocking tops from the garter belt. But she stopped what she was doing as soon as the men entered the room.

"You found him," she said, her voice clearly showing her pleasure. "Such a luscious young man. I've envied Pam for a year. Can I have him too? Does he have a nice cock? Let me see it."

"Strip, Cody," Gordon demanded, and Cody complied.

"Oh, sweet Jezusss, let me play with him, Gordon." She opened her arms wide. "Come to Momma. Let me suck it."

Cody hesitated, but Gordon growled, "You heard the woman. Let her suck you and then fuck her."

Cody walked toward the bed like a man going to the gallows. As he was crouched between her legs, kissing her mouth and breasts, as commanded, and fucking her deep, Gordon saddled up behind him, thrust his cock up Cody's ass, and controlled the pace not only of him fucking Cody but Cody fucking Geneva as well.

Cody considered himself lucky that Gordon and Geneva worked up a lust for each other that surpassed what they had for him. At length he managed to roll out from between them and Gordon attacked his wife, who laughed and writhed under him, like a wild woman as Cody slipped out of the room.

He went directly to his own room. Pam wasn't there, nor did he expect her to be. He packed and was out of the hotel, headed to the airport and back to Chicago within fifteen minutes. It would be harder for Gordon to give him commands in Chicago from the West Coast. Still, he knew it was only a matter of time until something had to give—unless he could find a way to counter Gordon—unless Cody could find a protector.

But Gordon was so handsome and so forceful. And he was still Mr. America muscular—and hung like a bull and virile and vigorous. Maybe it was time for Cody to come out. One thing was for certain: if Gordon got close enough to Cody to bark a command and wanted to get his dick inside Cody's ass, Cody would meekly open his legs to the man.

* * * *

"But we just went to an office Christmas party—and this one is way out in San Francisco, not Denver."

"I know," Pam answered, "but we can't skip this one. I certainly can't, and under the circumstances you can't either."

Cody's blood had run cold when Pam came home with an invitation to yet another Hayden Enterprise's management Christmas party—and this time in San Francisco, right in the lion's den. He had come to think of Gordon Clay as a lion—commanding, a king of beasts, but to be avoided at all costs. Cody knew he was weak. He dreamed of being fucked by Gordon, but there was too much danger involved, and he could see that if he came under Gordon's sway, he would be devoured and spit out as skin and bones.

Cody had checked the tabloids in fear for the week after he had run out on Gordon Clay and the man's demands that Cody come out of the closet and come to San Francisco—surely to lose his modeling career in its current form and be at the complete mercy of the cruel dominator—or be exposed by Gordon anyway. There hadn't been any exposure yet, and with each passing day Cody had increasing hopes that Gordon was bluffing or that he had turned his interests to some other young man.

But here was a summons to San Francisco—the invitation was to a party at the San Francisco Hayden Key Club and Gym, managed by Geneva Clay, but Cody knew it really was a trap set by Gordon Clay.

"What circumstances, Pam? I don't see why I should be at the beck and call of Geneva Clay." More to the point, he couldn't see that Pam could allow him to knuckle under to Gordon Clay, especially if it involved Cody publicly declaring as gay. That, in essence, is what Gordon was demanding he do. It wasn't just to come to the West Coast and lay under Gordon at that arrogant man's bidding. Gordon had told Cody that, the West Coast being what it was, he wanted Cody to take modeling accounts with gay-oriented companies. The sexy ads now would be Cody in suggestive positions with other men rather than women. This wouldn't be any better for Pam's career than it was for Cody's. There would have to be a nasty breakup and divorce in public and Pam still would suffer from the backlash.

Gordon wanted Cody to do gay male porn movies too—to be submissive on film to other dominating men. "Very tasteful; expensive films distributed only to those who can pay for them," Gordon said, but the image he wanted to give Cody was diametrically opposed to the one Cody had already established for himself.

"Look at the invitation—if we can call it that—more of a summons, I'd say. It's from Ty Hayden himself, and he is quite clear he wants you at the party."

"Me?"

"Yes. You know what this means, don't you? We've discussed this possibility before."

And, when Cody didn't answer, Pam continued. "It stands to reason it would come to this. He's actively bisexual, and he's a randy old goat. He's seen you occasionally at parties—most recently last week in Denver. And you model in the ads for the gym companies. He asked me about you several times last week. He said he heard you were submissive to men. I knew he wanted you to be, so I didn't lie to him."

"But he's fucked you already. We've already paid our dues to the man."

"It seems it's your turn to be fucked by him. We've discussed this already. We've agreed that both of us would give the man whatever he wants. He's already had me a couple of times. Now he wants you. I wouldn't be surprised if he forced Geneva to host this second office Christmas party just to get at you. I should have seen it last weekend. After you'd left and flown home—without telling anyone, including me—he asked where you were and was irritated that you hadn't stayed."

"God, how did we get into this situation, Pam?" Cody asked. "How did we fall so helplessly under the control of an old man like Hayden. He must be fifty."

"He's fifty-two. And he's in great shape. You saw him shirtless last weekend. He's a good advertisement for his own line of sexy gyms. And you don't know the half of it. He's what you like; he's hung like a bull, and he'll fuck you to exhaustion. And you'll please him, just like I've done more than once, to assure our cushy lifestyle here in Chicago. There's something about what he likes . . . but, no, I'll let you discover that for yourself.

"Now, go tell Sally that we need air tickets for Friday out to San Francisco, returning on Monday morning. And buck up; we're swingers. You're a swinger. If Ty Hayden had picked you up in a bar and showed you his erection and his bankroll, you'd have gone with him without a whimper. We've already discussed what we'd each do when he wanted either one of us."

Cody dearly wanted to tell Pam that it wasn't as simple as that—that there was the added danger of being in San Francisco with Gordon. He hadn't told Pam how great a threat Gordon was to their cushy lifestyle in Chicago, and he didn't think there was anything Pam could do about it even if he told her. There was still Ty Hayden and his demands.

That was Cody's real problem—the dominating people around him and his natural submissiveness to them. It wasn't just Hayden and Clay, it was Pam too. When she barked a command at him like a general as she just had done, Cody knuckled under and meekly did her bidding—just like he now did by going out to the business manager's office and starting the ticketing process for San Francisco.

The times they had fucked were when she had wanted it from him or wanted him to ensnare another woman. She had flatly told him that she wanted to use his dick, and as little interested in women as he was, he had laid there while she rode him, willed himself to stay hard, and ejaculated on command.

At least with Gordon Clay—and with Ty Hayden, if Pam's description of his equipment could be believed, Cody could attain sexual pleasure from being dominated and fucked.

* * * *

"Oh, God, oh shit. Yes, fuck me. Fuck me hard. Fuck me deep! Yes, Gordon, YES!" Cody was ashamed of himself for letting loose this much—and this easily—but he couldn't help it. Gordon Clay was growling commands, and Cody was knuckling right under. Not that there was any choice now, though. Cody was trussed up like a lamb to the slaughter. For Cody, though, being bound soared him higher into the clouds. He had a fixation of being taken whether he wanted to be or not—by muscular, big-cocked men.

Gordon was bringing all of these fetishes of Cody's to bear on him. Cody, once Gordon got him alone—and especially once Gordon got his dick in him—was helpless to resist.

He had no choice in what he knew Gordon's plans were for him now, with the presence of Rashad Jackson, the black bull stud, manager of the Houston gym, who Cody had watched fuck Pam against a wall at the Denver Christmas party—the black stud Cody had wanted to fuck him. And not just the presence of Rashad, but also of the photographer, firing off photos—photos that Gordon declared he had every intention of, first, using to blackmail Cody into working for him and then to send around to the porn studios to help get Cody into gay films.

Gordon was on his back on a bench press in the San Francisco Hayden Club gym, while the office Christmas party was roaring away at the other end of the sprawling complex. Cody was stretched on his back on top of Gordon, his torso arched and his buttocks rolled back so that Gordon could have most of his hard cock buried in Cody's passage. Cody's wrists were bound together and were wedged behind Gordon's neck at the top edge of the bench, providing a headrest for Gordon's neck. Cody's legs were raised and spread, with his ankles tied off on the arms of a barbell frame.

Cody wasn't going anywhere until someone released him. He was trembling with fear-laced pleasure of being totally at Gordon's mercy. Whatever happened now wasn't his fault. Few men other than Gordon had given Cody all he desired like this—including a black bull spreading Cody's thighs with his knees.

The photographer had fired off shots of Gordon, hands grasping Cody's thin waist, pulling Cody on and off Gordon's cock. Cody couldn't help himself, even knowing that frames were being shot and a video camera was running. The big-cocked, muscular man was dominating him, fucking him hard and deep, and he was bound, helpless to the onslaught of the man. It was just the sex the Cody liked best.

He particularly liked that the big black bull, Rashad Jackson, was kneeling between his and Gordon's spread legs and giving him head while distending and crushing his balls in a big, black fist. An overpowering black man giving him pain and sex, dominating him. Perfection.

It was all good—at least until Gordon barked out, "You too, Jackson. We'll fuck him together."

Cody whimpered in less than a good way—in a distinctly fearful way but still arousing enough for Cody to fire off an ejaculation. Still, he tried to writhe away from Gordon—uselessly—as Jackson stood, still close, between their legs, and rolled on a Trojan Magnum.

"You gonna come for me again," Rashad muttered. It wasn't a question.

Cody had had every intention of staying away from Gordon at this party. His plan was to latch onto Ty Hayden as quickly as possible, let Hayden do what he wanted with him, and catch the next plane back to Chicago, just as he'd done at the Denver party.

But there was no Ty Hayden at the party. There had been an office emergency in Denver and he hadn't shown up.

They were in Gordon Clay's jurisdiction now. He'd met them at the airport. He'd barked for Cody to get in the back of one limousine and when Pam came out of the arrival hall, having been distracted by Geneva, she was handed into the second limousine by Geneva.

Pam had been taken to the hotel attached to the San Francisco Hayden Key Club. Gordon had fucked Cody in the limousine into moaning submission en route to the Clays' mansion with Gordon's own form of a torture chamber in the basement, where Cody had been laced with sex-enhancing drugs, hung from hooks, and his body abused in every way that wouldn't show as bruises later in the evening for the party. All the time he informed Cody of the contract he'd sign the next morning to transfer to San Francisco and fall into the plans Gordon had for him.

Cody was completely cowed—having no backup plan to Ty Hayden not being here—and was expertly fucked and dominated by Gordon. Once Gordon got his mammoth cock inside Cody, Cody was lost to him. Even the flogging was arousing to him.

They weren't at the party long, with Pam trying to pull answers out of Cody on where he'd been and why Cody arrived alone, on the arm of Gordon Clay. Pam had thought he'd been with Ty Hayden all afternoon and early evening—and wanted to know why Cody was so sluggish and glassy eyed, before Gordon commanded that Cody come with him, and they arrived in the gym to link up with a naked and magnificently erect Rashad Jackson, and a photographer.

Cody weakly objected as he felt the bulb of Rashad's cock pressed to his asshole on top of Gordon's already-buried cock. He began to thrash around as best he could, knowing that he couldn't take two mammoth cocks at the same time— not without more preparation—until Gordon growled, "Stop fighting it. It will be easier. Relax. Take it."

Grinning, Rashad bent over Cody's chest and grasped Cody's sides with big, black mitts positioned above Gordon's hands holding Cody's waist. Cody tried to relax, as commanded, and panted hard, as he felt Rashad's cock try to enter him on top of Gordon's. The bulb penetrated him, but It just wasn't happening without more preparation. The two

116

cocks were too big. Although Cody had been doubled before, it never had been by cocks this size.

At that moment, Geneva, Gordon's wife, entered the gym and stripped down to basic, voluptuous Geneva. She went to one of the large-frame exercise contraptions that provided support for a multiple number of exercises. She chose one that spread her legs and pointed her trimmed cunt at the men on the bench.

Rashad lost interest in trying to double Cody and went over to the exercise frame. He found a position facing Geneva, with his legs spread, under hers, and both of them suspended in the air. They selected a shared exercise where they were both swinging, attached at the pelvises, with his dick buried in her box. The energetic swinging of the two in concert were providing cries and moans from Geneva, grunts and groans from Rashad, long and deep thrusts, and vigorous friction.

Both Gordon and Cody were watching the performance closely and Gordon was timing the slamming of Cody's passage on his cock with the increasingly wild swings of the couple on the creaking and shuddering exercise frame. Gordon was grunting and Cody, lost in the fuck, was crying "Yes, deeper, harder!"

The photographer was running around snapping off photos and rolling film in frustration of which direction to film in and what the best angles were.

All four fired off at once in explosive orgasms. It was more than the exercise frame could take, though. Rashad jumped free as it collapsed, but Geneva was under it as it came roaring down to the floor.

Gordon climbed out from underneath Cody, barking at the photographer, "Untie him."

Quickly freed, Cody ran out of the room with Rashad right behind, the latter running for help, as Gordon went to start pulling steel off his wife.

Cody, however, did exactly what he'd done in a similar circumstance in Denver the previous weekend. Finding clothes, he then hustled Pam up to their hotel room, rummaged around for what he needed, and an hour later, they were in the San Francisco airport, each headed in a different direction.

* * * *

Of course Pam and Cody had to return to San Francisco the next weekend—the day after Christmas—for Geneva's funeral. There was no question that Cody was going, under the circumstances, and Pam showed up just to check on how Cody was doing. He hadn't seen her since they'd flown off in separate directions from the San Francisco airport.

The two met up about half way to the gravesite, where Cody had to cling to her. He was walking bowlegged and in a haze. Cody couldn't help but notice that Rashad Jackson was walking on the other side of her and holding her arm possessively.

"You and Rashad?" Cody asked.

"He appeared at the airport when your plane was taking off," she answered. "He came to Chicago with me. He's been a big comfort."

"I'll bet he has been," Cody said.

Pam caught that he was a bit miffed. "Is everything—?" she started to ask, in a whisper, because a large group of mourners—many from the various Hayden enterprise holdings—were moving from the cars to the gravesite. She changed what she was about to say. "Cody, you know about me and black studs."

"Yes, I know," he answered through clinched teeth. It wasn't that he resented that Pam was fucking the black bull. He wanted Rashad to fuck him too, and it almost had happened. "It's not that . . . oh, God, you were right. I've gotten no rest," Cody answered. "The training to it was brutal. But I think it will work out. I can manage and am beginning to enjoy it. Don't know when—or if—I can come home, though."

Cody looked up toward where the family was sitting beside the grave. As far as he knew, Gordon hadn't released any of the photos or videos he'd had taken on the fateful day a week before. But then, with the funeral arrangements and all, he hadn't had time to do much of what he threatened to do—which relieved Cody. But Gordon was boring his eyes into the young male model as the three of them—Cody, Pam, and Rashad—approached the gravesite, arm in arm.

Gordon nodded to Cody to acknowledge he was there and also, Cody knew, to lay down a marker that they had unfinished business.

The ceremony was brief. While the coffin was being lowered, Pam turned and walked in one direction. She looked around for Rashad to follow her, but he was wavering, walking closer to Cody toward the cars. Cody wasn't surprised. The last time they'd seen each other, they both were in compromising positions—on tape—and there had been a tragedy. Cody wasn't surprised that Rashad might like to say something to him.

But Gordon arrived, pushing between them, as they approached the line of limousines.

"My car is up there, at the head of the line," he growled at Cody as they reached the road. "We've got business to do—you have a contract to sign. Go to the car and get in."

They had reached a limousine, the back door to which opened as they arrived. A voice boomed out from the interior. "Cody is riding with me. Rashad is too. Get in, lads."

Gordon recognized the voice and froze, letting his possessing hand drop from Cody's arm.

Ty Haden continued speaking. "I understand you have some photographs and videos that I'll want to have all copies of, Gordon, and that you won't speak of them again—to anyone. Cody is with me now. I'll not have him publicly exposed."

Gordon stood there, dumbfounded, flanked, and defeated, as Cody, who had flown not to Chicago from San Francisco the previous Saturday but to Ty Hayden in Denver, climbed gingerly into the back of the limousine behind Rashad.

On the way to the airport to return to Denver, Cody did what he'd been in training to do throughout the previous week to win a new sponsor—one with power over Gordon Clay—he'd held his legs open for Ty Hayden's favorite form of fuck—the double penetration. As Ty Hayden sat in the middle of the limousine's backseat and Cody sat in his lap, Hayden's monster cock buried up his passage, and Cody faced away from Hayden, Rashad crouched and came in between their legs.

This time his cock easily joined Hayden's inside Cody's passage—the training had been rigorous, the reaming wide. Although he was growing used to it, Cody writhed and sobbed and begged, first, for mercy, and then for deeper penetration and more vigorous stroking while the two worked him in counterthrusts. He had quickly learned what turned Hayden on the most and kept him in bed and interested.

Cody had repeatedly been reamed by two cocks at the same time over the preceding week to where he could take two bulls at once with little effort. Hayden had promised to keep Cody's preferences a secret publicly and to protect him against Gordon Clay's threats—and the service he would be providing for Hayden as long as Hayden wanted it, wouldn't show in Cody's modeling gigs.

As for Pam, she was getting the job security she wanted, she had been the one who told Cody he needed to lay under Hayden, and Rashad was just a temporary fix; Hayden had more studs to join him inside Cody's ass back in Denver. Rashad could return to Pam the following week.

Becoming Key West

"Are you lookin' for company, Doll?"

I riled at being called a "doll." I turned and looked at the bartender who was leaning over the bar and smiling at me. He was a real swisher—wouldn't have gone out on the street up in Baltimore. But, of course, no one else in this dive would have, except me, I guess. I definitely was out of place in my pressed khakis and sports shirt. Key West was a long way from Baltimore in 1970, and that wasn't just in miles. I almost wondered how I had gotten here—and why I'd come. Still, behind those black-painted lips, he was good looking. Much too young for what I was looking for, though.

And what was I looking for? Hell if I knew. I just knew that something called me to a place like Key West, suddenly becoming known as a place for a certain kind of person to be, after Karen died. Ten years married to my boss, who insisted that I change my aspect for the allowance to keep coming. Which I did. Ten years straight.

"No, no, thanks," I said. "I'm meeting someone here." I almost said "hooking up with someone." I should have said that. I needed to learn the lingo if I was going to stay here. That "if" was up in the air, though. Maybe Key West was too much, too out there. Maybe after ten years I couldn't get back on the wagon—or would find I didn't want to anymore. Good thing I had the bungalow on a six-month rent to purchase.

"You've been sittin' there for a half hour and nursin' two beers," the bartender said. "A big, handsome, strappin' stud like you shouldn't have to be alone that long in here. that isn't Key West."

I smiled wanly at him, and said, "I was early." And I was, and nervous as hell. And if I'd known I could just walk in here and get it, I wouldn't have, out of frustration at being here a month and nothing happening, responded to the escort service ad in the underground newspaper. I'd never had to pay for it before in my life. But there are a lot of changes in ten years.

The bartender was probably just jiving me on. I was pushing forty hard. Nearly everyone else in here was half my age. Sure, I'd gotten the eye more than once. But I probably looked like a sugar daddy to them. When I parked the red '66 T-Bird convertible up on Duval, the car had gotten more notice than I had.

"I take you for a power top, Stud," the bartender continued. "You don't see anything else you want to spike in here the next hour, I get off then. I'll show you a real good time."

"Umm, thanks, but I think he's here." A young guy was at the door, looking around. And he appallingly fit the description. I was hoping not.

"You mean Cory? Yeah, he'll suck it out of your balls good." With that and a wave at the young man at the door and a finger point at me, the bartender moved down the bar.

"John?" the young man—maybe too young, I thought, certainly not the twenty-four I'd been told—said as he came up to me.

I wasn't John, of course, but I had told the escort service I was. Oh, God, why was I paying for this humiliation? He wasn't anything like I would want to fuck. Not that he wasn't good looking and trim. He was—but in a cute way. When I was going with men, I was going with men men. And he too couldn't have walked the streets of Baltimore in 1970. He was small, short, and thin, showily dressed as the whore he was—tight micro shorts, a mesh T-shirt—a sleeve tattoo covering his right arm, rampant in color. And the piercings. An eyebrow, the right ear—and I'd been told what that meant—and, I could see through the mesh of his shirt, both nipples and his belly button. Who knows where else? His hair was spiked and frosted. He screamed bent-wrist homo. He looked a lot like many of the young guys on the dance floor in this bar. The Key West lifestyle, apparently.

And surely he wasn't legal. I needed to end this. This was a terrible idea. I needed to bow out, get back to the bungalow, pack up my artist supplies, and run back to Baltimore. I owned the advertising agency now—by way of Karen's death; she'd been twenty-five years older than I was; bought as her boy toy—I wasn't just one of its commercial artists anymore. Why had I felt I could be freer now, could get back on the wagon?

He came in close to me, between my knees as I swiveled the bar stool toward him. His eyes were a rich, chocolate brown and drew me in. Without saying anything he unbuttoned the top two buttons of my shirt and ran a hand in to palm a pec. "My, you're a big handsome one, aren't you? Hard pecs. Spend most of your day in a gym?"

"Listen, maybe this wasn't . . ." I gave a little jerk. His other hand was cupping my package, rubbing. I immediately responded.

"Big and handsome, with an emphasis on big," he said in a low, sexy voice. The hand came off my chest and he took a swig of my beer.

"Listen," I said again. "This might have been a mistake. I haven't . . . in ten years."

"It's like riding a bicycle, Stud. Where are you fucking me? Here, in back? They've got rooms. On the beach? Backseat of a car." He later told me he'd rushed me for fear I didn't have to pay for it—that half the guys in the bar would have gone with someone looking like me for free.

"Oh, God, not here," I exclaimed, looking around at all of the gyrating bodies, with the loud noise. No room in back could get away from this. This wouldn't happen in Baltimore in 1970. "I booked a room in a motel around the corner, but . . ." He dragged me off the barstool.

"Let's go then."

* * * *

He was right. It was like riding a bicycle.

He was as light as air, and pliable, and flexible. I was up on my knees on the bed, with him draped on my front, one of my hands cupping his chin, holding the back of his head into my chest, nestled between my pecs. My other hand was on his lower belly, pressing in with each thrust up his ass to give it to him deep. His legs were streaming back from us, against my calves. One of his arms was thrown up and back, his hand gripping the back of my neck. He was jacking himself off with his other hand.

"Shit, you're gigantic. You're killing me!" he cried out.

"Slow down? Stop?" I queried, still nervous, not believing I actually was doing this.

"No man, I was just giving you the *Good Housekeeping* seal of approval. Give it to me deep. Biggest I've had. Fuck me hard."

I'm sure he said this to all the johns—I almost choked when it reminded me of the name I'd given him—but I *was* big and knew I was. In my earlier life I'd reamed many a young man a wider channel. I was surprised I wasn't doing it for Cory. He was so small and thin. And his cock was small. It was like fucking him was a sin. But other than the initial difficulty of penetration, he'd opened right up, sucked my cock right in, saying he wanted it, wanted it bad.

"Shit, man. Harder! Deeper! Faster!"

I lost all control and began to pump him hard, with him flopping around on my torso, held in check only by my strong embrace, I turned my face down toward his to find he was looking up at me with wild, needy eyes. We went into a deep kiss, he shot his load across the sheets, and I unloaded mine deep in his ass.

When I'd parked in front of the motel room, he'd said he didn't want to get out of the T-Bird yet. He'd bent over me, unzipped me, marveled at the size of my dick as he uncoiled it. The first thing he did with it was to pull the foreskin down to the bottom rim of the bulb, which got a groan and my attention real fast. I groaned again when he thumbed the now-exposed piss slit. And then it was like he was worshipping it, as he fondled and stroked it until it was hard and throbbing. Nervous and naïve about relating to a rent-boy, not to mention having my cock worked in the front seat of a top-down convertible in front of a line of motel rooms, I just dumbly looked down at the hand manipulating my cock. I gave a little jerk as he tried to work the tip of his index finger into my piss slit and his efforts were rewarded with a dab of precum, which he slathered around on the bulb of my cock.

Afraid that I'd fire off too fast, I had to arch my head back on the top of the seat, stretch my arms down the back of my seat, and think other thoughts—about the art spread I should be home painting even now, with a deadline looming. I groaned as his moist lips opened over my hard dick and he sucked on the head. My cock was hard, hard, hard and throbbing, and he tried valiantly to deep throat it, not being able to but coming close. I grunted my need and set my hips in motion, at first tentative rises, moving to strong upward thrusts, as he made a big, stationary O of his mouth and let me face fuck him. My hands went to the back of his head, pushing the head down as I thrust up. He was gagging, but going with it, and now he *was* deep-throating, his lips reaching into my pubes. Now . . . when . . . with a jerk and another and another and a deep sigh, I creamed his tonsils.

He sat up in the seat, wiping his mouth off with the back of his hand, and said simply, "God, it's big. They should mold a dildo off that."

Overwhelmed, I reached for him, pulling his face to mine with a hand cupping the back of his neck, and took him into a long, deep kiss, a kiss tasting salty—of my cum. This is something I most certainly would not have done in Baltimore. I was almost taken aback that I was doing this here, but then I reasoned that he was a rent-boy. I was paying good money for this. Ten years earlier I'd never have thought of paying for it. But payment deserved good service. It should put me in control.

My other hand fiddled around with the buttons on his shorts fly, flared the sides open, found his cock, and, as we continued in one, long, drawn-out kiss, I jacked him off. His cock was small but filled out pretty well when stroked.

When he'd shot off, I pulled away from him, still cupping the back of his head. His eyes had a dreamy expression. I didn't know if that was something he'd trained himself to do for a john or not. Probably so. Still, it was sexy as hell. All of his paint and hardware were evaporating in my mind. I was seeing through to a desirable young man I very much wanted to fuck.

"Shit, man. No one's done that for me before. That was good." He sounded genuine, but who knows?

"Is this it, then?" I ask. "I give you your money now, and you split?" If it was, it was worth it—after ten years of pretending straight.

"You haven't fucked me. You're paying to fuck me. You said you had a room. I'll go in with you . . . if you want. If you really do have a room."

He dozed after I fucked him, draped on the front of me. When we'd ejaculated, I'd released him and let him fall to the bed, and he'd propelled himself up to where he was stretched out on his belly. He turned his face up to me, whispered, "God, you're built big. I took a big one," and closed his eyes.

I leaned over and ran my hand down the crevice between his butt cheeks. I followed with the other hand and spread the cheeks apart. For some reason I wanted to see my cum dribbling out of his hole—some sort of affirmation that I'd put it there. The hole hadn't closed; it was wide open in a big O shape, a couple of inches of pink, still rippling passage wall visible, leading down into the depths of him. And the cum was more than a dribble and glistened, caught in the beam of the light over the bed. Cory sighed and stirred, but he didn't wake. I resisted the urge to mount him again, but I wasn't ready yet. I wasn't hard enough.

Ten years without, and there, see, *I* reamed that hole. *I* put that cum in that hole. Just like riding a bike. Back in the saddle again. Even if I had to pay for it.

Taking my hands away, I sat there at the end of the bed, cross-legged, and watched him snooze. I'd done it. When I was hard, maybe I'd do it again. After ten years I'd fallen off the "straight" wagon. Of course I'd had to pay for it, and he wasn't anything I would have picked. I'd always gone for the college preppy or athletic types. Clean cut. And bigger. Someone closer to my own size. A football or basketball player. Someone who could hold his own. Not like Cory, who

I'd manipulated at will. I had trapped his small, thin body in my arms, stuffed his ass, and fucked the shit out of him.

Why was it I felt so satisfied, so powerful, so aroused . . . still? What had I paid for? I thought, as I felt myself going hard again. How many times? Could I remember? I padded out of the bed and over to my trousers. Taking two more twenties out of my wallet, I dropped them on top of what I'd put on the dresser, for him to see, before we'd undressed—me nervously so.

While I was up, I looked around frantically for something to sketch on. That's what I did. I was an artist. Nothing like I wanted to sketch now, but this was now, here. I found a couple of pieces of motel stationary and a pencil by the telephone. A Gideon's Bible in the nightstand.

After fifteen minutes I had captured him, stretched out on his belly, in repose. But as I finished the sketch, my hands were shaky. Having him in a sketch wasn't enough. I had to have him again, totally.

His eyes shot open and he grunted and groaned, as, stiff-armed above and stretched out over him in a pushup position, I penetrated his ass and slid in deep before starting to pump.

Murmuring, "Shit, it's big. Gigantic," he sleepily spread his legs, rose on his knees, reached under to grasp his cock, and began to meet the rhythm of my thrusts with counterthrusts of his own. "Fuck, it's big. Yes, Yes, like that. Harder. Deeper. FUCK ME!"

The headboard began to rock against the wall, the springs of the bed were squeaking. After ten years I was doing a second—fucking a sweet little honey hard.

I lay on my back on the bed, propped up against the headboard, my legs crossed, and my uncut cock in "big slab of meat" repose across one of my thighs. I was smoking a cigarette and watching Cory move around the room, fidgeting with his hair in the bathroom mirror, finding and pulling on his clothes.

I looked down the line of my body. It was still half hard, despite my age. And well muscled. My dick, serviced and satisfied, but laying, docilely across my thigh—not so docile, though, as the more Cory flitted around in the altogether, the more the "big guy" was stirring. My balls, heavy and drained—also satisfied and aching a bit streamed out from under the root of my cock. My bush, strawberry blond, redder than what was on my head, chest, and arms would have to be trimmed now, I thought, if I was getting back on this wagon. My dick looked even bigger with a trimmed bush, and I'd let mine go unruly.

I was fairly purring my satisfaction.

"What's this then?" Cory asked, picking up the sketch. "This is me."

"Yes, yes, it is. That's what I do. I'm an artist."

"This is good, man."

"You can keep it. I have you in my brain now. I don't need it. And speaking of that, if I call the escort service, can I have you again?"

"Have me again, as in fuck the wadding out of me?"

"Yes, if I call your pimp again, can I fuck you again? Screw you? Spike you? Ream you? Nail you?" Why is it that everything in Key West had to be stated so baldly?

"Yeah, I guess," he said, already at the door, his hand on the handle. "That's what the agency is for. But I don't know if you'd get me. I'm thinking of leaving town."

"Uh, OK," I said to the door closing behind him. I guess I knew what that meant. Not as much the stud with him as he had been letting on. Well, I'd been telling myself that all along. He was just a whore. He told me what I wanted to hear.

Deflated, I punched out my cigarette in the ashtray on the nightstand, rose from the bed that didn't seem as much the bed of roses now that it had ten minutes before, dressed, and drove back to the bungalow. Parking in the two-car carport stretching across the front of the lot, I walked back along the sidewalk running down the side of a long, narrow exercise pool, on one side, and the guest bedroom on the other. I entered the combination living room, dining room, and kitchen overlooking the end of the pool and a small terrace backed by an edge of luxuriant tropical foliage and back to the room behind the kitchen that I had set up as my art studio. The master bedroom was beside that, looking out over the terrace and the end of the pool. All in all it was a good house setup for me, I thought.

128

It wasn't even midnight yet, and I worked best late. I stood in front of a blank canvas, turning my mind—or so I thought—on the ad campaign artwork that needed to be done by the next Tuesday.

So, how did it really go? I wondered. That first time after ten years. The man sex I had come to Key West to pursue—that I couldn't have done in the world I'd lived in in Baltimore for the past ten year.

The sex had been good. Incredible—at least the part of getting my rocks off. Even ten years ago I hadn't often fucked a guy twice, back to back—let alone with a blow job session up front. My balls were drained, my dick very pleased with itself. I relived in my mind the moaning of the little piece I'd fucked—and how often he'd told me how big I was. The blow job was the greatest. I'd rarely gotten that even before Karen's dictum—I certainly didn't get them from Karen. In the early days it had mainly been jacking each other off and on to the main event.

But not my type at all. All those piercings. Everywhere, even in his taint, I'd found. Of course, the response I'd gotten by teething or pulling on those was interesting. The flaming-statement hair. The small cock and balls—the small size of him altogether—other than the hole that opened for me. Well, the size had turned me on, especially when combined with the opening of his ass. Being a lot bigger than him—everywhere—and the feeling of overpowering him. Watching what I was packing penetrate him. That had been arousing. It was arousing now. I was hard again.

I looked up at the canvas, ready to start painting. But, to my shock, I'd already filled the canvas with paint. How long had I been ruminating? What had I painted?

It wasn't anything to do with the ad agency. It was obscene, pornographic. Luscious, arousing. I set the paint brush down and cupped my hard cock. I was naked. That was no surprise, I often painted naked late at night. But I was in throbbing erection.

The painting was of Cory, but in no pose I remembered from earlier in the night. He was on a bed, on his belly, but raised on an elbow, looking directly into the viewer's eyes, his eyes swimming in satisfaction, fulfillment, cum. The body was small and thin, but beautiful, sexy even with every piercing and the sleeve tattoo in place. His far leg was stretched out, almost straight, the near one bent, covering any sign of a dick. The buttocks were two perfect pert globes, but they were jutted a bit up and parted—parted enough that his asshole was evident—and prominent—open wide and puckered. I had painted globes of white cum dribbling down from the hole.

It was a Cory who had just been royally, satisfyingly fucked. The look in his eyes affirmed that.

I stumbled back, falling into a canvas chair. My eyes glued to the canvas—to the gaping hole with the cum dribbling down—to my cum and the hole I had reamed big. I cupped and squeezed my balls with one hand, and with the other, I pushed the foreskin of my penis to below the rim of the bulb and pressed my index finger into the piss slit, producing both precum and a groan. I then masturbated my throbbing dick to a high-arcing ejaculation.

* * * *

Key West is a small island. Still, it seemed rather a long drive along the Atlantic coast of the key from my bungalow in the historical district to a grocery store. I had rounded the curve on the northern end of the key, by the airport runways, when I came upon a cut, blond hunk in just a low-slung Speedo and flip-flops bumming a ride. Nothing strange in a cut, blond hunk sighting in Key West, but there was nothing out here but scrub and runway to the right and sand and sea to the left. It was going to be a long walk for him. So, I stopped beyond him and let him walk to me.

"Thanks, man. Great ride," he said, as he got in the car. Another frosted blond with rings in his nipples and right ear. But this one was athletic in body build. He was admiring the red '66 T-bird convertible, even after he got in, running his hands over the top of the door frame and the dash on his side, and turning around to look at the back. "A convertible with a backseat. Neat. Bet you get a lot of use out of that."

"Sometimes I forget it's back there," I answered, not sure what to say. The car was mine. When I was in it I was behind the wheel, not in the backseat.

"I'm Tag," he said, as I got started down the road.

"Tag?"

"Yeah, as in 'Tag, you're it.'" He laughed. I smiled, not getting it. "Tag is a word down here for being fucked," he added.

"Where you going, Tag?" I asked, ignoring his last explanation.

"Wherever you take me," he answered. But then, when I turned my head and gave him a quizzical look, he added, "You picked me up to fuck me, didn't you?"

"No, what gave you that idea?" I asked, shocked. "I picked you up because it was a long walk from where you were to anywhere."

"You are a top, aren't you? I saw you the other night—in the Wave bar. You left with Cory. So, you're a top, aren't you? And a real stud of one even if you don't dress Key West. Not long here, are you?"

"No, I haven't been here long," I answered. I glanced over at him and almost drove the car off the road. He had the waistband of his Speedo pulled down under his balls and was stroking his cock. "Where did you say you wanted to be dropped off?" I asked again, pretending I couldn't see what he was doing.

"The backseat of this car would be nice," he answered. "I asked if you were a top. I think you are. You're a real stud. If you went with Cory, you must be a top. If you're a top you could tag me. Get it now? And you wouldn't have to pay for it like Cory made you do, I'm sure. You're too stud looking to have to pay for it in Key West."

"Yes, I'm a top," I said, wearily.

"You get a lot of tail here in Key West? You look like you do."

"Not so much," I answered.

"You need to signal it."

"What do you mean, signal it?"

"See, I've got a ring in my right ear. That means I take cock. You need to put one in your left ear—and maybe dress down more, to show the goods better. Then you'd get all the tail you could handle. I bet you've got a nice package. Yes, you do."

He had his hand on my crotch.

"Don't do that. I'm driving."

"Then pull over somewhere. Holy, Jesus, you got a whopper!" He'd unzipped me and pulled my cock out. I hardened in his hand.

"Hey, you'll run me off the road. Oh, shit, oh fuck!" He had his mouth on it. I pulled over into one of the parking strips by a beach and leaned back in the seat, groaning, as he gave me head.

"There's a beach a mile down the road with off-road parking, under some palm trees. That's where I want you to take me," he said when he came up for air. "I want to see if I can take this honking big cock—in the backseat."

I had to push the passenger side of the front seat up as far as it could go for me to fit in the rounded corner of the backseat with Tag sitting on my cock. I positioned him facing me, and kissing me as he fucked himself. Guys were coming up from the beach—all cut, blond hunks—and gathering around to watch us fuck and to run their hands over the finish of the T-Bird. I think the interest was divided between watching Tag, crouched over my hips, rising and falling on my cock, while we kissed, his arms around my neck, while I grasped his waist and helped guide the fuck and the attraction of the red T-Bird. The interest seemed to shift to me, though, when Tag came all of the way off my cock a couple of times to show how long and thick it was. Then several were muttering that they wanted to get in on the action. By the time I shot my load, three guys had sat in my lap and risen and fallen on the cock and a couple had begged me to take them home and bang them properly.

Looking around afterward, I wasn't able to pick out which one was Tag—they all were blond, cut, athletic hunks.

Welcome to the Key West lifestyle. For the first time I thought of the groceries in the trunk, many of which would be ruined now. I'd have to go back to the store.

But first—a couple of the cut blonds wouldn't leave. They said they wanted me to do them on the beach. So, what the hell, I went down on the beach with them and banged them properly, one after the other. I wasn't sure, but one of them could have been Tag. It suddenly occurred to me what he'd meant about being tagged.

132

I was starting to get used to the Key West lifestyle. I'd have to get me one of those earrings in my left ear.

* * * *

"Will you have any more soon?"

"I don't have any; not for a while," I answered, my mind on how I was going to have to ratchet back on these paintings because my stepson Billie was visiting on spring break from the University of Maryland and was bringing a friend. I'd gone wild in recent weeks, picked up the Key West spirit in spades. Too wild. I probably needed to ratchet back even if Billie and friend weren't visiting. The paintings and charcoal sketches I'd brought to the gallery today were more because I needed to get them out of the house.

"They sell really well," the gallery owner said.

"That could only happen in Key West," I said, with a laugh.

"No, there's a market for explicit gay art many other places," the gallery owner answered. "Perhaps it's just kept in a back, back room rather than here, where it's only in the back room, and the door to the back room is open. Your paintings are scintillating. So realistic. Just like you were there."

Real, not realistic, I thought. Some of it, I had to believe, thanks to the quick recognition my new earring in the left ear had brought me. No more speculation in bars.

I turned to look at what I had brought today. A dance scene at the bar. Young men gyrating and flirting. The spotlight on one young Jamaican, with his dreadlocks thrashing about his head, down on the small of his back on the dance floor boards, holding his ankles, obviously doing a spin, his face joyous, the other dancers swirling around him. Very sexy, the gallery owner had said. Even though it wasn't the usual sort of the art I was selling through the gallery, he said he knew who would snap it up. I knew too. It was the same man who had bought the companion piece a couple of weeks before—of the same Jamaican, on his back, holding his ankles, his legs spread, his dreadlocks fanned out over the floor, perhaps on the same dance floor. But naked, his long, black cock laying up on his belly, a dribble of cum at the head. His hole exposed, reamed wide, cum flowing from the opening.

That painting had lodged itself in my mind, right after I had pulled away from dropping my load in the Jamaican, who was lying on the small of his back on a cube in a back room of the bar and holding his legs open for me.

And the second painting, of a young, dark-haired man, with black lipstick, on his back, lengthwise, on the top of a bar—the very bar where he was a bartender—his legs spread and bent, his back arched, a dreamy, but slightly pained expression on his face, his hole gaping wide and bubbling over with cum. The expression of totally, over-the-top fucked.

"All three will go fast," the gallery owner said, reaching for the third one I was still gripping in my hand. "That one's unusual, but very nice."

"I've decided I'll keep this one for a while," I said, looking down at the painting of a man's muscular torso—Roman style, in that the arms are raised, but stop at the biceps, and the meaty thighs end at midpoint. The torso is twisted a bit to one side. It's not the torso of a young man. A man in his late thirties or forties—although I knew it to be precisely thirty-nine. Very well muscled. And if it weren't for the tattooing across his chest, the viewer's eye would inevitably go to—and remain at—the long, thick, uncut cock and drooping ball sac with the two large, distinct balls weighing it down. The tattooing was distinctive enough to arrest the attention, though. Red roses, backed by green leaves, in a V, the long upper edge extending along the top of the bulge of the pecs, and then coming down between the pecs in a V. One isolated rose teased the side of the belly button. A startling feature was that the roses surrounded, but didn't come within a half inch of the taut nipples and nickel-sized aureoles.

"Sexy, very sexy indeed," the gallery owner said.

"Thanks," I said. "I've got to go now, though. I have an appointment."

Carefully covering and returning the painting to the trunk of the T-Bird, I drove three blocks and parked in front of the tattoo parlor.

"There, one last rose to fill in," the tattoo artists said. "Hold still."

"You hold still," I said.

"It's hard to. You're in deep and throbbing," he answered, with a moan.

I was reclined back in something like a barber's chair, naked. Tony, the tattoo artist, also naked, was saddled on my cock and leaning over my chest, filling in the last of the roses on my chest tattoo.

"Oh, Christ, you are so huge," he whined. "I can't . . . I'll have to finish this later. Now. NOW!"

Rising out of the chair as he set the drill aside, I pushed him down on the floor in front of the chair, taking up a nearby chair cushion as I did so, and putting it under the small of his back. The young man was covered in a riot of tattoos, nearly every inch of him covered, other than the tops of his inner thighs, his shaved groin, and a few inches surrounding his puckered hole. Using the unshaved area as a target, I thrust inside him and started to pump as he arched his back, and cried out to the ceiling of the small, cluttered tattoo shop. His tattoos rippled, his own body undulating, as I fucked him.

"Oh, God, you're splitting me." And I almost did, taking him hard and deep, but pulling out to the surface to blast his hole with cum.

I already was posing my next painting—when I could get around to doing it. The first one with an external hint of a partner, I thought. The tattoo artist, sprawled out on the floor, his body rampant with color, his arms stretched out in a cruciform pose of surrender, of execution even, one leg bent, the gaping hole, slathered in cum, prominent, raised on the chair cushion, the other leg coming up and toward the viewer of the canvas. And the new touch—a hand, my hand, gripping the man's ankle, holding the leg raised and spread.

* * * *

I was padding nervously around the patio. I'd already done twelve laps of the pool so I wouldn't hear them, but they were still at it when I came out of the pool. I had been determined to cool it when Bill and his friend were here. I'd thought they'd be at the beach most of the time—and they were, I guess—but not all of the time. I'd looked forward to the time to catch up on my commercial art, but all I wanted to do was go into the studio and do the painting of the tattoo artist. No, that was a lie. I wanted to do a painting of Bill's friend, Danny.

The young man was so luscious—and such a flirt. And a screamer. Bill was fucking him in the guest bedroom now, and Danny was giving a running commentary of how good he was getting it.

They both were athletic hunks. On the lacrosse team at Maryland. Bill was from Karen's first marriage, and knowing how I would be if she hadn't bought me and could boss me around, Karen kept Bill off at school during our entire marriage. He had never appealed to me anyway. Too arrogant, too self-confident. And, as I now figured out, another power top. We could never have done it. Well, maybe we could have jacked each other off in frustration of nothing else being appropriate.

But I had never really gotten to know Bill. Karen had kept us apart. From photos, I knew he was a hunk, but no more. So, I didn't know that when he said he was bringing a friend to take advantage of my living in Florida for their spring break, that he was bringing someone to lie under him. A guy, not a girl.

From the moment, they'd entered the house, though, Danny had flirted with me. A really nice piece he was, too. Greek. Mediterranean dark and sultry.

"Oh, you have an earring," he said as they entered, "In the left ear." He said it like he knew that was a raging signal for a top at the time. And, of course it was, which is why, in my going wild, I'd had the piercing done.

"Already gone Key West, Gene?" Bill asked, as he passed me, obviously not caring about my orientation—and quickly, since it wasn't long before he had Danny on the guest bed, screaming his lungs out—establishing his orientation with me. The arrogant little prick.

I'd already gotten a painting off them, though, cracking the door and seeing them, in my mind's eye, in a Yin-Yang ball of fuck. I'd done an abstract sketch of them with the dueling cocks being hard to miss by anyone looking for them—and possibly not seen by anyone not looking for them.

I'd done everything I could in the two days they'd been here to lower key myself. I covered the rose tattoo with dark T-shirts, and I wore baggy, knee-length gym shorts. There wasn't much I could do now about the earring. I just hoped that the meaning of the signaling was local to Key West and not the same up in Maryland. None of that deterred Danny from touching me when and as he could.

Today, I was on my last nerve. I was aroused by their sexing, hard, and frustrated. I dove into the pool again. When I was on my return sixth lap, I came up for air to find Bill standing there.

"I'm going out for smokes and beer. You're out of beer. I'll be gone for a while. I think Danny would like to have company."

Shuddering, I came up out of the water and slowly toweled myself off. I wouldn't do it. I'd dry off and go to the studio. There were so many commercial art projects that needed attention.

I stood in the guest room doorway, looking at Danny on the bed. He obviously was expecting me. He was on his back, two pillows under the small of his back, his legs spread and bent, his hand stroking his cock, his hole open and glistening with Bill's cum, pointed at me. His head was propped up on more pillows so that he could clearly see me in the doorway. What was going through my mind was knowing that I could open the hole more for him—that I wanted to.

"Shit, a roses tattoo," he murmured. "Gorgeous. Sexy. Don't make me wait. Screw me."

I pushed my bathing suit down and stepped out of it.

"Oh, holy shit, man. I don't know. Billie is big. But you're huge. I don't know, man. Maybe . . ."

But by then I was on the bed, rising up between his legs, covering him, and lowering my lips to his. I took him into a deep kiss and we rocked back and forth, my cock rubbing up and down his heaving belly. His was moaning and groaning at the decibel rate of a diesel engine, as we rolled around the bed. He locked his arms around my back and his ankles around the small of my back and moved his pelvis hard against mine. Arching his back and crying out, I felt his cum shoot out over my belly. He relaxed his grip and went slack, letting his legs and arms stretch out.

"Sorry," he whispered. "Did Billie tell you I was a fast shooter."

"No, he didn't," I answered.

"So he didn't tell you I was a fast reloader too."

"No, he didn't. Did he tell you that I could split you apart and that I could fuck you all night? We're going to make you a bigger hole, Danny."

"Ulp! Oh, God, Oh holy shit," he cried out, as I positioned my cock head and started the thick invasion.

"Oh holy shit, oh holy shit. You're enormous," Danny screamed, as he grabbed for his ankles and spread and raised his legs wide.

I fucked the shit out of him for a good twenty minutes. By the end he no longer was screaming, he was babbling and moaning softly. He no longer was holding his ankles either. He was a rag doll. I held his ankles while I missionary fucked him. And I held him up with an arm under his waist while I doggy fucked him.

All along I was wondering what painting this would make. When it came to me I hauled him off the bed and over to a straight chair with arms. I hooked one of his legs chair back and let him put the other foot on the floor, with his leg bent. I pushed his head down in front of the chair seat so that he could be looking back at me.

The resulting painting got across how exhausted and fully surrendered he was, his eyes showed how total the fuck had been. And only I knew it, but the cum streaming out of the gaping hole that was the focal point of the painting was from two men.

* * * *

The sun on my body felt good as I lay out on the beach near the airport and luxuriated over my full recovery. I was the only one on this section of the beach between two rock outcroppings that went nearly down to the water. I had been laid up for several weeks. I probably shouldn't have done it, but I wanted my transformation to Key West style to be complete. This was the life I wanted. I wanted the proper, straight life of Baltimore irrevocably rubbed from my soul.

I'd sent most of the commercial art work projects I had back to the agency in Baltimore to be reassigned. As I owned the agency now, I could do that. I was concentrating on my "after sex" paintings of young men now—not on the collecting of images for a while now, but my mind was spinning more.

I had been dozing—sleeping really—with my arms stretched over my head, when I woke to a rough hand blindfolding me. I tried to pull my arms down, but they had been handcuff over my head and staked. I started to cry out, but a ball gag went into my mouth. My bathing suit was pulled down my legs, and I heard the intake of breath and the word "huge."

He was sitting on my chest. I knew it was a he, because his cock was thumping against my belly. He was heavy, probably large. The cock rubbing against my belly certainly seemed long and thick.

He grabbed my ankles and jackknifed them up and over my shoulders, rolling my pelvis up. And then for an eternity he was sucking my cock and balls and eating out my asshole. I then was writhing and screaming through the ball gag as he worked his cock inside me—I'd never had a cock, but he certainly seemed huge. I was lying there, panting hard, when it seemed like he was inside me to the root; he was panting too, and I think I heard him mutter, "Tight as a virgin. Love it." I wanted to scream that I *was* a virgin to this, but I knew it wouldn't make any difference to him.

It had hurt like hell. But now that he was in, I could feel my walls stretching to accommodate him. His cock was throbbing, and a certain pleasure mixed in with my pain to realize that I had a man inside me and I'd managed to take him. I always had topped, but I'd often wondered what the bottom felt. Pain, of course, although that was becoming manageable. Something else—the knowledge that I was possessed, that another man was throbbing inside me, had wanted to be inside me, that I was part of an intimate connection—a different part of it than I'd ever been before. In its own way the feeling was exhilarating—arousing.

Could I bottom—well, could I enjoy it? Silly question now. I *was* bottoming for this man who was assaulting me. And in a perverse way I was giving pleasure through the screen of pain. The pain already was becoming manageable. Bottoms had told me that it could send them on an arousal high, even with a cock as big and all-consuming as mine—as this one was. Whatever, I knew I was fucked now. If he released my arms, I knew I'd grasp him to me, open myself to him as much as I could, and beg for a completion. It was no good wanting any less at this point.

I wondered how it felt to be filled with cum. I knew how I felt when I did it, but how about when another man blasted my insides with hot cum. Did I hope this man would give me that experience? Perhaps I did—if only the pain would go down to a little less.

Without withdrawing from me, he pulled my legs down and hooked my ankles on his shoulders. I felt the ball gag being removed, and I gasped deeply and then worked my jaw to loosen the tight muscles. I couldn't talk yet. I didn't know what to say—or to scream. He was inside me already. It's not like I wasn't into male-male sex. Just not this end of it. But it certainly was a new experience.

"So, how's the fantasy so far?" the voice asked—a deep bass voice. He seemed calm, not a wild man at all. "Having a good time?"

"You're in too deep. Too much pain. Too big," I whimpered. I didn't know what else I could say. I couldn't indignantly tell him he couldn't fuck me. He already had his cock in me. This was no fantasy; this was real.

"You're one to talk of big," he said, with a low chortle. "I'm not anything big like you are. So, too much pain for you? This is your fantasy. We can't help that."

"Yes," I gasped, "too much pain."

"For now, maybe. There is that better? Play the prostate a while."

"Yes, better." He had pulled the bulb back to the prostate. Anything was better, and I could actually feel pleasure creeping in under the pain as his glans rubbed across my prostate, and I felt the cum starting to rise.

"I'm going to fuck you now," he muttered.

140

Fuck me now? What was it that he already had been doing? And then I understood. He was beginning to move in and out inside me, pumping my channel. I should know this. I did this to men. The cock was rubbing over and over my prostate, bringing forth flashes of pleasure and the need to shoot. He was stroking inside me, but no deeper than the prostate. I did this to myself sometimes—with the dildo I'd bought on the shop on Duval.

I sighed and trembled in his embrace.

"Like that?" he asked. "Can you manage it better now?"

"Yes," I murmured. His lips came to mine for a kiss, and I liked that too. I knew he was moving the cock deeper in his stroking, but the pleasure was still slowly washing over the pain. And then a bit faster and deeper. He was pumping my ass, while he stroked my cock with a hand, and he was kissing my lips, and my throat, teething my nipples. I shuddered and felt my pelvis involuntarily going with him. I'd felt this so often with the men I fucked—the point of surrender, of going with the fuck. Of wanting the fuck. And now the pain-pleasure balance was tipping in favor of pleasure. Now is usually when the men I fucked begged for it.

"Yes, yes. please. Work me, fuck me."

"You want it now, don't you?"

"Yes, don't stop. I want to come; I want you to come . . . inside me."

"I'm in almost as deep as before," he said. "You want it all?"

"Yes, yes, give it all to me. I can take it."

And I could. There was pain, but there was pleasure, and I was pulling the pleasure through the wall of pain. Faster, faster came his strokes. Harder, harder he pulled on my cock. And then I ejaculated. And if anything, that made me relax, open more to his cock, and he was fucking me deep, continuing on to his ejaculation. The infusion, the spouting of his seed inside me was an incredible feeling. I wanted the fountaining to go on forever, but of course it lasted only for a few seconds.

I whimpered.

"Liked that?" he asked.

"Yes," I whispered.

"Want it again?"

"Yes," I answered before thinking. Wanted the pain of the first invasion again? Not on your life. The feel of his hot cum filling me? Yes.

"In a few minutes," he whispered.

My answering whimper was probably taken by him as disappointment that he couldn't fuck me again, right then.

After half of an eternity of being held close with him kissing me and tonguing my throat and chest, he pulled out of me, stood up, and reached down and lifted my legs until I was rolling up onto my shoulder blades. Scissoring my legs, he worked his cock inside my hole again. And then he brought the legs together, holding the ankles together. The cock fit was incredibly tight, but the pain wasn't anything like it had been before. When he began to pump, I lost it and writhed under him, panting hard, and, to my disgust, my mouth, betraying me as much as my body was, was murmuring, "Yes, yes, fuck me, fuck me, fuck me." He tensed and then jerked off his load inside me, as I was shooting off as well.

Then he let my legs down, and left me there.

The next I knew, I was being freed and a familiar face appeared above me. "Cory?" I asked, tentatively. "I haven't seen you—"

"John? I didn't recognize you at first with the tattoo and earring. And this. When did you get this?"

"The cock ring? The Prince Albert?" I asked. "Weeks ago." I didn't mention that I'd had myself circumcised too to show off the PA. It was my way of going "all Key West."

"I love it. I want to fuck myself on it. But what sort of fix have you got yourself into here?"

"I have no idea. Some mad assaulter. Bound and gagged and fucked."

"Fucked. You ever been fucked before?"

"No, never."

"You sore?"

"Yes, of course."

"A big one?"

"Felt like a baseball bat."

"So, now you know how a big one feels."

142

"Yes, I guess so. Should I be reporting it or something, though?"

"Reporting it? What, you didn't know this is a Beach Attack hookup spot?"

"A Beach Attack? What's that?"

"Beach Attack is a Key West sex game—for guys who want to simulate rape—as giver or taker. This is one of the spots they use. Look, you set your towel down in front of that stake up there. If you brush around in the sand there, you'll find the cuffs that go with it. You put your towel down and laid down right in the spot one does who wants to be bound and taken in a Key West sex game."

"Oh." What else could I say? So much still to be learned about the Key West lifestyle.

"You never called for me at the escort service."

"I didn't think it would get me anywhere. I took what you said when you left the motel room to be a kiss off."

"It wasn't. It was that you just were so big. I couldn't take my next appointment. It scared me."

Nothing was said for the next few moments, as he was trying to swallow my cock. I laid back and moaned and listening for the tinkle of the PA on his teeth.

"Mmmm, I like that," he said, coming up for air.

"But does it still scare you?"

"What do you think?" he answered, as he moved a leg over my midsection, positioned his hole on the cock, slowly sheathed himself, and started to rise and fall on the cock.

"Do you want to see my house," I murmured later. "And my name isn't John. It's Gene."

"I figured it wasn't John. Sure, I'd like that. And the paintings. I heard you were doing sex paintings. They're all the rage."

* * * *

Cory had been with me for two weeks. He still went out on jobs, and I didn't stop him—part of my developing Key West lifestyle—but he spent long enough in my bed to keep me happy. Each time in bed, he taught me a new position and

I, in turn, was able to pull passion out of him that he said none of his johns did.

Truth be known, I didn't give up cruising; I went cruising too occasionally, without him. I didn't bring anyone but him back to my bungalow. I found places to fuck them in place—to keep them at least a heartbeat away from me. I had gone pretty far down the road of "Key Westing," though: an earring, a big tattoo, a "dirty pictures" job, casual fucking—even my stepson's boyfriend, circumcision, and a Prince Albert. The truth be known, I even was frosting my hair a bit to add in highlights and using skin cream to try to slow down the inevitable aging. I walked around naked in my home and with just short shorts and flip-flops in public, and I returned flirty stares—even followed them up on occasion far enough to get my dick inside another man.

I still had it—in fact was refining it, thanks to Key West. Once I got my dick inside a man, none complained, and I had more referrals than I could handle.

And I'd even, now, had another man's dick inside me—and the more and more I thought about it, the more and more I thought I could enjoy that. Was it really all that painful, considering the eventual pleasure? Would it be that painful if I did it again—and again? Was I too chicken to find out? Surely the Key West way would be to go with the flow if the situation naturally presented itself.

So, how was that? In less than six months moving from imposed straight, to power top, to versatile.

When he'd first come into my bungalow, Cory had been awed that so many of the sketches and paintings I had were of him. I fucked him on the floor that afternoon, despite the pain of my own very recent experience, and he reveled in looking around of the artwork featuring him well fucked as I was fucking him well. Then I painted him in the pose I'd left him in when I'd filled his passage with cum. That painting had gone for a pretty penny.

Since that day, I'd ruminated on the fucking I had received for some time, but when Cory came into the studio and looked at what I was working on one afternoon, he said, "That's you, isn't it? The gaping hole with the cum dribbling out is your signature, I know, but those legs raised and brought

144

together at the ankles—those are your legs. There's that birthmark of yours, there, on the thigh."

"Yes, that painting is of me."

"You thought much about that fucking you got?"

"A little, I guess."

He caught me in the lie immediately. "Just a little? A little is enough to weeks later be painting it? Did you like it?"

"I don't know if 'like' is the word I'd use." I didn't want to admit that, increasingly, it was the word I thought.

"But you got hard and you jacked your load when he fucked you, didn't you?"

"Yes. A couple of times."

"So, you liked it."

"It was something new, I guess."

"So, you liked it; you'd do it again."

"Probably." That's as far as I was willing to go—even with myself at this point.

"You want to be fucked again, don't you?"

"Yes," I admitted.

"I could arrange that for you. Get any cock size you want. Rough or vanilla. You know this is Key West. You know that anything goes here. If you like it, do it."

"I'll keep that in mind. But I hear the doorbell."

I opened the door to a muscular, bald hunk. A regular Mr. Clean. "Yes?"

"I'm Stan. I'm a fan of your artwork. And I'm the guy who spiked you in the Beach Attack game on the beach near the airport a couple of weeks ago. I followed your T-Bird home. I think you want me again, and I can't get you out of my mind. Can I come in and fuck you again?"

I lay on my back on the bed, my legs spread and bent, my hands gripping Stan's biceps as, standing on the floor, leveraging off his feet and leaning into me between my legs, Stan hammered me hard and deep. I was arching my back and crying out, "Yes, yes, fuck me hard!"

There was pain again, but not nearly the pain as before—and more pleasure. The pleasure added of knowing who was fucking me—a big-cocked muscle man. Wanting his dick inside me. Exercising hard to give us both pleasure and

145

release. I was taking him deep. I could handle it. We were one beautiful, synchronized fucking machine.

I'd never known I wanted this too—that I could be versatile. And not just versatile, submissive, and fucked hard.

Cory nudged in between our chests, coaxing Stan to rise up more. The smaller man positioned himself on my cock, and the three of us went to town—Stan pounding me in the ass and Cory riding my cock. As Stan was pumping cum into my channel, I was thinking about how I was going to depict this in art. Probably an abstract that brought you deep into the painting before your blushed and said, "Oh, my, it's three studs fucking."

Later, the three of us sitting around the kitchen island, eating sandwiches and drinking beer—all of us knowing we'd soon be doing it again, the telephone rang.

It was Chris from the ad agency in Maryland—my ad agency. The man I'd left in temporary charge.

"When are you coming back, Gene?" he said. "There are decisions to be made up here. The art work is backing out."

"I don't think you'd recognize me if I came back, Chris."

"What? What does that mean?"

"I've been fully taken over by the Key West style." I turned my face toward Stan and winked. He winked back. "I don't think I could even be allowed to walk the streets of Baltimore now."

"What are you saying?"

"Send me the paperwork that makes you managing head of the agency. Hire another commercial artist or two. Just send me profit checks. I'm all Key West now."

I turned to Stan and Cory after disconnecting with Chris and almost did a double take and laughed. The robe Stan was wearing had come open. He was perched on a bar stool and had a hand on his cock, working it up for our next workout in the bedroom. He wasn't so big. His cock was bigger than Cory's certainly, but he was no championship stud—not compared to me in any way. I'd felt taxed by a normal-sized cock. God, did I still have a lot to learn and prepare for in the Key West lifestyle.

Oh, well. It was a start. I had time to work my way up. I wondered if Stan had ever been fucked—and by someone as hung as I was.

I, Mannequin

I came to with a jolt—literally—Dwight was standing over me, naked, except for those horn-rimmed eyeglasses he hadn't taken off in the living room either. He was leaning down and jolting my nipples with a vibrator with a big, globular head. I was flat on my back, legs together, and arms straight out from my side like someone being crucified—and I could feel my legs and arms, but they were tingling from something other than the effect of the vibrator and I could only move them with great effort. It wasn't effort I wanted to invest at the moment, because I was still trying to figure out where I was, how I had gotten here—and why.

Sensing my head would soon be immobile from whatever was paralyzing the rest of me, I swiveled it enough to see that we weren't in Dwight's living room anymore, but in some sort of work room. Idiotically, tailor's shop is what first entered my mind, because there were four or five male dummies hanging on stands around the edges of the room, facing the wall. Or a medical examination room, I thought, because there was a tan and green-enamel examination table behind me. A wheelchair was a couple of feet off beside me. That must have been how he got me in here. He wasn't much bigger than I was. I would have been dead weight unconscious.

The dummies gave me a double take, as they all had big holes where their assholes would be with plastic tubes attached behind the holes.

What is this shit? I wanted to scream at Dwight. I had marked that I'd fuck on the first date on the Internet hookup dating site application. And we were almost into it when I blacked out in the other room. When Dwight did something to make me black out. And when he had done something to make my systems start to close down—not my ability to feel; my ability to move.

But, as far as getting on with it, Dwight was getting on with it now. He was kneeling below me and had pulled the red silk jock strap, which was the only thing I was wearing, off my legs. I had worn it for him—for him to slip off my body—or not, as he could fuck me wearing a jock strap without pulling it off. It had been for his pleasure. But he didn't need to be doing any of this immobilization shit. I had clearly marked that I'd fuck on a first date—and that I was a submissive—that all he had to do was get it in me and I'd go all docile for him. Even that I'd take it rough. I'd marked all of those boxes.

He grasped both of my ankles, bent my legs, and placed my feet flat on the floor. It seemed that he could place my body parts where he wanted them, and they'd stay, but I couldn't. I felt his hands feeling up my inner legs from calf up high on my thighs, and he was nudging the legs open wider.

I screamed inwardly, which came out only in moans and groans, as he applied the bulb of the vibrator under my balls. I writhed inside my skin, but remained paralyzed—and increasing so—on the outside, as the vibrating ball rolled across my balls, and up and down the sides of my erect penis and down under, at my ass opening rim. I could feel it all; I just couldn't move anything and react to it. I did react to it eventually, as he held the vibrating bulb to my piss slit until I shot my load.

Hey, Dwight, this was OK, I called out in the silence of my brain. This was kind of sexy. It made me hard; I shot my load. I would have let you do this without being paralyzed. I'd signed up with the hookup service because I was tired of vanilla fucking. I wanted something jazzy like this.

Dwight then pushed his knees under my buttocks to raise my pelvis to his entry, slid his hard cock into me, and fucked me, in long, languid strokes. He was manageable and I wasn't particularly being violated; I had marked on my application that I would fuck on the first date, and I had every intention of letting Dwight fuck me when we'd been paired up. I even was good with the vibrator. I'd signed up with the hookup service, marking the fetish and rough boxes, because I'd gotten tired and frustrated with my soccer coach's vanilla fucking in the backseat of his Honda Accord when he could get away from his wife and kids.

So, all of this incapacitating stuff was so unnecessary, I kept screaming on. But Dwight, concentrating on varying the stroking of his cock inside me, didn't hear my internal-only voice and probably didn't care.

With a sudden movement, Dwight was out of me and pulling himself up on his feet. He did a fast pull of the condom off his cock and I thought, here it comes. Is he going to hit me in the face or somewhere else with his cum? But he didn't shoot off then. I watched out of the periphery vision of my now-paralyzed head as he stumbled over to one of the male mannequins, Stuffed his cock through the hole in the dummy's ass, grabbing its hips in his hands, and pumped the transparent plastic tube until, with a deep groan, he ejaculated in that. I clearly could see the spurt of the cum in the tube.

OK, so he doesn't want to come with a condom on.

* * * *

"Your profile says you have modeled."

"Yeah, if you could call it that," I had answered. He seemed to be interested, for the first time really that we'd been on this date. Not that he didn't give the impression that he'd get around to fucking me, but after the movie, we'd been sitting at this outdoor café with him talking all sorts of technical scientific stuff that I couldn't understand and was having trouble giving him the idea that I was fascinated by.

Dwight had said to meet him at the movie theater. We were starting the date by watching the new *Star Wars* movie. No introductions or anything, just meeting near the box office. He paid, so it was OK with me—getting to see a *Star Wars* movie for free was a pretty good date right there. He paid for everything, of course, as I'd signed up at the Web site as a submissive bottom and he'd signed up as a seeking top. The one who dominated paid the fee.

There was something during the movie, during the lull periods in the action, although there weren't many of those. The usual gripping of my knee and thigh, moving to tracing my cock through the material of my jeans with the murmured, "Nice; we're gonna have fun," and me returning the favor, finding what I could feel of his cock OK, but nothing to write home about. A kiss and a whispered, "I want to be inside you so bad," even when the lighting on the screen went real dark. But nothing in the way of conversation more than a phrase here and there to get my cock interested.

He gave a couple of grabs on my knee at the café too, took a foot out of his loafers and pushed his toes up under the hem of my jeans leg for a few seconds, but nothing else other than that except for telling me about some of his high tech projects where he worked in Palo Alto. I guess he was about thirty-five and some sort of genius engineer. A nerdy type. His body and face were nice enough, but he wore those horn-rimmed style of eyeglasses, seemed quite serious—and maybe a little keyed up-intense.

All I had going for me was majoring in soccer and lacrosse at San Francisco State, as a sophomore, and being vanilla fucked by my soccer coach, so I didn't do much of the talking. That I'd put modeling on my activities list on my hookup site profile seemed to have gotten his interest, though.

"It's just for the Christmas season," I said. "I did it last Christmas and have been hired to do it again this Christmas. At Macy's. We model clothes in the department store window, standing real still and then changing pose on a signal. It draws in a lot of people coming down to see the window displays and then going in to buy something."

"So you play like you're mannequins?" I could swear he was licking his chops, and the grip on my knee was almost painful. But it was also short lived. His hand was traveling up my inner thigh.

"What's a mannequin?"

"It's sort of a dressing dummy. It's a fake person, like what you are simulating you are when you stand in the department store window. It's what people think they are seeing until they see you move, and that's why they're surprised and amused. So you act like a mannequin?"

"Yeah, I guess that's what I do in that job." It came out as sort of a squeak, because he was gripping my junk through the crotch of my jeans. This was more action than I'd gotten in the darkened theater.

"If you're finished with that hamburger, maybe we can go back to my place. It isn't far." He was breathing heavy and maintaining the grip on my dick and balls.

"Yeah, sure, that would be fine."

"And are you going to suck my cock and let me fuck you?"

"That's what this date is about, I thought."

Dwight lived in a high-rise apartment building with three levels of garages under it. He said the building was only two-thirds sold out, so there were plenty of parking spaces in the garage. I followed his Chevy Camaro in my old Mustang, and we parked in a secluded, badly lit part of the garage.

His living room had a sofa facing a gigantic flat-screen TV. He told me to get comfortable on the sofa and he put on a gay action vid, featuring Dirk Caber fucking the shit out of Johnny Rapid. I wedged myself in the corner of the sofa and kicked off my sandals and, without preliminaries, Dwight was sitting close to me on the sofa, pulling my T-shirt over my head, had his hands on my belt buckle, and was kissing me all over my face, lips, throat, and nipples.

As I gripped the hem of his polo shirt and pulled it over his head, he went up on his knees in the sofa, grabbed my hips, turned my back to the arm of the sofa, and brought my legs up onto the sofa. He had unbuckled and unzipped me and had flared the sides of the jeans open and pulled them down low on my hips. One of his hands cupped the red silk pouch of my jock strap and the other wrapped itself around the back of my neck and brought my face in for a deep kiss.

This was moving along nicely.

He was stretched out on top of me and dry humping me, and I reached down, unbuckled and unzipped his trousers, and pushed both trousers and briefs down low on his hips, freeing his cock, so that nothing, really separated us from real fucking, which could be managed even with my jock strap in place. I badly wanted him inside me—a man who wasn't my soccer coach. I wanted to see how another man would be.

"Fuck me, fuck me now," I murmured, trying to move this along even more nicely.

Meanwhile, he had pushed my jeans farther down onto my thighs. His cock pressed in under my balls, still covered by the pouch, and I tightened my thighs around the cock, with us still in a deep kiss and him dry fucking me between the thighs and under the pouch.

I tried rolling my pelvis up to him. Just a little adjustment and he'd be inside me. But he put a palm on my belly and pushed me flat on the sofa cushions again.

I was breathing hard and ready to have a good time, counting down to him having his dick inside me.

Still wearing his horn-rimmed glasses, Dwight started kissing down my body, as he pulled his cock out from between my thighs and moved his body down the line of the sofa. It didn't take him long to be sucking on my cock through the red silk of the jock pouch. I groaned as he pulled the waistband of the jock down under my balls and opened his mouth over my cock, managing to deep-throat it. Yeah, this is nice, I thought. OK, let's do this before the main event.

He grabbed my hands in his fists, holding me captive there, and I turned my eyes to the vid of Dick Caber pounding Johnny Rapid's ass in a standing fuck against a wall, moaned the attention given my cock, and moved my pelvis, languidly face fucking Dwight's mouth cavity.

When I had come, Dwight came off the sofa and walked around to the arm behind me. He grabbed me under the pits and pulled my shoulders up onto the sofa arm. My head was flopping over the side of sofa at just the right angle for him to shove his cock in it, and, raising my arms and holding his hips in my hands, I held him steady and started returning the favor of the blow job.

When he was throbbing and hard as he was likely to get, he pulled out of my mouth.

Here it comes, I thought. I turned over on the sofa, my shoulders still on the arm, and went up on my knees, presenting my ass for a doggy fuck. My eyes went to the TV screen, where Jack King and Sebastian Young were now

153

double fucking Johnny Rapid. But I felt no hands grip my hips, no body come in behind me, no hard cock penetrate my ass. Dwight wasn't back there—or still in front of me. A wave of frustration and confusion surged through my body. I'd come here to be fucked. This was the moment I expected to be covered and fucked.

"I thought we'd take a break and have a beer." Dwight was padding over from the breakfast counter between the kitchen and the living area. He had two beers in his hands. He handed me one, and stood behind me where I now sat on the sofa. I was drinking mine slowly, engaging in a bit of a pout that I wanted him to notice but not like I was doing it for him to notice. His beer went quickly, the bottle disappearing somewhere, and he had his hands on my shoulders—and then traveling down to where his fingers were tweaking and squeezing my nipples. His chin rested on my shoulder and his lips were close to my ear.

"Johnny Rapid's really getting pounded by both of those guys, isn't he?"

"Yeah, he is," I said, splitting my attention between the vid on the TV and the playing of my nipples by Dwight's fingers. I want to be pounded too, I screamed in my mind.

"You ever been doubled like that?" Dwight whispered into my ear.

"No, never. I don't see how he manages it," I answered with a croak. Dwight was driving me wild with the nipple play. I was hard again.

"Maybe you'll try it one of these days," he whispered. I only half heard him, because his hands were in my pits again, pulling my body up on onto the low back of the sofa. I was balanced on the sofa back, the bottoms of my shoulder blades hitting below the rim at the back of the sofa, and my legs bent and my feet in the seat cushions of the sofa.

Dwight was hard too, and maneuvered his dick in my mouth again and then leaned over my chest with his, captured my hands in his again, and swallowed my cock. We both sucked cock until we both came—Dwight for a first time, me for a second—but me first this time.

As he pulled his cock out of my mouth and creamed my face, I realized that I was feeling woozy.

And then I blacked out, becoming conscious next in a room lined with mannequins with holes in their asses, some sort of medical examination table, and a large-bulbed vibrator making love to my nipples, with my whole body tingly with sensation but not responding to my commands to move.

* * * *

Manipulating me like a rag doll, Dwight had moved me up to the examination table. I couldn't imagine what exam would have involved the position he put me in. I was lying belly down, my weight being taken on my chest. My wrists were bound to the side of the table, my legs were bent and spread behind me and at a higher level than my chest.

Once more I was screaming inside, because Dwight was behind me and between my spread legs and was using the vibrator on my nuts and dick and asshole rim.

The torture there stopped, although I was getting to where I almost missed it. This wasn't my soccer coach's vanilla fuck. This also wasn't quite what I had in mind when I clicked the "fucks on first date," "fetish," and "rough" boxes on my hookup site profile—but it certainly was an experience. Dwight was dragging one of his mannequins over to under my hanging head. He pushed it down, belly down, on the floor and then turned, stuck his thumbs in the sides of my mouth, stretched my mouth open, and inserted his half-hard cock. I was powerless to do anything other than let him use my mouth to pump up his cock.

When he was at the desired hardness, he went down on the floor, hugging the torso of the mannequin to him, and fucked the mannequin's ass to an ejaculation. Strangely enough I watched him fuck the mannequin with interest rather than disgust and it was arousing in its own way when I reasoned that he had gotten me off first and might do so again. Why should I care if he finished with a dummy rather than me, if he finished me. And he'd finished me repeatedly. I'd leave this date with my balls drained and with something more sensual to think about than being slam-bang-thank you, son, gotta get home to the missus vanilla quick fucked in the backseat of a Honda Accord.

Dwight disappeared for a while after that. I have no idea where he was and what he was doing. My body was paralyzed. I could feel everything, but I couldn't move anything.

* * * *

Dwight had unbound me and dumped me to the side of the examination table. He made some adjustments and then dragged over a mannequin that he had fashioned a knobby plastic dildo on as a penis. That probably, I thought, was what he had been doing while he was out of my line of sight. I knew he had stayed nearby because he had been humming happily.

The mannequin went on its back on the surface of the examination table. Then I babbled internally as Dwight got me positioned, facing up on the examination table. The mannequin's penis—the dildo—went into my ass, not all that easily, and not without me huffing and puffing inwardly and moaning outwardly. My wrists were bound at the sides of the table and my legs were put in stirrups that spread, bent, and raised them—like I was going to get an OB/GYN exam.

Dwight, humming, purposely came into my line of sight so that I could see him strap on the knobbly surfaced extender sheath that enlarged his cock both in width and length.

I screamed bloody murder internally as Dwight came between my legs and worked his enhanced cock in over the mannequin's buried dildo. To add to the excitement, the mannequin's dildo penis was a vibrator. It was really rough going for a while, but eventually I got into it, was accommodating it, was actually enjoying it, and was looking forward to doing it again sometime. It was good enough that I fired off another salvo of cum.

I would have liked to have had the use of my muscles, though. I knew how to ripple my passage wall muscles over a man's cock and I could have helped maintain the rhythm of Dwight's stroking.

Exhausted, I drifted off after I had ejaculated once more—more times in one session than I ever had before. I don't know if Dwight finished off inside me or in one of the mannequins. I also didn't care much one way or other. He had finished me, repeatedly. And that was good enough to me to be the name of the game.

When I came out of the paralysis and was able to regain full control, I was dressed again and lying across the backseat of my Mustang in the dark recesses of the parking garage. Dwight's Camaro no longer was parked beside my car.

* * * *

Dwight was visibly startled when he answered his door a week later, late in the evening.

I raised a six pack of beer. "Whatever you put in the beer before, it's fine if you lace the beer I drink before you fuck me again—if you want to fuck me again," I said. "And as long as you finish me repeatedly I don't care what you need to do to finish yourself. You can be rougher on a second date, too, if that turns you on—and if it finishes me off."

Rehabilitation System

Leonard, eyes wide open and glazed, panting and moaning slightly, lay on his belly on the bottom bunk in the prison cell, his eyes glued to Big Phil, perched on the desk across the cell, his feet on the floor, his legs spread, naked, slow-stroking his cock back toward full erection. His eyes also on Leonard, gauging where they now stood. Leonard was still wearing his prison T-shirt; his sweat pants were in an entangled pile on the tile floor at the side of the bunk. Phil's prison T and sweats were neatly folded on the table.

Leonard, in for lewd behavior—being caught, for the third time, sucking a man's dick in a library restroom where Leonard worked shelving books—had just lost his male virginity.

"First thing you need to do on the inside," his lawyer had told him after sentencing, "Is to find a protector. You're just the sort who will have a miserable time and be all torn up inside if you don't."

"A protector? Torn up. I don't understand."

The lawyer told him and the young man's eye went big and he began to tremble.

"You're an effeminate gay man. I know it's brutal to say, but you have to understand that you are as close to a woman as men inside are going to be able to get to. They will make do—with you. That's inevitable. Giving their cocks suck isn't going to be good enough for them. It's a choice of a dozen men or one. You'll have to give it up for the protector,

158

but then it will only be him. Do you understand? You got yourself in this mess, Leonard, you need to do what you can to survive it."

Leonard had shuddered, but he slowly nodded his head. "I understand, but how—"

"I have connections in the prison. I'll make the best arrangement for you that I can. But then it's up to you to hold onto the protector. Do you understand that? He will be the only thing standing between you and the hospital."

"Yes, I understand," Leonard said, meekly.

Phil Lindstrom had been meek too when he'd entered the prison, a jewelry store owner who was in for five years for receiving stolen goods. He had been thirty-five and was pushing forty now. He was about to be released into an interim work program, but nobody was telling Leonard that.

Phil was of Norwegian stock—tall, of sturdy construction. When he'd entered prison, he'd been overweight and timid, confused on how he could have gotten here, where he'd gone wrong, and spending much of his time reorganizing his approach to life. He hadn't had any idea he was receiving stolen jewelry. He'd taken it on consignment, trusting a friend. The friend was the target of a "make an example" sting operation, though, so they threw the book at Phil too.

When he'd entered Woodward Prison, Phil hadn't faced the decision that cute little Leonard had, because of his intimidating size, being grossly overweight, his age, and because his was a white-color crime. He didn't run with thugs—at least not then. Once he'd showered communally a couple of times, though, it wasn't the size of his belly at the time that mattered. He had young men who had been fully indoctrinated in the sexual system in the prison coming to him to ride him.

Phil had been largely asexual before coming to prison. Never married, his nose perpetually to the grindstone to keep his jewelry store profitable, his few layings with women had been unsatisfying to him and challenging to the women. His experience with men, buried in his youth by his determination to be "normal," had, however, been more satisfying. He didn't know before coming to Woodward, where trapped men had essentially two choices for release—their own hands or their

159

fellow prison mates' bodies—what aroused him. It didn't take him long in Woodward to discover what did, especially when young men were begging him to lie on his back and let them ride his cock.

Sexual dominance in a men's prison gave a man power. Three years after he entered the prison system, thanks to endless hours in the prison gym, he was much more of a man to be reckoned with than the one who entered prison. His natural abilities and determination at organizing, his age, the height and mere muscular physical presence of him now, and where he stood in the order in terms of equipment, taken him to the top of the pecking order in the prison population, He now even was looked to by the guards to help maintain order—which they rewarded with perks.

Perks such as Leonard. "Fresh meat" is what they called new "scared rabbit" prisoners who looked and acted like Leonard did.

"You OK, Lenny? You can take it?"

Leonard answered with a groan, but then he nodded his head and whispered, "Yes, it was fine."

"You have two choices now, Lenny. You know what it entails. You can stay here, bunking with—and under—me, or you can go into the general population and take your chances. I can arrange either. Which is it?"

"I want to stay here, with you," Leonard murmured, his lawyer's advice screaming in his head.

"You know what it means then. Wherever, whenever I want."

"Yes, I know what it means."

"Most other men out there have smaller cocks than I do. You could find a protector more easily managed—maybe. Although, I got to tell you that protectors are established by the inches they have—and not just in height and wingspan."

"I'll stick here, please," Leonard answered in a small voice.

"Tell me you want it again, then."

"I want it again," he said, with a huge sigh.

Having stroked himself to full erection, and slowly rolling a Trojan Magnum on his cock, with Leonard shuddering at the sound of it snapping in place, Phil moved to the bunk and slid in on top of Leonard, pressing Leonard's legs apart with his knees. Leonard whimpered, closed his eyes, and grabbed up gobs of prison blanket, as Phil put a beefy forearm under Leonard's belly and brought the young man up to his knees.

He turned Leonard's buttocks toward the light coming in from the side of the bunk and spread the young man's butt cheeks to view his previous handiwork. He always enjoyed seeing the gaping hole he'd reamed for a first time. Sorry I don't have a camera to record this, he thought. Turning the buttocks back into place, as Leonard groaned and whimpered in anticipation, Phil positioned his hips over the young man's buttocks and let the bulb of his cock rest at the entrance, moving it around to rim Leonard's hole, disengaging to run the underside of his hard cock up the young man's crack and rubbing across the hole, before returning to rimming him, listening to Leonard's heavy panting.

This was Phil's favorite time of the foreplay. Not the first time, but the second. Teasing the hole with his cock head, his partner knowing now, as he didn't the first time, what was to come.

"Please, please," Leonard whined, his body shuddering at the rim play.

Phil didn't know what Leonard meant by the "please," and he didn't care.

The slide inside was easier for Phil now, with the hole still gaping from having been reamed within the hour. But the soreness of having taken someone Phil's size for the first time didn't make the second time any less painful for Leonard—at least initially, before he accepted his fate and relaxed his body.

"You OK Lenny? You taking it OK?"

"Yes, OK," Leonard answered through clinched teeth. It wasn't OK, but it would have to be OK—and maybe in time it even would be good.

With a grunt, Phil entered him deep and immediately started pumping hard, muttering, "There's no easy way for you to get accustomed to this."

Leonard writhed under him, with Phil covering his mouth with a hand to reduce the noise level, until Phil had established a steady rhythm and then, resigned and pleasure beginning to fight with the pain, Leonard settled down, reached under his belly, and began to stroke himself to completion.

Finished and going up on his knees, Leonard sprawled under him and moaning, Phil pulled a piece of chalk out of a crevice at the end of the bunk and leaned over Leonard's gasping body as Leonard followed his movement with his eyes, not knowing how soon Phil would want to be inside him again. Phil reached over to the wall the bunk was pushed into and added two stroke marks to three rows of marks, marked off in fives, that stretched the length of the bunk.

When first seeing those, Leonard had thought that Phil was counting the days he'd been in the prison cell. That wasn't at all what Phil was counting.

"You OK, Lenny? You OK with it?"

"Yeah, I'm OK," Leonard answered through a whimper.

Phil palmed the young man's butt cheeks and spread them again. He leaned down and blew on the hole, which elicited a moan from Leonard and caused the hole to open like the lens of a camera for him, ready for his cock again. He'd get around to that in a bit. If you're breaking fresh meat in in this prison, you needed to get it done fast. Yeah, he thought, a shot like that would made a good ending for a video.

* * * *

"I may have found a job for you, Juan."

"I hope so. I'm desperate, Mr. Lindstrom," the young Hispanic man answered.

"As I understand it, you have to find something within the next two weeks or go back to Woodward to serve out your sentence."

"Yes, sir, that's right. I'll take anything at this point."

"That's good to hear. There are two functions to the job. It's in a auto repair garage and you've been trained for that, haven't you?"

"Yes, sir. At Woodward. I started about the time you left the prison. You were head of the auto repair studies, weren't you?"

"Yes at the end."

"And what's the other part of the job?"

"What were you in for?" Phil asked, leaning across the desk that was in his combination office and bedroom in the work program half-way house. He'd been in a position of authority and trust when he'd left the prison for this program himself, so he had been given a job to place other guys in the program in jobs. Auto mechanics had been the skill he himself had mastered while in prison, so he got young men like Juan here, who also studied auto mechanics, to try to place.

"Ah, solicitation—prostitution," Juan answered.

"You were a rent-boy, right?"

The young Hispanic hesitated, but he finally answered in the affirmative. "But I don't understand what . . ."

Phil was giving him a hard look.

"Oh, the guy with the job wants to fuck me." Juan's voice made clear that he was miserable that his crime had been raised.

"He wants to fuck whoever he gives the job to, Juan. And not just once. He wants a bedmate as well as a mechanic. I've shown him your photo and your rap sheet, along with those of some other guys here needing jobs. He's interested in you. You've been selected over others. We can't find employers without revealing what the potential employee's crime was. This employer asked for a young prostitute when I talked to him—one that would take his cock along with the job."

"But this is supposed to be a rehab program; I didn't think it was supposed to send me back to what got me in prison to begin with." It came out of Juan in a whine.

"Life is tough, Juan. We have to build on the skills we have. Maybe when you have proved yourself as a mechanic, you can trade for a job without other strings attached. But you're within two weeks of going back in the slammer for another year. Which will it be? This or the prison? I have other guys I can offer this job to if you don't take it."

"This, I guess," Juan said, in a whisper. "Where and when do I have to go?"

"It's not sure yet. The employer wants to see what he'll be getting—not the auto mechanics part; the other part."

"He wants to fuck me before he decides?"

"He wants some form of evidence. A video of you will do, he says."

"He wants me to do a solo? On a video. How do I get a video done."

"We can do it right here, Juan. There's a bed over there, and, if you'll look over there and there, you'll see video cameras set up. We'll take the film right here. But not just a solo, Juan. A solo will be nice, but he wants a film of another guy fucking you." Phil was unbuttoning his shirt.

"You? Here?" Juan asked, almost hyperventilating because Phil had stood up from the desk, unzipped his fly, and fished out a monster cock.

"No time like here and the present," Phil said cheerily. "Strip and go over to the bed, please. I've got to get the cameras turned on."

Juan was small of stature and Phil was large boned, especially the bone between his thighs. Juan had been a prostitute, though, and was nailed regularly in prison, so he took it like a champ and gave the camera a good show.

After a solo act completed with an ejaculation, Phil planted himself on his back on the bed, and Juan climbed onto his midsection, pointed toward Phil's feet, and rode Phil's cock until Phil decided that the film needed some spice. First, he pushed Juan's torso down between his legs, laced his legs under Juan's arms to hold them out and immobile and locked his ankles behind Juan's neck. At Phil's command Juan hooked his ankles onto Phil's shoulders on either side, Phil held Juan's legs close into his side, and then he subjected Juan to a rocking fuck, raising his torso a bit and rocking back and forth, controlling the stroking of his cock in Juan's ass.

This was not the time for Juan to raise any objections. He reverted his thoughts and actions back to his earlier life. He had been a prostitute; he *was* a prostitute. Nobody was fooled that the system would give him a real opportunity to change. He gave Phil and the cameras whatever they wanted.

After several minutes of this, Phil changed the position, while keeping his cock in Juan's channel. He pulled Juan's torso up to where it lay on Phil's chest. He put Juan into a full Nelson hold, with Juan's fists pressed into the coverlet on the bed, and then he laced his legs through Juan's and lifted and spread them. One of the cameras got a straight shot of the thick root of Phil's cock, as he stroked deep inside Juan's hole and Juan writhed and groaned at the deep fuck.

When Phil was ready to come, he pushed Juan down to the floor at the end of the bed, sat on the end, grabbed Juan's head, and held it in place as he jacked off on Juan's face. He made Juan clean off the cock with his mouth—and turn his head toward the camera, with Phil cupping his chin, and smile for the world out there.

"There, I think that will get you the job," Phil said, as he looked down at Juan, who had collapsed in a heap onto the floor at the end of the bed.

Later, Phil retrieved the film from the cameras and spent some time at his computer desk splicing up two copies of a single film. "Good enough for the Internet," he muttered, which was good because, although one copy was going to the auto garage owner, another one was going on a subscription site Phil had opened up on the Internet as soon as he'd gotten out of prison.

Just as he thought would be the case, the garage owner loved the video—and, ultimately, loved having Juan in his bed. He passed on his appreciation to some of his friends, and when Phil left the half-way house to reopen his jewelry business, he received an award for the number of men in the program he'd managed to place. No one, though, remarked how many of the men he placed had been in prison for prostitution.

* * * *

Phil looked the young man standing before him across the jewelry story counter over from head to toe. He looked down on his luck, but he also looked presentable. He sported a ring in his eyebrow and a few tattoos were in view, but there were clients who would like that—especially if there were more piercings and tattoos. A slim build, but the mounding in his T-shirt indicated sufficient muscling. He did look desperate.

"I'm not a pawn shop, son," Phil said. He made sure he said that these days and watched the follow up. He didn't want to get trapped in a sting again.

"No, I want to sell it outright."

"I couldn't give you anything near its worth if the deal is just for the necklace."

"I don't understand."

"How desperate are you? I could ask you if you stole this piece and even if you said no, I could give you maybe $60 for it. If you throw in something else of value to me that costs nothing for you and that you have more of, I could just not ask you where you got this and I could give you $900 for it."

"$900? What else could I throw in?"

"Well, you could come back to the back and I'd provide a meal—and let you take a shower, and I'd even wash your clothes for you. You could have a lie down and then I would pay you $900 and take this necklace from you."

The young man gave Phil a sharp look. "You want me to lie down for you. You want to fuck me, don't you?"

"What did you do for your supper last night?" Phil asked. "Was it worth as much as I would pay you? You take your position right across the street from here, son. I see you getting in men's cars. What would you be doing for me that you don't do for strangers in cars whenever you can?"

"$900, eh?" the young man said, seriously contemplating the deal now. "For a fuck."

"For whatever I want in a three-hour span, starting with the meal. And an hour of it on camera."

As soon as Phil had been released from the work program, he'd come back and reopened the jewelry store. It wasn't the store, though, that was making the big profit. There was a small apartment in the back of the store, and Phil had set it up as a film studio with equipment to enable him to create films and to put them up on his subscription Web site. He made three times the money from that operation now than he made from the store front.

"I don't know," the young man said.

"You'll be done before your customer rush tonight out on the street, and how much do you think you'll make from that?—and you'd still have this necklace to unload. It feels hot to me. I wonder how hot it is and how much you'd like to be arrested for prostitution and have this found in your possession. Tell you what, I'll up it to $1,000, but you'll have to sign a release for the film, and, as I said, when the clock starts ticking on the deal, it will be three hours I have to do as I want with you."

* * * *

The young man, who said his name was Jack, to which Phil said, "OK, if you say so," sat, naked, at the table, a three-quarters-finished peanut butter-and-jelly sandwich on a plate in front of him. His chair was pulled back from the table and he was slouching down in the chair, his arms thrown back over the chair back, and his head, likewise, arched back. Phil was sitting in a chair close to and at the side of him, watching the expression on the young man's face as he slowly beat off Jack's cock with his left hand. His right hand was buried between Jack's thighs, with two fingers in Jack's ass.

Phil was quite pleased with the young man. He wasn't muscle bound by any means, but he had a good body, he was attractive, the red hair on his head and bush were an interesting red, and he did have more tattoos and piercings: little bar bells in his nipples and a colorful tattoo covering a shoulder and his right pec.

The young man gave a few jerks, told Phil he is was going to come, and then did so, his spunk arcing up and landing on the remnants of his peanut butter sandwich.

"Take a shower and clean yourself out," Phil said. He watched the young man pad toward the bathroom, admiring the curve of his buttocks. It would look good on film.

"Hey, whatyer' doin'," Jack said when, naked, Phil slipped into the shower with him.

"I paid for three hours of whatever I want," the older man said. "Now, down on your knees and suck me off."

"Wowser," the young man exclaimed from below Phil's chest. "You didn't tell me what you're packing. You think you're going to nail me with this?"

"I know I am. You signed a waiver already, and I don't think you're leaving anytime soon. I took your clothes. Now, shut the fuck up and suck."

Several minutes later, Jack exclaimed. "Hey what now? What are you . . . oh, shit. Oh FUCK!"

That's what Phil did, he bent the young man over at his waist, demanding that he grab his ankles with his fists, and then fucked him from behind under the cascading water from the shower. Jack was an experienced prostitute. After the first bit of complaining Phil was too big for him, Phil no longer was too big for him and just stood stationary, while Jack moved his ass, fucking himself on the monster cock.

Phil got more artistic on the bed, under the lights and the quiet whirring of the cameras. Phil fucked Jack from behind, both of them on their knees on the bed, with Jack's legs streaming behind Phil's; Phil embracing Jack's torso from behind, one hand cupping Jack's chin and arching the young man's head back into the hollow of Phil's shoulder, where their lips occasionally could meet, and Phil's other hand cupping, fondling, and squeezing Jack's balls, while Jack slowly jacked himself off. When the fucking became frenzied, Phil pushed Jack down, shoulders and cheek to the bed coverlet, grabbed his hips, and pistoned his channel hard to a shared ejaculation.

A second go had them both on their butts, their torsos propped up on the elbows, the two facing each other, while their pelvises met in the middle, their legs streaming around the other man's hips, Jack's butt cheeks resting on Phil's upper thighs as, his cock buried in Jack's ass, Phil thrust his cock forward rhythmically and Jack thrust his passage forward in synch to take the cock as deep as he could. Phil decided that this was one experienced street prostitute and that he'd have to sign him on for follow-up vids.

Later, Phil sat on the side of the bed, with Jack reclined in front of him, his hands on the floor and his legs streaming back around Phil's hips, while Phil clutched the young man's hips and pulled his ass channel on and off his cock.

Near the end of the three hours, Jack, exhausted, lay on his belly on the bed, his right leg stretched out straight behind him and his left leg bent and thrust out to the left. Phil had just come off his back, having covered him close and fucked him deep. Jack was panting softly and moaning almost inaudibly. Phil grabbed one of the video cameras and commanded, "Grab your cheeks with your hands and spread them. There, that's nice."

He filmed a close-up of Jack's hole, reamed extra large for Phil's specifications. That shot was becoming a signature closer for Phil's Internet films.

Before he left, Jack signed for two more filming sessions, and after Jack left, Phil took the necklace to the hidden safe in the back of a bookshelf. As he figured it, the necklace was worth $5,000. Jack obviously had stolen it, as he didn't have a clue what it was worth. Phil would have to be careful unloading it, though, and he probably wouldn't get more than $3,000 for it on an out-of-state sale.

He moved on to splice together the various camera angles of his session with Jack so that he could get it up on the Internet by 11:00 p.m., the start of his clients' favorite browsing time.

* * * *

"You've done very well in reaclimating, Phil," his probation officer was saying.

Phil didn't fully hear him. His eyes had gone to a swishy young man flouncing around the open-cubicle room the probation officers worked in. He seemed to be some sort of mail clerk. Phil had seen him in a gay bar on 4th Street, though—more than once. And he'd left with different guys— all obvious tops—each time. Phil wanted him for the movies. He'd make for variety, especially if he squealed when he was penetrated.

"Excuse me? What were you saying?" Phil asked.

"Your rehabilitation has gone well. A classic case of success. You came through your imprisonment well, have kept your nose clean, and are back running your jewelry store. It's a breath of fresh air against so many other cases where a man has come out of prison a more hardened criminal than he went in."

"Yes, I'm grateful for the system having brought me back on the path and rehabilitated me so well," Phil said, his

169

eyes still following the flighty young man around the vast room of shelf-high cubicle walls. His mind was planning how he would blackmail and fuck the mail clerk to the best advantage on a film for his Internet subscription site. Maybe in a side split, holding one of his legs straight up and showing his thick cock working in and out of his small hole, Phil thought. The clients would eat that up. But should he do it before or after he went up to northern New York to unload the necklace he had bought from Jack along with other pieces he had acquired on the sly?

Slave to Two Hung Masters

I became the sex slave of two big-cocked masters in Bangkok. Not simultaneously. Neither would have acceded to shared control. But one after the other. I tried to fight them off initially, but once they had nailed me to the quick and bathed me in their cum, I went docile and let them do whatever they wanted with me.

I was not a promiscuous submissive—well, not before I arrived, traumatized, in hedonist Bangkok in 1976, having been chased all across Southeast Asia by forces that wanted to kill me. But I *was* a submissive to men, and, whether or not I wanted to admit it, to big-cocked, dominating men.

I was a field reporter for UPI, the international news agency. I was in Saigon in April of 1975 to report the fall there. And then I was in Phnom Penh, until the last, later in that same month to cover the invasion there. I even made the bloody coup in Bangladesh in August of that year, being confined to my quarters for seven months afterward, not sure whether I would be freed to leave or put on trial under suspicion of being a CIA spy. The coup had been credited to that Agency.

I was dumped out in Bangkok in the spring of 1976, glazed-eyed, jittery, and contemplating death—in time to stand at the gates of Thammasart University on October 6th to watch the Thai Army mow down the students and hang their ringleaders from tree branches and set their bodies on fire on the Saram Luang parade ground in a failed democracy coup before the Thai king opened the gates of his palace to give what remained of the students sanctuary.

I should have been pulled home, but instead, I fought off the horrors of what men could do to each other by pulling up the latent desires I had suppressed over the years, finding the gay bars of the city, and spiraling to the heights of licentiousness in a giddy "whatever brought short-term pleasure" unleashing of desire, celebrating life as long as I was able to live. A gay bar with active sexual activity was not hard to find in Bangkok in the mid '70s—nor is it now, for that matter.

I had been fucked before, mostly during times of tension in military situations in Vietnam and Cambodia, where desperate men clung together, not knowing if there would be a tomorrow. The soldiers were fit, virile, and as needy as I was. These invariably were furtive couplings on the moist ground or on cots in tents, still fully dressed in combat gear, which started with hugs, furtive kisses and then occasionally moved to mutual hand jobs or blow jobs. On rare occasion it ended, with the sound of unnerving and desperation-inducing gunfire near or far, with the fumbling of belts and zippers. And with me turning my face to the open tent flap to eye the bursts of light and sound of the restless night "out there," while, hard and throbbing, he entered me from behind, deep, and held me close. Both of us striving to forgot where we were in the pain-pleasure of the ultimate connection and intimacy that can exist between two frightened men. Usually, as keyed up as we were, it took no more than five thrusts, and his cock was withdrawing and he was adding his cream to the buildup of other stains on the material of my fatigues. It gave us relief from what was happening around us for that moment in time—and a release of the tensions of our bodies.

It wasn't sex as much as it was calming therapy—a statement that, among so much death, the two of us still lived—that we still could shoot our loads. That we could receive pleasure and release of tension even under these circumstances, no matter how brief or fleeting.

But I never engaged in sex regularly before I went whole hog with it as therapy for war shock in one of the back rooms of a Bangkok club. I had drunk far too much and let

172

men touch me far too intimately when The Major, a heavily muscled, hung, black bull, who was assigned to JUSMAG—the Joint U.S. Military Advisory Group—got his cock in me in a struggle that was both emotional, made moot by my being half drunk and him being a massive, muscular soldier, and physical, as I had never taken a man as thick and long as he was. I continued to struggle weakly and ineffectually when he was fully saddled and pounding my ass, but once his cream flooded me deep, I lay there, docile, panting, and watching him with my eyes.

I had convinced myself that I'd only done it in the field as a form of desperation and an escape from the horrors of combat. I had reasoned with myself that I wasn't really "that way"—that I didn't need it. The Major took any guilt from the act in the back of the Bangkok club away from me. He gave me no choice. I didn't give him anything. He took it. At least that first time.

He stood away from me after he'd unloaded, the huge meat of him hanging between his legs, dripping his cum, still half hard, and stared down at me with the unspoken question of "What will you do next?"

"Do you want to leave?" he asked me in a gruff voice.

I pulled myself up on the bed in the room and, panting hard, turned onto my back, bent and spread my legs, rolled up my pelvis, and grabbed for and spread my butt cheeks, showing the massive black bull standing over me a still-gaping hole, dribbling with cum, that The Major had just reamed to his specifications. With a low, guttural laugh and a "I didn't think so," he came down on his knees between my thighs, possessed me again with his cock, and fucked me deep. I lay docile, under him, no struggle or resistance now, completely open to him, while he fucked me again—and again. Signaling full surrender, as he held me to him with an arm under my waist, I let my torso recline back on the bed and my arms open wide, in defeat, and resting docilely on the surface of the bed.

He took me home to his walled house off Sathorn Road and fucked me through the night, dominating me with his muscular, fit, virile, and vigorous body and his ever-ready big, black cock, daring me to resist. His sex slave now, I just lay there and took everything he did to me.

After that, I was his. He could do anything he wanted with me. When he entered a room, I went down on my back and opened my legs for him. I denied him nothing. Once at a pool party at his house, I lay on a pool bed and opened my legs to eight men in succession—simply because The Major told me to—and because he wanted to brag to other men that he possessed a sex slave.

When he was unexpectedly assigned away from Bangkok, I didn't mourn, though. I resolved that never again would I be sex slave to a cruel master, no matter how well-hung he was, and I substituted going to a gym for the trips to the gay clubs. It was a gym for gay men, though.

* * * *

I put my efforts to releasing tension and blocking out the situation in Southeast Asia, to the extent my job allowed, by toning up my body again. I had come to Bangkok trim, well-muscled, and cut, from moving in the field with soldiers and exercising constant in my Bangladesh confinement. I was in as good a shape as any twenty-five-year old could be. The Major had said that he was drawn to me not only by my looks but also by my toned body. I hadn't gone to fat since coming to Bangkok, but I wanted to be in top shape again. So I applied myself to the muscle-building machinery of the gym floor, tempered with the cleansing of the sauna, and the release of the Thai-particular massage.

The Thai masseurs at the club gave full-body massages, which invariably concluded with an oiled dick, tension-relieving hand job and balls squeeze. The hand job came with the regular contract and supposedly was based on the claim that a release of old semen to make way for fresh was good for the body and thus a legitimate part of massaging it. For a bit more money in the contract, which we weren't told about but had to learn by word of mouth or by following the moans and peeking in on massages in progress, the masseur would give you a blow job, would ride your cock, or, if you were inclined, would dildo or fuck you. It seemed that any masseur—all Thai men—at the club was prepared to fulfill any of the contract specifications.

I hadn't known about the extra contract options when Kassem became my regular masseur, and I even opened my eyes wide from a pleasant doze near the end of my first massage, when, the rest of my body oiled up, Kassem started oiling up my cock and assured me that, yes, he would be stroking until I ejaculated and that this was part of the regular massage—releasing tensions and clearing the balls, which also were oiled and had the cum teased out of them by hand manipulation.

Kassem's massages progressed to more sensual services over the year without my having to add to the contract, once I'd found out about the option. I didn't even have to think whether I wanted to pay extra for the option. I was still being fucked regularly after The Major was transferred—it was just in more casual settings avoiding a strong dominator and with more normal-sized cocks. And slowly, although Thailand was still under curfew in the wake of the October 6th coup, the tensions of wartime coverage were seeping away from me. But Kassem added the extra service on his own. During one massage he was complaining to me that his mother's kitchen had burned down. Thai country houses often had the kitchen separated from the main house for this exact reason. I asked him how much it would cost to rebuild and that perhaps I could loan him the money (which I took as a hint to offer when he'd told me the story to begin with). The cost was less than $100 in U.S. terms.

"Hell, I'll give you the money," I said. And, bowing his gratefulness, he said he'd work the amount off. At the end of the massage, as I came close to an ejaculation from the stroking of the oiled cock, Kassem finished with a balls-squeezing blow job. The next time, with me on my back, and his hand having worked me into an erection—more of an erection, I should say, as the regular massage invariably gave me an erection—Kassem came up on the table, straddled my cock, and rode me to that evacuation of my balls that I was told the gym routinely and unabashedly ended massages with. Thereafter, Kassem established a revolving routine for ending my massages: hand job, blow job, cock ride, hand job, blow job, . . .

The gym workout part of the contract didn't become the focal point of my continued membership—the massages did. I liked the workouts on the machines, but I didn't particularly like the attention I was given by the other gym members and the temptation this entailed. The gym was completely gay men; Bangkok in the '70s was all-out "anything goes as long as it's pleasurable" hedonist. I could be on a weight machine huffing and puffing from raising weights, and a couple could be right beside me on a weight bench, fucking. Invariably fucking—sometimes double penetration—was going on when I entered the sauna. The signal for wanting company or not in the individual shower cubicles was whether you closed the shower curtain or not.

I could resist most guys, but after the black bull major and having learned to take him, I found myself attracted to other tall, muscular, hung, arrogant, demanding, and possessive men—exactly the ones I was determined not to give my life over to ever again.

Magnus Amundsen was just such a man, and he took up a campaign to get his cock inside me. The Norwegian UN contingent military officer—in Bangkok to protect the interests of various UN offices in the city during the unrest in Southeast Asia—was a six foot seven, 240-pound, forty-plus year-old Zeus, with the hardest of muscular bodies and an "I'm God, open your legs for me" attitude.

When I was on the exercise floor when he was there, he saw himself as my spotter. I permitted him this role far beyond when I realized what he wanted. He aroused me and scared me at the same time. I knew he was a dominator, but I couldn't allow myself to fall under the sway of another The Major.

I knew he was monster hung because he left his shower curtain open and made sure he was working his cock anytime I walked past. I knew he was a cruel dominator because I heard the groans and moans of his masseur whenever Amundsen was being given a massage at the next cubicle over from where Kassem was working my muscles. And Kassem told me that Somdet was the masseur of choice for Amundsen because he was the one who could sheath the man's cock least painfully.

I knew he came here to fuck young men—there was nothing about his own body that could be developed or enhanced further—because he had fucked a young Canadian on the bench press next to where I was doing squats soon after I started at the gym, and I'd walked into the sauna on a later date to see him spiking an American teacher from the International School.

I knew he wanted me, because, increasingly, his spotting included touching and fondling me more than being there to keep a barbell from falling on me or me falling off the parallel bars. He also always seemed to be coming in or out of the shower when I was, and flashed me with his huge cock. I let that go too long, probably. Just as he made sure that I knew how low he hung and how hard he could get, he learned far more than was necessary about me one evening. He had me kneeling on one knee, my other foot on the ground, on a bench on the exercise floor. I had been doing curls with pretty heavy weights, and he was close behind me, supposedly spotting me. As I set the weight down, I realized just how close behind me he was.

Amundsen exercised as much in the altogether as one could get without being naked. He wore a jock strap and gym shoes without socks. He was an exhibitionist. He wanted all of the men to see how beautiful his body was—perhaps as a goal for all of them to strive for. I saw it as advertising, though. I think that's why he was pursuing me. For all other submissives working out at the gym, he had to do no more than stand before them, hands on hips, and give them the eye and they'd lay down on a bench and open their legs to him, even though they knew they'd be screaming bloody murder at the effort to take his cock. I didn't respond this way. So, I was a challenge.

And here he was behind me, thinking, no doubt, that this was his time to make a move. He embraced me with his arms, one hand cupping my chin and pulling my head back into the hollow of his shoulder, the other hand pushed under the waistband of my gym shorts where he was hefting and measuring the size and weight of my balls, discovering my cock was cut, and finding that he could encircle the base of my cock with his big hand and rub the side of the bulb with the tip of his index finger when I was still hardening. I certainly could

177

feel the hardness at his cock at my back through the jock pouch.

I was struggling against him, at least until he started stroking my cock inside my gym shorts, which made him laugh. Any minute he'd have me bent over the bench, surrounded by all the other guys working out on the floor, and would be banging me in a doggy fuck. How embarrassing it would be, considering the judgment I'd passed on other young men I'd seen letting him fuck them in public. I couldn't give in to him, I knew. He was just another form of The Major. I couldn't let him get inside me deep and bathe me in his cum. I didn't want to be a slave solely to one man again.

Someone laughed a hee haw laugh out at the reception desk, which startled Amundsen and allowed me to slip out of his grasp and stumble back to the changing room, foregoing the massage and a shower—just needing to get away, to avoid the temptation heaving through my body to just go back, lie on a bench, spread my legs, and let Amundsen have his way with me.

He didn't prevent me from leaving the gym that night, but he followed me back to my apartment, me in one tuk tuk and he in another. I was aware he was there. When I reached my third-floor apartment, I dared not turn on the lights. I went to a window overlooking the street and watched him, leaning against a lamp post, smoking a cigarette, and looking up at my building. He remained there for an hour. I remained at the window, stroking my cock. I didn't really think I took a breath all of the time he stood there. I was warring with myself—leave him standing there or admit the inevitable and bring him back up to the apartment, to my bed, to deep inside me?

I had seen him fuck other young men. I knew he would fuck me as roughly, as totally. I shivered at the thought, whether in anticipation or fear, I dared not contemplate.

No more than a week later, I was in the sauna, a towel wrapped around my hips, when Amundsen entered. Two men were fucking over in the corner, and I had been about to leave, but Amundsen placed his large and powerful body between me and the sauna door. He gave me a cruel smile and let his towel drop. His body was achingly magnificent, his cock in half erection. He stood there for maybe twenty seconds, making sure I took in his body and his rising need and determination. Then he reached over and snatched my towel away.

He laughed, knowing I would be hard—and I was. I was aching for him.

"You want me; don't pretend you don't," he growled.

If he had come to me—into me—there, in the sauna, I would have spread my legs, rolled up my buttocks, and received him. Instead, though, another young man, the Canadian, entered the sauna, naked, perched up on the shelf on the wall to the left, and spread his legs. Amundsen gave me a grin and then turned, crouched down, thrust his cock inside the Canadian, and started to pump. The Canadian flopped about in ecstasy under the assault, his eyes bugging out and his mouth formed in a big O.

I fled the sauna, padding quickly to the shower cubicles, jerked the curtain closed behind me in one of them, turned the shower on, and masturbated to completion under the jet of water. I arrived at the massage cubicles twenty minutes early, a towel around my waist, and had to wait on one of the lounges in that section's waiting room for Kassem to be free.

Kassem's massage was thorough. I was hard throughout, and he kept giving me little strokes to keep me hard all the time that he was working the other body parts. I was so oiled up that I was afraid I'd slide off the table. There was nothing amateur about a Thai body massage. Everything was worked hard and everything felt so much better after the masseur had finished torturing it. The same could be said of the cock and balls—and for the little special thing Kassem always did for me.

Tonight he massaged my front first, and after he'd worked over everything on this side, he latched onto my hips and pulled me to the end of the board. This wasn't difficult as heavily oiled as I was. He bent and spread my legs, placing the feet down at the outer and bottom edges of the table. He encircled my cock with one hand and started a slow stroke, and, in that special little thing he did for me, he entered my ass with a finger of his other hand. I sighed and moaned. A second finger went in. This sometimes was done before, but not usually. But it was pleasurable. He was able to find and give attention to the prostate. His mouth came down on the cock head, and he had started sucking me off. My sensations focused on the cock, so that I wasn't really aware that the third and forth fingers had gone in until I felt his knuckles at my rim. Kassem had long, sensuous fingers, a thin but strong hand. More than one finger was working my prostate. He took his mouth off the cock, which he had been deep-throating, and, one after the other, swallowed my balls, and sucked on them.

My pelvis-thrust-up ejaculation reached for the ceiling of the room.

The hand was pulled out of my ass, and he told me to turn over on my belly and scoot up the table. He gave a deep massage to my arms, my back, and legs, but he didn't spend as long on them as usual. Instead, he kneaded my butt cheeks until I wanted to scream, parted them, and blew on my hole. I tensed up and he told me to relax. He ran his fingers over the hole and thumped it with a finger tip until I did let the tension flow out of my body and felt my channel opening, the entrance going slack. The lubed fingers went back in the hole and he was moving them in and out, at first slowly and then more rapidly. I moaned and reached back with my hands to spread my cheeks and the hole opening.

I hadn't gotten the butt play before. I hadn't told him I was a submissive bottom. He must have heard that from elsewhere, because he most certainly was giving me the extra service that I'd heard bottoms got with their massage.

He told me he was going to use a dildo on me, and I didn't tell him no. He pulled my body back down the table, hooked my ankles on his shoulders, and then started working my ass with a dildo. I pulled my legs back down and raised a bit on my knees, enough to get a hand under my belly. I jacked off again while he was opening the passage ever wider with the dildo.

When I had come, the dildo came out and he pulled me back full onto the table. "More back work," he said.

I felt the weight of a knee at the small of my back, and two strong arms going under my pits and then up into a full Nelson hold. My torso was immobilized. This was a standard massage move. My shoulder blades would be arched back, with the knee buried in the small of my back, I would hear a crack, and my spine would be in full alignment. The knee came out of my back and went between my thighs, pulling them apart, which was not part of the standard movement.

Someone else was in the cubicle, because other hands were pulling my legs up and hooking the ankles on the shoulders of whoever had me in a full Nelsen—and now had my body stretched and curved like the runners on a rocker. The body on me was larger than Kassem's—much larger. The arms holding me in a full Nelson were much beefier.

The bulb, a massive, throbbing bulb, of a cock was at my hole, resting just inside the puckered rim, Kassem's finger and dildo work having opened me up significantly. I knew it wasn't Kassem. I knew it was Magnus Amundsen, having bribed Kassem, and coming in as a substitute masseur.

I knew I was going to be fucked thick. I fought to keep my passage relaxed, open.

Amundsen started rocking our bodies back and forth, his cock entering me deeper with each revolution of the rock. I struggled against him and did some mouthing off, none of which brought any help. Increasingly, I didn't want help and my struggles grew weaker the deeper inside me that he moved.

It took him nearly five minutes to hit bottom with his cock, and another ten minutes of rocking before he released his seed inside me.

I had not wanted to lose control to another man like this ever again, but my body—my passageway—betrayed me. I hadn't had a man so totally big-cock-possessing me like this since The Major. As if my walls had been starving for throbbing stretching to the limit, the muscles undulated over the invading club, making love to it, pulling it in, and rippling over it as I panted hard, frightened that the walls wouldn't hold, but also willing it to invade deeper and deeper, which, relentlessly it did. My passage wanted the big cock. I ached to be possessed and fucked like The Major had done it.

The bulb throbbing at the quick of me, as possessing as The Major's had been, the betrayal came pouring out of my slack mouth. "Yes, yes. Fuck! Shit! Nail my ass to the table!"

I knew my surrender would be full if I gave in to this Norwegian stud. I was back with The Major, the master. Except that this was a new master. All resistance was futile, any decisions on what or who I had inside me were no longer mine to make. When he had seeded me the first time, I would be his to command. Just like with The Major.

The Norwegian laughed a low, gravelly laugh, and began to pump. At the point of ejaculation, I gave voice once more to my new master. "FUCK yes, give me your seed. I am yours! Do what you want with me!"

When he was done, I lay there, panting, no fight in me. He had given me all of his cock and had cum inside me. I was his now. He realized that or at least suspected it.

The question was "Now what?"

He went back on his haunches between my thighs, as I panted and recovered. His hands went to my oiled back and arms, and he massaged them, not doing as well as Kassem, but doing well enough.

The world was waiting for something. After conquering me, he hadn't left. He was still kneeling between my thighs and massaging my torso. I knew I had totally surrendered to him and he could do whatever he wanted with me now. Apparently he wasn't sure, even though I had cried out his victory, my surrender.

I turned on my back, lifting a leg over his head, but not bringing the ankle back down any further than his shoulder. Lifting the other ankle to his other shoulder, I now was facing him, completely open to him. Moving my arms above my head, I gripped the top edge of the table and raised my hips off the table, bringing the bulb of his cock back to my dripping ass opening, while giving Amundsen a look of surrender. In supplication to him, I was presenting my ass passage for his pleasure.

"Do what you will. Fuck me again. Do anything you want," I whispered, which elicited a hard look from him. I had asked for it. He hadn't stated that I was going to get it. This was not yet a slave-master relationship as he evidently wanted it to be.

Moving up with his knees, he slid them under my buttocks, reached down and under with his hands, squeezing and separating the orbs, pulling my hole open to the maximum it now could offer. His cock slid inside me and he pumped me deep, vigorously, and hard, as I grunted and groaned and moaned and cried out variations of "Nail me. Nail me hard" and "Yes, yes, fuck me! Fill that hole!"

There was no question now that I was totally his—not just in my mind. In victory, before coming but after I had done so again, with Kassem moving his hand between us and beating me off, Amundsen went up on his feet on the massage table, bringing me up with him, his cock still buried and thrusting inside me, his hands gripping my hips, my legs hooked on his hips, and my body streaming down to the surface of the table, my hands thrown over my head, gripping the top edge of the table. He fucked on for fifteen more minutes, adding cum to his previous deposit.

We lay there, stretched out on the table, Amundsen pulling me into his belly. One arm was under me, his forearm bent toward me, his hand gripping my throat. His right leg was thrown over my calves, holding me in place, my buttocks jutted back to his other hand, palming my butt, two fingers in my ass, digging, pulling back, digging again. His face was over mine, his eyes looking intensely into mine. Kassem was gone now. Most of the lights in the ceiling floating above the tops of all of the cubicles and sections of the club were off and no sounds could be heard to cover my heavy breathing and whimpering.

I tried raising my face to his, to go into a kiss. He jerked his head up. It wasn't going to be that kind of a fuck, that kind of a relationship. I let out a little yelp as the third— and then the fourth—finger went into my ass. I tried to raise my right leg to open my hole more to him, but he held me in a vise grip with his leg. He twisted and lowered his mouth to my left nipple and chewed on it. I stopped any semblance of struggle. I was his, to do what he wanted with me. Obviously he was testing and demonstrating that.

I gave a little cry as he pushed his hand into my ass up to the knuckles, spreading his fingers inside me, testing the limits of the stretch of my channel. He began to hand fuck me. I did everything I could to relax. I knew I couldn't ask him to do anything he was doing. I knew the whole point was that he was in control and my role, as his slave, was just to take it. He was going to test my limits in this way to assure himself that I would take it. I closed my eyes and worked on controlling my breathing as he fucked me with his hand—a larger one than

Kassem's had been, the knuckles bruising my rim, my channel walls in convulsions over the unnatural invasion.

He pulled his hand out, and turning me to belly down on the table, he grabbed my wrists in his fists, forcing my arms over my head, saddled himself on my hips, thrust inside me and fucked me hard, brutally to his third ejaculation. I laid there and took it, silently. I dare not tell him I was enjoying it, even though, on several levels I was. I just lay there under him, taking the big-cock fucking. It didn't matter that I'd taken his cock twice already. It seemed to grow with each fucking.

He really was no different than The Major was. He had campaigned to conquer me. As soon as he had nailed me to the quick and bathed me in his cum, he was my master and I was his slave. He would use me cruelly now, and I would let him. My arousal would be highest when he did.

Not unlike The Major, to drive home and brag of his domination, Amundsen took me back to the UN barracks that night and shared me with whoever wanted a piece of me. I opened my legs to any and all—because he told me to.

I never blamed Kassem for giving me up to Amundsen. I'd known it was going to happen. After it *had* happened, I would not have wanted it any other way.

A sex slave to two successive big-cocked masters for the entire time I was assigned to Bangkok.

Tea with the Prince

June 1929, Tokyo, Japan

I was straining for him to start. I ran my hands down his hard-muscled back from the shoulder blades to his buttocks, pushing his trousers down further on his buttocks and clutching at the orbs, willing him to start the stroking. He was inside me deep and I was panting hard for him.

He spoke from the hollow of my throat. "I . . . we need a favor of you."

A favor? What in the hell was this? He had me on the floor of his hotel room, my legs spread and bent, him lying on top of me between them. My trousers and briefs off, my shirt open to the work of his lips and teeth on my nipples. He was inside me, goddamnit. Why wasn't he fucking me? Why was he picking a time like this to speak of a favor?

"Fuck me," I murmured. "Give me your cum."

He continued, as if he didn't hear me. "A prince, a professor at Tokyo University. We need his permission to get into the private art collection in Kyoto."

Private art collection. He was speaking of the homoerotic art he wanted to see during this university study tour to Japan. This whole study tour was probably because he wanted to get into that collection of homoerotic art in Kyoto. That was what Professor Tyndale did on the side himself—sketches of men fucking. And Tyndale was good at it. He had shown me his art that first time, that old "Come up and see my

185

etchings" ploy, and it had aroused me so well that I'd laid down and opened my legs to him then—and whenever he wanted me to since then.

"Fuck me," I whined. The professor was old—maybe in his late forties—and gaunt and ugly. But he had a good cock. I wanted his cock now. Not just inside me. Stroking. To pump me deep. To fuck me. to blast me with his cum. To make me come too.

"He wants me to come to tea with him. To bring a young student with me. A willing young student. He says he likes young blond men."

"Please do it; do me now," I whimpered.

Tyndale cupped the side of my head, ran his fingers into my blond curls and kissed me on the lips. Coming out of the kiss, he gave me three slow, deep, long strokes. I buried my fingernails in his butt cheeks, arched my back, and, through pants, cried out, "Yes, yes, fuck me!"

But he held there. "I would be there too. He wants sketches done. Will you do us this favor? The study group needs to see this collection."

"Fuck me and I'll do anything you want."

He began to stroke, establishing a steady, deep beat. Lost to him, I arched my back, as his lips went to my nipples, and ran my hand up and down his back from his shoulder blades to his buttocks, digging my claws in at the down thrust. I panted and set my pelvis in motion in a counterthrust, writhing under him, no thoughts in my mind of anything but that staff working my passage.

He tensed, held, and ejaculated in two bursts, holding for three after spurts, creaming me deep inside as I purred and sighed and ran my fingers up into his hair, pulling his face to mine for a deep kiss.

Tyndale went up on his knees between my thighs and looked down into my eyes.

"We meet him at the Meiji Shrine tomorrow at 3:00 and he'll take us to wherever he wants to perform the tea ceremony," he said, adding, "You haven't come yet. Masturbate yourself for me, please. I want to see you come."

Dutifully, I encased my own hard cock in my hand and began to stroke it. He slipped his hand under my buttocks, and

I felt one, and then two, fingers enter my ass, search for, and finding, the prostate.

My eyes went to his now-slick cock, slick with his own cum. The best feature of him. It had only gone half flaccid and was thickening again as he watched me masturbate and he fingered my ass. I knew he was going to fuck me again. That knowledge drove my arousal, and minutes later I tensed, arched my back, and shot my load. Immediately, he was lowering his body to mine again, entering me, grabbing my knees in his hands, rowing my legs, moving them back and forth—pushing them wide apart as he thrust in, pulling them together as he drew back.

In ecstasy, I arched my back, threw my head back, and in a panting voice of total surrender, whispered to the ceiling, "Yes, yes, fuck me," as the pumping of his cock picked up speed.

* * * *

The first indication I had that the man we were meeting was anyone of importance, even though Professor Tyndale had said he was a prince, was when our car was let through in front of the shrine when all others were being kept back. There were three black Duisenberg limousines lined up in front of the Torii—the ceremonial gate—of the shrine, and burly Japanese men in black suits cordoning off the area.

At the top of the steps up into the first shrine hall stood a small-stature, mousy-looking Japanese man, graying hair, wearing wire-rim eyeglasses and a black, tailored suit, complete with vest and top hat.

Professor Tyndale leaned over and whispered, "Prince Satsuma," in my ear.

It was obvious to me then that the man was of some import because a crowd had gathered behind the imaginary line the black-suited guards had set and were bowing their heads in the prince's direction. This was a chore for them, because as soon as Tyndale and I stepped out of our car, I became another focus of attention, and those in the crowds were doing what they could to look at me too. I had grown used to the attention in Tokyo, because, with the exception of a contingent of jackbooted Nazi Party Germans roaming the streets of Tokyo during what later proved to be secret pact talks between the Japanese and Germans, blond young men were few and far between in Tokyo in the later years of the 1920s. And it was supposedly good luck to touch blond hair. So, I was getting a lot of furtive attention during this university art class study tour to Japan, the last, we were told what probably would occur in a while, as the flames of war were building in Asia.

So, this little man was going to fuck me in order for Professor Tyndale to have access to a collection of homoerotic art in Kyoto, I thought. Piece of cake; he was such a runt, I thought. He was all mousy diffidence and refinement as he showed the two of us through the shrine, with his guards clearing the spaces so that we had a private tour. During the tour I had to reassess my impression that he was a weak runt. He led me from space to space with a grip of steel on my arm that belied his looks and his weak, tinny-voice precise English that showed him to be a professor type as well as a prince.

As we stood in front of a massive reclining Buddha in polished wood, he stood close behind me. With one hand he pointed my attention to the *fundoshi*—the loin cloth—the statue was wearing and the subtle peeking out at one side of the bulb of a cock. He moved his other hand around my belly and down and was fondling my package. He also was holding me close into his body from behind.

I look sharply to the side to catch Professor Tyndale's attention to what was happening, and he just smiled, shrugged slightly, and gave me a furtive palms-down signal. Obviously the permission to view the art collection wasn't a done deal. There was a checking out of the goods phase. I stood there, dutifully, in front of the Buddha of the Peeking Penis, while the short and wiry Japanese prince felt up my body from my throat to my knees with strong, searching hands. Tyndale and the bodyguards stood, pretending not to be watching, as if nothing untoward was happening.

Satsuma grunted and turned, and we were making our way back to car park, the prince and Tyndale in front of me. I heard Tyndale lean over and ask, "Satisfactory?" and the prince answer, "Quite satisfactory indeed."

* * * *

We were sitting on eight-inch-deep, silk-covered cushions with a low tea table between us. Professor Tyndale was sitting across from the prince and me, his sketch book and charcoals at his side. The prince was sitting very close beside me.

In addition to two ceramic tea pots and three cups for tea sitting on the table between us, other objects, one of which had me hyperventilating, were set off to the side. There was a bowl of fragrant oil, a six-inch strand of ivory beads with a tiny eyehook at one end—and a clear-glass knobbly dildo, very definitely a dildo, as it was slightly curved up with a vein on the underside running across the knobs and the head on the end undoubtedly was in the form of a penis bulb.

Nothing was said about the added implements. The conversation was quite refined, with the prince providing a step-by-step explanation of the tea ceremony. The surroundings were sparse, but richly appointed, the setting definitely Japanese, with shoji screens and niches with Ikebana—flower—arrangements in them. There were few pieces of art on the walls; what was there was homoerotic and was lit. A Roman-like bronze sculpture was in one corner of the room. It was of two torsos, rather than the usual one, armless and legless, accentuating the muscularity of the torsos. The torso in front was in erection, the bronze plate of this hanging low from the bottom of the torso plate. The torso in front was slightly turned so the root of the cock of the one behind could be seen buried in the ass of the one in front.

Nothing was being hidden about the reality that this was the house of a man who fucked other men and that I was going to be fucked.

The house itself was a conundrum and screamed of refinement, wealth, and power in Japan. The estate took up a whole block in a bustling downtown area of the city. The grounds were so covered in manicured and landscaped foliage that the house could not be seen from beyond the grounds and the city could barely be heard from the house. The house itself was set on a small man-made hill in the center of the property. The surprise was that the house obviously was the design of

189

the American architect Frank Lloyd Wright. The prince explained that Wright had accepted the commission to design it, the original house having burned down, while he was building the Imperial Hotel in Tokyo, which had been completed six years earlier.

Once inside, the blending of Japanese tradition and Wright's style was shown to be perfection.

After we entered the house, both Professor Tyndale and I were led off to a room walled with shoji screens, floored in tatami matting, and overlooking a walled pocket garden with a small pond surrounded by rocks and foliage. The pond turned out to be a tub of fragrant, steaming water, where we were bathed (and embraced, kissed, and fondled each other) before being dressed in silk *yukatas*—robes—Tyndale in white, me in a rich red—with only one-material-length fundoshi wrapped and knotted underneath.

The tea ceremony was long and involved, and my tea came from a separate pot than the one the prince served Tyndale and himself from. It didn't take me long to figure out why. Almost immediately upon drinking the tea, I began to feel all tingly, warm, weak, and ultra sensitive to the touch all over my body.

The ceremony over, servants, with well-formed, muscular bodies, and wearing only fundoshis, appeared, heads bowed and not looking at any of us, and turned the tea table so that it was at the opposite side of the prince from me. They took away the tea implements. They left the bowl of fragrant oil, the string of beads, and the glass dildo.

Tyndale rose and I started to do so as well, assuming he'd take the lead in showing me what I should do. But he motioned me to stay in place, and the prince put an arm around me, in which I again was surprised at the strength of him, and held me in place, pulled close into his side. The servants carried the bolster Tyndale had been sitting on to the far side of the room, and he settled down there with his sketch book and charcoals.

As pedantic as the prince had been about explaining every aspect of the tea ceremony—other than the drug he was using on me—and as long as the ceremony had taken, I expected a longer phase of getting down to sex. But it didn't happen that way.

It started with a kiss on the lips, but while that was happening, the prince was brushing his blue-silk yukata open—only to expose his cock and groin. He already was in erection. With a hand cupping the back of my head, he made my eyes lower as we came out of the kiss to ensure that I saw what he had uncovered. I shivered and gave a little moan. He may be a small man, but there was nothing small about his cock. It wasn't thick, but it was long, long, long. It was upcurved, in angry erection, accentuated as it was stained red; and it had a thick Prince Albert ring in the bulb.

Upon being assured I'd seen the cock, which he could have told from my intake of breath, the start of light panting, and my low moans, he grasped my left hand and pulled it around, nudging me to take the cock in my hand, which I did. Directing me only by movement, not by spoken command, he signaled that my fist should be open and loose, so that he could stroke his cock in the fist, which he started to do.

The fingers of the hand he had at the back of my head—his left—were buried in my blond curls, gripped my hair, and pulled my head cruelly back. With his right hand, he brushed my yukata open at my breast, and he possessed my left nipple with his mouth and teeth. His right hand then brushed my yukata open at my crotch and, with one deft pull at the knot of the fundoshi, he stripped that away and took my cock in his hand. His hand was slathered in oil, and I realized that he must have dipped it in the bowl of warm oil on the tea table. After slick-stroking my cock for a minute or more, he dipped his hand in the oil again and slathered it over my balls, letting it drizzle down between my crack, my pelvis rolled-up, and entering my ass with oiled fingers

I lay, trapped in his strong embrace, breathing heavily, all of my senses, sexually energized but feeling physically weak from the drug he'd given me, pinging on what his hands, lips, and teeth were doing to my body.

"Fuck me, fuck me please," I softly whimpered.

He made me come with his hand stroking my cock. Across the room, Professor Tyndale was sketching like crazy, tearing one sheet off when he was done, and moving on to the next, capturing each change of position initiated and controlled by the prince.

The prince moved into the next major change, turning me to face him more, with my groin totally exposed down and under to my hole, with my pelvis rolled up, my weight on the small of my back. My left leg was bent, the sole of that foot buried in the tatami matting. My right leg was raised straight up his chest, my ankle hooked on the back of the prince's neck. We were still mostly covered, with only his crotch, his pubic bush hair; a darker black than the grayer hair on his head, and his angry, long, upcurved cock still in hard erection, exposed. My left pec, with its puckered nipple, and my crotch area were exposed.

I watched, mewing softly, past the unavoidable screaming erection on the man, to the tea table, where he was spinning the head of the glass dildo in the bowl of oil. I watched in fear, and arousing anticipation, as he slowly brought the dildo out of the bowl, moved it to my hole, slowly penetrated me with it, and fucked me. At first in a slow stroke seeking out every surface inside me and then hard and vigorously until, me straining against an embrace I couldn't escape, I gave him another ejaculation.

I was still trying to bring my pulse under control from that when I was forced to watch him pick up the string of ivory beads, dip them in the oil, and attach them to the ring in the bulb of his cock. With no further preparation and certainly no explanation and no time for me to try to relax to it, the prince turned his pelvis toward mine; dipped his hips; came back up with his beads-enhanced cock head, deftly targeting my entrance; and plunged up inside me. The dildo had opened me up to where I easily took the girth of him, but my eyes popped open from the effect of how deep he could get up into me.

I cried out and tried to writhe out from under him, but he was too strong for me. One hand was arching my head back with a grip in my head hair. The other was gripping my left thigh and holding my leg out. His cock, the beads aswirl, was pumping my passage hard and deep.

Tyndale was busily sketching on his pad. I knew that the resulting sketches would become part of the prince's homoerotic art collection—and maybe find their way eventually into the Kyoto collection that Tyndale was so hot on seeing.

I didn't really care at that point. The little Jap was giving me the fuck of my life.

He moved me to the position of kneeling over the bolster, my elbows on the tatami matting on the other side of the bolster. My yukata was pulled up and gathered around my waist. The prince was naked, except for his glasses, his body wiry and thin, but his muscles hard, and his small size accentuating the angry length of his cock, the beads drooping down to the tatami. Kneeling at an angle behind me to give Tyndale a shot of my buttocks and erection and drooping balls between my spread thighs, the prince leaned over and ate out my ass, distended and squeezed my balls, and milked my cock through my legs. He mounted my ass and finished me off in a good ten minutes of stroking and swirling the ivory beads inside me.

He left us then, Tyndale finishing up his sketches and me laying in a heap, belly over the bolster, and moaning and purring having been finished royally—in more ways than one.

When a servant came to usher the professor out of the room, I started to rise, having difficulty doing so because of how deeply I felt the prince still inside me in the form of my rippling passage walls and his cum seemly in my stomach. But Tyndale signaled me to remain.

"You are staying here until we return from Kyoto," he said. "You are to help the prince in a project of his own."

If his project included more of his cock work inside me, that didn't bother me a bit, I thought. But then I looked up to watch Tyndale being escorted out of the room, I saw, entering the room, one of the jackbooted German Nazi generals who had been roaming around Tokyo. He had a big smile on his face, he was lightly slapping his leg with a riding crop, and he was unbuttoning his brown uniform shirt.

* * * *

December 9, 1937, Nanking, China

193

I moved the pillow from underneath the small of my back and placed it under the other pillows behind my head. After reaching for the cigarettes and lighting up, I looked down the line of my naked body, my legs still spread and bent, and watched the German colonel dress in the black uniform of the Nazi Party. This was the first time I'd seen Heinrich Krentz dressed thusly. He'd told me that it was for expediency. The less-dressy khaki uniform of the Chinese Nationalist Army that he had been wearing as a secret German adviser to Chiang Kai-shek's Chinese Nationalist military was folded into a suitcase set on a nearby chair.

"Do you really have to go, Heinrich?" I asked. "Is it really not safe here?"

"The Generalissimo left two days ago. The Japanese 10th Army is closing in on the city on two sides. I haven't been released by Berlin as adjunct to the Chinese yet. I must follow them to Chungking. You should come as well, Wilhelm. I can guarantee your transport."

"Can I leave on the 15th?" I asked "The university is being packed out to go to Chungking. I have students I'm responsible for."

"That might work. But not much longer after that—especially for your Chinese students. The reports say that the Japanese march from Shanghai has been brutal. No prisoners taken; no one left alive along the track."

"Surely that's just propaganda."

"I wouldn't count on that. In fact, I think you should leave with me today."

"I have responsibilities. But I'll miss you until I can catch up with you in Chungking," I said.

And the strange thing was that I *would* miss him. He was my third lover—no, master—in the eight years since I'd been forcibly taken back to Germany from Tokyo after Prince Satsuma had given me to the Nazi generals who had ravished me mercilessly. I had been beaten so much into submission that I raised no objection when I was hustled back to Berlin with them—I had come to accept and then to seek the rough sex. In time, I'd been given more freedom by the general who controlled me and even permitted to go to the university in Heidelberg to complete my art degrees.

When Heinrich brought me out to China with him on his adviser tour, I was given a professor position at the University of Nanking, and we lived together as partners. I'd almost completely forgotten that I was once an American with free reign of my life. I even was more used to my German name, Wilhelm, now than the name I'd been given, William. And the Toliver surname never was used anymore. I was documented as Wilhelm Krentz, Heinrich's son. For social purposes the father and son relationship was established. Only a few of the Chinese servants knew I slept in Heinrich's bedroom, under him or that sometimes he lashed me to a pillar, flogged me, and then fucked me still tied to the pillar.

We were believable as father and son, I suppose, if you considered that Heinrich had been quite young when I was born. We were both Teutonic blonds, qualified for the master race. And qualified in more ways than hair color too. Both of us were blue-eyed and of strong, handsome features. Our body styles were different—his tall, solid, muscular, hung, and mine more lithe and trim and on the shorter side, but we were similar enough for me just to be considered to favor my mother more than my father.

That he was muscular, hung, virile, and vigorous was enough to keep me satisfied with the third German Nazi Party member who had virtually owned me for the last eight years. At twenty-seven, I was lucky to have a god of a man of forty-four, like Heinrich, serving as my protector and master.

His manner changed when I said I'd miss him. In some ways I was more master of him than he of me. I could arouse him quickly, and as I lay there, naked, reaching for my half-hard cock, and giving him a "come hither" look, I could see his resolve on leaving me melt. He had fucked me twice after we had awakened that morning—more times the previous night— as if he couldn't pull away from me and leave me here in Nanking.

"Do you really have to leave right now? You don't have another half hour?" I asked.

When his trousers hit the floor, I saw that he already was in erection. I barely had time to snuff out my cigarette in the ashtray on the nightstand before he was upon me, turning me, coaxing me up on my knees at the end of the bed.

"Yes!" I cried out as he entered me strong and deep from the rear, grabbed the hair on the back of my head, arching my torso up toward his face. He fucked me hard and brutally, as all of the Germans had.

Just like the Japanese marching on Nanking from Shanghai—taking no prisoners.

* * * *

December 13, 1937, Nanking, China

"Professor Krentz? Wilhelm Krentz?"

"Yes," I answered, standing at the door, maintaining a position between me and the students in the art studio who were packing up art supplies. A Japanese officer, backed up by several soldiers, all with rifles drawn with bayonets attached to them. There had been sounds of gunshots and screaming as the Japanese soldiers had spread out across the university campus, having easily broken through the city defenses, such as they were, that morning. The government and most of the Nationalist army had already drawn off into the interior of the country.

"You are Wilhelm Krentz, German citizen?" the Japanese officer asked again.

"Yes," I answered, not really lying anymore, I suppose, as I had been in German hands for the last eight years and no American had come looking for me. I handed over the papers that Heinrich had made sure I had documenting me as a German with German government and Nazi Party connections.

I'd asked Heinrich before he left why he was so adamant that I have these papers.

"If the Japanese see these before they shoot you, you should be safe—if you don't leave Nanking in time. The Chinese don't know, but Germany—the Nazi Party—has a secret pact with the Japanese. We're allies. Our leaders in Berlin just want to be seen backing both horses in this war until we can see who will win."

I obviously hadn't left Nanking in time.

"Yes, these papers are in order. Come with me, please."

"My students. I have a responsibility for my students," I said. But soldiers had already stepped forward, taken me in hand, and were dragging me down the hall. Other soldiers entered the art studio. I was only half way down the stairs when I heard the shots and screaming, the screaming quickly cut off. I nearly collapsed on the stairs, screaming myself in despair, anger, and frustration, but strong hands carried me out of the building and loaded me onto the back of a canvas-covered truck.

I was taken into the foreign quarter, which was nearly deserted, except for the scurrying about of Chinese civilians, most being pursued by Japanese soldiers—and most being run down and dispatched within my sight until I pulled back from the back of the truck and also in my hearing, which I couldn't deaden and was forever after haunted by.

The truck stopped at a stone villa, built in the Western style, and, dejected and my wits dulled, I was taken up the stairs and to a dining room. The table had been pulled to the wall and a low table supporting a Japanese tea set was in its place. Cushions were spread on the other side of the table, and at one side of these sat an elderly Japanese man in a blue, billowy silk yukata. He lifted his head and I sucked in air. It was Prince Satsuma. He was grayer now, in his early sixties, but he still was trim and his back was ramrod straight. He was nearly bald.

"Come, take tea with me, William," he said simply, gesturing to the cushion beside him, as the Japanese soldiers who had brought me here melted out of the room. "Please take off your clothes and put that yukata on before you sit by me," he said.

"How . . . why . . . ?" I stammered.

"It doesn't matter. It only matters that I found you in time and that you are safe with me. Come over to me. We'll take some tea and then I will be inside you again. I've often thought of you, the sweetness and yielding nature of you. I have a room back in Tokyo lined with drawings of you being taken by me and other men. Very sweet and invigorating. They had helped keep me young—my *chinko* hard and vigorous. You'll be interested to know I still can fill and seed you."

And he could. Resigned to giving him what he wanted, I sat by him, brushed the folds open at his groin, and found him still capable of an erection and with the Prince Albert ring in the head of his cock. As he rolled over on top of me, I brushed my yukata open, bent and spread my legs, rolled my pelvis up, and took him deep inside me.

We stayed in the villa—in hiding it seemed—as the city died around us. Satsuma never left the villa in the five weeks we were there. He wore a general's military uniform but I could see no invasion or occupation force that he commanded and later could testify he was at the Rape of Nanking but couldn't attest to him having had any part in it—quite the contrary. He rarely was anywhere but on top of and inside me. I could hardly say at a military inquest that he was that close to me all of the time, though.

After five weeks of looting and raping across the city, the pillage seemed to die down. There really was no one left to rape or rob. Only then did he say, "I think it's safe for us to leave now."

We did, in a staff car, taking us all the way back to Shanghai and then by ship to Japan. In Japan, after enjoying my body for two more weeks in the room he told me about where sketches of me being fucked were hung, he had me driven to the American embassy and repatriated to my home country.

After what I'd seen and heard in Nanking, there was really only one thing I could do from there.

* * * *

September 15, 1945, Tokyo, Japan

I sat, ramrod straight, in the passenger seat of the jeep, while the soldiers jumped out of the canvas-covered truck behind me, pulled open the leaning gates of the park-like block in the middle of the bombed out Japanese capital, and then fanned out over the grounds, avoiding the cavernous holes dug out by Allied bombs.

My driver drove me up the winding road that had once trailed artfully through landscaped gardens, gardens that now were both overgrown and beaten down by bombs. I took in my breath and nearly teared up as we got within view of the palace that had once been a breathtaking Frank Lloyd Wright creation. Only one wing stood now, the central part of the building having taken a direct hit from an Allied bomb.

As I got out of the jeep and motioned a couple of the soldiers to come with me, the irony didn't escape me that I now was doing what had been done to and for me back in Nanking eight years previously. I had come for a prince, to escort him safely through a city in turmoil.

We entered the building and I felt I knew the place. Indeed, I had been held prisoner in this wing for weeks as the German generals were given free rein in ravishing my body to their brutal needs and desires. Halfway down the corridor I brought the escort to a halt and spent a few minutes in the room where, sixteen years earlier, I had repeatedly been hung from an overhead beam and flogged and imprisoned in stocks and fucked. The prince had occasionally taken me as well, but he had me taken to more comfortable quarters to fuck me, and his attentions were almost soothing and love-like in contrast to the German generals he was trying to impress by gifting me to their sexual pleasures. I, of course, had never heard from or about Professor Tyndale again. For all I knew he was still roaming the private collection of homoerotic he had sold me to access.

My thoughts were conflicted. I could do an ineffectual search and let the prince go uncaptured. He had saved me in Nanking. But would that be doing him any favors? I doubted he would be the focus of military trials. He quite possibly would be examined and then let free. But perhaps he should be put on trial for having given me to the Germans in the first place. I never revealed how I had gotten from Tokyo to Germany and then back to China.

Prince Satsuma was right where I assumed I would find him. He had described his "William" room to me well enough in Nanking that I could walk directly to it. He was sitting on cushions behind a tea table in the center of the room.

I stopped the accompanying soldiers just outside the door, as a lieutenant announced, "Major William Toliver, of U.S. Army Intelligence"—a position I had risen too based on my facility with German and personal knowledge, which was put to good use, of the hierarchy in the Nazi Party. After that introduction, I told my escort they could go back to the jeep, that we would be out in a few minutes. I had spied something that settled my quandary on what to do here.

"You're looking divine, William," Satsuma said in a crackly voice. "The uniform becomes you, although I always preferred you naked."

"I've come to take you back to our headquarters, prince. I have no idea whether you will be kept or for how long. But you must understand that there will have to be an investigation of your wartime activities."

"I understand," he said. He sounded so tired—and old. And he suddenly, at seventy-two was, in fact, at-the-end-of-his-rope old. Despite how he had used me, I found I no longer felt any bitterness toward him. He also had saved me in Nanking and, most important, hadn't, as far as I could see, had anything to do with the Japanese carnage there.

"Do you understand, completely?" I asked. "You were in Nanking, as a general. It's a matter of record. If you go with me, I will do what I can to separate you from what happened there, but you were there, so the questioning will be difficult."

"I do understand. But I don't think it will matter. Not unless your justice is swift. Come, can you come sit by me one last time and take tea with me?"

"We don't have much time," I said.

"No, there isn't much time," he said. "But, please, one last time."

I went over and went down, cross-legged on the cushion beside him. There were two tea pots and he poured our tea from separate pots. That there were two tea pots and that he served us separately made all the difference in what I would do here. He was taking the responsibility and decision out of my hands. We drank.

In the silence that followed, I could hear him sniff back a tear. "If only . . . one more time."

I reached into the folds of his yukata. As old as he was, he still could achieve an erection. As he softly moaned and sighed, I stroked him to a dribbling ejaculation that didn't take long to accomplish. As he came, though, he coughed, sighed, slowly collapsed back onto the cushions, and expired.

I knew I'd have to make sure the tea in the two pots was carefully preserved and analyzed—and I would have to ensure that I expressed surprise at what had transpired here.

Beware the Coach

"Is one of those male figure skaters down there your son?"

She knew damn well that one was my son—and which one; the other one was her son. Gail Culbertson didn't know me from Adam, I'm sure, because she was East Coast U.S. and I was homed in Japan. And my son had left the circuit with an injury before hers appeared at Nationals and then went out with injuries for a year too.

That's what our sons had in common. Both now healthy, they were trying to make a comeback from foot injuries.

"Yes. The smaller, shorter one doing the backspin." I pointed to Ken, who, I was happy to say, was doing a brilliant backspin. It was perhaps unfortunate that her son, Chad, was doing a nearly equally brilliant flying camel. He could have jumped higher into it, though, and with his long, elegant body he should be able to learn that. It would impress judges and audience alike. I could teach him that. Until now I had coached my son. Gail Culbertson, who coached her own son, had missed that chance. Her son could be quite the figure skater with a better coach.

"I thought he was Japanese."

By that she was saying I clearly wasn't Japanese, which I wasn't, and this undoubtedly was part of her ruse in trying to convince me that she didn't know I was Ken's father and coach.

"His mother is Japanese," I answered, keeping my voice friendly. "We live and train in Tokyo."

"You weren't thinking of asking Sergey Tsarevich to coach him, were you?"

Yes, of course I was. That's what Ken and I were doing in Colorado Springs. Tsarevich always kept an older skater trying to rejoin the hunt in his stable and he'd brought three of them back to national and international placings. Ken and I were here precisely for the same reason that Gail Culbertson and her son were here—Sergey was down there by the boards watching our sons going through practice routines, trying to work themselves around the three women also practicing on the ice, and trying to get chosen by Tsarevich over the other one.

The question was why was Gail Culbertson trying to hide that she was Chad's mother and coach?

"Yes. My son was out for more than a year following foot surgery. Tsarevich has made medal winners out of returning skaters. Ken is trying to get in his stable."

"But aren't you worried?"

"Worried about what?" I asked.

"Well, Tsarevich has a reputation, I've heard. If I were a male skater's parent, I think I'd be worried."

"Are you saying—?"

"I wouldn't want to say anything. But it's no secret that he dominates his male skaters—beyond the training aspects. Look at Miles Stinson and Avery Adams, for instance. Both skaters he coached. I'm just saying . . . well, beware the coach, I guess I'm saying."

"And both of them were coached to international medals," I said. So, that was her angle. Scare my son off with rumors of homosexual domination to give her son free sailing with Tsarevich.

"Yes, but at what cost down the road, one wonders," she said, and then immediately moved on. "Look at that other skater. Wasn't that the most elegant triple axel you've seen? He's such a stylish skater."

"Yes he is," I answered. And indeed her son's skating was elegant. But the jump was slightly underrotated. If his current coach couldn't see that and get it corrected, he never would be able to come back. It wouldn't bother Tsarevich at this point, of course. If he chose Chad, it's exactly the sort of shortfall he'd believe he could correct. The situation with Chad screamed of needing someone other than his mother to coach him. Someone other than Tsarevich, though, if I could do anything about it. Beware the coach was right. I was savvy enough to beware of Coach Culbertson, and she needed to beware of coach Wilton too—of me, Ken's coach, Jim Wilton.

"Well, just keep what I said in mind—and what's best in the long run of life for your son," Gail said, as she heaved a big sigh and started to move away, heading for the exit. What she had intended to do, she probably thought she had done— to lay uncertainties and concern.

Except that I wasn't buying. Ken and I already had our strategies in hand.

"Yes, thanks. You've been very helpful," I said to her as I watched to ensure that she was headed for the exit of the ice skating arena and didn't appear to have any more arrows in her quiver to release on this visit.

* * * *

"Mr. Wilton," Chad said, in surprise, when he came out of the showers.

I had waited for this moment on purpose—to get him in an awkward position, with just a towel around his waist. And I was amused to see that it was tented. The sound of men having sex in a room off the male figure skaters' locker room was unmistakable to me. I trusted that Chad could hear it too as he was taking his shower and that it had had an effect on him. He might even have jacked to the sound—or at least fantasized to it—while he was in the shower. His eyes were flashing like he was turned on.

Or maybe they just flashed when they saw me. I don't know any reason why they wouldn't. I was known as a handsome—even a sexy Mediterranean aspect—man and I kept in top shape. Forty-five had proven to be a good age to appeal to these younger male figure skaters: men of maturity and solid bodies and sexual experience. I had almost laughed in Gail Culbertson's face for her innuendo about Sergey

Tsarevich's demands on his male skaters. I fuck all of the male skaters I coach too, except for my son, Ken. Tokyo is just too far away from the States for a reputation like that to take hold.

"You know me?" I asked. So, his mother, Gail, hadn't clued him in on her strategy of pretending not to know me. I invaded his space more than one normally would do for a young man wearing only a towel and maneuvered him up against a massage table. I didn't want him uncomfortable as much as aroused.

"Yes, you're Ken's father," he said. "And a skating coach in Tokyo. I saw you sitting by Takio Koneshi this year when he took silver at the Grand Prix of Japan—and then the silver again in China."

"I watched you out there practicing just now," I said. "You've become quite an elegant skater. Too bad you came here for nothing."

"What do you mean?" Chad asked.

"You're not going to be taken on by Sergey Tsarevich."

"I'm not? How do you know that?"

"You can hear it yourself. I'm sure you knew what Tsarevich would want from you—would take from you—if he took you on. But you've come too late. He takes only one 'come back' skater a year. Come, let's take a peek in the room next door."

When we had, Chad was downcast. It was easy for me to maneuver him back to the massage table.

"You are good, though, far better than before your injury time out."

"Do you think so?"

"Yes. You deserve to be back on the circuit. You're that good. Well, with a few minor corrections of your technique."

"What do you mean, minor corrections?"

"Your jumps. Most of them aren't completely rotated. You have the ability to be in the air long enough to do it; you just won't be receiving full credit. You come down sooner than you should. And you don't get your ass down nearly enough in the sit spin." I had used that example on purpose, as it gave me a chance to touch his ass—and to leave my fingers there, on top of the towel. He either didn't notice or didn't object,

205

because he didn't pull away. The shudder I sensed in his body suggested that he knew I was touching him there.

"Your current coach hasn't noticed those minor flaws?" I asked.

"No, she hasn't," he said, the concern clear in his voice. He was following me.

"You do deserve a higher-level coach. I think I might be able to help you."

"You can? Maybe you could coach me to work out these flaws?"

"Better than that, you know who Sandra Elerby is, don't you?"

"Oh, shit, yes. She's coached dance teams to the worlds."

"She does singles as well. And she's top notch at dance moves. You already have elegant lines and the start of really good presentation skills. That's my specialty too, but she would be great with it."

"Well . . . but—"

"And she's here, in Colorado Springs. She's up at the Broadmoor Hotel, at the Ice Skating Hall of Fame, for a meeting. I know her. I could take you up there."

"You could. You say I have elegant lines."

"Yes, certainly. You have become a hard-bodied man since your injury. You had some body fat before and you've grown taller. Here, let me show you. Your shoulders and biceps are well defined now. Your chest is filled out—not overdeveloped—but distinct, sensual, sexy, even, to the audiences when your nipples are taut like they are now. It will earn you presentation points with the judges and applause from the audience that they won't even understand what they find so appealing. And your belly is flat, a sexy plate of hard muscle now."

He was panting slightly and trembling as, while I was pointing out this feature and that, I was running my hands over his body. And intent on learning and flattered and encouraged by what I was telling him, he was letting me feel him up.

"And your legs . . . here, let me hop you up on the table." I lifted him and set him down on the edge of the table. I returned my hand to his belly and used it to untie the knot in

206

his towel so that the towel fell away from his body. He was in full erection—but, then, so was I—but I said nothing at that point.

I continued with the foreplay that he was at least pretending was a professional assessment of the strong points of his body in terms of winning him points on the ice.

"Firm and strong thighs," I said, running my hands up the inner surface of both, gently coaxing them apart. He spread his thighs at my touch, and I fancied I could hear him sigh— which came in stereo as fucking was continuing in the adjacent room. "But not so muscled that they would come across as thick. You must do exercises to keep them perfect, just like this." I was taking and raising his legs, one after the other and gliding my hands up the calves and the thighs, back down and then up again. I let the legs come down, still spread, with my hands high up in the crease where the inner thigh met the groin. I let my thumbs move under his ball sack.

"Yes, you have elegant lines. With the right dance coaching and improved techniques, you will be a sexy bombshell on the ice. You're a sexy bombshell off the ice." I leaned into him and touched his forehead with mine.

"Coach," murmured. Not explaining, but not having to. His voice was full of need.

"And you'll nicely fill out a large cup," I said, grasping his cock, and feeling him tremble under me. "Despite your grace, you'll be seen as a manly skater. You'll have women spectators openly biased toward you—and some men secretly, as well."

"What . . . what . . . ?" he gulped. "What will you want for helping me?"

"I think you know what I want, Chad. I want the same thing I know you were prepared to do for Sergey to convince him to take you on. It's a question of how badly you want it. We both know you want it. We both know what else you want."

We held there for a good fifteen seconds, and when I moved my face down to kiss him, he closed his eyes and raised his face to mine. When I extended the kiss and enclosed his cock in both of my hands, he shuddered, but his half of the kiss became more intense.

Pulling out of the kiss, I murmured, "Your cock is hard, Chad. You are saying you'll give me what Sergey would have gotten, aren't you?"

"Yes," he said in a low, slurred voice.

"I am hard for you too. Unzip me, take it out, and stroke it to full hard."

As he did that, I fondled his balls with one hand and then instructed him, "Put your ankles on my shoulders and roll your hips up to me." I wetted the fingers on the hand I wasn't stroking his cock with and, as he rolled his hips up, moved my hand up under and beyond his taint and penetrated and worked his asshole with, at first one, and then two and three fingers.

"Oh, fuck, fuck, fuck me, coach," he murmured. He was moving his ass on my fingers. "Put it in me. Fuck me. Fuck me hard. Fuck me deep."

I took his mouth back in a kiss. His hands left my cock and he was gripping my sides hard and trying to pull me into his body. I handed my cock and moved it into position, rubbing it up and down his crease and across his hole, as he panted and his fingers opened and closed on my flesh.

"Fuck me. Stick it in me. Split me," he pleaded.

I moved the cock to where the bulb was at his entrance and pressed in, just enough to bury the glans.

"Yes," he cried out, arching his head back. I would have been worried they'd hear us in the other room, if Chad's voice wasn't overridden with declarations from the other room of "Yes, yes, yes. Like that. But deeper, harder. Fuck me harder! I'm gonna cum! Shit, you're gonna fuckin' split me in two!"

Once I had the bulb inside Chad, though, I stopped and held him in position. He was panting hard and whimpering. He would have let me bareback him—right here in a locker room where anyone could have walked in on us. If I had any question he would let me do whatever I wanted with him, that question was answered.

I pulled out of him and stepped back. "Not here. Not for what I want to do to you. My van's outside. We'll fuck with more privacy in my van. And we need a condom—or two."

He shuddered at the "or two."

"Then I'll take you to meet Elerby."

* * * *

Ken walked out of the shower, with only a towel around his middle, to find the coach, Sergey Tsarevich, standing there, arms folded across heavily muscled chest. He was wearing only skin-hugging tights and his bulge was one that confirmed legends, the tubing of the cock and the curve of the balls clearly discernible. The man was half hard.

So far, so good, Ken thought. The Russian had been right behind him coming into the locker room and had stood there, scrutinizing Ken's body as he undressed to go to the shower. And here he was, still in the locker room, after Ken had showered.

"I wish to speak to you," Tsarevich said. "Are you really Ken Wilton, the skater who started on the circuit five years ago and left for over a year after foot surgery?"

"Yes, of course. Why do you ask?" Ken said. He knew why the man asked.

"You don't look old enough to be on the senior circuit. If I didn't remember you from before I wouldn't believe it. What nationality are you?"

"You remember me from before? I'm interracial. My mother is Japanese; my father Spanish-American." Ken was encouraged. The man had known of him from before.

"Yes, I had my eye on you from your first skating at the lower ranks of the seniors. You had promise, but you needed work. I wanted you then. I may want you now."

Ken hoped that the want was for more than his skating. His father had told him in no uncertain terms what he'd have to do to get Tsarevich as his coach. He'd have to let Tsarevich seduce him. Tsarevich would have to want to seduce him. And then, Ken would have to keep the Russian interested to maintain his position in the man's stable and to get the training attention Ken would need to become a gold medalist.

"You have an androgynous look about you that we can exploit if I take you on. You must float in air, though, and you must have specialties that other men aren't doing—some that come over from the women skaters and some, perhaps that go back in time."

He was already planning how to package Ken. That was a good sign. It was time to grasp the man's sexual interest as well. As if it was an accident, Ken's towel dropped. He remained in position long enough for the man to get a good look at his fully naked body from the front—Ken had given the Russian more tease looks at him while he was stripping for the shower. Then, in fumbling for the towel, he turned to give Tsarevich a butt shot. He even managed as he pretended to struggle to pick up the towel to pull a butt cheek aside. The intake of breath from across the room assured Ken that Tsarevich had taken in the hard work Ken had been coached by his father to put into opening his hole with a thick dildo.

"Come into my office," Tsarevich said when the towel was back into place. "If you are to work with me, you will have to put yourself completely in my hands. I will assess your attributes and skills from the ground up, starting now. And I will only make my decision after a detailed assessment and after I'm completely satisfied that you are fully mine to form and use. Do you understand?"

"Yes . . . master."

Tsarevich, who had been preceding Ken into the room off of the men's locker room stopped, looked around, gave Ken a piercing look, and smiled. Score a point for Ken. The man had appreciated being called "master" rather than "coach."

"Give me that towel and go stand in the middle of the room. I am going to closely examine your body. There are strengths and weaknesses in a man's body that serve or hinder a skating style. If you come with me, I will give you a new style—one that goes with your ethereal beauty. You were technically not bad out on the practice ice, but your style is all wrong. It's too masculine and heavy. We will make you into a thing of beauty on the ice. A male Michele Kwan. Da?"

"Whatever you want." Ken said, standing, naked, in the center of the room, legs and arms spread a bit as Tsarevich glided over his skin and tested and prodded his curves and creases and his musculature. The man was lost in mutterings of what he liked and what he intended to correct and improve.

Ken got the distinct impression that Sergey liked more than he disapproved of. He was breathing heavily and his tights were seriously tented. Toward the end of the examination, Tsarevich peeled the tights off and threw them to the side. He ended his examination standing close to and in front of Ken. He was grasping Ken's cock with his hand. Ken was erect.

"If I take you on, your body will have to be sculpted in a perfect balance of visual perfection and function. As I said, you will float over the ice. Your jumps will be higher than any other man's in relation to height and you will rise into them effortlessly. Thus, your thighs will have to be perfectly formed to give you power without making them look fat. And flexibility. You will have to have flexibility approaching a woman skater's. I want you to do split jumps—not just full splits—to the four sides of the arena in one pass—which will be your signature move—but stag splits too—leaping toward the front like a stag with legs high off the ice and bent back and your arms raised in the air. No one does those two split moves anymore. You will make them gasp by doing them.

"And spins. Your sit spin will be lower to the ice than any other man's and you will do an ankle hold, leg straight up from your side, as Sasha Cohen did it, and at least a half Beallmann, catching your blade with your leg raised behind, if you can, or at least your calf. Do you understand? This conditioning will be very hard, but you will do it if I take you. And you will be a winner. Do you understand and accept?"

"Yes, master."

"And you understand that I will take you. I will fuck you. I will fuck you daily. Fucking in demanding positions will be part of your flexibility training."

"Yes, master."

"And I am going to fuck you now, before I decide whether to take you on."

"Yes, master."

"Let me check your flexibility" Perching Ken on the side of a massage table, Tsarevich grasped the young skater's ankles and manipulated his legs—first high above his head, pulling the young man's butt to the edge of the table, then folded up into his stomach. Lastly, he spread and raised the legs wide, moved in between them, thrust his cock inside Ken's

211

hole, as the young man jerked and gasped, and started to pump him. His mouth went to Ken's and they kissed deeply, as Ken threw his arms around the Russian's neck. Tsarevich creamed Ken's inside and Ken only then realized he'd been barebacked. His father had warned him of this, though, telling him that it was what the Russian would demand.

They held there for a few minutes, both panting. Ken felt the Russian going hard inside him again, though. Without further preliminary, the significantly larger and much more powerful Russian grasped Ken at the waist, pulled off the table, and rotated his body so that Ken was draped on Tsarevich's front, his head down to the floor—but at the level of the Russian's groin.

"Show me you can do the splits. Put your legs in the splits position." Ken complied. "Now suck my cock and do a good job of it." Ken complied. And he gasped and moaned and groaned as Tsarevich attacked his cock, balls, and hole with his mouth.

Tsarevich fucked Ken for several minutes from the back, his cock buried up in Ken's hole and his hands palming Ken's pecs, holding the young man's body close into his. Ken had an arm stretched back and around the Russian's neck, and they had their faces turned to each other in a kiss.

And then Tsarevich fucked Ken more athletically, with Ken suspended off to the side of a massage table, his arms behind him, supporting him on top of the table, and the Russian standing and facing him, holding Ken close into his body, with Ken's legs hooked on the Russian's hips, while the Russian fucked him in slow, deep strokes and the two watched the effect of what was happening to them in the other's eyes.

Then it was back to the Russian standing, with Ken draped in front of him, Ken's legs bent back to twist around the Russian's thighs, and Tsarevich immobilizing Ken's arms in a full Nelson hold.

Tsarevich creamed Ken's channel there, having fucked Ken bareback with the declaration that as long as he was being coached by the Russian, no other man would be inside Ken. Ken had already spent his load twice by that time.

The Russian laid Ken on the massage table again, saying, "You did well. Yes, I think I will take you on."

Ken didn't have much time to celebrate, though, because Tsarevich went on to say, "Before we fuck again, you must be hairless. There will be no hair on you other than on your head. We may keep the shoulder-length hair for the androgynous look. Or we may not. But the rest of the hair. It goes. I shave you now."

"Yes, master," Ken answered in a tired voice of surrender. "Anything you want to do to me."

It all got saved: pits, the dusting under the pecs and down to the belly, the pubes, the forearms and calves. Even the rim of his asshole. Tsarevich held Ken's cock as he shaved in the privates, and Ken ejaculated for the third time.

They were in their second fuck session when Jim Wilton and Chad Culbertson heard them from the locker room. Ken was standing sideways next to the massage table, his right leg raised and resting on the table, his body twisted around to the left, as the Russian, standing behind him and fucking him from behind had both hands clutching Ken's throat. The Russian was pounding him hard and deep.

"Yes, yes, yes. Like that. But deeper, harder. Fuck me harder! I'm gonna cum! Shit, you're gonna fuckin' split me in two!" Ken was crying out.

* * * *

I sat back on my haunches just inside the backdoor of my specially configured van and smoked a cigarette as I watched Chad Culbertson look at me with both fear and arousal in his eyes. I'd just finished eating out his ass and sucking his cock dry after tying him off. His hole was gaping open for me—and twitching. He wanted me inside him. His back was on a low, carpet-covered cube I kept in the back of the van for the purpose of putting a man's ass at a good angle for my penetration.

His arms were pulled over his head, with his wrists tied off on an anchor behind the front seat. His long, elegant legs were split straight out from his body, with his ankles tied to anchors on the side walls of the vehicle.

His ass was twitching, causing the dildo I had stuffed in his ass to wave at me. His ball gag was going to muffle any sound getting beyond the van walls where I'd parked it in a lot a quarter of the way up Pike's Peak, deserted at night because anyone would have to be suicidal to be tooling around the switchback curves of the top half of that mountain at night.

I had explained everything I was going to do. He had said he wanted it—that he'd do anything to get a coach who would put him on a winning track again. I'd even made him crown my cock with the condom. And I'd taken cell phone shots of him doing it. I wasn't going to get into the type of trouble Sergey was headed toward—not being able to approve that the skaters were willing to trade fucking for training.

Putting out the cigarette, my cock ready because I'd been jerking off while I smoked, I came off my haunches, crouched my way to him, grasped and spread his butt cheeks, pulled the dildo out, skewered him with my own hard cock, and pumped him vigorously to an ejaculation. Once inside him, I let loose of his buttocks and worked his cock with one hand and his nipples with the other, as he writhed as he could under me and did what he could to respond to me vocally through his ball gag.

After I gave him a rest from both of us ejaculating, I unbound him, but only to bind him again, belly down, with his nice long legs tied together around the thighs and calves and tied off at the anchor behind the front seat, his body inclined toward the floor of the van at the near end of the cube. His arms were stretched out to the side and tied off on the inner walls of the van.

Mounting his ass in reverse, I fucked him facing the front of the van. When I felt myself ready to blow, I pulled out of him, slipped the condom off, came around to his head, grabbed his hair and pulled his head up, relieved him of the gag, came on his face, and made him clean my cock with his mouth.

While I was fucking him, I made a decision. He wanted a higher level coach so badly that he was willing to do this. I would have liked to fuck him more conventionally and passionately, but I was testing him—testing how far he would go.

He apparently would go wherever a coach wanting to trade fucking for training wanted to go.

I felt bad. Sandra Elerby wasn't up at the Broadmoor Hotel. I had no idea where she was. I was going to dump him here on the mountain and let him find his own way back—arriving too late to undermine my son's campaign to sign with Sergey Tsarevich.

But I was being a heel. The guy wanted this chance so much. And he was good. He was really good. I hadn't been lying in any of the things I said he needed to correct—all minor—to be champion class—or at least a contender if he could stay on his feet during a program when it counted.

I sat and held him, both of us crouching on the cube, until he stopped trembling.

"I'm as good at what you need as Sandra Elerby is," I whispered. "You're good, really good. I can help make you great. You let me fuck you when I want to, I'll take you back to Tokyo and train and enter you without expense to you. What do you say?"

"Yes . . . master," he whispered back.

It wasn't disloyalty to Ken. I thought that Sergey could make Ken the gold medalist that Chad couldn't quite become. But I'd do everything I could to get him there. I'd make sweet love to him every day, and he'd be all the more advantaged to be half a world away from that bitch of a mother he had.

Fist of Gold

I think it was the rumble of the engines of the Air France S.O.30 Bretagne commercial airliner flying into African airspace, reaching out for a landing in Bamako, Mali, that brought up the memory as I dozed. Or maybe it was my returning to Africa for the first time since departing from Morocco for the Anzio Invasion eight years previously. Or the images surfaced by looking at the animated slender hands of the Italian businessman sitting beside me. Of maybe it was all three.

The rumble was reminiscent of the sound of the German tanks grinding by too close to us as we hid beside the narrow macadam Italian road. And the chatter was Tony, another GI of Italian origin, egging me on to rise from our hiding place when the tanks were abreast of us. "Come on, Lieutenant; they won't be able to see us from inside those tin cans," I heard him saying, waving his hands in front of me. The sound of someone standing in the aisle of the plane, opening and closing a briefcase in the overhead bin—snap, snap, snap—translated into the machinegun fire that mowed us both down.

After that I was in an entirely different world, a world of white and red and moaning and pain. A hospital ward in Naples. Of pain and more pain—in my thigh and torso and shoulder—and the maddening repeat of "You were the lucky one," when I damn well knew that Tony wasn't the lucky one if I was still alive and he wasn't. And of Miranda, the nurse, with smiles and encouragement, laughter, cheery English accent, and kisses and more when I regained my mobility. And of Tom, the orderly, understanding, flirting in his own way. The Australian Tom of the "No worries" at my involuntary hardening during the bed baths and massages. Tom of the slender, relief-giving hand. Tom of the magic hand and introduction of the closed, stretching fist.

"What river is that down there?"

"Excuse me?" I asked, coming out of my remembrance doze.

"Oh, sorry. Were you asleep?"

"Just dozing, and thinking of the past," I answered. "What did you ask?" He was a handsome man. Maybe in his forties. Dark and sensual looking, the graying sideburns only adding to his attractiveness. Trim, but well muscled, expensive Italian suit—and those slender, expressive hands with the long, groomed fingers. The hand with just the right breadth across the knuckles. He had a hand on my thigh as he leaned over to look out of the window. It was all so casually done, but it was as if he knew I wouldn't mind having it there—or higher even. It was as if he'd seen the magazine that had fallen out of my briefcase for just a moment—and perhaps he had. He either had or he was supremely self-confident—and forward. We had eyed each other as early as the departure lounge in Paris, and I'd felt a jolt of electricity go up my spine when I saw that we would be seatmates in first class, the seats here being wide and deep and having high backs that made each side section seem like a private cubicle.

"I asked if you knew what river that was down there."

"It's the Niger. We'll use it as a landmark as we fly into Mali and land at Bamako."

"Oh. Have you been here before? Do you have business in Mali? Sorry, my name is Antonio Corti. I'm a mining engineer. Here on business. My first time here."

"Kyle Kendrick," I answered. "I'm an archeologist, here to consult on a Mali Empire dig. And, no I haven't been to Mali before. I've rarely been to Africa—other than Egypt, of course, which I don't really think of as Africa, but which, of course, it is. I was in Morocco a few years past, though."

Why did it seem like I was chattering? It was as if I was nervous. Well I *was* a little nervous. We seemed to be in our own private capsule here, there was so much about him that was attractive to me, and it seemed like he was sending subtle signals that he felt the same. Slow down; take a breath, I admonished myself.

"The Mali Empire? There's history here?" he was asking.

"Oh, yes, there was quite a powerful empire here—based on the gold trade—for a good eight hundred years starting about 800 AD. Not my specialty. But my former professor at Oxford believes there are enough similarities between the Incas and what he's found here for me to be useful."

"Oxford? But you're not English, are you? Or French?" He was giving me a warm smile. He'd taken his hand off the top of my thigh, but it lay against the side of the thigh on the low console between us, the fingers spread out against my leg. I looked down at the hand, and so did he. He didn't take it away and I made no move to move my thigh away from it. I knew now for sure that he was signaling, and I strongly suspected he knew that I knew.

Who was to make the next move, I wondered. But then, when I didn't move my thigh away, I was signaling too, I suppose. I had made the next move by not moving my leg.

I smiled back. What can I say? He was a handsome man, with slender, expressive hands, slender enough across the knuckles. Even though Miranda and I knew the score between us and what both of our preferences were, when I was at her family's country estate in York and even more at the family townhouse in London, I was on a pretty tight leash. I was in the wilds of Africa now, and I'd come when Sir Geoffrey Bentham, my mentor at Oxford, had called because of what he had been to me and had initiated me in. Maybe, though, my expectations for when I reached Geoffrey were clouding my judgment of what was happening here, with this gorgeous man. Any questions there, though, weren't going to mean that I was going to back away from this moment. I had come for more of an adventure than consulting on an archeological dig on the banks of the Niger forty miles outside of Bamako.

I keyed in on this man's signals because I had been revved up for it since I'd received Geoffrey's letter of invitation.

The fingers of his hand spread and acquired more pressure. I moved my thigh into them, thus spreading my legs a bit. I looked at his hand again, then up into his face, and, finally, lowered my eyes, dipping my head a bit. A signal of submission. His grip tightened in recognition of my acquiescence. I moved my hand to where our fingers were touching. As far as I was concerned, the deal was struck. If he wanted me, I was his.

"No, I'm American," I belatedly responded to his question. "My graduate studies were at Oxford."

"Ah, American. I see that you have a cane and walked with a limp when you climbed the stairs into the plane. A war wound, perhaps?"

"Yes," I answered.

"Does it—?"

"It aches from time to time but it doesn't keep me from functioning in any way I want," I answered, anticipating the question. "In any way," I repeated.

"Good," he said, moving his hand to on top of my thigh. Again, I permitted him that intimacy. I looked around. The only way we could be seen was if someone was in the aisle immediately beside us and we'd been told there might be unexpected turbulence and to stay in our seats, if we could, with our seatbelts on. As I was in the window seat and in my seatbelt, I had the sensation of being under his control already.

My tolerating him resting his hand on my thigh was enough to signal that I'd permit him other intimacies, should the opportunity arise. He was signaling domination. He was a top. Again, I moved my hand there too, this time wrapping a finger around his middle finger. I couldn't get any clearer or more intimate under the circumstance—or so I believed—than that.

"I was in Southeast Asia—Thailand—for the duration of the war," he said. "I'm Italian, from Brindisi," he added.

We were conversing in innocuous terms on one level, but we were already fucking on another level. But even the words we were exchanging were a probing. He was fucking my mind.

He wanted me to know he wasn't in Europe for the war. The Italians were Axis; the Americans were Allied. I didn't want to tell him that I'd been in the Italian campaign, marching from the tip of the peninsula, at Anzio, as far as the monastery at Monte Cassino, before I was wounded and taken to Naples, where my war ended. We had bombed the shit out of Monte Cassino, an Italian historical treasure. He wouldn't want to know that. I wanted him only to hear of my softness, my openness, my willingness for him to enter me—deep to my core. I picked up the hand he had laying on my thigh and gently squeezed the fingers together with my hand, running my fingers over the span of the knuckles. A new level of enquiry on my part.

Another signal—a very special signal. I wondered if he would recognize it and would still be interested. Not every man was. Few men were willing to do this service, even if, in my case, it greatly enhanced passion.

"You have very nice hands," I said. "Slender. I'll bet there is less than a nine-centimeter span from knuckle to knuckle." That would be no more than three-and-a-half inches in American and British terms. I looked into his eyes, wondering again if he would pick up on, correctly interpret, and respond to the signal.

He smiled back. "Yes, I believe the span is no wider than that. I can make that useful . . . for someone who has such a wish."

He already knew he could fuck me. We were exploring other possibilities now. None of what we were exploring, even if we had to pull back, meant that he couldn't fuck me.

"Yes," I said, still stroking his knuckles, "I believe the span is no wider than that. I can make that useful."

I gave him a sharp look. He knew exactly what I was talking about. "I believe you must be a very rare young man," he said.

"Who is always on the look for other such rare men," I responded.

When I put his hand back, it was on the inside of my thigh and I closed my thighs on it. He left it there, opening and closing his grip on the inside of my thigh rhythmically. My legs started to tremble to his touch, and they gave out on me, falling open, surrendering to him.

"May I?" he asked. He was turned in his seat toward me, both giving me his full attention and obstructing any view of our laps from the aisle.

I didn't make any form of negative gesture.

Boldly, he coaxed my legs wider, pulling my left leg over to on top of his thighs. He moved his hand to my crotch, tracing the line of my hard cock, gripping me there, returning to opening and closing his grip, but this time directly on my cock through the material of my trousers.

"Give yourself to me. Put the seat back," he murmured to. "Relax. Don't fight me. Close your eyes. Concentrate on your core, on the pleasure you feel there."

I did put the seat back and closed my eyes, but it took a few minutes for me to relax as he continued to feel me up. Involuntarily, my own hand went to his crotch, feeling him there, albeit not nearly as intimately as he was fondling me. He too was hard—and massive. I clutched the hardness I could feel.

I filled to where he could grip the shaft and slow stroke it. "Nice," he murmured. "Very nice. Thick and long. Relax and let it harden. Think of us alone, in my hotel room." His thumb found my bulb and he rubbed me there. I moaned softly.

"Relax. Let it go," he whispered in my ear. "Give yourself to me. Don't hold back. We can take longer later." With a jerk, I came inside my briefs. He knew I had; the wetness had come through the material of the trousers, although it would dry and not be noticeable when we deplaned. He rubbed his thumb on the wet spot and thus on my bulb still and I continued to leak cum for several long, sighing seconds. He gave my crotch a pat, pulled his hand away, and I opened my eyes to see him smiling with his thumb in his mouth.

He straightened up in his seat and continued talking in a conversational tone just as if we hadn't just had sex, just as if he hadn't brought me to and past a climax. He lifted my hand off his crotch and set it down on my thigh, as I pulled my seat back into an upright position.

But we *had* had sex—or at least he'd brought me to having had sex. And we both knew that if he wanted to have sex again, I would give in to him—that he would take his pleasure from me in more taxing ways. He moved immediately into establishing that we would meet In Bamako for sex.

"Are you staying at a hotel in Bamako or heading directly to your dig?" he asked.

What could I do except take his lead and act like what had happened hadn't? "I'm being met," I answered. "I have been given the option of staying the night in Bamako, though, and am tentatively booked at the Le Grand Hotel."

"Aren't we all?" Corti asked, with a winning smile. "Do stay the night in Bamako. I'm sure you'll find it very satisfactory. You're an unusually handsome young man. I'm sure you will find the servicing at Le Grand quite satisfying. Perhaps we could take dinner together if you didn't have other plans."

He'd called me a young man. He had me at that. It perhaps was for no other reason than I was within two months of losing my youth—turning thirty—that I was answering Geoffrey's call to come to him in Mali. I was scared of what I would become after thirty. I'd always been the desirable, handsome young man. What was there after thirty?

"Dinner would be very pleasant," I answered, trying to keep my speech nonchalant but still trembling inside, "if my reception party doesn't insist I go out to the camp tonight."

"Ah, tonight," Corti said, giving me another sunny smile. He leaned into me and whispered. "You must stay in the city tonight. I know you now. Tonight we will know each other totally. And you will have my fist if that is what you want. I am an expert in the art of pleasuring men with the fist, I think you'll find. I can prolong your pleasure as long as you can take it." I shuddered as his hand moved up to brush my basket, which made me yearn for his touch, and then he pulled it away, both of us seeing the stewardess starting down the aisle to announce that we were preparing to land in Bamako.

Corti helped me descend the stairway onto the Bamako tarmac, his support as much hindrance as help, but I sensed that he wanted to demonstrate possession by having an excuse to put an arm around my back, and, as long as I would get what I wanted out of him, I could feel the arousal of being the submissive. I allowed him to manipulate me rather more than I needed. The intimacy kept me hard. I already was hard.

Geoffrey had written me that I wouldn't have any trouble identifying the reception party at the airport, and he was right. He'd already told me that he'd hired Mandinka tribesmen for the dig because of their long association with the area and an unbroken line of connection with the Mali Empire. I'd looked the name up to discover that, along with the Masai of Kenya, the Mandinka were the tallest peoples on earth, ranging up to seven feet tall. Two ebony men, looking very dignified and swathed in cloth, stood head and shoulders above everyone else in the reception hall. I knew even before I saw the sign with "Kendrick" on it that the taller of the two— reaching possibly six feet ten inches—was holding up that they had come for me.

They were handsome creatures in their own way. Seemingly beanpoles, with elongated features, until you stood next to them and found that they were as muscular as most men—just that everything was stretched out. And clean. I had thought of them as being covered with dust, but their bodies were pristinely clean and glowing with health.

The taller of the two, and obvious leader, identified himself as Tejon Darany. He was quite dignified of carriage— and reserved, although perfectly civil. He spoke impeccable English. His French also probably was impeccable, but since mine wasn't, I couldn't assess him on that. The other, shorter—if something around six feet eight could be considered shorter—and younger man was identified only as Modibo. He spoke no English and only broken French, so our exchanges were awkward, brief, and rare. He obviously was under the wing of Tejon, as he looked to the older tribesman in all matters and only shyly at me. Of the two, he was the more handsome in Western terms, but these two men were so exotic that I couldn't think of them in Western terms.

Tejon didn't seem the least bit upset when I told him I wanted to extend my touch with Western civilization by spending my first night in Mali at Le Grand Hotel. He said that he and Modibo had places they could stay and families they could happily visit that evening, and, with very little other verbal exchange, he drove me to the hotel in a dusty Land Rover and said they would pick me up there at 10:00 the next morning.

* * * *

I was huffing and puffing—but in seventh heaven, albeit its pain wing—as Corti's knuckles rubbed against the rim of my ass entrance. He'd taken several minutes getting to this point, aided by gobs of the vegetable grease lubricant I had gotten from a market near the hotel. We were both naked and stretched out against each other on my hotel bed—on rubber matting I'd also found in the market.

Corti's body was beautiful, which speeded my arousal, and his quick erection indicated he was pleased with mine, as well. He had the olive skin of Mediterranean climes and was covered with an arousing pattern of curly black hair that swirled around his nipples and descended into his neatly trimmed pubic bush. The curly hair covered his forearms and thighs as well and curled in his pits, also neatly trimmed. Everything about his body spoke of grooming to accentuate his beauty. His body was thick and muscular, more of a Zeus than an Apollo—promising the experience of a mature man. And experienced he was; he didn't bat an eye about giving me the servicing and release that I sought. He knew what to do and how to give me the most pleasure from it.

He had started slow, sensually, running his hands over my body as we lay stretched out against each other when we were naked. He kissed and fondled my body, spending considerable time on the puckered bullet wounds on my thigh, torso, and shoulder. He wanted to know the circumstance of them, but of course I couldn't give him the specifics, so, instead, I murmured, "I want you to fuck me and then give me what I want. Then I'll give you whatever you want. Don't make me wait."

He didn't make me wait. His hands went to my thighs, coaxing them apart, pressing my legs to bend, my feet to go flat on the surface of the bed, and my pelvis to roll up, as he entered me with three fingers—I ached for more—and he gave me another one. Using the four bunched fingers, he slowly pumped me to a state of shuddering and begging for more.

"All in good time," he murmured. "I can't hold any longer for now, though." He pulled the bunched fingers out of me as I gasped at the loss of them, rolled over on top of me, entered me strongly, deeply, thickly and took me quickly and efficiently. At the crucial moment, he held, straining, and then relaxed and emitted a long sigh in the flow of his seed. He tensed again and ejaculated again. Then a third time. All that time, I held, also tensed, my fingernails buried in his shoulder blades, my mouth slack, feeling and reveling in every spurt of the cum of a supremely virile dominator.

"That was good, very good," he murmured. I beamed in the light of his approval.

"A few moments and I'll give you all that you want. Then I will take all that I want." I shuddered and moaned in anticipation.

After we had rested, he held me close into his body, with a towel-covered bolster under the small of my back, which elevated my pelvis. My right leg was bent and pressed into his chest. His left arm was embracing my torso; his lips were possessing mine in a tongue-down-the-throat kiss. I was gripping his left shoulder with my right hand and beating myself off with my left. He had four fingers and the thumb of his right hand inside me, moving them in and out, searching for, finding, and giving attention to my prostate.

He asked no question about what to do to arouse and please me. He'd obviously fisted men before.

"Please be careful," I murmured. "I want it, but I have my limits."

"Limits we must both respect and challenge," he whispered, "for therein lies the pleasure for us both. My ultimate pleasure is knowing that I've given you maximum pleasure." He pulled his hand back and then pressed in again. I arched my back and moaned.

"Yes, yes. More. All of it."

I jerked my mouth away from his, arched my head back, and gave a little cry of "Shit!," then "Fuck!" and then another and another cry, each more dirty, unguarded, expressive of being fully serviced, as the knuckles of his slender hand breached my rim and his fist was inside me and bunched to stretch my passage to the limit. He expanded and contract the fist, a knuckle pressed into my prostate. Expand, contract. I dug my fingernails into his biceps. "Oh, god," I moaned. He stifled further exclamations and sobs by taking my lips in his. Expand, contract. I involuntarily tried to pull away from him, but he held me too tightly. Expand and move a fraction deeper. I tore my mouth away from his, arched my head back, and cried out to the ceiling. "Oh, fuckin' shit!" I shot my load, and he pulled his knuckles back out of my ass almost immediately. He had known exactly what to do to give me the maximum pain-pleasure in my ejaculation.

And he knew when the overwhelming pain would flow back in unless he prevented it.

He held me there, in his arms, holding my eyes with his. "Is that the way you want it?" he murmured.

"That was . . . it," I whispered, being at a loss for what to say, feeling both completely worn out and satiated. Never had I been so much on the edge, crossing into the divine, as with that. He was a master of the art.

"Well, here it comes again," he growled, holding me tight, as I writhed under him and began to pant in response to the pressure of the fist.

Afterward, we kissed deeply again, and when he pulled away from me, he murmured, "And now may I take my full pleasure of your body?"

"Of course," I responded. "I think I am too weak to resist anything you do now anyway." I laid back, fully prone on the bed, my arms outstretched.

He laughed.

"Are there any limits now to what I can do with you?"

"Try me," I answered, pulling my feet up prone on the bed under my bent knees at the nudging of his hands and raising and rolling my pelvis up with just the touch of the palm of his hand at the base of my spine. My legs were spread wide, and I gripped my buttocks and spread them—completely open to him now—as he rose, turned, and pressed his knees in between my thighs.

He did try me and test me and completely master me— fucking me effectively, efficiently, totally, and exhaustingly into the dark of the night. He made me feel young and flexible again. He pumped me and seeded me incessantly, again and again and again.

Throughout the night I lay there, completely open to him, soft at the core and vulnerable, taking the cock deep, hard, vigorously when he wanted to completely dominate me and bucking with him as we came close to climaxes. He murmured constantly that I was giving him all that he wanted, which was only right. He had given me all that I wanted.

Before he left in the first streaks of light before dawn, he told me how long he would be in Bamako and where he could be reached.

"If it becomes convenient, I would like to use you again," he said.

"I would like that too," I responded. Normally I would think that his choice of "use" was a translation problem, but he had, in fact, used my body as a vessel of his methodical, efficient lust, and I had come countless more times—to where my balls ached at the total draining and demand for fresh production—for him before he was finished. That he had used my body seemed to be a perfect description that I could not object to or complain about. I had certainly used his hand to get myself off on. Everything after that was icing on the cake.

* * * *

"I didn't see your dig reported anywhere. And I looked in a lot of media sources for it."

It was evening and we'd had dinner out under the stars. It looked like we were going to be doing a lot of things under the stars. There were tents, in two circles, but except for the communal tents and Sir Bentham's, they didn't look too commodious. We—Geoffrey Bentham; his French colleague, Perrin Tolbert; and I—were sitting around a fire pit in the circle of our tents and the communal ones. The Mandinka workers were in the circle of tents that intersected our circle at a tent assigned to Tejon Darany. Tejon and Modibo were still in our circle, passing out after-dinner drinks and cigars. The rest of the Mandinka were in their circle. Drums were softly playing, matched by low chanting by male voices. Some of the tents were lit up internally, casting shadows through thin material of what was inside. All very atmospheric. I was in Africa. The sky overhead was a cobalt blue, the stars seemingly suspended just a few feet over our heads.

"I should hope to God you didn't see mention of this dig—or tell anyone you're coming here," Bentham blustered. "This is really hush hush. There are few in the Mali government who know about it either."

Bentham was sitting within fondling distance of me, which I sort of expected him to have gotten around to doing before now. He was my dominating top when I was at Oxford after the war. And he was a power top with perhaps the biggest dick in England. He had to fist me just to be able to screw me later.

But I had to admit that the last five years, since I'd seen him last, hadn't been kind to him. He was gaunt and looked emaciated. And he had a wildness about his eyes and spoke more rapidly than I'd known him to do before—like he was on borrowed time. How old would he be now, I wondered. Funny that I hadn't wondered about that when we were together in Oxford. He'd said a few times then that he was twice my age. But now it seemed like maybe that was off, like he was more than twice my age. He looked well into his late sixties now.

But then, maybe he was waiting for the others—the Mandinka servants and his colleague, Tolbert—to leave us before he became intimate with me.

"So, what is it about this dig that's so secret and important, Geoffrey?" I asked. "I trust that, since it's close to the river, the site is buried."

"Tejon, go fetch the treasure box, please. Then you and Modibo may retire," Bentham said. Then he turned to me. "You've heard of the writer named Rihlah, haven't you, Kyle?"

"I believe so. The Arab who traversed northern Africa early in the fourteenth century and wrote of his travels."

"The same. He wrote of a Temple of Kongoba, but although there is a village by the name—just over the hill there—no one but he wrote about a temple."

"And you have found the temple site?"

"The site, yes, I'm sure I have. But I don't think it actually was a temple. More of a storehouse. I don't think the

Malian guides leveled with him when he asked what the edifice was."

"Storing what?"

"What is Mali famous for? What was its leading trading good during the Mali Empire? Do you know?"

"You think that gold was stored at this Kongoba site?"

"Not was. Is. Ah, thank you, Tejon. I'll just show our colleague here what we have and then you can take it back."

Bentham opened the rectangular box that was more than a foot long and took out a solid gold rod. It was nearly a foot long, an inch and a half wide up the base, and a good three inches or more at the bulb.

"A dildo?" I said, with a laugh. "Is this a supersized phallus?"

"A dildo perhaps," Bentham said, smiling, "but look again. You of all people should recognize what it is."

I drew in my breath. It wasn't a phallus at all. It was a stylized arm rising up into a fist.

"Is that . . . ?" I asked, with a stammer.

"Yes, I believe this is an ancient dildo in the form of an arm and fist," Bentham said. "Tejon thinks so too. There are rituals among the Mandinka that go back to that era. They are, as you can see, an outsized race—outsized in nearly every way. Many of their rituals were sexual. Thank you, Tejon. You and Modibo can retire now."

I watched the two, swathed in billowy cloth, walk to Tejon's tent. Bentham had said they were outsized in every way and my mind was savoring what that could mean. Not in every way, I would have said. As with all men, I had assessed the knuckle span of both of the Mali tribesmen when they had met me at the plane. Both had slender hands and were within my tolerances.

This, of course, increased my interest in both of them.

I watched them go into the tent and one of them light a lantern that illuminated the interior of the tent, making a form of shadow play for we voyeurs as their figures moved about the tight space, both of them having to bend over for head clearance.

"Where did you get the gold object?" I asked. I thought it would be unprofessional to refer to it as a dildo, although that quite obviously was what it was—a fisting dildo.

"Where do you suppose? Right here, where we're digging. This could be from the golden trove of the Mali Empire." He had put his arm around me, and a hand went to my thigh. I looked over at the Frenchman, and he was watching us. "I wanted to share this discovery with you, Kyle," Geoffrey said, and then he brought my head in for a kiss.

Tolbert had his eyes on us but didn't flinch. Of course he would have been told what Bentham and I had been to each other. For a fleeting moment I wondered if Geoffrey wanted Bentham to have me too—if there was some sort of deal between them for Bentham's presence here at the dig.

I opened my lips to Geoffrey. I wouldn't deny him anything he wanted of me. He was my mentor, my first serious lover. A man with a cock that filled me to near bursting. A man who knew how to use his fist.

"I've missed you, Geoffrey," I whispered when he'd released my lips and I'd immediately kissed him back to signal total submission. He moved his hand to my basket. I was happy to be able to show him that I was hard for him.

"How is it with Miranda?" he asked gently.

"Oh, you know Miranda. It's much like always. Affectionate in public. Beyond that, you'd have to ask Veronica."

"She's still with Veronica?"

"Yes," I answered. I didn't have to guard my voice from bitterness. I was glad Miranda had someone and mostly left me alone.

"And you, Kyle. Who are you with?"

"I'm with you at the moment," I said.

"I meant back in England. Have you not found someone else? Someone who takes care of your needs?"

"No one measures up to you, Geoffrey," I answered, knowing he would know what I meant as well as I did.

"It pains me to hear you say that, Kyle."

"I'm sorry. What do you mean by that?"

"I'm old and I'm sick, Kyle. I couldn't get it up anymore no matter what drug I took. I was hoping that you had found someone who satisfied you. I didn't want you coming down here thinking that that was why I sent for you."

A man who satisfied me? I was satisfied last night. But that was just a transient Italian. Neither one of us talked about anything that wasn't fleeting and casual. And damn right I'd come down here expecting more—expecting what I'd gotten before—from Geoffrey Bentham. Why else would I come to a place like Mali?

"I asked you to come down so that you could be in on this find with me—so that you could benefit from it. It's all I can leave you, Kyle. But I invited Perrin down too. I think you'll enjoy him."

Ah, so I wasn't off the mark.

I looked over at the Frenchman. He indeed was a hunk. Maybe thirty-five. Old enough to control and teach me a move or two. But I had looked at his hands earlier in the evening. I always look at the hands of a man who attracted me. The two Mandinka tribesmen, Tejon and Modibo had elongated, slim hands, in keeping with the elongated nature of the rest of their bodies that I had viewed. The Frenchman's hands were broad, at least four, maybe more, inches across at the knuckles. I could never . . .

But then, at Geoffrey's signal, Tolbert was bringing his chair over close to mine, on the other side from Geoffrey. Also at this point, I realized that there was something going on in Tejon's tent. The two figures, made quite clear in silhouette by the lantern light, were standing close together. They just now were pulling the last of the billowy cloth off each other's bodies. They looked like stick figures, even though I knew they both were well muscled. They seemed to be moving to the rhythm of the drums and the chanting of the other tribesmen in the other circle too, and I realized that the tent would be as much a shadowbox from the other side as from this one.

The two came together in an embrace and a kiss and then Modibo's body—identifiable because he was shorter—arched back and Tejon went down on his knees, while supporting Modibo's body in standing with hands gripping the young native's buttocks. It was clear that Tejon was giving Modibo head and helping him to remain steady even though arched back, his palms on the dirt floor behind him.

It was equally clear that Perrin Tolbert, bent over my lap, had unbuttoned me, taken my cock out, and was giving me head. Geoffrey had an arm around me and was unbuttoning and releasing my shirt with the other hand. He sucked on my nipples while Tolbert sucked on my cock. I raised my leg and hooked it on Tolbert's shoulder to signal acceptance, compliance, complicity. Tolbert was going to fuck me while Geoffrey watched, and I was going to comply.

Was this some sort of double ritual, I wondered. But I was too taken up with it to wonder much.

Geoffrey leaned down and pulled my shorts and briefs off my legs.

"You and Perrin are going to enjoy each other," he whispered.

"Yes," I replied.

Modibo was on his back on a cot and for the briefest moment I saw the shadow of a monster cock in length standing straight up from his groin. And standing over him, stroking an even larger one, was the shadow of Tejon.

Geoffrey and Perrin manipulated my body to where my crotch was lying across Geoffrey's lap and my head was in Perrin's lap, where he was offering me a quite large cock to suck. I managed to turn my face while I sucked, though, to where I could watch the shadow scene in the tent.

Tejon wasn't fucking Modibo—at least not yet. Modibo's left leg was on Tejon's right shoulder and his right leg was bent. His pelvis was raised off the leverage of his right foot, and Tejon's left arm was extended down to Modibo's pelvis. He was fist fucking Modibo. The music from the other circle was becoming more frenetic.

I could feel Geoffrey's fingers at my ass entry. They were heavily greased. He was working his hand into my ass.

"I'll give you what you want and then you'll give Perrin what he wants," Geoffrey said. "For now watch the shadow play."

I cried out as his knuckles breached my rim. My cry was accompanied by one in the tent, where Tejon must have gained his own entry. I panted hard and sucked hard on Tolbert's cock as Geoffrey started to move his hand inside my ass. Expand, release. Expand, release. Working me almost as expertly as the Italian had.

Then I saw in the tent that Modibo was holding up an object in his right hand. It was the Fist of Gold Geoffrey had shown me earlier. His left hand came out of Modibo's ass, and the right arm went down. I watched the gold fist enter Modibo and the young native writhe, crying out as it rhythmically fucked him. I writhed and cried out as Geoffrey fist rhythmically fucked me too. Expand, release.

Modibo and I came nearly simultaneously and the music in the tribal circle beyond stopped abruptly and Geoffrey withdrew his hand. The light went out in the tent. I saw no more, as Tolbert rose from his chair, pulled me up, threw me over his shoulder, and marched me to my tent.

I was exhausted, completely spent.

In my tent, Tolbert threw me down on my back on my cot, slapped my legs apart, and came down between them. He thrust his huge cock into my ass, reached up to grab my wrists and force my arms over my head, latched his lips on mine, and banged me hard into heaven and the next day.

Geoffrey stood at the open flap entrance to the tent and watched Tolbert and me rutting like barnyard animals.

* * * *

"Are you all right?" Geoffrey was looking at me over his glasses the next morning as we ate at a table by the fire pit, the embers of which still glowed red under the gray ash. "I hope that last night wasn't too—"

"I only wish that it had been just you and me. It was OK because you put me in the mood before Tolbert fucked me."

"I've done what I can by you, Kyle," Geoffrey said. "I can't help it if there's not much I can do anymore. I'm afraid not being able to get, let alone sustain, an erection has completely stifled my libido. I can only approach feeling sexual pleasure in watching others now. I did obtain pleasure from watching Perrin fucking you last night. You took him splendidly."

233

"I was happy to please," I said, taking a big bite of the fried eggs Modibo had cooked up for us.

"You wore poor Perrin out. He is still snoring away in his tent. You certainly pleased him."

"I was more concerned with pleasing you. I wanted to see you get better results from stroking yourself. I was performing with the Frenchmen for you. I'm sorry it didn't happen. You had gotten half hard, I could see, with the little ritual Tejon and Modibo performed in the tent."

"Yes, that almost did it for me. I would like to do it one more time before I die."

"You sound morose about that. Surely you're not dying, are you? I know you don't look well, but—"

"Yes, Kyle. I'm afraid I am dying. I've been given just a few more months. I'm not sure I can hold on even that long."

"Then why this?" I asked after a few moments of silence to process his news. I couldn't get all weepy, though; I knew he wouldn't want that. He was a man of reality and acceptance. "Why spend your last few months here in the Mali Savannah rather than at Oxford, among those who respect and will honor you?"

"You mean other than having the pleasure of watching Perrin breed you so masterfully? I doubt that's something I wouldn't see in Oxford."

"It's there," I answered. "You fucked me better than that when we were both in Oxford. There are others doing it there now, I'm sure."

"Oh, do you think so? I like to think we were the last of the superior Oxford fuckers. But seriously, I've never felt so alive as in the bush, at an excavation. I want to feel alive right up until I die. I've always felt bad about you, Kyle—about taking advantage of you and using you—and developing that fetish you have. Not being able to come without the fist before penal penetration. I believe if I just hadn't—"

"You liberated me, Geoffrey, and taught me how high into ecstasy I could go." "Penal penetration." I could have laughed if he hadn't just given me such bad news. He always was the scientist. Only when he was in high heat could he drop that veil and be a primeval man. I hadn't lied. He'd taken me with abandon when we were together in Oxford. And I had

234

been able to do that for him at one time too. I just wished I could do it for him one time more.

"And you did the same for me," he was saying. "I want to leave you with something—something tangible that will support you in life. I hate seeing you controlled as you are by Miranda and her family."

"I didn't exactly get kidnapped into the situation," I said. "I want to have a comfortable life with the means to do as I like. Miranda's leash is a long, loose one as long as I'm not in England, among her circle of friends. There she doesn't want me to embarrass her. She knew what I came here for. She was well rid of me for the time I'm here. There wouldn't be many of her friends streaming through Mali."

"Still, it's my concern I have to reach peace with, Kyle. That's why I want you here on this dig. It could set you up for life."

"Set me up for life? If there is gold here, what will we get beside recognition? This is Mali's gold."

"Some part of it, yes," Geoffrey responded, speaking carefully, deliberately now. "But if my calculations are correct, there will be more than enough for those in Mali who are in the know and for those involved in the dig as well."

"Surely, you're not suggesting—"

"We really need not go into this now," Geoffrey said, interrupting me and changing the subject. "I believe you enjoyed Tejon's show with Modibo last night as well as I did."

"Very much, yes," I answered. "If that hadn't been transpiring when you fisted me, I don't think I could have gone with Perrin Tolbert."

"Why is that?"

"The span of his knuckles. I can't consider a man with a span of over three-and-a-half inches. It doesn't really matter if he's just doing cock work. The fisting is too integral with it all for me. And It's just a matter of self-preservation with Tolbert. Just seeing how broad his hand is dampened my arousal for him. You mustn't give me to him again without the preparation of a tolerable fist."

"Ah, as I said, something I feel responsible for. You require a man with a big cock but a small hand. Difficult to come by."

"Nothing you should worry about, Geoffrey, and not all that difficult. There was an Italian on the plane coming to Bamako . . ."

"And how long had it been before that? And didn't you come here so eagerly because you thought I could give you relief?"

I didn't answer that. I turned to a sudden interest in what was left of my fried eggs.

"What happened in Tejon's tent last night . . ." Geoffrey said, ". . . did you not wish that was you under Tejon, taking his fist and the Fist of Gold and his enormous cock? Do you know he's nearly a foot long and those magic three-and-a-half inches in girth? Think of not just a bulge of that diameter inside you, but the whole length of a cock nearly a foot long filling your passage at that diameter."

"I must remember to tell Modibo that his eggs were delicious," I said, not being able to look at Geoffrey. Yes, of course, I wished that it was me with Tejon the previous night. Watching them while Geoffrey and Perrin worked me over was what set me up for being able to ride the Frenchmen's cock as wildly and for as long as I subsequently did.

"I think . . . I think I might have been able to reach an erection and maintain it long enough to have an ejaculation if it had been you under Tejon, Kyle." But then he sighed, murmured an, "Oh well."

"You want to watch Tejon fuck me? You think that may give you enough of an erection to fuck me too?"

"You put it so baldly," Geoffrey said.

"If it will give you release, I'll gladly do it," I said.

"We'll just have to see what transpires," Geoffrey answered, trying to sound breezy, but I could tell that my offer affected him deeply. Then he changed the subject. "Would you like to see for yourself the prospect of what can be found at our excavation? There's gold just below the surface. It's like it works its way up to us as we dig down to it. It wants to bask in the light of day."

"Yes, I'd like that very much," I answered.

"I'll have Tejon drive you over there. Modibo will put together a picnic lunch for you."

Tejon was coaxing me to raise my pelvis up with a hand cupping my right thigh, signaling for me to bend my leg and plant my foot on the ground under my bent knee to raise and roll my pelvis up. I knew what he wanted me to do and I did it. My left ankle was already hooked on his right shoulder. I knew why. His face was buried in the hollow of my neck. I knew he wouldn't kiss me there or on the lips. I knew this was primeval ritual, not affection, with him—unless it was affection for Geoffrey. He was slathering my ass with vegetable grease. I knew why. I knew what he was going to do. I was panting, afraid of it, but wanting it.

We were lying in some sort of animal's wallow next to a watering hole that had been carved out of a stand of elephant grass some six and seven feet tall, the stalks densely spaced, the stalks of the wallow underneath us. Carved out by some massive animal or animals—probably elephants; maybe rhinos. I had no idea whether either was native to this place. No one would know we were there unless they were flying low overhead or unless, like Geoffrey Bentham, they were crouching in the elephant grass, peering through it, watching and anticipating what Tejon was going to do to me. An enclosed world of just Tejon and me, panting, me moaning in anticipation. Geoffrey watching from behind a line of Elephant grass stalks, his heavy-hung cock out, being stroked, showing signs of life.

Tejon's freed shaft conjured up images of the elephant or the rhino, and I shuddered in anticipation of sheathing it. I knew I would be sheathing it.

I wasn't doing this just for Geoffrey. I would have submitted to this anyway, but if there was a chance for Geoffrey . . .

I cried out as Tejon entered me with four fingers, up to the knuckles. It wasn't just he and I panting now; Geoffrey was sucking heavy, ragged breaths in and out and had moved closer, just a few lines of stalks between him and the wallow.

Tejon's thumb was thrumming my rim. I knew what he was going to do. I felt him tuck the thumb in and apply pressure. My mouth opened wide in a silent scream and I arched my head up. Looking over at Geoffrey I could see his cock beginning to stiffen. I knew what Tejon was doing; Geoffrey knew what Tejon was doing. I tensed but then, at Tejon's command, relaxed and made a rumbling sound deep from within my belly when the knuckles breached the rim and his fist was inside me. I let out a long "Ahhhhh," as the fingers opened and he rubbed my prostate and inner walls with his fingertips. The fist expanded, contracted. Expanded, contracted.

A sucking noise and the feeling of profound loss as the fist pulled out of me and the drawn-out whimper as it pushed back in. Out and in. Fucking me with his fist. I knew what Tejon was doing to me. I was hard as a rock. It took great effort not to blow, but I worked at not doing so for fear that he would stop fucking me with his fist if I did.

I had known what was going to happen as early as back in the camp when I saw the facial expressions shared between Geoffrey and Tejon before Tejon drove us off in the Land Rover. I knew also because the box housing the Fist of Gold was laying on the backseat beside the picnic hamper.

He did take me to the dig first, and we did scrape the earth a bit. And nuggets of gold did come out of the earth. For all I knew they had been salted there to impress me and raise my enthusiasm. I needed neither. My thoughts were elsewhere—steaming ahead to where Tejon's fist and then his cock would be inside me. And the Fist of Gold as well.

Tejon had stripped down to a loin cloth to dig in the earth. The loin cloth left nothing to the imagination. He was longer and thicker than any man I had ever sheathed before—even Geoffrey. Again the image of an elephant or rhino. And he was only half hard as we dug, me down to my shorts as well. The looks he gave me told me all. The looks I gave him begged him to get on with it.

When it came time, there was no build up, no foreplay. No request. No permission given. No "will you?" or "I want." He simply walked over to me, put his strong hands on me, slung me over his shoulder, and carried me into the dense elephant grass. Five feet in and it was just the two of us in the world. Twenty feet in and he could have had his way with me, murdered me, of he wanted, and I'd be missing for all time. Forty feet in was the wallow and the edge of the watering hole.

He held me tighter and I opened my mouth in a silent scream again as he breached my rim with the thickest part of the Fist of Gold. I panted hard and let out little yip sounds as he fucked me, both shallow and deep, with the gold staff.

I looked over at Geoffrey, whose cock was lengthening and hardening, as, through slitted eyes and licked lips, he watched Tejon fuck me with the Fist of Gold.

When I couldn't take it anymore, I exploded, my cum arcing up onto my chest and Tejon trumpeting a tribal victory yell. He'd been chanting in the native tongue of the Mandinka all the while he was fucking me with the Fist of Gold.

It was a ritual with him—and because Geoffrey wanted him to. None of it was my choice with him. For some reason that heightened my arousal.

He extracted the staff, and I had the presence of mind to lower my left leg from his shoulder, place both feet flat on the matting of elephant grass stalks, the thighs as spread as possible, and my pelvis raised as high as possible to give him a straight angle for his entry.

I knew what came next. It's what came next in the tent shadow play. It's what I wanted to come next.

I tried to regulate my breathing, relaxing my channel as much as possible to be able to take him inside me. He came between my thighs on his knees and grasped and spread my butt cheeks with his hands. I howled in pain and ecstasy as he entered me with an erection that was every bit as long as the Fist of Gold and as thick all along its entire length as the thickest section of the Fist of Gold. Never had I been stretched this much by a cock. Never had a cock reached so far up my channel. I turned my head toward Geoffrey, not really being able to see him for the glaze descending over my eyes. My mouth opened wide for a long, rolling howl, as Tejon began to pump me, fucking me hard and at length to his own ejaculation that flooded my passage and oozed out of my hole.

As he withdrew, there was Geoffrey, displacing Tejon between my thighs, hard—hard enough to enter me and to fuck me in the lubricant of the heavy vegetable grease and Tejon's cum. He only managed to stay hard for a few moments of stroking and his ejaculation was weak, but he was crying with relief and joy when he jerked and seeded me.

He stayed inside me, flaccid, but still filling, and kissed my face, my mouth, my throat, and my nipples, muttering "Thank you, thank you" over and over again.

* * * *

True to his prediction, Geoffrey was dead within two months. But in that time he regularly arranged for Tejon to ravish my body with his hand, cock, and the Fist of Gold while Geoffrey watched, and twice more Geoffrey was able to harden enough to enter me and ejaculate as well. On his deathbed he declared that he was satisfied leaving life this way.

Before he expired we managed to recover a fortune for everyone in the know of the Mali Empire gold at Kongoba. More than half of it went to a selected number of Mali officials, who were helpful in getting my share and that of the Frenchman, Perrin Tolbert, out of the country. I have no idea where Tolbert went from there and what he did. He was a sexy man, but just too wide across the knuckles. Tejon and Modibo went in together on a café in Bamako. The other Mandinka workers were delighted to maintain silence for what they received, not knowing what a small amount it was compared to the total haul.

Geoffrey got a share of the take. There now is an extra mausoleum in the supposedly closed Holywell Cemetery, next to St. Cross Church, in Oxford, England. It seems that Mali government officials aren't the only ones who can be bought off.

I stayed for an extra month in Bamako after shipping Geoffrey's body off to England and sending Miranda a note on my plans to buy into an Incan civilization excavation, where we found some gold but nothing like what we found at the Kongoba dig. What kept me in Bamako and at the Le Grand hotel was the extended stay of the Italian mining engineer Antonio Corti. He loved making love to me with the Fist of Gold and the mood it put me in to gave him all that he wanted. He wanted his cock inside me too, fucking me hard and deep. As long as he gave me what I wanted, I lay there afterward,

240

open and vulnerable to him, soft at the core, surrendering to the want of his cock.

I left for South America satiated if sore and not walking straight—but with the confidence that the Incan and Mali Empires had been similar enough that I'd find some distant descendants of the Incas with slender hands and big cocks that would know exactly what to do with their hands, the Fist of Gold, and their cocks.

Misdelivered Mail Male Sex Training

Allen came to the window of his Maple Street bungalow and looked out at the driveway at the unmistakable sound of the purring of an expensive sports car. He had arrived in time to see Jack unfold his elegant six-foot-four frame out of the red Porsche Carrera convertible and run his hand through a thick mane of auburn hair with frosted highlights. The man was a real hunk from his Italian loafers sans socks; up through his tight designer jeans that were extra tight over his athletic thighs and bulging crotch; up to his casual, but cashmere and obviously pricey, polo shirt, which showed off his gym-honed pectorals to perfection.

Turning from his car, Jack saw Allen standing in the window, also quite handsome in dark, Mediterranean looks, if smaller of stature and a lot less wealthy in dress than Jack was. Allen's shorts and T were run of the mill, although they showed his body off to near perfection for his size. The most expensive item he was wearing was a red silk jock strap under the white shorts that, purposely, showed through the white of the shorts.

Jack smiled and waved and lifted a wine bottle in one hand—most likely an expensive wine, which they'd have for dinner before turning to beer later. As he'd done before, Jack made an O with the fingers of the hand not holding the wine bottle and, making sure Allen could see the gesture, pumped the neck of the bottle in and out of the O he'd created. Like, no one watching could miss what that meant. He laughed and headed for the door.

Allen didn't know why Jack always did this. They both knew Jack was here to eat Allen's steak dinner, watch Allen's TV, and fuck Allen's ass—in that order of priority. This was Jack's form of slumming. The two had met in a pickup game of soccer at a gay men's sports club. Jack had been the game's attention-getting superjock—until the smaller Allen had shown him up by deftly eluding him and going for a couple of goals. In a fit of pique Jack had cornered Allen afterward in a rarely used row of lockers separated by a bench and fucked the stuffing out of Allen to show him who was boss.

Since then Jack had come to Allen's bungalow on Maple Street nearly every other Sunday afternoon, eaten the steak dinner Allen provided, watched Allen's TV, and fucked Allen to, again—perpetually—show him who the boss was. If anyone had told Jack it also was because he liked fucking Allen's ass, he would have given them a blank stare.

It was no different this Sunday.

They talked a bit through the dinner Allen served at the table in the small dining area forming an L with the kitchen off the living room, but it was mostly about sports and Jack thinking of turning his last-year sports car in for this year's model. It occurred to Allen that he'd never been told where Jack worked and why he had all of this money—and why he kept coming back to eat Allen's steaks and fuck him. They had nothing in common really. Maple Street was literally on the wrong side of the tracks in this town. Jack could be the county judge for all Allen knew. He did know that Jack was at least four years older than his own twenty-three, but that didn't bother him. It just meant that many of Jack's reference points to life weren't the same as Allen's.

Neither had Jack asked what Allen did for a living and why he could afford to live even in a small bungalow like this on the wrong side of the tracks. Allen had inherited the bungalow from an Army officer—Allen's CO in Afghanistan. Afghanistan had been a scary and turbulent place, where one constantly didn't know if there would be a tomorrow and where men lived in combat situations closely with other men. The popular saying was that there were no atheists in foxholes. The parallel saying in Allen's company in Afghanistan was that there were no straights in foxholes—that the tensions and opportunities involved led men to each other for comfort and release. That certainly worked out to be the case with Allen. He was leaning gay anyway before he went to Afghanistan, but Allen's older, combat-worn lieutenant, had initiated Allen at the age of nineteen in one of those foxholes—had fucked Allen six ways from Sunday and made Allen his slave.

To the lieutenant's credit, when both of them had been drummed out of the army, the lieutenant brought Allen back to the States, sent him to college, and then promptly died and left Allen with this bungalow—as well as with a job as a counselor at a half-way house for released prison inmates. His program was especially involved with the gay ones, and he'd been given a membership in the gay men's club where he met Jack because of his work.

Jack had been Allen's first since the lieutenant had died during Allen's second year in college. Allen had gotten some form of affection and plenty of control and direction from the lieutenant. So far that's what he got from Jack as well. He had no idea why he kept waiting to see if there was more that would come his way some day.

Dinner was timed to end before the start of the Eagles and Redskins pro football game coverage on the TV. And the start of the game found Jack out on the sofa in front of the big-screen TV on the living room wall, while, behind him, Allen moved dishes, silverware, glasses, and serving plates from the dining room out to the kitchen. Jack had drunk most of the wine he had brought himself at dinner. Allen pulled a bottle of cold beer out of the refrigerator and approached the back of the sofa with it.

Jack was engrossed in the TV. Allen waited for the end of the kickoff and reached over and slid the cold bottle down Jack's chest. Jack had taken off his jeans, shirt, and loafers and folded and stacked them neatly on the seat of Allen's recliner. This left him wearing only a pair of FU e=fu8 Pleasure Pouch briefs. Allen only knew that because Jack had told him at dinner what designer underwear he was wearing this time and

244

pushed in trouser waistband down to show Allen the logo on his undies, which was Jack's form of foreplay. The play had heated up momentarily when, in turn, Allen told him he was wearing a red silk jock strap of unknown brand that he'd gotten in an adult sex shop.

"It may be strawberry flavored," Allen said.

Jack had made him strip his shorts off so he could feel Allen's jewels through the pouch, but that done, after an exploratory sniff for the scent of strawberry, he'd moved off on another topic.

"Thanks, babe," Jack said, taking the beer. He pulled Allen's hand down to his crotch with the other hand, which also brought Allen's mouth down to his. They kissed, with Allen noticing that Jack's eyes were targeted beyond his head to the TV set, where a commercial was winding down.

"Feel me hard, babe? This is all for you. Half time. I can't wait." He released Allen's hand as the TV coverage returned to the game.

Going back to the kitchen to clean up the dishes, Allen couldn't help but think, If he's so hot for me and can't wait, why are we waiting for half time? Allen wouldn't have minded Jack fucking him on the couch while the game was going. The lieutenant had done that many times. And, what the hell, Philadelphia and Washington weren't even local teams.

After cleaning up in the kitchen, Allen stripped down to his jock strap and came back into the living room with two more cold beers in hand. He handed one to Jack, who pulled him down onto the sofa without taking his eyes from the TV set.

They embraced and kissed and did some fondling, but it was perfunctory, with Jack giving the priority of his attention to the football game and Allen doing most of the fondling. Jack was more of a wham-bang-thanks-a-bunch guy than a fondler.

Jack showed more attention when Allen had gotten his fu briefs off him and had bent over and deep-throated Jack's cock, which was hard to do. Along with all of the other perfections of Jack, he was horse hung. And this was why Allen was here, bent over him, and sucking his cock. Jack was the only man Allen had had since the lieutenant died, and he was a hunk. Allen wasn't proud about where he got it and what he had to do to get it.

During halftime Jack delivered in his own way. As the teams were leaving the field, he showed that he'd brought a DVD to fuck by and popped a scene in of a big guy fucking a little guy, the big guy in Roman soldier costume, and the little guy dressed as a servant slave.

When he came back to the sofa, Jack pulled the smaller Allen up, turned him sideways to the sofa, set his chest on the arm of the sofa, with his head and arms reaching for the floor, slapped Allen's thighs apart and brought him up to his knees on the sofa cushion. He then went to town sucking Allen's cock and balls and eating out his ass while Allen moaned, remembering why he had Jack over every other Saturday. Jack spent more time finger fucking the hole than licking it.

Six minutes of this and then Jack snapped on a Trojan Magnum and mounted, penetrated, and fucked Allen hard and deep, with Allen squirming under him and luxuriated in the pain-pleasure of being taken by a hung man. Jack didn't even bother to strip Allen of his jock strap. He just moved aside whatever was in his way for what he wanted to get at, just as he'd done when he was eating out Allen's ass.

Once in position, Jack drove his cock in, causing Allen to yelp and his eyes to go real big and his mouth to form a big O. Jack held for twenty seconds to give Allen a chance to adjust to the cock. Grabbing a handful of Allen's hair, Jack arched Allen's torso back to him and bit Allen on the side of his neck. It always started in anger like this—as it had that first time, in the locker room, when Allen had scored two embarrassing goals on Jack.

Regardless of Jack's motivations for fucking him, Allen had loved the position, forced onto his chest on the bench, with Jack grabbing his ankles and forcing his legs spread and bent back over Allen's head, as Jack pushed himself between Allen's legs in reverse and fucked brutally down into him.

It had been that exotic position as well as the domination and the thickness and depth that Jack could reach that had Allen agreeing to see Jake again, to invite him over for dinner and to watch a game on TV, and to nail Allen's ass to the sofa—never again in as exotic a position, though.

"Be good to me, Jack," Allen whimpered.

"I'm always good for you." Jack answered, with a low laugh. Allen couldn't dispute that, there being no one else to compare with Jack's periodic visits since the lieutenant had died. And then Jack leaned back, grabbed Allen's wrists, and arched Allen's back by pulling his arms tight behind him. It was time for Allen to go to pain-pleasure heaven, whispering for Jack to give him mercy when he actually wanted exactly what Jack was doing—pounding his ass hard and deep and fast— just like the lieutenant had done.

This was Allen's time to focus his eyes to the TV screen. As Jack was preparing his ass for mounting, Allen watched the Roman soldier on the screen pick the slave up, reverse the smaller man's body on his, and eat out the slave's ass while, suspended upside down on the front of the soldier, the slave sucked him off. And while Jack was fucking him, the Roman soldier had the slave draped on the front of him right side up this time, the slave's arms immobile in a full Nelson, the slave's thighs spread on those of the solider, and the soldier fucking up into the slave's ass.

The slave was completely at the mercy of the brutal hunk of a Roman soldier. That's what Allen dreamed of as well, being held completely in thrall of a demanding hunk.

As nice as it was to have a long, thick man inside him, Allen thought, the slave on the screen was getting more exotic action than he was. Maybe six minutes of painful ecstasy—of being truly alive—and it was done.

As halftime was winding down, Jack pulled out of Allen, jerked his body up and reversed it on the sofa, and ripped his condom off. "On the face," he commanded.

And that's where he shot his load.

Allen cleaned off in the kitchen while Jack did so in the bathroom and was back on the sofa and engrossed in the TV as the second half started.

Allen had hoped that Jack would stay around and go into the bedroom with him after the game, but Jack hadn't done so before and he didn't do it now.

"Gotta see a man about an investment portfolio," he said at the door. "You were great, babe." And then he was gone.

Yeah, great, Allen thought. He went to his bedroom, stretched out on the bed, slipped off the red silk jock strap, and masturbated himself, thinking of the action in the Roman DVD and letting the lyrics of the old Peggy Lee song, "Is That All There Is?" run through his brain. Six minutes of building arousal and six, maybe seven minutes, of walking on the clouds, and that was it. The steak had not been cheap. Allen considered that he might as well have hired a rent-boy—one who gave both commands and attention. Allen fully realized he was a needy submissive.

Still, the lieutenant, much older than Jake was, didn't last for more than five minutes. That was at a time, of course. The lieutenant came back at him after a rest. And then again— and again. By the third time, the fuck was the way Allen dreamed about—him exhausted and totally malleable to whatever the lieutenant wanted to do to him. And the third time was always the lieutenant at his most cruel and demanding. That was nice.

* * * *

Allen had to ask about the back room and how you got there. The door was pretty well camouflaged. The greasy-looking-skin guy behind the counter had given him a knowing look and popped his tongue in the side of his cheek but had shown Allen where the door to the adult section of Sam's Costume Dreamland was located.

Allen had learned about the place at work, where he overheard a couple of guys making jokes about the place. What they had said about what you could get at the costume shop had worked on Allen for a couple of days. He needed some sort of pizzaz going in his life. The porn stars in the Roman soldier film Jack had running while he fucked Allen had been having more fun than Allen was having. If nothing else, Allen decided that when he took matters into his own hands, he could be in costume and watching appropriate DVDs.

He wanted to see that Roman soldier film again. He wanted to be that slave the Roman soldier was fucking—even if vicariously. He wanted to get a copy of that film.

So, here he was, in Sam's Costume Dreamland. He'd picked up some costumes—an Indian loincloth and deerskin boots, a Navy sailor's costume, a Roman slave tunic, and a colonial dandy's blousy shirt, leather boots, and tight britches with a codpiece that opened all the way back to the ass—and set them on the counter for the smirking clerk to process. Then he needed DVDs to go with them, so he found the courage to ask the clerk about the rumored back room.

He wandered around in the back room that, the rumor having been right, had an extensive collection of DVDs and sex toys. The business office was off to the side of this back room. There was a big picture window and a door between the rooms—and the manager was sitting back there. From what Allen could see the manager was a towering, thuggish, muscular ogre of a man, somewhat like Allen's lieutenant—with a bald head, bull-thick neck, and hairy forearms. He'd glance at the man in the office occasionally and find the man always watching him, moving from the desk to standing in the door, leaning on the frame with crossed arms. Allen might have found that intimidating, but, instead, he'd been aroused by it—the hint of domination and cruelty in the man.

Being a little nervous that he was being closely watched—although understanding why a patron in this section would be—Allen quickly picked out the DVDs that went with the costumes he was buying and, as an afterthought, picked out a Jack-sized plastic dildo with knobs all over it, and went back to purchase his extensive "do it yourself" kit.

The next two evenings he enjoyed jacking off to DVDs as an Indian and a sailor, with a plastic dildo up his ass. It was something, but it wasn't everything.

On the third day when he went to the mailbox out on the street to retrieve his mail, he saw that he'd mistakenly gotten a letter addressed to a Samuel Strang at a house around the corner from him on Oak Street. It looked like a normal letter, except that on the reverse side from the address, down in the corner, in a tight little script, he saw written "Roman slave," and under that was "Saturday, 8 pm."

The inscription didn't mean anything to him, although it kept running through his brain, and he was ready to take a run anyway. He ran the misdelivered envelope around the corner to the mailbox of the house on Oak, which was much the same as his bungalow, albeit the foliage around it was thicker than around his house. The area had been a subdevelopment in the forties, so there was a basic general sameness to all of the houses tempered by time with some individuality. If his house reflected tired drabness, this one was a bit mysterious and sinister.

The next day the letter was back in the mailbox. Allen flipped it over. The same "Roman slave," with "Saturday, 8 pm" written under it, both now underlined in red. On the flap of the envelope had been added "I will take care of you."

Allen didn't immediately understand what it meant. But his dick did; it was going hard.

* * * *

The guy who opened the door of the Oak Street house to him at 8:00 p.m. on Saturday was the big ogre manager from Sam's Costume Dreamland. He was dressed as a Roman soldier in a pleated skirt; sandals, with laces up to his knees; and a full-torso breast plate in a shiny gold metal that showed a muscular, cut torso sinking down to cover the lower belly. He wore thick gold-metal bands on his wrists. Allen arrived in a simple tunic going down to mid thigh over a tied loincloth and sandals, with laces up to his knees, covered with a trench coat.

Allen had taken a wild guess and had, surprisingly, been right. He even had envisioned the costume store manager in the role of the Roman soldier, he realized, now that he saw the man in costume. The whole scenario was enveloped in a dreamlike film that enabled Allen, going completely submissive, to just float along with it now.

"I'm Sam and you are Allen Brice—and you've come here for a fantasy fuck," the man said in a deep voice. "Come in and lose the coat." He already was unlacing the breastplate, with his torso, when the armor was lost, proving to be no less muscular and cut, if thicker and more mature, than the breastplate, which he tossed aside.

"On your knees, slave. Blow me," Sam commanded. Allen sank submissively on his knees before the man with a low moan. It was all a dream, of course, but the dream was one

250

he wanted to be in. The soldier wore no loin cloth under the short skirt. He was a bull, thick, hard, and of slightly longer than average length. His bush was coarse, unruly, and a brighter red than the hair was as it rose up his chest and arms and didn't quite reach his head. He held Allen's head close in both hands and manipulated it as Allen's mouth gagged and slurped in taking him to a pulled-out-and-cream-the face shoot off.

"Follow me and slither on your belly. You're a Roman slave and I am your general and master. I have conquered your people and now I will thoroughly subjugate you to my will and pleasure."

Allen trembled with anticipation and the novelty both of how arousing this sex role playing was and how readily he'd recognized and fallen in with it as he slithered along the floor into a room where there was a Roman couch with a plaster column behind it and a small, carved-wood table supporting an earthen-ware jug, an earthen-ware wine cup, an earthen-ware plate with a bunch of red grapes on it, and a huge earthen-ware dildo. Across the room from the Roman couch was a wall TV, running the same Roman soldier porn scene, over and over, that Jack had brought to Allen's the other night.

Jack hadn't been able to locate that exact DVD at the store and had been disappointed at the failure to do so. Here it was—for him to enjoy as he was being mastered. He certainly hoped he wouldn't wake up before he'd been thoroughly fucked.

Sam, the Roman soldier, picked up the dildo and showed it to Allen, who had reached the center of the room and propped his torso up on his arms extending to the floor. His eyes were on the Roman soldier and the earthen-ware dildo. His look was wary. The dildo looked larger than anything he'd taken before.

"Do you recognize who I am?" the man asked.

"Yes, the man from the costume shop."

"You looked apprehensive when you were in the shop. Are you afraid of me?"

"Yes, I little."

"Afraid I will be cruel?"

"Yes, a little."

"Does that arouse you?"

Allen didn't answer, but he lowered his head in submission, a signal understood by them both.

"Good. We will share a mutually beneficial relationship. Remember that no matter what the role we are playing, I am the master and you are the slave. I own the store. I am the Sam of the store's name. I know who you are. Allen Brice. I know what you bought in my store. For instance, I know you bought a version of this." He rotated the dildo. "You bought a size eight thick. Have you used it on yourself yet?"

"Yes," Allen answered haltingly.

"This is a size nine. I am a size nine."

Allen shuddered.

"I got the impression from watching you in the store that you are ripe for some excitement in your sex life. If I'm wrong, tell me."

Allen didn't answer, which was an answer.

"I want to be quite clear," Sam continued. "Not many have followed my command at the door the first time. I take that as an indication of how badly you need what I can give you. And this surprises me. You are quite good looking and have a perfectly formed body and a sweet, soft mouth. You are a bit small in stature, but there are many men, including me, who see that as arousing. And yet, here you are and there you were in my shop—buying fantasies. Tell me, do you open your legs for men?"

"I have," Allen answered.

"Have you possibly lost a lover recently and are having trouble replacing him?"

"Yes."

"You've found someone but he isn't fulfilling your fantasies?"

"Yes, that's right."

"But is a satisfying sex partner otherwise?"

"In most respects."

"I am not looking for a slave," Sam said. "I will not possess you permanently. But I am able to give you what you want—and possibly help you get more of what you want from your sex partner—or enable you to find more satisfactory sex partners. If that's not what you want, you may slither on out of the house and thank you very much for the very nice blow job at the door." He paused, giving Allen a chance to withdraw. But Allen stayed put. He'd decided before he came that he'd carry through with it if this was what he thought it was and the other man was presentable.

Sam was very presentable in many ways—he certainly was horse hung—and in many ways reminiscent of Allen's lieutenant.

"You bought a size eight thick dildo in my store. I like to think that the men who shop there underestimate their needs. As I said, This dildo is a size nine extra thick. If you stay here, I will be fucking you with it."

Again Allen made no effort to move.

"And I also will fuck you with this, also a size nine." He pulled his own cock out from underneath his short skirt. Allen had been intimately introduced to it at the door already, but it didn't look any less formidable now in full erection.

"So, we will begin," Sam said, sitting on the side of the couch. "Come, serve me wine and feed me grapes. I am a Roman general and your master, back from many months on the campaign trail. I brought you back with me, one of the last survivors of a vanquished people. I saved you from being ravished and dispatched by my soldiers. I saved you for myself. You have not yet been touched in that way by man. I have saved you to do that myself.

"I haven't had a man in those months, as the marching and fighting have taken all the energy I can give. I am home now, bathed—and I fucked the bath attendant—and massaged—and I fucked the masseur—and I am here now, hungry for wine and food and more young, virginal male pussy. I seized you to be my personal servant to serve me at the dining couch—both in delivering food to me and riding my cock.

"I am here now, to use the present I bought for myself. I am thirsty and hungry—and randy. Serve me this wine and then feed me these grapes. I will take care of deflowering you myself. Be aware that you know exactly why your life was spared thus far, what you were brought to do for me, and that your life hangs in the balance of doing it well.

253

"Pour me wine and hand me the cup. Yes, like that, but don't withdraw from me. Stand there, between my spread thighs, as I drink the wine. Fondle my cock with both of your hands. Yes, like that. Your job is to keep me hard, knowing that my intent is to take your virginity from you—fully and brutally. I am back from the cruel battles. My need and intent is to ravish you. But you are resigned to it—glad to be alive. Willing to please me to remain alive—knowing that if you don't please me, you won't live."

Allen was totally into the role play, panting already, thinking of the impending loss of a virginity he no longer had. Thinking of being the property of this rough-handed man, intending to fuck every ounce of his pleasure out of an untested, smaller slave.

"Put the wine cup back on the table. Pick up the grapes."

Trembling, Allen complied. Sam pulled the young man in between his spread thighs, and pulled Allen's tunic over his head, leaving him only clothed in a tied loin cloth. Sam's face went to Allen's belly, which he nuzzled and kissed. Moaning lightly, the slave stood his ground, murmuring, "Yes, master, yes," and putting his hands on the Roman's bald head. He shuddered as the Roman general pulled on the knot of the loin cloth and it fell to the floor. Grasping the slave's buttocks, the soldier parted the cheeks, moved the calloused middle finger of each hand to and into the young man's virginal hole, and swallowed and began to work the slave's cock, bringing an ejaculation out of the young man in short order as lost as he'd become in the role play.

"Keep your body perfectly straight while you feed me the grapes," the general growled, as the slave exclaimed in surprise at being easily lifted and raised over the soldier's head as he reclined on the couch. The strong Roman used the slave as a straight-bodied dead-weight lift over his body. He lifted the slave up from his body and then brought him down, whereupon the slave would place a grape in his mouth. Every third feeding the general took the slave's lips with his and transferred the grape for the slave to eat. After several rounds of feeding, the general commanded the slave to part his thighs and remain close on top of the general's stretched body as the two exchanged grapes in their mouth. Telling the slave to close his thighs on the cock, the general dry fucked the slave's thighs while they finished the grapes.

Looking over at the TV, Allen saw, to his surprise, that this was part of the porn film Jack had shown him the other night. It just wasn't a part of the scene that Allen had seen before.

As the TV scene continued, Allen moaned, knowing then what came next. The general came off the couch with Allen in his arms, spun Allen's body around so that he was head down toward the floor but draped on the front of the Roman general's body. As in the film, the general told the slave to do the splits with his legs and then started munching on the slave's asshole with his mouth, while the slave, holding onto the general's legs behind his knees, sucked the general's cock.

Constantly in the mind of the slave—and in the mind of Allen, fully invested in this role play—was the need to please the Roman general, to give him whatever he wanted, to be totally submissive and responsive to prolong his own life.

Raising and turning the slave's body with ease, the Roman grasped the young man's back to his chest, pulled the slave's buttocks up, while the slave locked his fists behind the beefy soldier's neck, and set his passage down on the cock. The slave then twisted his calves around the general's thighs, while the general put the slave into a full Nelson hold. The appropriate cries and begging for mercy that followed came, by the power of suggestion and the tale being woven, from a virgin being debauched. Relentlessly, mercilessly, the general fucked the whimpering and groaning slave to an ejaculation.

As the Roman recovered his erection, he took the moaning and fully submissive slave to the couch, laid the young man down, clutched the slaves throat to keep him flat and subdued, put the slave's left ankle on his right shoulder, and fucked his ass with the earthen-ware dildo.

At some point the position was adjusted a bit, with the general turning to be on top of the slave and the dildo was exchanged with a real, churning, shooting cock.

Sam left Allen stretched out on the couch, panting and sighing and contemplating how satisfying and exotic the role-playing fuck had been.

It wasn't too long, though, before Sam reentered the room. He was wearing football gear—or most of the equipment. He had on tight, silken football britches and athletic shoes with cleats. The pants had a big bulge at the crotch, which Allen could attest probably was all Sam, with a codpiece that laced up. He had hip protectors wedged into the waistband of the pants and was wearing shoulder pads. The rest of the heavily muscled chest and six pack and armor-like flat belly were raw Sam. He had dark smudges under his eyes and a mean look in his face.

He held out another set of silken football pants and said, "Here, put these on and come in the other room."

"This isn't any of the costumes I bought in your store," Allen said.

"I know what you bought in my store. What we just did—the Roman scene—was your fantasy. This one is mine. Get up and put these pants on and come into the other room."

The next room was small, and all it had in it was a huge wall TV, which now was rerunning the Philadelphia-Washington football game from the previous weekend.

Good, Allen nonsensically thought. He never had seen the final score of the game. He had spent the third quarter jacking himself off because Jack hadn't taken care of him, although Jack held him in his lap and penetrated him with two fingers, rubbing Allen's prostate, to help him come. In the fourth quarter, Allen had been too busy pouting and shoveling beer bottles at Jack to keep track of the score.

"Here, you're going to be hiking this," Sam said, as he handed Allen the strangest-looking football Allen had every scene. It looked more like a monstrously thick cigar. Allen shuddered when he realized it was a thick dido.

"I've always wanted to see this done in a real game," Sam said. He was busy unlacing his codpiece. "I've done it in pickup football games. We're going to do it right now. This is my costume fantasy for the day. You're the center and I'm the quarterback. Get down in your stance, facing the TV set."

Allen went down into a center's stance, his trembling hands holding the fake football in position, ready to snap it back to the quarterback. As Sam counted off numbers, he worked fingers into the seam of Allen's football pants and split

256

the silky material along the seam running from Allen's belly to past his asshole. Allen felt his cock and balls drop, and then Sam was pressing his cupped hands under Sam's taint and cried out "Hike."

Instinctively Allen hiked the ball back into the hands of the man crouching over his spread legs as he bent over to the ground. An arm went under Allen's belly to hold him up in a bent-over doggy stance, and Allen cried out and huffed and puffed as Sam fucked him, first, with the football dildo, and then with the real thing, grasping and milking Allen's cock toward the end to give them a nearly mutual ejaculation.

* * * *

The next Monday Allen went to the mailbox at his house and discovered another misdelivered envelope destined for Sam Strang on Oak Street. With trembling hands, he turned the envelope over. In the bottom right corner, a notation had been written: "Indian brave" and, below that, "8 pm Wednesday."

Wednesday evening Allen was scheduled for a pickup basketball game at the gay men's sports club that he hoped Jack would go to. The role-playing fucks at Sam's house had him keyed up and his juices flowing. He felt sexy and more open to the possibilities with other men than before. He was interested in taking risks he hadn't taken before. There was a thug of a guy who had hit on him at the club but that Allen had been afraid to risk. He didn't come out for the pickup games on Wednesdays, though. He was there on Thursdays. Allen thought he'd give the guy a try—all because of how Sam had opened him up to possibilities.

Allen was interested in seeing Jack again too. He felt that Sam, in just those two sessions, had loosened him up, made him sexier. He wanted to know if Jack would notice that—and would give him more attention.

There was no question where Allen was going on Wednesday evening, though. Sam met him at the door in full war paint. He was wearing low-rise deer hide britches, with a laced-up codpiece, moccasins on his feet, a breast-plate bone chest shield, leather bands dripping in rawhide strings around his biceps, and a feather headdress.

Allen wore a loin cloth and moccasins. He didn't wear the loin cloth for long, though. With a movie of Indian gang banging a white old-West cavalry soldier blaring on the wall, and tent-like walls around three sides of an area with a floor-to-ceiling pole in it, the Indian chief lashed the young brave to the pole, wrists bound high over his head, lightly lashed his naked body with a many-pronged rawhide whip until both he and the young brave were hard as rocks, and then unlaced his codpiece to free his erection, held the brave's legs straight out from his sides in a splits, and fucked him from behind to completion.

For a second "go" at him, the Indian chief staked the brave who Allen was portraying out spread-eagled on a mound of dirt in his backyard, face down in the dirt; tickled him with feathers, saying they were providing the effect of the ants from the hill the brave had been staked on; and, eventually, mounted the brave's ass and rode him like he was a horse loping across the prairies.

Thursday, the misdelivered letter in Allen's box gave the fantasy as "Plantation owner's son; time for company," with the date of "Friday" and time of "8 pm."

So keyed up was Allen over the prospect of another role play that he went to the sports club's Thursday pickup basketball game. He found out that the thug who had been propositioning him was a policeman named Larry. In a remote corner of the locker room—on the same bench that Jack had originally fucked him, Allen let Larry handcuff him to a bench, his arms over his head and a gym bag under the small of his back to give Larry's cock a good penetration angle, while Larry slapped him around, squeezed his balls until he wanted to scream, and gave him a brutal missionary fuck.

Lost in the fantasy of a prisoner being taken in his cell by a cop, Allen luxuriated in every minute of the taking. Most surprising was that afterward Larry told Allen he had been a lot of fun and that what he'd like to do to Allen would really stretch his limits. When he went on to tell Allen what that would be in graphic terms and asked for his phone number, Allen gave him his actual cell number.

Before Sam, Allen would never have submitted to the handcuffed fuck, let alone shown willingness to do something darker.

* * * *

"You are the step-son of a plantation owner on the Mississippi who has, along with your mother, gone to New Orleans for a week," said Sam as he led Allen back into a bedroom with a four-poster bed, with canopy, grasping the back of Allen's neck with one hand and latching onto one of Allen's forearms with the other. Allen was wearing the colonial dandy costume he had bought at the store—frilly and blousy white cotton shirt, tight britches, and something similar to ballet slippers on his feet. Sam was wearing coarse woolen britches and a Henley pullover shirt in the same coarse material. Playing on the TV on the wall was a DVD of a group of black bulls gangbanging a young white guy on a river bank.

"I am the overseer of the plantation and I have lusted for you for some time. You are flirty. You know I want you. You know you want men. I know you are mine for the taking. Your step-father and mother are gone. Your step-father has been preparing you for him to deflower himself and you have become increasingly receptive to that. But he isn't here. I am here. It is time for you to lose your virginity. And you are going to lose it to me."

Suddenly, without warning, when they reached the bed, Sam backhanded Allen across the cheek and Allen spun around and fell back on the bed at the foot of the mattress.

"You've been a little tease," the overseer growled. "This is your time." Pulling the britches and undergarments off the legs of the son of the plantation, the overseer pulled his own shirt over his head and, grabbing the young man's ankles, bent and pushed his legs up into his chest and rolled his pelvis up. The young man was still trying to catch his breath as the overseer attacked his cock, balls, and hole with his mouth. In short order, though the son of the plantation gave in to the attentions in little mewing sounds and soft moans.

The overseer turned him over on his back at the foot of bed, hooked one of the young man's ankles on his shoulder, and held his torso flat on the bed with an arm across his neck. He worked the young man's ass with the other hand, penetrating him with an increasing number of fingers until he had worked in four up to the knuckles. While the son of the plantation writhed under him and begged for mercy that was not forthcoming, the invading hand pumped him slowly, with fingers rubbing the young man's prostate. The young man yelped and fired his load as the knuckles breached the sphincter, pulling in the thumb as well, and sank in to the wrist.

Moaning deeply, the young man went limp as the overseer fist fucked him for a couple of minutes more before withdrawing.

"You've taken a fist before, haven't you?" Sam asked in a voice displaying some awe.

"Yes, but not for some time," Allen answered, his memories going back to the desperation and high arousal of his time in Afghanistan—of the other men in his unit who preyed on men. Of how rough they could be. Yes, he had been fisted before. Never had he taken it with so much want and need and sense of being fully possessed as he was doing now, though.

The overseer fucked him in a reverse position, the young man facing down, his torso streaming down to the floor from the foot of the bed, his fists buried in the carpet at the end of the bed to keep himself steady. His calves were on the bed, held there with the overseer's hands clutching his ankles. The overseer's trousers were flared and sitting low on his hips. His cock was buried, reversed, in the young man's channel and he was pumping hard.

"Break away," Sam muttered, "and head for the door to the corridor." Allen did so, coming up short, because the doorway to the corridor was taken up with the figure of a massive black man, wearing only torn and loose cotton britches held up with a rope. As Allen stood there, transfixed for the moment, the black man leered and unbuttoned his fly, and a huge cock flopped out.

"You have two choices," Sam barked. "There's a door over there. If you run through there and get to the front door of the house and touch it, you're safe and the role play is over. This is Jamil. He's playing a slave on the plantation who has lusted after you as much as the overseer has. The overseer has

260

said he can have you after the overseer has fucked your virginity out of you. If you want the black slave to have you, try escaping around the other side of the bed."

Allen scooted around to the other side of the bed without hesitation, where the black bull caught him, forced him down on all fours, shredded his shirt in pawing his chest, covered him, mounted him, entered him deep, and fucked him.

The black bull was bigger than anyone Allen had taken before, but he'd just taken a fist, so he could manage. The experience of being power fucked like this by a black man sent Allen up to heaven, as he grunted and groaned in the effort to remain open to the churning monster cock.

When the black bull came up to standing, he brought Allen with him, still deeply skewered on the black monster cock. Allen held close to the black man's bare chest, with his hands locked behind Jamil's neck. Jamil's hand were under Allen's thighs, keeping his legs bent, not reaching the floor, and spread.

Sam walked over close to them, his cock still erect and in his hand. "Have you ever been taken by two men at once?" he whispered as he came in very close to Allen, between the young man's spread legs. "I know you can take it if you agree to it."

"Yes, I've been doubled. Yes, I want it." Allen answered, licking his lips and his mind going back to the trenches and the lieutenant—but not only the lieutenant. A sergeant as well, in combination with the lieutenant—after opening him up with a fist. Just like now.

"If you decide you don't want it, we'll let you break loose and head for the front door," Sam said. Allen let loose of his hold on Jamil's neck, Sam's chest being close enough into him that he wouldn't fall, and he embraced Sam, bringing Sam into him.

"Both of you, now," he begged in a husky voice.

Allen pressed his head back into the hollow of Jamil's shoulder, raised his face, and howled to the ceiling as Sam worked his cock inside him on top of Jamil's and started to pump. Allen writhed in the throes of the pleasure-pain ecstasy of the exotic feel of having two hung men working him at the same time, his mind racing back to the trenches and of being shared by the lieutenant and sergeant, the two of them making him forget where he was, the danger he lived under, the horrors of Afghanistan. The fisting he'd endured earlier helped him take the two cocks—as did the emotional pleasure of knowing he was taking two, one of them a black bull.

* * * *

Saturday morning there were two envelopes in Allen's mailbox. He'd staked out his living room window and thus was able to see that it was the greasy, thin clerk from the costume store who snuck up and put the misdelivered mail in his box. One envelope, like the others, was addressed to Sam's Oak Street house. The notation on it was "rent-boy lap dance," with the time set for 8:00 p.m. that night. Allen looked on that with disappointment. That evening was a regular visitation session by Jack. He would be sorry to miss the lap dance fantasy.

Except that he didn't miss it. The other letter, addressed to him from Sam Strang on Oak Street, contained the note, "If Saturday is the time for a visit from your sometimes lover, cancel that. You must learn not to be taken for granted and he must learn not to take you for granted. This is training for him as well as you."

"What do you mean I can't come over?" Jack had said on the telephone. "This is our regular Saturday."

"I'm sorry. I have other plans. Maybe next Saturday."

"I may not be available next Saturday."

"Then it would be a pity for us to miss a fuck," Allen responded, saying good-bye and disconnecting before Jack had time to object further and after saying, "I'll call you to check on whether you want to come next Saturday."

Sam met him at the Oak Street house door at 8:00 p.m. He wasn't in any particular costume. When he shed his coat, Allen was wearing his red silk jock strap, the lace-up sandals from his Roman costume, and a red sequined vest that didn't meet across his chest.

"You said this was a learning experience for me—and should be for my lover too," Allen said to Sam at the entrance.

"Yes. I could tell from watching you in the store and from what you bought that you needed to move up levels from where you were in sexual activity," Sam answered. "Little did I know that you've been up many levels at one time—that you both were fisted and doubled before—and what you need is to recover them."

"What is there in this for you?" Allen asked.

"I get a luscious little piece to play with," Sam answered, "At least until you've regained all of the expertise you once had and the assurance that you deserve and can get better than you've been getting."

"And the lesson for today?" Allen asked. "A lap dance seems pretty tame compared with being doubled by you and that black bull."

"It isn't the intensity of it—it's the lesson that it's the sexual arousal and release that is the focus, not the partner you're with."

They entered the living room, and there, in a straight chair in the center of the room, sat the beanpole, gawky, greasy-haired clerk, just in gym shorts. He was hunched over slightly, his chest concave. From the tenting of the gym shorts and the grin on his ugly face with the pronounced Adam's apple, Allen could tell that he was ready and looking forward to the session.

"Dance for him, blow him, and ride his cock," Sam directed. "Your role is that you're a rent-boy in a sleazy club trying to get money out of any man who wants a lap dance—and more money for more service. Phil here has money. Your job is to make him part with his money. He'll reward you periodically as long as you are doing him well. Remember that the training is to be able to be a rent-boy—focus on the sex acts and the rewards to be won, not the client."

Allen crouched over Phil's lap and bumped and grinded for him to music and two TV screens of rent-boys giving ugly old men lap dance fucks. He got his first big bill by taking Phil's head in his hands and giving him a deep French kiss, more for rubbing his chest on Phil's and moaning during the dance. Even more for kneeling between Phil's spread legs, pulling the man's gym shorts off his legs, and sucking him off, taking the cream on his face, and cleaning that and Phil's cock off with his tongue.

Phil took over in the fuck. Sliding Allen's jock strap off as Allen rose from the blow job, tucking his arms under Allen's knees and flipping Allen backward. Phil's arms were strong and he was able to pull Allen's crotch up to his face and, while he was recovering his own hard, he sucked on Allen's cock and balls and ate out his ass. When he was recovered, he let Allen down to do a few more gyrations of a lap dance and then took charge again, positioning his cock bulb at Allen's rim.

"He's going to fuck you now," Sam said. "He's not the handsome hunk you usually need to open for. His cock is big, though. He's going to put it in you."

"Yes, yes, fuck me," Allen whined, taking Phil's head between his hands and kissing him on the lips. "Give it to me hard, big boy."

Phil held Allen's body at the waist and slammed it down on the cock. Lift up and slam down. Repeating it for as long as it took for him to bottom. Yelping and writhing, Allen settled down, collapsing like a rag doll and completely docile before Phil started the serious pumping, letting Allen's body arch back to the floor, while Phil gripped his hips and pulled him on and off the cock in swift, powerful, deep strokes.

"Yes, yes, give it to me. Fuck me hard!"

Phil held off on ejaculation for almost forever—some time after Allen had shot off again—before he filled the bulb of his condom, leaving Allen in a sighing, purring heap at his feet.

At the door on the way out, Sam said, "Remember that. Their looks don't always match their sexual prowess. Phil could make you his willing sex slave if I let him—and I can see in your eyes that you recognize that. So, when you are in your rent-boy role, don't judge a client by his looks or even his diffidence. I'll bet this lover who doesn't fully satisfy you is an Adonis."

"Yes, he is," Allen admitted.

"To be satisfied by him, you will need more than a pretty face and a big cock from him. He'll have to want to fuck you so bad that he'd give you the attention you need. And remember for your own pleasure, Allen, that it isn't how handsome the man is or whether he is, it is that he has his cock inside you and that he knows what to do with it when it's in there. Keep your mind on the fuck."

* * * *

The follow-up instruction on misdelivered mail on what he was to do on Tuesday evening was more in this vein. "The Smallwood Rest Stop. Do two ugly truckers."

The first one was a pudgy man old enough for the fringe of hair on his head to be turning gray. Allen had bellied up to a urinal at the notorious rest stop on the highway to which he had been directed. He waited until an obviously interested trucker came in and moved into the urinal next to him. They held there longer than necessary for a guy to take a piss and long enough for them to signal each other with their eyes.

The older man turned toward Allen enough for Allen to see that he was in erection. Allen turned as well, and the man reached out and touched his cock, which helped it go harder. Allen had managed to harden up by running the image of ugly Phil and what he could do with his cock through his mind repeatedly. With effort, he found that the experience itself, this setting, was enough to arouse him. Allen reached over and more aggressively took the man's cock in hand.

"Can I suck you off?" the man asked in a tentative voice.

"I'd rather you fucked me," Allen answered. "Do you want to do that?" The man nearly lost his teeth in that offer.

"The stall over there," Allen said.

The man sat on the toilet, his pants down around his calves, and, sans shorts and briefs, Allen sat in his lap, facing him, and bounced up and down on the man's cock until the trucker came. The trucker had a very nice cock, Allen found, and he had a technique of kissing every inch of Allen's internal walls with its bulb.

Afterward Allen offered his ass to a tall, thin guy in flannel shirt, jeans, and cowboy boots leaning up against the side wall of the toilet building in the shadows and smoking a cigarette. They were around at the back of the building, between a huge air handling system and the back wall of the toilets before Allen realized that it was Phil, sent by Sam to check on whether Allen had carried forth with the assignment.

Allen raised his arms over his head, pressed his chest against the back wall of the toilets, and jutted his naked buttocks back into Phil's hands. Phil went down on his knees behind Allen, spread Allen's cheeks with his hands and attacked Allen's asshole with his mouth. He snaked a hand between Allen's spread thighs, milked Allen's cock, and fondled, squeezed, and distended Allen's balls until Allen gave him his cum. Then Phil mounted Allen's ass, gripped his hips, and fucked him hard for twenty minutes before coming himself, leaving Allen a puddle of putty in Phil's hands. They went back to the car Phil and driven, got in the backseat, and made out like teenagers after the prom, with Allen winding up on his back across the seat and the toes of one foot wedged into a side hook above a door and the other hooked on the top of the front seat, while Phil lay on top of him between his spread legs. They worked each other's mouths while Phil was pounding Allen's ass again.

Ugly is as ugly does, Allen was taught—and Phil did anything but ugly. Allen had to assume he'd gotten passing marks for his rest stop lesson.

* * * *

Thursday night rolled around again. Finding Allen at the gay men's sports club once again for a pickup basketball game—and maybe something else to pick up as well. These manufactured role playing games of Sam's had really opened Allen up. He was looking for it more broadly and actively than before. He was coming out of his mourning period for the lieutenant—or at least what the lieutenant had given him sexually—and he had to credit Sam for pulling him out of the lethargy. Allen couldn't say it was grief or even mourning for the lieutenant himself. It was more starting to come out of the need for someone else to give him commands and to start expecting and seeking pleasure himself.

The irony was that it was Sam giving Allen roles to play and commands that was moving the young man not to need them so much anymore.

The basketball game was fine—and Allen *did* get propositions. This after all *was* a gay men's sports club. But there was nothing on offer that excited him and he was coming to realize that he needed and deserved excitement. Specifically, Larry, the cop, and his handcuffs and forceful fuck hadn't shown up.

Allen left in an "oh, well" mood. And he must not have been paying much attention because half way home a revolving red light pulled up behind his car and he saw that, indeed, he had been going ten miles over the speed limit. It was in a school zone too, but that didn't really matter. It was after 10:00 p.m., and the school was closed. Allen was guided over into the school parking lot and in side-by-side spaces under a stand of trees by the police van.

"Please step out of the car," an authoritative voice boomed out when Allen rolled down his window. The man with the voice was shining a light in Allen's face, blinding him, but Allen recognized the voice.

"Larry?" he said.

"Turn the ignition off, step out of the car, and go over to the back of the van."

As Allen walked to the back of the van, which wasn't a police vehicle—it just had a temporary red light on top of it— Larry stopped the light and tossed it in the front seat of the van.

The back of the van was tricked out with carpeting; soft lighting; music loud enough to, Larry said, drown out screams coming from inside the van; sex toys; and a restraint system. There also was a TV suspended on the window between the back of the van and the driver's compartment; it was running a DVD of a cop fucking a prisoner in the back of a police van.

Larry was wearing a police uniform, but, as Allen stripped down and got into the back of the van, Larry opened up his shirt, unzipped his trousers, climbed in the back behind Allen, and shut and locked the van doors.

Larry put Allen on his knees and made him lick all the way down from his hairy barrel chest, past his heavy belt with the gun and truncheon holsters, into his unruly pubes, and then to take the erect cock in his mouth and give it suck. Allen sucked the cock greedily, aroused by the fantasy fuck Larry was providing, which was better than Allen could have imagined himself for this evening.

Allen huffed and puffed, gasped, whimpered and his eyes watered, as, wrist handcuffed to ankle on either side, bowing his body almost painfully, Larry put Allen on his belly on a carpeted cube in the middle of the van bed, and fucked his ass with a greased nightstick while both watched the action on the TV screen.

Later, Allen now on his back and spread-eagled in four directions with leads going to anchors in the four corners of the van, Larry crouched between Allen's legs and fucked him to a mutual ejaculation.

It was what Allen had come out this evening hoping to find, so he didn't complain; he cried out for the exotic fuck.

The only damper of the evening was that, as Larry released him, Allen saw the store bag that the DVD cover was in. It came from Sam's Costume Dreamland. What was the relationship between Larry and Sam, Allen wondered. Was this all part of the education program Sam had set up for Allen? Was Larry part of the fantasy role playing, operating under Sam's command?

Was Larry even a real cop?

Allen was so taken by this experience that, frankly, at this moment he didn't care.

* * * *

On Saturday afternoon, Jack called Allen in a panic.

"You'd said maybe I could come over today. It's the Army-Navy football game. You haven't answered my e-mails, though."

"I wasn't sure I wasn't doing something else today," Allen said.

"Doing something more important than me? You love me fucking you."

"You've got a great cock, Jack. But you're not using it enough on me. Yes, I love what you do to me for the six or seven minutes you're doing it to me. If you come over, you'll have to give me more of a fuck than that—and pay attention to me when you're doing it."

"Hey, I'm aching for you here. My balls ache they need it so bad. Nobody takes it like you do."

"Maybe because nobody but me lets the ball game take priority. And I'm not doing that anymore either. I've got a great meal planned for you, but if you're coming over, it will be early, before the game, to be pumping inside me for fifteen minutes at least and giving me attention when you do—and you have to get this done before I feed you—and before the game starts. And after the game, you have to take me into my bedroom and bang the hell out of me. You might even have to spend the night on top of me."

"Is that what you really want? I don't know what's come over you. You want me to—?"

"Take me into my bedroom, yes—no TV, no competing attention—and bang the hell out of me."

Allen watched Jack unfold from his new, blue Porsche Carrera convertible—seemingly identical to the old one except for the color—and walk up to the front door. He was carrying a bottle of wine, but he didn't do the old "fuck you" routine with it. He looked quizzical and a little worried. And he'd arrived an hour and a half before the coverage of the Army-Navy college football game was scheduled to start on the TV.

Allen met him at the door. "Here, strip, and put these on. Leave the waistband flared and your cock out. You get a blow job for showing up early." He handed Jack a pair of combat boots and camouflage baggy fatigue trousers.

"What's this . . . and what are you—?"

"It's Army-Navy game day. And we're going to play a game of our own. You're Army and I'm Navy. Good news; it's your lucky day. Army gets to fuck the shit out Navy today."

The lower half of Army fatigues had gone to Jack. Allen had met him at the door, wearing the naval uniform he'd bought at the costume store: a white tunic, with blue scarf, white bellbottom trousers, and a seaman's cap.

"Here. While you're dressing, I'll go ahead of you and strip off the bellbottoms." When he did so, he was wearing his red silk jock strap. "Remember this jock strap. Last time you fucked me without taking it off me. This time you have to take

269

it off me—and get me hard and make me come in the process—before there's any dinner or the TV is turned on."

Jack sat at the dining room table, his hands on Allen's head under the table top as Allen knelt between his thighs and his mouth bobbed up and down on Jack's erection. Jack moaned in a way he'd never done before. Much of this was because a quarter of the way through the blow job Allen took his mouth off the cock and wove a tale from underneath the table of what they were doing.

"Since you were here last, I learned a thing or two about the erotic help role playing can give to a fuck. I want more out of you, Jack, and I know you have it to give. In turn, I can take you higher than you've been before—I can give you a high that surpasses your football team winning on the TV.

"We are playing private Army and Navy, you and I. For starters, this blow job starts off our game. I'm going to work your cock until you come. But you aren't going to come right away. When you want to, I'm going to back you off, and then when I resume, I'm going to take you higher than you went before when you wanted to shoot. And then again."

Jack moaned, not only in anticipation of the play but also because Allen was stroking his cock and pressing his pinkie finger into Jack's piss slit.

"What we are playing is a Naval admiral coming to visit an Army installation. I am the admiral's young aide. I am a virgin, but I am aching to be debauched and I have decided the time is now and the lover who will pop my male cherry is you. You are a handsome, young Army lieutenant, the general's aide who is immediately turned on by me. We are meeting at the officers' club. One wing of the officers' club has visiting bachelor officers' bedrooms.

"While the general and admiral confer at one end of a conference table, you and I have exchanged needy looks at the other end of the table. I slip under the table and give you a blow job. The general and admiral, although their presence heightens our arousal, don't know what's happening under the table. It's a fantasy; they don't need to know. You then carry me to the BOQ and have your way with me. Every position you take me in—and they should be athletic and exotic—I'll give you a different form of a Cowboy ride.

"We will count the times we come."

With Jack groaning the effects of anticipation of this role play, Allen quickly completed the blow job. "One for you."

In the bedroom, fully invested in the role play, Jack tied Allen's wrists together with a belt while Allen protested that he didn't really mean for his teasing to go as far as a cock the size of Jack's up his ass—and Jack just laughed at his protests. He then tied the other end of the belt to one of the legs of the bed at its foot. Allen's body was stretched up the bed, and Jack moved Allen's left thigh over his right leg, giving a reclining Jack access to Allen's hole. Jack moved the butt crease strap of the jock strap aside and ate out Allen's ass until he was begging for more. Slipping the jock strap off Allen then, Jack turned him, returned the favor of the blow job, alternating with the sucking of Allen's cock. He finger fucked Allen's hole while sucking him off.

"One for you," Jack announced at Allen blew his load with a jerk and a whimper.

"Number two coming for me," Jack declared. Pulling Allen up to his knees, his ass high in the air, Jack mounted and rode him high in a bulldog fuck.

Maintaining Jack's interest, Allen rode his cock in a reverse Cowboy, Allen riding a reclined Jack while facing his feet. Taking advantage of reverse positions, Jack put Allen on his belly, couched Allen's head between his feet, grabbed Allen's ankles with his hands, and fucked Allen's passage in reverse.

Number two for Jack; numbers two and three for Allen.

They fucked through dinner. They fucked through the Army-Navy game. They fucked through twilight and into the night.

They slept in starts and stops between fuckings, but Jack never suggested they leave the bed to do anything else—other than Jack fucking Allen on top of his dresser and, again, with Allen belly down on an ottoman.

They lost count, and by morning, they didn't give a shit how many times it had been for either of them. They just knew they both liked playing this game with each other.

271

"What can we do next time?" Jack asked.

"I'll see if a can scare up pirate captain and cabin boy outfits," Allen answered, knowing already that Sam's Costume Dreamland stocked them.

"Saturday after next again?" Jack asked, his face showing a puppy dog expression.

"How about next Saturday?" Allen said.

"Even better," Jack responding, doing a convincing version of a dog pant.

Allen was exhilarated. He was getting what he wanted from Jack now. This should satiate him, he thought.

But on Monday morning he went to the mailbox on the street in front of his house only to pull out another misdelivered envelope addressed to Sam Strang on Oak Street. Down in the corner on the flap side were written the words, "Three on one hiker." Under that was written, "Belleview Park parking lot, Wednesday, 5:30 pm."

Three? he thought. Sam, Jamil, and Phil? Out in the woods. All of them on me? Oh, shit. Oh, fuck. I can't wait.

And, indeed, when, at 6:45 on Wednesday night, when Jamil pulled out of him and turned him onto his back in the mossy patch between two oak tree roots and Allen, his hiking shorts gone and his hiking shirt torn to shreds on his body, looked up at the twice-spent cocks of the other men standing over him, Sam and Phil, Allen could only purr and bend and spread his legs to beg for thirds.

The Lighthouse Keeper

I stumbled out of Rock Hudson's trailer in the high desert town of Marfa, Texas, on the set of Giant *and into the arms of Stewart Whitaker. The* Giant *production had started in Keswick, Virginia, supposedly represented as located in Maryland. Warner Brothers had licenses to film two movies in Central Virginia in 1956, and I was the heartthrob in the other movie, a Civil War epic called* Honor Above All Else, *which wrapped up filming while* Giant *was still being shot in Albemarle County.* Giant *was a hit;* Honor *wasn't. But I was riding high in those days and had caught the eye of Hudson. He assured me that the problem with* Honor *wasn't me—that I was superb in the film clips he had seen. I was flattered that he had looked at the film clips—that he took the time to pull me aside, place his hand on my arm, and assure me that I had been good in the film. Unfortunately, as films go sometimes go their stars as well, and my career peaked with* Honor.

The flattery given me in that trailer led to where such things sometimes lead in the presence of a major movie star.

Needing a drink badly after leaving the trailer, I went straight for the Fandango bar on Marfa's main street. Stewart Whitaker, the gossip column writer, was there, dark, handsome, muscular, and brash. With me still in a daze from my first experience with a man, he invited me to sit with him. I remarked that I'd just seen him in Virginia. Admitting that that was true, he'd said that he'd followed me to Texas from Virginia just as I had followed Hudson. Three drinks later, I'd staggered under his guidance to his hotel room, and he fucked me mercilessly with an eight-inch cock.

It had been nothing like that first time. Being invited into the trailer and offered a drink. Him standing there in a silk robe, a gorgeous man, an icon, holding a crystal glass of scotch out to me. Smiling down at me where I was sitting, nervous—honored but nervous—on the end of a studio couch. He had told me what he wanted from me. He told me in Virginia. And here, in Texas, I have come to his trailer. I have followed him to Texas and come to his trailer—just to say yes.

The sash of his robe coming loose and drifting to the trailer floor. The robe brushing open. Me gasping. Him solicitously, gently taking the glass of scotch out of my hand, saying I am trembling so badly it will spill. Don't be afraid, he whispers to me. Cupping my chin and looking deep into my eyes, waiting until I wanted it before lowering his lips to mine. I somehow become unbuttoned, unbuckled, unzipped during the kiss, my trousers and briefs sliding off my legs as I closed my eyes and savored the taste of scotch on his lips.

Going back on my elbows as his hands glide down my shuddering body—to my thighs, my inner thighs. Coaxing them open to him with slender, insistent fingers. His hand encircling me. The other at the back of my head, arching my head back with a tug in my hair. His face over mine, his eyes boring into mine, his throbbing staff at my entrance, my pelvis instinctively rolling up to receive him. Someone in the room is whimpering. Could it be me? I raise and spread my legs further, grasping the edge of the couch with the soles of my feet. I blot out the pain as he slowly enters me, enters me, enters me and holds, while, panting, I struggle to open fully to him. I pant harder as he starts to move, in, out, deeper, in, out. His hand pressing my torso down on the studio couch and remaining there, his face still over mine, as he moves deeper, slides faster, thrusts harder . . . All I can think of is what an honor this is—to give my virginity to a man—to this man— crying out at the warm flow of him when, inevitably, it comes.

Aiden dropped the wrench on the steel catwalk surrounding the Sea Isle lighthouse in Delaware Bay and shook his head to clear it. It was no good dwelling on what had gotten him here when the light needed to be fixed before dusk. He'd been working on it all day, and it was frustrating the hell out of him. There wasn't much room to work up here and it was hot as Hades. He was stripped down to his briefs to combat the heat. He was a muscular young man—still young. His movie career hadn't lasted for more than five years. Like Icarus, he had dared to soar too close to the sun. But he'd been at the top, blond movie star handsome, perfectly formed body, a combination that made the teenage girls scream and won him beefcake roles. He had never worn a shirt throughout any movie he'd been in.

He'd gone through all of the mechanical courses that went with lighthouse keeper when he'd chosen this as an escape, as a way to drop out of the world. Why couldn't he get this light going? And why was he drifting off into reliving a past that he couldn't change. A past that had ended for him nearly a year ago in the summer of 1958.

Aiden sighed, deciding that there was nothing for it but to unscrew the crystal cover and delve deeper into the mechanism of the light. But the cover hadn't been off since he'd arrived—and who knows for how long before that? The screw he started with seemed to be stripped. His mind wandered again as he worked on it.

Please go slow, I had begged when we were stretched out against each other on the bed in Stewart's room, naked, and he was stroking my cock. The size of his cock had frightened me silly. Why, you've been fucked before, haven't you? he asked. Not before this evening, I'd answered. He'd laughed and then had gone slow, stroking me and then sucking me and working my hole with lubed fingers and his mouth until I'd ejaculated. He'd coaxed my legs open then, lain on top of me between them, and I'd grunted and groaned—and would have cried out if he hadn't been covering my mouth with a hand—as he worked a cock inside me that was thicker and longer than I'd taken earlier in the evening. He started slow, as promised, but, getting excited, he rode me hard near the end. He gave me his cum in three blasts deep inside me. That, at least, had been the same as earlier in the evening. Afterward, I'd said I was headed back to L.A., and he said that, strangely enough, so was he—that perhaps we could fly out to the coast together. Once in L.A., he claimed two drawers in my dresser and a section of my closet and fucked me on the sly on a regular basis.

The screw wouldn't come off. In frustration, Aiden hit the iron base of the light with the wrench, and the light miraculous came on and started to revolve.

It was dark when he came out of the shower four flights down in the tower. It was too late to dress, so it again was just bikini briefs. It didn't matter. He was all alone out here—purposely. He did his evening calisthenics—he did them three times a day to keep in shape—fixed his dinner on the level below that of his bedroom, and sat in front of the fireplace of the living room in the addition at the base of the tower and whittled away at his wood while his stereo blasted mind-numbing—also purposely—classical music.

Wood whittling had been the pastime he'd taken up when turning to the solitary life of a lighthouse keeper. He whittled on wood. Sometimes he didn't even think about what he was whittling and let it take whatever shape it wanted. He was surprised and a bit disturbed by the piece he had completed and had polished up earlier today. He'd almost thrown it into the fire—almost. But he hadn't. He'd polished it until it glistened.

When he looked up from whittling, he saw that it was nearly midnight. He had to be up by 6:00. There was work to do—maintenance work on the lighthouse, maintenance never being finished, and there was the garden. He grew his own vegetables. Wouldn't his fan club be aghast at how he lived in isolation and grew much of his own food? If he had a fan club that cared. Stewart had taken care of that.

He went to bed, stripping off his briefs before climbing in bed. He closed his eyes, fondled himself for a few minutes and fell into full-fledged, writhing, sweaty masturbation.

Stewart and I are lapped, facing each other, my thighs on top of his, each embracing the other, his eight-inch dick inside me, on the bed in the master bedroom of my Beverly Hills mansion. He is miffed at me, saying that he waited in vain for the invitation to the premier of my latest movie, Love in the Shadows. *He was holding me tight, refusing to fuck me, even though he already was inside me, and I was begging for it. I tried to reason with him. Rock had just been outed—by his own wife—in the June 1958 edition of the* Hollywood Reporter, *although the charge didn't seem to be taken seriously. I knew it would lead to a relentless witch hunt, though—that the rest of us would have to cool it. Stewart said we'd cool it then, and he started to pull out of me. Begging for the fuck, I'd agreed to put him on the premier guest list. He pushed me back on the bed then and fucked me hard, deep, and long, giving me all eight inches. My agent nixed the invitation, though, the next day.*

His cock filled and stretched me when he fucked me. No one could work me like Stewart did. No one else did except in casual pickups in anonymous bars in anonymous towns I passed through, where the man wouldn't recognize me—where he was only interested in if I had a hole that would open for him and accommodate him. Even my movie star looks didn't mean anything in the darkness of a fleabag hotel room at night. All I was to these casual partners was a fast-opening hole and a cock hugging passage. None fucked me like Stewart did. Eight thick inches, fully possessing me, hitting all of the sensitive spots as it worked inside me. Stewart: handsome, muscular, hung, virile, vigorous, arousingly cruel, demanding, dominating. And, ultimately, vindictive.

Having shot his load toward the ceiling, Aiden groaned, turned over on his side, and drifted off to sleep, facing a day much like the day before and the day before that—unending monotony. But by his choice.

* * * *

"So, I found you. And in tip-top shape, I see. Playing the role of Robinson Caruso? I think we have quite enough movies on that theme already. It's only been five years since we were gifted with the Luis Buñuel version."

"Scott," Aiden said, surprised to see his former movie production colleague stepping out of a motorboat at the lighthouse pier. He would be surprised to see anyone other than the old geezer from the biweekly supply boat lash up to the lighthouse pier. He had been working in the vegetable garden and was instantly embarrassed that he was just wearing a pair of now dirt-splashed briefs. He hadn't looked in the mirror for days. Surely he had mastered the scruffy, unshaved look.

Scott Drayden was a movie scriptwriter, some four years older than Aiden was. He had worked on Aiden's earlier movies when they had both just been starting out in the business. They had hit it off and palled around with each other, each making an attempt to work each others' films after that. But Scott also had been one of the people in Hollywood who had turned his back on Aiden when, in July of 1958, Stewart Whitaker had written his blockbuster "Male Hollywood Stars I

Have Slept With" exposé in the wake of the beginning of the Rock Hudson scandal. He hadn't named Hudson; he had featured Aiden Allen, though. Aiden's movie stock had dropped like a boulder, and, by mid August he had completely disappeared from not only Hollywood, but also the face of the earth.

Scott had disappeared from Aiden's presence even before that.

Aiden had been so happy to see Scott that he initially forgot all that, but he soon recovered and his reception became guarded. "What brings you out here, Scott? You can hardly say you were just passing by."

"I almost passed out trying to get the motor on this boat operating."

"I can look at it for you," Aiden said. "I've had to become quite the mechanic. Have you tried hitting it with a wrench?"

"What?" Scott said, clearly confused.

"Never mind," Aiden answered. "Why are you here? You didn't just coincidentally drift here when your engine stopped."

"I want to take you away from here, Aiden. I have a proposal."

"Take me away from this paradise?" Aiden asked, with a laugh, opening his arms to take in the quarter acre of lighthouse base that he lived on. "I must show you my empire. Come. Give me fifteen minutes to shower and find some clothes and I'll walk you around and show you why I couldn't possibly give up this life."

To Scott's credit, he followed Aiden around the lighthouse, asking questions with respect, not criticizing or making fun of any part of the life Aiden had retreated to. It wasn't until after Aiden had fixed him supper—which Scott also tactfully didn't complain about—that they settled down in the lighthouse living room before the fire and talked seriously again.

"What is it, Scott? You couldn't drop me soon enough last year. Why is it that you are here?"

"I'm moving to Italy," Scott said. "Writing scripts for Italian movies. They don't have enough heartthrob leads there.

I thought you might like to move to Italy too. As I remember you speak passable Italian."

"My mother's parents were from Milan," Aiden said. "They never learned English, so I learned some Italian out of respect and self-defense. I wanted to know what they said about me and my acting; they never held back and were the best movie critics I'd ever encountered. I've had too few honest people my life."

At this, he gave Scott and pointed look, but the man wasn't rising to the bait.

"But you know I can't get back into movies," he added.

"Others are doing it. Just pick a new stage name. No one will know—and even if they do, they won't care. It's not the Communist scare that you were involved in. Stewart isn't in the picture anymore. Memories are short. Rock is still taking leading roles. If he can survive the scandal, so can you. You just haven't given it a chance."

The reference to Stewart tugged at Aiden's heartstrings—and, truth be known, at the wall of his nether passage too. It's not easy to wipe out the memory of a thick eight-inch cock. "I didn't wish death on Stewart," Aiden said. Another actor, as ruined by his exposé as Aiden had been, had shot the gossip columnist dead. He was headlining in Folsom Prison now. "I was stupid to go with a gossip columnist," Aiden said.

Scott didn't disagree with him, which raised his hackles again, and Aiden said, "I don't know why you are looking out for me now, Scott. You dropped me like a hot potato when Stewart's article came out, just like everyone else did."

"I couldn't say anything—for your own good."

"My good, or yours? We palled around too much. You were afraid to be painted with the same brush. Can't get too close to a queer in Hollywood these days—almost as bad as being in bed with the Commies."

"No, I was afraid that our friendship would be used against you—to add fuel to the attack on you."

"I don't understand."

"I was under threat too, Aiden. Some of my former lovers were threatening to out me too. And if they had and I was linked to you, it would have made your life even harder than Stewart's article was making it. There was only that one allegation about you. The same story from two separate sources and you're a cooked goose."

"Former lovers? Outing you? Are you telling me that you are queer too, Scott?"

"Of course. How could you have missed it? How could you have missed how much I ached for you, but couldn't do anything about it because you obviously were with Stewart, and Stewart wasn't someone you crossed?"

"Oh. Well, that's ironic. Learning that now that I'm out of that lifestyle."

"Out of that lifestyle? You showed me what you were doing with wood—the objects you were whittling. What's this object, Aiden?"

Aiden looked at the object in Scott's hand and his heart skipped a couple of beats. It quite clearly was a penis—a thick and long one. Had he carved that? He hadn't been conscious of doing that. But there was no mistake about it. It was the object he'd finished carving two days ago and had polished up to a satin finish the previous day. And it wasn't just a penis, he was aghast to realize. It was a particular penis. It was life size, albeit oversized. It was at least eight inches long, and thick, and it had those three veins running up the shaft and the slight upcurve that Stewart Whitaker's cock had had. It was a dildo.

"Have you been fucked by a man since last summer, Aiden?"

"No," Aiden answered. "You're the first man to come ashore other than an ancient mariner who delivers my supplies and he usually just hauls the boxes out onto the pier and never leaves his boat."

"Have you used this dildo on yourself?"

"No." How could he say that that was Stewart's cock, the size and thickness of it, Stewart's cock down to the veins in it? Or did Scott suspect that it was?

"Why not? Why not take your pleasure despite whatever the public thinks?"

Aiden didn't have an answer for that.

"Where is that bedroom that takes up a whole floor of the lighthouse?" Scott asked.

Aiden, naked, was lying on his back on the double, brass head-boarded bed on the fourth level of the lighthouse. The light from the revolving beacon overhead was showing up at one window in the stuccoed wall before disappearing and, after a moment, showing up in the window across from it. Aiden's arms were pulled over his head, his wrists tied to the brass rungs of the headboard.

Other than the brief flashes of light reflecting off the white walls of the circular room, the room was dark. The only sounds other than the distant grinding noise of the light revolving on its base, were the sounds of Aiden's low grunts and groans and of Scott's moist kisses.

Scott, also naked, was positioned lower against Aiden's body. His cheek was on Aiden's trembling belly. Aiden's right leg was trapped behind Scott's back, with his ankle hooked on the back of Scott's neck. Aiden's other leg was spread to the side and bent, his foot flat on the surface of the bed, but rocking back and forth, causing the former movie star's pelvis to move. Scott's left arm was under Aiden's waist, his hand helping to keep Aiden's left thigh raised.

Scott's right hand was holding the base of the wooden, lubed-up dildo, which was six inches inside Aiden's passage and being rhythmically pushed in and pulled out, with brief stops for the bulb of the dildo to punish Aiden's prostate.

At seven inches, Aiden arched his back and moaned deeply. One more inch and it would be Stewart fucking him.

Scott dipped his head lower, and tongued up Aiden's erect cock from base to glans, after which he swallowed the cock and began to suck it. He worked the dildo progressive harder, pumping faster, digging deeper, pulling it completely out, and plunging it back in.

Eight inches. Aiden arched his head back, bowing his spine, and cried out to the wooden beams overhead as he shot his load and creamed the back of Scott's throat. Pulling the dildo out immediately, Scott rolled over on top of Aiden, stuffing a pillow under the small of his back to elevate his pelvis. He thrust inside Aiden's passage with his hard cock and immediately started to pump. Aiden moaned at the realization that Stewart Whitaker hadn't been the only one who had an eight-inch plus cock.

For a good fifteen minutes the noise level in the room went up: Scott grunting and breathing heavy as he grabbed Aiden's hips and worked hard to dig deeper, stroke harder and faster; Aiden moaning and crying out, "God, yes, fuck me. Fuck me harder"; and the frame of the old brass bed making the most noise of all, the brass headboard banging rhythmically against the wall and the springs of the bed screeching, bouncing and scrunching under the punishment.

The fucking went on all night, as if the two of them were trying to make up for the years of relating to each other without realizing that the other one was aching to be a lover.

In the early morning light, they were stretched alongside each other, Aiden on his back, and Scott on his side. Scott's left arm was under Aiden, his hand cupping the side of Aiden's head, turning it to Scott's face for good-morning kisses. Aiden's pelvis was still elevated by pillows, and Scott was slowly working his ass with the dildo.

When Scott had showered and come down to the living room, where Aiden had set a fire in the fireplace and had cups of coffee ready, Scott entered and sat in the wing chair across from Aiden's. Aiden was fondling the wooden dildo.

"So, Aiden, have you given thought to coming to Italy with me and getting back into movies?"

"You haven't given me much time to think about that. You'd had me thinking about other things—like whether I was going to survive that master cocking of yours."

"You want the number of the complaint department?" Scott asked.

"Absolutely not."

"So, what do you think? About Italy? About me and Italy? About me fucking you into the next century—on movie sets all across Italy?"

Aiden's eyes went to the wooden dildo. He let his hand slide from root to penis. Then he turned and threw it into the fire.

"What was that? That was a nice piece. We made good use of that."

"You wouldn't understand, and I'm not going to tell you," Aiden answered. "But I don't need that. I've got you now. I guess I need to brush up on my Italian."

~

About the Author

Habu is one of the pen names of a former supersonic spy jet pilot, intelligence agent, male model, movie actor, and diplomat. A wild youth in Southeast Asia was spent enjoying whatever sexual opportunities came his way, and much of his gay male writing is about recalling incidents from those days and inventing ones he'd perhaps have liked to experience. He now leads a very quiet and ordinary happily married family life.

An American, he is a published mainstream novelist and short story writer under another name and in another dimension of his life. He has written or cowritten (with Sabb) approaching 1,000 published short stories and over 100 published erotica e-books, primarily of gay fiction but also memoir, straight fiction and ménage fiction. His hand and creative writing can be seen in stories and books by habu, sr71plt, Dirk Hessian, Shabbu, and Stephen Kessel—among unrevealed others that might surprise readers. The fictionalized GM memoir *Flying High, Diving Deep* is loosely based on his life experiences. He can be found at the adults only gay male site BarbarianSpy.com, which he shares with Sabb and Dirk Hessian.

Our authors always like to receive feedback, and appreciate it when readers post reviews at distributors and other sites.

BarbarianSpy
FOR LITERARY HEAT

Not all books listed below may currently be on release.
* indicates the book is available in paperback and e-book.

BOOKS BY CHRIS CROSS
Multisexual Adult Romance
Pulaski Square
Chocolate in Vanilla (MF)
Christmas with Chris (MMF) (MM) (MF)

BOOKS BY ALEX LOCKHEED
Transgender Romance
Meeting Jenna
Transgender Other
Being Sarah

BOOKS BY DIRK HESSIAN
Xtreme Historical Erotica
Ancient Times (Print only Bundle)*
The King's Men
Shores of Tripoli*
Prophecy of Noto
Pretender's Fate

General Historical Erotic Romance
Ridden West
Deliver a Virgin
Clouds and Rain
Confederate Gold
Puttin on the Ritz
To the Hessian Hills
Fire Down the Valley*
Constantinople*
The Beautiful Way*
Blue and Gray
Colonel's Treasure
Beginning of Time
Labyrinth

BOOKS BY HABU
Gay Erotica
Memoir Faction
Flying High, Diving Deep*
Xtreme Erotica
Fist of Gold
Liaisons
Chain Gang Banged (Short Story)
Tramp Steaming*
Escape to Girne
Silas' Choice*
Last Call
Choke Hold
Apyko: The Greek Pimp
Visits of the Schlange
Second Coming: Emile La Cour Unleashed*
Vortex: Sacrificed by Curiosity*
Dark Angel Sounding (in e-book & included in
Sounding:Ultimate Control paperback)*
Sounding: Ultimate Control (Print Only)*
Sounding Five (in e-book & included in
Sounding:Ultimate Control paperback)*
Romance
Finding a New Sam
Bangkok Summer Seduction
The Photograph
Inevitable Case
Turn to Love
Rain Check
Built for Pleasure (Sci Fi)
Danny's Choice*
Pull of the Groove
Sugar n Spice Christmas
Friday Nights with Lenny (Christmas Romance)
Snowy, Snowy Nights (Christmas Romance)
Tank n Bull
Sail to the Sun
War Letters
Ravens Roost

Caribbean Cruise Top to Bottom
Arena Stage
Trading Partners (Valentine's Day)
Four Coins
Lower Than the Heart (Valentine's Day)
Brambleton
Gotta Keep Trying
Finding Amnad
Platres Conclave
Other Novels/Novellas
Syrian Ram
Temptation's Clutches*
Descent into Chaos
Escape to Girne
Journey Through Abilene
Harmony and Dissonance
Stallion Station
Racing With the Devil (espionage suspense)
Prepared in Cape Verdi
Gilded Cage
House on Park*
Anything for Ambition
Dance of the Ravishers
Hard Knocks U*
My Neighbor's Spa*
Man's Man: Tales of a High Priced Gay Hooker*
Trip Money
The Indian Doctor
Sailorboy
Home to Fire Island
Murder Mysteries
All Fools Day Foolery (Mike Kavanagh)
Inevitable Case (Mike Kavanagh)
Vanishing Laura
Death on a Ping Pong Table
Clint Folsom Mysteries Compendium Volume 1*
Death to Blonds - Stolen Judgment (Clint Folsom
Mystery)*
Clint Folsom Mysteries Compendium Volume 2*

Gay Erotica Anthologies
Earth Cry*
Shunga
Habu's Christmas Balls
Eight in D*
DevilMENt
Silas' Choices*
Stallion Station (A Novella in Parts)
Eleven to the Dogs*
Fifty Seventy*
Spy Tails 001*
Spy Tails 002*
Doubled*
Doubled Again*
Tails in the Tropics*
Tails in the Med*
Tails in the West*
Rough Riders*
Grab Bag 1*
Grab Bag 2*
Grab Bag 3*
Grab Bag 4*
Grab Bag 5*
Grab Bag 6*
Grab Bag 7*
Grab Bag 8*
Grab Bag 9*
Beyond the Beaded Curtain*
Habu's Christmas Balls
The Sporting Life*
Fetish Galore!*

Literary Gay Erotica
Cairo Surrender*
The Handyman*
Homeward Bound
Journey to Mirage*

Bisexual/Menage/Multisexual Erotica
And Eat it Too
Two Men, One Woman*

Every Which Way
Summer of Denial
Death on a Ping Pong Table
Cruising Gigolo
13 Ways for Halloween
Luther*
The Indian Prince*

BOOKS BY SABB

Driver Reliever
Hiring in Hollywood
The Legend of Holleystone Grange
Surprise Encounters*
She is He
Wrong Man
Loyal to his King
Barbarian Tales - Book One - Traveler's Tales*
Barbarian Tales - Book Two - Journeys Begin*
Barbarian Tales - Book Three - The Inheritance*
Barbarian Tales - Book Four - Road to Persepolis*

BOOKS BY SHABBU

Velvet Interrogation
Finding Jason
Dirty Pool
Operation Black Jade
Cigars!*
Angel in the Barn
Gayly Complicated*
Despoiling David
The Tree of Idleness*
I Met a Man
Rough Road to Happiness

BOOKS BY STEPHEN KESSEL

Gay Romance
The Forever Man
Two Chances

BOOKS BY KIM BLACK

Lesbian Romance
Transfixed on Tammie (F/T lesbian)